The Kiss

A kiss? Lauralee wondered desperately to herself as Dancing Cloud's lips moved toward hers. What harm was there in just one little kiss? She so badly wanted to feel his lips upon hers again. He had such beautiful lips, so soft and gentle.

Dancing Cloud framed her face between his hands and gazed down at her. "Lauralee, my woman, allow my kissing you," he said huskily. "Passion is not so much an emotion as it is a destiny. It is *our* destiny to come together, as one."

Lauralee's heart pounded fiercely within her chest. Her throat was dry. Her knees were weak. She prayed to the good Lord that Dancing Cloud's kiss would not bring back the horrid memories she'd tried so hard to forget.

She wanted to enjoy the kiss.

She wanted to enjoy *him*.

All of him!

ALSO BY CASSIE EDWARDS

WILD ABANDON

by

Cassie Edwards

A TOPAZ BOOK

TOPAZ
Published by the Penguin Group
Penguin Books USA Inc., 375 Hudson Street,
New York, New York 10014, U.S.A.
Penguin Books Ltd, 27 Wrights Lane,
London W8 5TZ, England
Penguin Books Australia Ltd, Ringwood,
Victoria, Australia
Penguin Books Canada Ltd, 10 Alcorn Avenue,
Toronto, Ontario, Canada M4V 3B2
Penguin Books (N.Z.) Ltd, 182–190 Wairau Road,
Auckland 10, New Zealand

Penguin Books Ltd, Registered Offices:
Harmondsworth, Middlesex, England

First published by Topaz,
an imprint of Dutton Signet,
a division of Penguin Books USA Inc.

First Printing, November, 1994
10 9 8 7 6 5 4 3 2

Printed in Canada

I dedicate *Wild Abandon* to some special
people from Mattoon, Illinois, my hometown:
Mayor Wanda Ferguson; JoAnn Homann;
Ann Diepholz; Evelyn Donnell;
my husband, Charlie; my son, Brian;
Tiffany Schrock, and Bob and Doris McDowell.

—Cassie

Lauralee, take my hand,
Let us walk this world together.
Mother Earth created you,
Within you lies the sun, the breeze,
And the sacred fire.
I feel the passion as I touch you,
Warmed by the fire within.
Dancing Cloud, I never knew inner peace,
Not until you taught me.
Love to me was a stranger.
Now my soul rejoices,
My warrior, my love, my life.
I will love *you* forever,
Till my days on this earth are over.
Lauralee, be my wife forever.
Make me whole. I love you so.
With a sigh she promised,
Yes, you own my very soul.
Mother Earth smiled at her children
As they spoke their sacred vows.
Their destinies were charted,
In the gods' most sacred plaque.

by Deanna K. Phillips,
a Mattoon Poet/Author
and my cousin
—Cassie

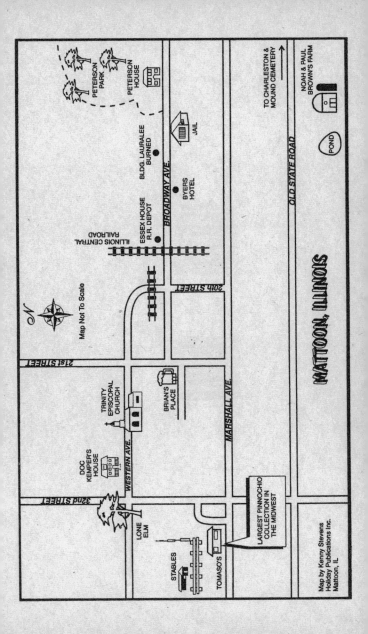

1

The brave man is not he who feels no fear,
For that were stupid and irrational.
But he whose noble soul its fear subdues;
And bravely dares the danger nature shrinks from.
As for your youth whom blood and blows delight,
Away! with them there is not in their crew
One valiant spirit.

—WILLIAM SHAKESPEARE

Tennessee—1865.

The rains had become continuous. The mud was deep.
The rivers were overflowing, the roads nearly impassable for wagons. The colors of the uniforms of this
Civil War regiment were scarcely discernible through
the layer of mud and grime, the mood of the soldiers
matching the gray that they had worn so nobly this past
year during the war.

The horses upon which many of the soldiers rode
through the dismal, rainy day, grunted and blew steam
from their nostrils as they attempted to make their way
through the ankle-deep mire.

The soldiers walking behind the horses, their steeds
having been shot from beneath them during the last
ambush, cursed the Yankees beneath their breaths.

The war was officially over, but not inside the hearts
of those who had given up so much for a victory in the
South.

They coughed, sneezed, and clutched themselves
with their arms as chills raced across their cold, wet
flesh. They had now gone three days and nights without sleep except for those brief moments that had been
snatched at the watering places.

Lieutenant Colonel Boyd Johnston surveyed his
men. His aching, cold fingers tightened around the

horse's reins, helpless against what had happened to his regiment.

He drew his eyes from the sick, downtrodden men. He looked over at Joe Dancing Cloud, a Cherokee Indian who had joined his regiment a year ago. Although Joe was only eighteen years old, he had fought as valiantly as a man of thirty.

Long before the war a bond had grown between Boyd and Joe Dancing Cloud, one that fathers and sons sometimes never achieved during a lifetime. He hated saying goodbye to the lad, fearing he would never see him again.

"Damn shame, isn't it, Joe?" Boyd said, calling Dancing Cloud the nickname that he had given him when he was ten years old.

"The surrender of Lee and Johnston?" Dancing Cloud said in perfect English. For the most part he and his people attributed their knowledge of the English language to Boyd Johnston, who before the war had been an Indian agent assigned to look after Dancing Cloud's Wolf clan of Eastern Cherokee.

"Yes, the surrender," Boyd said gloomily. "But when our forces suffered greatly in the valley campaign of 1864, after the Battle of Cedar Creek, I saw the end then, Joe, of everything that we had fought for."

Dancing Cloud's jaw tightened and his dark eyes narrowed angrily. "Surrender is not a noble thing, *o-gi-na-li-i*, my friend, but unavoidable after the collapse of the Southern railroads," he said flatly. "All of Lee's regiments began to suffer from slow starvation. This, together with Sherman's victories in Georgia and the Carolinas, undermined the morale of our soldiers. When desertions began, it was *then* that Dancing Cloud saw the true end for the Confederacy."

He looked over his shoulder at his Cherokee warriors who had moved valiantly onward even when they knew that the North had all but won the war. There had been no deserters among the Wolf clan Cherokee faction of the Confederate troops who, when not fighting, made their homes in the Great Smoky Mountains.

Although they were worn and weary, their stomachs distended from hunger, they had been true to their word and had stayed loyal to the South, to the end.

Dancing Cloud became lost in thought, recalling the day that Boyd had come to him attired in the gray uniform of the Confederacy.

The young Cherokee had not seen Boyd for three winters at that time. He was surprised to see that he was no longer coming to the Cherokee in the capacity of an Indian agent, but as a soldier who held much rank with the Confederacy.

Boyd had come to tell the Cherokees that in order to protect them from other dishonest leaders who might ask them to join the fight, he had gotten permission from his superiors to ask his friends to enlist in his infantry regiment.

Boyd's motive was to keep the Wolf Clan of Cherokee out of danger.

James Talking Bear, Dancing Cloud's chieftain father, had seen no other way than to allow his son and his warriors to go to war. Better it be with Boyd Johnston, than total strangers.

Dancing Cloud's eyes became troubled when he thought of his father, mother, two younger brothers, and baby sister. He said a silent prayer to the Great Spirit that they were all safe from those who were in the mountains now who did not belong.

Dancing Cloud and his warriors had joined the fight. He felt that by aiding in the war he could secure respite for his people. His ultimate hope was that they might be allowed to remain in their own mountain country.

If he had rejected the offer to fight, he feared that the whole force of the Confederate troops might come down upon his people in one fell swoop.

Until recently, Dancing Cloud had felt that he had succeeded well enough. Just before the news of the end of the war had reached his regiment there had been reports of deserters from various parts of the Confederacy who were arriving in numbers to hide in the mountains where the Cherokee lived. Those deserters preyed on the innocent, robbing, killing, and performing other outrages.

"Joe, I said from the beginning of the war that if I lived through it, I would have done enough to be satisfied to spend the remainder of my life in retirement with my wife, Carolyn, and daughter, Lauralee," Boyd said, interrupting Dancing Cloud's train of thoughts. "Soon you and I will say goodbye, but not for long. I shall bring my daughter and wife to the mountains. It's high time they get to know my Cherokee friends."

"It will be good to have you at our village again," Dancing Cloud said. "My family will share their lodge and laughter with your family."

"Joe, do you fear for your family's welfare?" Boyd asked. He wove his fingers through his wet shoulderlength brown hair, to smooth it back from his narrow face. "I have never feared so much in my life as I fear for my family now. Did they survive the damnable Yankees? I have heard of such atrocities committed by the Yankees that makes my blood run cold. When I entered the war, I thought Carolyn and Lauralee would be safe enough on our land in Tennessee. It was on the very edge of the mountains, set deep into the forest. I hope to God the Yankees didn't spot it as they marched their way south."

"*Ii,* yes, I fear for my family, as well," Dancing Cloud said somberly. "But we shall both know soon. We have almost come to the intersection that marks our departure. You will go your way. My warriors and I shall go ours."

"Joe, you served well for the South," Boyd said, reaching over to give Dancing Cloud a fond pat on the shoulder. "You are a splendid specimen of Indian manhood. I trust and admire you more than one hundred white men put together. Your father taught you well. He has a son to be proud of."

"*Wa-do,* thank you, Boyd." Dancing Cloud was humbled by how his white friend felt. "Your words reach my heart with pride. They will live there, *i-go-hi-dv,* forever, in a corner always reserved for my feelings for you."

Dancing Cloud then followed Boyd's lead and drew his steed to a stop where a road sign had fallen, which had at one time given directions to towns in four directions. The sign, destroyed during the ravages of the war, lay in a heap of mud and debris.

Boyd gave an order over his shoulder for everyone to dismount.

Dancing Cloud looked over the weary men. For so long they had been continually drenched with rain, seldom able to dry their clothes. The nights had been bitterly cold, and blankets had been as scarce as tents. Sickness pervaded the unit.

Taking a black cape from his saddlebag and draping it around his broad shoulders, Boyd gazed at length from one man to the other. He then began to talk in a tone filled with emotion.

"Soldiers, it is with much pride and affection that my heart has accompanied you in every battle of this war," he said, a hush having fallen over everyone.

The men did their level best to refrain from coughing and sneezing so they could listen to this great leader who had been forced to bow down to defeat, yet very heroically.

"You men continually rendered a service that displayed the highest quality of devotion and self-sacrifice, which proves your character of the warrior-patriot," Boyd continued. "Your battle cry will forever ring loud and clear through the land of the enemy, as well as your own."

Boyd paused and bowed his head toward the ground, then looked once again at his quiet, devoted followers. "But the time has come to part, to go our separate ways," he said thickly. "The war is over. Let us begin anew. Hold your chins high to those who will mock you as losers. In our hearts we must always remain the victorious ones, for we never failed at what was expected of us. Soldiers, one and all, I bid you farewell. Should we meet again, it will be my pleasure."

Everyone remained quiet.

There was a sudden commotion at the side of the road. A man stepped into the open from the fog that was just creeping in over the rain-drenched land. His red hair shone like the sun. His eyes were cold and blue as a leaden sky just before the first signs of a storm on a summer day.

Everyone grabbed for their weapons, but the man held his hand up in the air and shouted that he was a friend.

The color of his uniform gave them cause to doubt that. Through the mud and grime that covered it they could see that it was blue.

Boyd and Dancing Cloud stepped slowly and cautiously toward the man. Dancing Cloud's eyes looked warily on either side of the stranger for others to follow out of the fog.

"Lieutenant Boyd Johnston of the Twelfth Tennessee Regiment, sir," Boyd said. "And where do *you* hail from?"

The red-haired, blue-eyed man paused. "My name's Clint McCloud," he said in a low, guarded voice, obviously not saying which regiment he hailed from. "I've lost my way from my troops. Might you allow me to travel with you for a while? Might I even travel on horseback for a few miles? I'm bone-weary. I doubt I can travel another foot."

"You're a Yankee," Boyd drawled out suspiciously.

"As you are a Rebel," the man drawled back, his eyes narrowing into thin, blue slits. "But the war's over. The colors of our uniforms no longer matter. Right?"

"In most cases," Boyd said, his voice low and measured.

"And why would mine be different?" Clint asked,

his hand inching toward the pistol holstered at his right hip.

"You tell *me*," Boyd said, taking a step away from Clint.

Boyd looked past the Yankee, into the rolling fog. He was sure that he had seen movement. This man wasn't alone after all.

Dancing Cloud had also seen the movement in the fog.

But before he could react quickly enough, the red-haired, blue-eyed Yankee had drawn his pistol and was aiming it straight at him.

When Dancing Cloud saw the flash of the pistol's report, he thought that he was experiencing his last moments on this earth.

He was stunned speechless when Boyd stepped in the way and was shot, instead.

Dancing Cloud gasped when Boyd's body lurched with pain as the bullet made contact in his left shoulder. He grabbed for his friend and held onto him. He turned and watched in disbelief when several Yankees came from the cover of the fog and began an attack on his regiment.

Bloodshed erupted on both sides. Bodies fell right and left. The screams of pain were like shocks of white lightning bouncing through the air.

Dancing Cloud laid Boyd down on the ground. He peeled aside the black cape to see how badly he was wounded. When he saw that it was only a flesh wound, he sighed heavily with relief.

He started to rise and enter the battle but stopped and stared at what he had never expected from his warriors. Those who had not been killed were so furious over their brothers' deaths they were scalping the downed Yankees.

A throaty cry sliced the air, a cry that seemed frozen in time. Dancing Cloud looked quickly around and found Clint McCloud standing there, his eyes filled with the horror of what he was witnessing.

Dancing Cloud was torn with what to do. He did not want his warriors to continue scalping. Yet if he took the time to stop them, this one lone survivor would escape.

For a moment Dancing Cloud and Clint McCloud's eyes met and held, their eyes speaking words of hate that their mouths could not at this moment say.

Then Clint McCloud grabbed one of the Confederate horses, mounted it, and rode away.

Dancing Cloud grabbed his pistol and took a steady aim on the fleeing man. One shot rang out and he realized that he had not killed the Yankee.

But he was certain that he had shot him square in the thigh of his left leg. The Yankee would lose a lot of blood. Gangrene might even set in before he reached a hospital.

Clint McCloud looked over his shoulder and shouted at Dancing Cloud as he rode into the veil of fog. "You savage!" he cried. "I'll get you. Some day I'll find you and you will pay. Not only for shooting me, but for allowing your savages to scalp . . . my . . . men."

His voice trailed off.

Dancing Cloud turned and stared down at the bloody massacre and swallowed hard. The scalps that had been removed had been tossed in a pile. One of his warriors was setting a match to them. The others watched, their faces somber.

Boyd leaned up on an elbow and stared blankly at the fire as it burned into the leaden sky. "My God," he whispered. He became pale and gaunt as he shifted his gaze and looked at the men who had died needlessly. "The war is over, yet it is not, or perhaps never shall be."

Dancing Cloud knelt on one knee and examined Boyd's wound again. "This should be seen to soon," he said. He looked slowly around at his dead brethren, and at those who were wounded. He felt helpless since he had no way to gather herbs to doctor his friends.

Nor was there a white man's hospital nearby. And all medical supplies had long been used up.

"There is no bullet lodged in my flesh. I'll be fine," Boyd said, groaning as Dancing Cloud helped him up from the ground. "And you?"

Dancing Cloud's eyes met with Boyd's. He became humble again in the presence of this man whose heart was big. "Because of you I am alive," he said thickly. "I owe you a debt that I may never be able to repay."

Boyd nodded and smiled. He held his shoulder as he began walking toward his men. "We'd best see what we can do to get everyone back on their feet who can stand. Their loved ones are waiting on them," he said. "Thank God we at least got this far without being totally wiped out by bushwhackers."

Dancing Cloud watched Boyd move through the wounded, and dead. He vowed to himself to find a way to repay this man for his kind ways.

Some way.

Some time.

Some how.

He *would* find a way to repay this man for saving his life.

He turned and looked into the rolling, thickening fog. Beyond that wall of gray, high up in the Great Smoky Mountains, his people waited.

His head bobbing, occasionally drifting off to sleep in the saddle, his shoulder now numb from the loss of blood, Boyd was only scarcely able to recognize his way back to his plantation. He had parted ways with his regiment and was on his way home.

The rain had stopped and the sun was out, revealing to him that the land was scorched as far as his eyes could see.

Not only did he witness the charred remains of all of the farmhouses that had stood in the way of the Yankee soldiers, he saw way too many bodies of innocent peo-

ple, children and grown-ups alike, to stop and bury
them.

And he didn't even have the strength to see *to* the
Christian burial for those unfortunate people. He
scarcely could stay in the saddle now from lack of
sleep, food, and medical attention.

Yet he kept on going, the fears mounting inside him
now over what he was going to find when he reached
his home. He doubted there would be any home left to
recognize.

He choked back a sob and wiped tears from his eyes.

Nor did he now expect to find his daughter and wife
alive. It was foolish, he condemned himself, ever to
have left them.

But he hadn't left them totally alone. There had been
his slaves, among them a big, muscular black whose
devotion to Carolyn and Lauralee was beyond that
which was expected of him. He would have killed anyone who came near them.

"Jeremiah, oh, God, Jeremiah, I hope you were
enough for their protection," Boyd said, his throat
growing drier as he got closer and closer to his home.

One turn in the road and he saw the devastation . . .
the ruins . . . the charred wastes of what had been his
house, outbuildings, and gardens.

There was nothing left to recognize.

"Carolyn?" he said, his voice choked and drawn.
"Lauralee?"

There were no voices to answer him.

Then he saw the remains of a man. It did not take
much thought to realize who this was. He recognized
the silver bracelet on the man's wrist. He had bought
this for Jeremiah as a thank you for being so dependable.

Jeremiah was dead. Then what of his wife and
daughter?

He hung his head and retched. . . .

* * *

After he had left the regiment behind, Dancing Cloud had stopped long enough to shed the clothes of a soldier, down to just a pair of breeches. He was bare-chested and he wore no shoes, feeling and tasting freedom for the first time since he had gone to fight for the South.

Determinedly, anxiously, Dancing Cloud continued to work his way up the mountainside on his roan. He felt elated to be back to this region of luxuriant flora, with its great red-spruce forest, its clear air, its breathtaking sights.

He looked over his shoulder at his Cherokee friends, some wounded, some not. They moved as anxiously as Dancing Cloud, thinking of families and friends.

He turned his eyes back to the narrow path. There was almost impenetrable thicket and tangled undergrowth on the slopes and ridges, with an exceptional variety of flowering shrubs, mosses, and lichens, and a lavish display of purple-pink blossomed rhododendrons and azaleas.

Among the rushing streams that spiraled down from the summits and ridges of the mountain, were such trees as hemlocks, silver bell, black cherry, buckeye, yellow birch and tulip.

Every now and then he would get a glimpse of a black bear, or a browsing white-tailed deer. He enjoyed seeing the foxes as they lurked around beneath the trees, sniffing out a ruffed grouse, or turkey.

And above him, many colorful songbirds flitted about, as though welcoming him and his returning warriors.

The farther he rode up the mountainside, the hazier it got, the very reason the mountains had been given the name—the Great Smoky Mountains.

His heart beat like a drum within his chest. He again softly prayed that he would find his family as he had left them a year ago.

Dancing Cloud sank his bare heels into the flanks of his horse and he sent his steed in a faster trot, having now found the path that led to his village that lay in a sheltered cove and valley only a short distance away.

As he got closer and could see through the break of trees ahead, the sight that he had prayed would not be, was. Only a portion of the log homes of his village remained.

Dancing Cloud emitted a loud groan when his weary eyes discovered that his father's larger cabin no longer stood near the center of the village.

But he was relieved to see the Wolf Clan Town House still standing. Within its walls burned the sacred fire of the Wolf Clan of Cherokee. It had been kept burning while so much had gone wrong for his people.

As Dancing Cloud grew closer, he saw so much more that made his heart ache. His father was standing at the edge of the village, a blanket draped over his shoulders. He looked as though ravaged with time, himself. He leaned heavily against a long, wooden staff, his eyes appearing empty.

His father did not even seem to notice that Dancing Cloud was approaching. There was no joy in seeing his son, only a remorse that seemed to lay heavy in the air, reaching Dancing Cloud as though he had just entered a thick thunder cloud, all black and dreary.

Dancing Cloud drew his steed to a halt and slid out of the saddle. His heart pounded as he ran to his father and embraced him. He grew cold inside when his father did not seem to have the ability to respond.

"*E-do-do,* Father, it is I, *Dancing* Cloud," his son said as he took a shaky step back from his father. "I have returned from the war."

He looked past his father and searched with eager eyes for the rest of his family. When he saw none except his aunt, Susan Sweet Bird, he placed his hands at his father's lean, slumped shoulders.

"*E-tsi? I-go-nv-tli? I-gi-do?*" Dancing Cloud said, his voice breaking. "Mother? Brothers? Baby sister? Where are they, Father?"

His father's dark, haunting eyes became level with

Dancing Cloud's, proof that his son's words had finally penetrated that blank wall that had seemed to have enveloped him.

"Dead," his father said, his voice vacant of emotion. "Dancing Cloud, Yankees came. They took. They burned. They killed."

Despair swam through Dancing Cloud. He swallowed back the urge to retch. He shook his head in an effort to clear it of the thoughts that were spinning there.

"They were deserters? Bushwhackers?" he finally managed to say.

"No, my son," James Talking Bear said bitterly, the name James having been given to him by Boyd Johnston. "It was a full regiment of *soldiers.*"

"Soldiers?" Dancing Cloud said, stunned. "They came and . . . and . . . ?"

"They came and took my heart with them when they left," his father said mournfully.

"Confederate or Union?" Dancing Cloud said, his insides stiffening.

"Bluecoats," James Talking Bear said, nodding. "The one with hair the color of the sun and eyes the color of the sky. He led the bluecoats into the slaughter of our people. When he left, he laughed."

Dancing Cloud's heart seemed to turn to ice at the description of the soldier. It was surely the very same man who had led the ambush on Dancing Cloud's regiment a few days ago.

Now he wished that his aim had been more accurate. In the back!

He should have shot the heartless Yankee in the back instead of the leg.

Silently Dancing Cloud once again vowed to find Clint McCloud one day and make many wrongs right.

But not now.

Perhaps not for many winters.

For now he was needed to help put his father's life

back together again, as well as his own, and the people
who depended on his chieftain father's leadership.

Dancing Cloud placed a comforting arm around his
father's shoulder. "Come," he said thickly. "Your eldest son did not die at the hand of the *ha-ma-ma-* enemy Union soldiers. He has come home, to mend
things for you, and our people."

"Your father's insides are dead," James Talking Bear
said, his voice breaking. "How can that ever be
mended?"

"With much *tsi-ge-yu-i,* love, Father," Dancing
Cloud said, drawing him closer to his side. His fingers
tightened against his father's shoulder. "I am here. And
I have much love to give you, Father. Much *tsi-ge-yu-i*
love."

When his father looked over at him, tears misting his
usually bright and brilliant dark eyes, Dancing Cloud
felt as though his very insides were being torn from inside him. His father had always prided himself in his
nerves of steel and his ability to withstand all sadness
and challenges. In one instant, in one heartbeat, that
had all changed, and because of that, Dancing Cloud
was suddenly a changed man, himself. He now knew a
bitterness within him never known before.

Vengeance.

One day he would avenge this that had been done to
his family.

Suddenly flashing before his mind's eye were the
faces of his mother, sister, and brothers. He was glad
that he was able to see them as smiling, for any more
sadness today would perhaps be too much for him to
bear.

2

My life closed twice before its close;
It yet remains to see
If immortality unveil
A third event to me.

—EMILY DICKINSON

St. Louis, Missouri—1880.

It was a sweltering day in late July. Sweat pearled along Lauralee Johnston's brow as she entered the veterans hospital, the humidity causing her long and flowing coppery-red hair to kink up into tight ringlets. Although she was not a registered nurse, she helped out at the hospital as often as she was needed.

Soon to turn twenty, she would be expected to leave the orphanage where she had lived since she was five to seek her own way in the world; to seek her own destiny.

But Lauralee had found some comfort and a safe haven within its walls. It had helped alleviate the pain of the past that had left deep scars caused by the Civil War.

Lauralee would never forget her mother dying so violently during the war. She would never overcome her loneliness and despair of being abandoned outside her burned-out house until a priest had come along and had taken her to his parish at the St. Louis Children's Home.

There Father Samuel had given her shelter from the rest of the damnable Civil War, a war that had snatched everything from her.

Her mother.

Her father.

No one could bring her mother back to her. She had been dead since the bluecoat Yankees had arrived at her house. They not only looted it, they killed her mother.

The only hope that she had lived with all of these fifteen years was that her father would find her and take her into the safe cocoon of his arms.

Yet she had decided long ago that he had surely died during the war.

But even though she had been only a child when she had last seen him, his memory still lay soft and sweet in her mind.

She remembered that day he had left for the war. He stood tall, wearing boots shiny black and a handsome gray uniform, with two revolvers slung in leather holsters at his waist.

He had not yet reached the age of fifty, but still had beautiful, long gray hair. His violet eyes had been hypnotizing as he had laughed and played with her.

His laughter lingered now, like a warm dance within her heart.

But Lauralee's ache of missing him made all of these memories hard to bear sometimes. She had only herself. She had to keep telling herself that.

And she would fend well for herself once she left the orphanage. She would become a nurse in a grand hospital. She would care for the inflicted, hoping *that,* in turn, might help slowly mend the hurts that she still carried around with her since the evil, blue-eyed, red-haired Yankee had . . .

She shook her head to keep the worst of her memories from surfacing. She hastened down the long, narrow corridor of the hospital, the skirt of her plain cotton dress sweeping her ankles. Each day she was anxious to come and spend time with the veterans of the Civil War, hoping that she might find someone who might have known her father.

Even now as she slowed her pace and started looking into the rooms as she passed them, she studied the faces of those who had only recently been brought there.

Of course she knew that it was foolish to believe that she might one day see *his* face among the ailing men. It was an impossible dream, a true fantasy, to believe that she might ever see her father again in *any* capacity.

She did not wish to see him ill. But if he could only be alive and *slightly* ill, enough to bring him to this very hospital so that she could get the opportunity to tell him that she was his daughter, that would be the same as entering the portals of heaven!

"Good morning to you, Lauralee," a priest said as he walked past her in his long and flowing black robe. "How are you faring on this fine day?"

"It's just a mite too hot for me," Lauralee said across her shoulder as the priest walked on past her. The sight of a priest always saddened her now, for Father Samuel had passed away a year ago. Their bond had become tightly entwined.

And now, as before, she was alone again.

"The humidity will pass," Father Edwards said back to her over his shoulder. "Just keep that pretty smile and pretend a soft summer rain is falling on your sweet face."

Lauralee laughed softly, then went to a desk and leaned over the shoulder of a nurse. "Are there many new patients today, Dorothy?" Lauralee asked, trying to read the names of those Dorothy had entered into a ledger.

"A few," Dorothy said, then closed the journal and looked up at Lauralee. "Dear, there's a man in room fourteen. He was just brought in moments ago. I haven't had time to check my charts yet for a name. He has pneumonia. He may not even last a week. Two, if he's lucky. Why not go and see if you can cheer him up? I'll be in shortly to check on him."

"You don't know anything about him?" Lauralee

said, forking an eyebrow. "His name? Where he's from?"

"Dear, I've been quite busy this morning, so, no, I haven't taken time yet to see about the man," Dorothy said, heaving an irritated sigh. "I can't be expected to know everything about every patient the minute they are brought to my end of the floor. Now can I?"

"No, I guess not," Lauralee murmured. She gazed down at Dorothy. This woman was not only lapse with her nursing duties, but also herself. She was dowdy. Her white dress showed signs of having not been washed in days. Her stringy blond hair was drooping over her shoulders. Her skin was blemished with scars left by pimples.

There was even a slight aroma of perspiration as Dorothy moved her arms about as she stacked ledgers on the top of a wooden filing cabinet.

Lauralee, however, took pride in herself. She always smelled sweet from a recent bath. Her freshly washed hair sparkled and shone, and her cheeks were rosy and dimpled.

She brushed her hands down her perfectly ironed dress, proud that she made a good appearance whenever she visited the ailing men. She smiled to herself while thinking about how she always drew a compliment or two from them as she entered their rooms.

Lauralee recalled how her mother had looked to her when she was five, and now she saw how much she resembled her whenever she looked into a mirror at herself. She carried that knowledge around with her with much pride and tenderness. She had loved her mother so much. She had never heard as sweet a voice since, nor had seen such a lovely, warm smile.

Not wanting to get into it with Dorothy, always having found it hard to tolerate her neglect of everything, Lauralee walked away. She hurried to the room where the new patient lay with pneumonia, his days on this earth now numbered.

Her heartbeat always raced when she was to become

acquainted with a new patient who might have fought side by side with her father. She always said a prayer to herself that this might be the day she would hear what she wanted to hear. That her father was, indeed, still alive.

The door to room fourteen was ajar and Lauralee could hear the labored, hard breathing. This was the breathing of someone whose each and every breath carried with it an intense pain. It was at this stage that many of them prayed for a swift end. Life no longer held within its arms anything warm or beautiful for them.

Lauralee tiptoed into the room. She stopped and peered through the gloom. The shades were drawn at the windows. A candle's glow on the bed stand was the only light by which to see.

The smell that met Lauralee was strongly medicinal. The sight of the thin, ill man covered by soft blankets was sad. Lauralee was saddened at the thought of him dying soon.

Except for her deep emotions and feelings for people, Lauralee had always felt that she could be a good nurse. When she realized that someone was gravely ill, she became overcome with pity and remorse for them.

Realizing that he was asleep, she moved softly and quietly. She stood over the bed and sucked in a breath of despair when she saw how gaunt this man's face was, and how bony his hands were as they rested above the blankets. His hair was all but gone, yet still showed signs of once having been gray.

As she looked down the full length of him, she knew that he had at one time been a very tall, and most likely a grand and handsome man.

"My father was tall," she whispered to herself, taking a cloth from a basin, slowly wiping his sweating brow. "But my father couldn't be this old. This man must be . . ."

Her thoughts were stolen away when the man slowly lifted his eyelashes and revealed entrancing violet eyes that mirrored Lauralee's. She gasped and paled, then shook the hope from her heart that finally she had found her father.

And this was not at all the way she had wanted it to be when she found him. This man . . . was . . . dying. She could not bear to think that she might find her father, just to lose him again all that quickly.

Boyd Johnston blinked his eyes over and over again as he stared up at the lovely woman standing at his bedside caressing his brow. His pulse raced. His heart thundered within his chest.

"Are . . . you . . . real . . . ?" Boyd whispered in a voice that held no strength. He slowly raised a shaky, thin hand toward Lauralee's face. "Tell . . . me . . . I'm dreaming."

So used to the elderly men making over her, Lauralee laughed sweetly and softly. "No, sir, you aren't dreaming," she murmured. "And since you are awake, is there anything I can get you? Would you like to have a drink of water? Are you hungry? Perhaps eating would give you back some of your strength lost to the pneumonia."

"No, I . . . don't . . . want food," Boyd stammered. "Let me look at you up close. Please. Go and lift the shade at the window. Let . . . me . . . see you . . . up close."

Lauralee's smile faded and her insides did a strange sort of flip-flop. This man. This stranger. He was not acting the same as the others had, after all, when they had opened their eyes and saw her for the first time. This man seemed to know her. He wanted to get a better look at her to be *sure.*

But it was foolish of her to make anything of this. She had been only a child when her father had last seen her. He would not recognize her now.

His eyes were the only characteristic that bore the slightest similarity between her father and this man.

And anyone could be born with violet eyes.

"All right, if you wish, I'll raise the shades,"

Lauralee said, feeling strangely weak-kneed as she went to each of the two windows and allowed the blaring sunlight to flood the room.

"Come to me," Boyd said, his voice weak and gravelly. "Come now. Step up close. Let me see you."

Lauralee hesitated, then went on to the bedside. "Sir, you are frightening me," she said, as once again his fingers reached for her face and he ran them over her features. "Who do you think I *am*?"

"My wife," Boyd said, a sob lodging in his throat. "Carolyn. My wife, Carolyn. Lord, how you look like my Carolyn."

Lauralee almost fainted as those words sank into her consciousness. She steadied herself by grabbing for the bed. She peered more intensely at the facial features of this man. If he thought that she was Carolyn Johnston, that had to mean that he had known her. Lauralee did lay claim to being the exact image of her mother!

"You also had a daughter, didn't you?" Lauralee asked, her voice quavering. She took his trembling hand and clasped it to her bosom. "You did, didn't you? You had a daughter. Her name was Lauralee."

She could feel the leap of his pulse as she clung to his hand. She knew that she had hit a nerve. She knew that she had found her father!

Tears flooded Boyd's eyes. "Lauralee?" he whispered. He tried to raise himself on an elbow but his weakness caused him to fall back onto the bed. "Are you my Lauralee?"

Lauralee could not hold back her emotions any longer. She bent to her knees beside the bed and leaned over and embraced Boyd, her body racked with heart-wrenching sobs. "Father," she cried. "Oh, Father. I never thought I'd see you again. I . . . thought . . . you . . . were dead."

The dreaded word "dead" came to her like a bolt of lightning. Soon he *would* be dead. She had only a short time to be with him, to relish, to form remembrances that could last until her own dying breath.

Bony arms enfolded her. Boyd's tears mingled with hers as she placed her cheek against his. They clung and cried.

They stayed that way until Dorothy entered the room, gruff and bossy.

"Heaven sakes, Lauralee. What are you doing?" Dorothy asked, gasping loudly. "Get away from the patient. Don't you have any more control of yourself, than that?"

Dorothy went to Lauralee and grabbed her by the arm and jerked her to her feet. "I'm going to report you," she snapped in a disgusted tone of voice. "We don't need someone like you sobbing and weeping over men you don't even know. What has gotten into you, anyhow?"

Lauralee jerked away from Dorothy. "Get out of here," she said, leaning to speak into Dorothy's face. "Do you hear me? Get out of this room."

Dorothy paled and stiffened. "What did you say?" she balked. "Are you actually ordering me around?"

"It's time somebody did," Lauralee said, taking Dorothy by the arm. She ushered her toward the door. "You are the one who is going to go on report. And as far as my father is concerned, never enter this room again. I forbid it."

Dorothy stopped and glared at Lauralee. "You are not in the position to forbid me anything," she snapped back. Her mouth dropped open. She turned and stared quickly at Boyd, then back at Lauralee. "Your father?" she said in a drawn out whisper. "This man . . . is . . . your father?"

Lauralee smiled down at Boyd. "Yes, after all these years, I've finally found my father," she said, then glared at Dorothy again. "Now please, leave us alone. I'll see to his needs. I'm aware enough about pneumonia to know what is required to make him comfortable."

Lauralee closed the door, then went and sat at her

father's bedside. She wondered about the gleam in his eyes, and the smile fluttering along his pale, thin lips.

"My daughter has grown into a little spitfire, I see," he said, reaching for her hand, patting it. Then he grew somber. "I imagine you had to learn how to protect yourself after what you must have been through."

He swallowed hard. "Tell me, Lauralee. Tell me all about it. And I don't have to ask to know that your mother is no longer alive. I sense it in your behavior. When did she die, Lauralee? Where is she buried?"

Lauralee could hardly find the words, or the courage, to tell him everything. But she knew that he deserved to know. Due to fate, he had not been able to return to his family before the Yankees destroyed everything that had mattered to all of them.

"Mother?" Lauralee managed to say. She rubbed tears from her cheeks with both hands. "Her grave is on the hillside overlooking the house. And even though I was only five, I knew to say a prayer over her grave."

Tears rolled down Boyd's cheeks. "She died when you were five?" he gasped out.

"Yes, not all that long after you left, Father," Lauralee said, her eyes taking in his gauntness. He scarcely resembled that once powerful, muscled man. "The soldiers came. One in particular was the worst of the lot. His hair was red. His eyes were piercing blue. He . . . he . . ."

She hung her head, then blurted out the rest of the truth of that dreadful day. "Oh, Father," she groaned. "The red-haired, blue-eyed Yankee raped Mother, then . . . then . . . killed her. I was hiding. He didn't know I was there."

After she finished her tale, she wished she hadn't told her father the most brutal part. His color had worsened, as well as his breathing.

Lauralee moved from the chair and sat down on the side of the bed. She swept her father into her arms. "Please don't blame yourself," she sobbed, as she could hear him beneath his breath cursing his absence that day, and all the days since. "You were called to duty. How were you to know that the war would be so horrible? And that the soldiers could be so devious? Please, Father, don't blame yourself. Don't you see? Your daughter is fine. I was raised in the orphanage that sits on the grounds of this hospital. The priests and nuns were good to me."

"An orphanage?" Boyd said, peering up at Lauralee as she moved out of his embrace. He could not get enough of her. Her face was exactly the same as her mother's. Small, oval, and exquisite, her eyes veiled with thick, dark entrancing eyelashes.

Yet there was something in her eyes that cut him to the very core—the lack of peaceful happiness.

"Yes, I was taken to the orphanage by a kind man," Lauralee said, nodding. "There I have lived until now. Soon I will be twenty. Then I will be expected to leave. Father, you and I will leave together. I will make you well again. We will be a family!"

"Lauralee, don't fool yourself into believing this ailing man will ever leave this hospital alive," Boyd said, coughing into his cupped hand. "As for you, I must find a way to see to your future before I die. It must be a future with family."

He paused, then grabbed her hands. "Sweetheart, you are such a beautiful young lady, as you surely were as a child growing into maturity," he said, his voice growing much weaker as he spoke. "Why is it that . . . no . . . one ever adopted you?"

"Father, I'm not sure if I should tell you." She smiled sheepishly at him.

"Tell me," Boyd said. "I want to know everything about you. Everything. Tell me, Lauralee, why you were never adopted? When you were placed with the other children, for people to choose from, surely you stood out from all of the rest as something sweet and beautiful."

Lauralee reached for a cloth and dipped it into the

water basin, then began absorbing the sweat on his brow into it as she caressed his clammy flesh.

"Sweet?" she said, laughing loosely. "No. Not many saw me as sweet when I was at an adoptable age. Instead, as a small child, I was labeled a 'rebel' and troublemaker. When people came to the orphanage to choose a child, I always hid away in a closet, the way I hid when the soldier came into our house that day during the war. After a while I had those in charge of the orphanage convinced that I didn't want to be a part of anyone else's family. Not when I had my own true Papa out there somewhere who would come for me one day."

"I would've had I known," Boyd said, choking back more tears. "Oh, but if only I had known where you were. I searched forever for you, Lauralee. But never as far as Saint Louis."

He coughed again and hugged his chest with his arms in an effort to ward off the pain. "And now that I have found you, it's too late," he said, giving her a look that caused her whole insides to ache. "I know my condition. I've had pneumonia before. This time I'm not strong enough to get well."

"I will make it so," Lauralee said determinedly. She rose to her feet. "I shall go and get Doc Rose. He'll make you well. I know it."

"Lauralee, come back here and sit down," Boyd encouraged, patting the bed at his side. "We've got your future to discuss, and we must do it while I am lucid enough."

Lauralee sat down beside him again. Her eyes were wide as he told her his plan.

"You have been alone without family long enough. You need to be with family," he said. "And I must arrange that before I die. Then I can die with a smile on my face."

"Father, I know you mean well," Lauralee said, knowing that she must face up to the fact that he *was* dying. All of the forceful intentions of telling him that he was going to live would be foolish, and would make it harder on him to know that she could not face up to the truth. "And I am touched by your concern. But I am no longer a child. No one would take me in at my age."

"Lauralee, I know that you are no longer a child," Boyd said, his voice sounding more and more drained. "But family is important. You need to experience the warmth and love of family."

"Father, perhaps that is true, but I know of no one who would wish to take me in, *as* family. And I want you to know that I have dreamed of being a part of a family for as long as I can remember. But I only wanted it to be with you. Not strangers."

"The people who I have in mind aren't total strangers," Boyd said, patting her hand. "Darling, I have a distant uncle. He and his wife are childless. When Abner and Nancy were young, Abner was too busy to get involved in adoption proceedings. And now they feel they are too old to adopt a youngster. Sweetheart, you aren't a youngster, and you are true *family* to them. We just never got together so that you would know them as a child. I'll wire Abner and Nancy. I'll tell them about you. You will have an immediate home to go to."

He paused, then placed a finger beneath her chin and drew her face down so that they were eye to eye. "You must promise to go to them," he said thickly. "Lauralee, promise me?"

"Only if you will go with me," Lauralee blurted out.

"Lauralee, you know as well as I that I have seen the last of my traveling days," Boyd said wearily. "And you know enough about things to realize that I am not on this earth for much longer. Promise me, Lauralee, that once I am gone, you will go and live with your Uncle Abner and Aunt Nancy."

"But I do not know them at *all*," Lauralee said, sighing heavily.

"They know *of* you," Boyd said, patting her hand.

"On my brief visits to Mattoon during my travels away from you and your mother before the war, I spoke of you to them. They hungered to see you then. But time was against those sorts of wishes. The travel time from Tennessee to Illinois is not a pleasant thing for a frail woman and small child."

"You say they make their residence in Mattoon, Illinois?" Lauralee asked, a part of her thrilled with the idea of becoming a part of a true family. Another part of her ached, now truly knowing that it would never be with her father.

"Yes," Boyd said, sighing when he saw that she was actually considering what he asked of her. "And Mattoon is such a lovely city. Abner Peterson. Judge Abner Peterson and his wife Nancy could be your parents until you find a nice young man with whom to make a family of your own. I know that even before I send the wire their answer will be yes. They will welcome you with open arms and hearts."

"Father, I don't know . . ." Lauralee said, still battling with herself over what she must do.

"You will go," Boyd said flatly. "And when I send the wire to Abner and Nancy, I shall at the same time see that a wire is sent to my friend Joe. He owes me a favor from way back. I am going to ask him to escort you to Mattoon."

"An escort?" Lauralee said, arching an eyebrow. Her jaw tightened. "I need no escort anywhere. I can very well take care of myself."

Boyd patted her hand again. "Honey, I know how you must feel about men," he said softly. "After what you went through, who wouldn't understand? But believe me when I tell you that you can trust my friend Joe. There's no other man on this earth like him."

Lauralee grew silent, fighting off remembrances of that fateful day of her mother's rape and murder. Men. She had grown up wary of most men.

Father Samuel had managed to change much of those feelings for her. When he had encouraged her to work at the hospital, where she was faced with men every day, gradually she had become less wary of them.

But to take a long journey with a total stranger?

The thought made cold chills ride her spine.

Boyd was lost in his own thoughts—of a young Cherokee warrior. Joe Dancing Cloud. He was now thirty-three, a mature man, and extremely handsome. Surely Joe would come and see to this old dying man's last wishes. He and Joe had been so much to each other through the years. They had met often to keep their special bond between them, a bond that would give Joe cause to come at Boyd's request.

I'm sure he will, Boyd thought to himself. He smiled slowly and looked up at his ravishing daughter. And wait till he sees my Lauralee.

Just maybe, he thought, just maybe his daughter and Joe might happen to fall in love?

Lauralee smiled back at her father, wondering what was on his mind that would make him take on such a glow, and make his eyes dance so?

3

Above the wind and fire, love,
They love the ages thru!

—R.W. RAYMOND

The wrinkled hills were alive with the yellows and blues of wildflowers. Joe Dancing Cloud tossed another rock into the creek that murmured and meandered through shallow, gravel-filled riffles behind his log cabin. Torn with what he should do, he was going over and over again in his mind the message that he had received from Boyd Johnston.

The message had said, "Please come. I need you. Boyd."

The address where Boyd had sent the letter from was a hospital in St. Louis, Missouri.

The fact that Boyd was in a hospital made Dancing Cloud realize the urgency that was needed to heed his friend's bidding. Perhaps he was dying. Boyd had not been all that strong since the Civil War; not since he had been wounded by the red-haired, blue-eyed Yankee.

The wound had not been life-threatening, but because Boyd had taken so long getting medical attention it prevented him from fully recovering.

And Dancing Cloud knew that in Boyd's weakened state he had fought pneumonia more than once these past years. Boyd had nearly died from pneumonia only a few moons ago while visiting Dancing Cloud.

Perhaps he was ill once again with the lung disease.

Perhaps this time he might not recover.

Ii, yes, Boyd just might . . .

Dancing Cloud did not want to think further about his friend possibly dying. They had kept in touch through the years since the war, their meetings always filled with peace and harmony. They had talked often about the war. Boyd had told Dancing Cloud that people are not destroyed because they are wrong; only because they are weak.

Joe Dancing Cloud had helped Boyd get over the loss of his family.

Dancing Cloud had in a sense became Boyd's family.

"And now he needs me as a father needs a son," Dancing Cloud said aloud.

"And, my son, you must go to him," Chief James Talking Bear said suddenly from behind Dancing Cloud, drawing Dancing Cloud quickly to his feet.

He turned to his father, concern heavy in his midnight-dark eyes as he once again saw his condition. A blanket hanging loosely around his shoulders did not hide his frailty. His leathery face was gaunt. His dark eyes were buried deeply into his flesh.

"*E-do-da,* Father," Dancing Cloud said thickly, placing a hand to his father's elbow. "Let me help you back to your lodge. You should have not come this far. It weakens you too much."

"My son, do you not know that your father is aware of the battle being fought within your heart and soul? Do you not know that your father is aware that since you received that message from Boyd Johnston you are torn with what to do?"

James Talking Bear leaned heavily on his tall staff as he walked slowly beside his son toward his cabin. The wind rustled the thin wisps of his gray hair that hung just past his shoulders.

He gazed over at Dancing Cloud, his only son. Always while looking at him it was like looking into a mirror image of himself those many years ago when

James Talking Bear was his son's age. Dancing Cloud's coal black hair was thick and flowing past his waist. His jaw, chin, and nose were strong. His eyes spoke of his stolid dignity and his triumphant courage. His son was tall and lithe, a man of inscrutable self-poise.

But even with all of those attributes Dancing Cloud had not yet shared marriage vows with a woman. Dancing Cloud had said more than once why he had chosen to delay taking a wife into his lodge to warm his bed. Guilt had followed him along his path of life since the Civil War. Dancing Cloud still blamed himself for having left his people to fight a white soldiers' war, leaving his Wolf Clan of Cherokee at the mercy of the Yankees, whom, in his absence, had swept down on them like the plague.

James Talking Bear had argued with his son often that Dancing Cloud was just one man. If he had even been there on the day of the massacre he could have done no more than what the others of his village had suffered through. He might have even joined those who had died.

Who then would be chief once James Talking Bear began his long walk in the hereafter?

It had been decided in council that James Talking Bear's son would follow in his father's footsteps.

The fringes of his buckskin breeches and shirt fluttering in the gentle breeze, Dancing Cloud stood at the door of his father's cabin as he waited for his father to enter, then followed.

James Talking Bear leaned his staff against the wall, then sat down in a wooden rocker before his fireplace. As he slowly rocked back and forth his old eyes watched the flames caress the wood on the grate in orange, satinlike streamers.

Dancing Cloud sat down in an overstuffed chair opposite his father and silently watched him, his eyes following his father's movements as he rocked in his favorite chair.

"*E-do-da,* Father," Dancing Cloud then said, drawing his father's eyes to him. "I feel that I must go to Boyd, yet *you* are *also* ill. I have many responsibilities here at our village. Yet I still feel a responsibility to Boyd. As you know, if not for him, you would not have a son to sit by the fire with you to talk. Boyd took the Yankee's bullet that was meant for me."

"And I will be forever grateful to Boyd for saving my son's life. My son, you must go to him. Go with my blessing. Do you not know that I understand a man's heart whose feelings are strong for a man who saved his life?"

"When we met in council after I received the message from Boyd, I discovered that some of our warriors resent me for even thinking about answering the need of my white friend, much less actually go *to* him," Dancing Cloud said, his voice drawn. "They say that I have turned into a white man, whose *heart* is now white."

"Those who judge you wrongly only do so because they wish to take your place as chief when this chief, your father, dies," James Talking Bear said solemnly. "I have learned long ago to close my ears and my heart to such jealousy. So should you, my son. Just remember this—there are many more who respect, than resent you. Those will be the warriors who will take their places in council with you when you are chief. The others? The door will be closed to them. Some might even be banished should they go too far in their comments that are born from jealousy."

"I wish to create no trouble among our people," Dancing Cloud said, bending to shove another piece of wood into the fire.

"You are not guilty of such a crime," James Talking Bear said, allowing the blanket to ease from his shoulders, to rest against the back of the chair. "You must go, my son. This is a good time for you to return the favor for your life having been spared. Go to Boyd Johnston. See what he requires of you. Do it. Then the debt will be paid once and for all. You then can return to your people and set things right in your life."

Dancing Cloud cocked an eyebrow as he looked over at his father. "What have I left undone that you are speaking of?" he asked softly.

"Would you not say it is time to take a wife?" his father said in an even and exact tone. "Would you not say that you have waited long enough to find a woman who could fill your lodge with sweet laughter? I have missed such laughter since your mother's death. I have thought often of taking another wife, yet none would ever compare with your mother."

"Then how do you think *I* can find someone that pleases *me*?" Dancing Cloud asked. "I also remember how special my mother was. I have yet to find someone as special."

"There will be that perfect woman for you if you will just start looking for her among the many that you have to choose from," James Talking Bear said, smiling. "But for now, my son, go and do your duty to Boyd Johnston. When you return, *then* you can start concentrating on choosing a wife."

"*Ii*, yes, perhaps it *is* time." Dancing Cloud nodded. "I have learned what is required to be chief. Through the years I have worked hard to better our people and have helped rebuild not only our village, but our people's hopes for the future. I no longer see fear and hesitation in their eyes. I see sunshine."

"And that is why you will be a great leader," James Talking Bear said, reaching over to pat Dancing Cloud on the shoulder. "Now go, my son. Ready yourself for the journey ahead. Ride with peace in your heart and do not burden your travels with worries of your father. I am in the twilight of my years. Soon I will cross over to the other world. That will be a time of joy for your father, not regret. I will again see your mother. We will walk hand in hand. Is not that a beautiful thought?"

Dancing Cloud went and knelt down on the floor before James Talking Bear. He hugged his father. Momentarily feeling as though he were a child again, Dancing Cloud lay his head on his father's lap.

"I shall miss you so, *e-do-da,* Father," he said thickly. "How I wish you were well enough to travel with me. I miss our times together while riding free on horseback. It has been so long, *e-do-da.* So very long."

James Talking Bear stroked his thin, long fingers through Dancing Cloud's hair. "I ride often with you, my son," he said, his voice breaking. "Did you not know that my dreams are filled with our joint adventures? While awake, my remembrances vividly recall our times together while on the hunt. Dreams and remembrances pacify this old father enough now, my son." He chuckled low. "And it is way less strenuous."

Dancing Cloud rose slowly to his feet. He placed a hand on his father's shoulder. "I will go now," he said, forcing his voice not to break with emotion.

"*Wah-kon-tah,* the Great Spirit will travel with you and keep you safe," James Talking Bear said as he gazed up at Dancing Cloud. "When you reach Saint Louis tell Boyd that my thoughts and prayers are with him."

Dancing Cloud nodded, then turned on a heel and left. His travel bags were already packed and secured at the back of his saddle. Without looking back, he rode from his village.

As he traveled down the steep mountain path, past gnarled cedars that clung to the sheer cliffs, he concentrated once again on the note that Boyd had sent to him. It had said that Boyd needed him.

"I wonder what he needs me *for*?" Dancing Cloud whispered to himself.

Vireos warbled and wrens chattered in trees overhead.

A heron eyed Dancing Cloud from a distant limb.

Water snakes and turtles sunned on rocks as he rode past a spring gurgling from the mountainside.

"What can I do that someone of his own skin coloring could not do?" Dancing Cloud whispered.

His curiosity aroused even more, he sent his horse into a hard gallop now that a straight stretch of meadow was reached.

The shades drawn closed at the hospital windows, Lauralee sat vigil at her father's bedside. His raspy breathing and his ashen color made her well aware of his worsening condition.

But she had seen this for several days now. Even *weeks*. And still he clung to life as though a lifeline were there, keeping him from sinking into the dark void of death.

"Oh, Father, is it because of the man you sent for?" Lauralee whispered, more to herself than to her father. He had not responded now for several days. "Is it sheer will that keeps you alive? Is it that important to you that your friend arrives to escort me safely to Mattoon? Lord, Father, I'm glad something is keeping you alive. We missed so many years of being together. Oh, but if only a miracle could be performed that could make you well again. We would share such wonderful times."

"Lauralee?" Boyd's voice was so faint she could scarcely hear. His eyes opened weakly as he turned to her. "Has he arrived yet, Lauralee? Has Joe arrived?"

So happy that he was awake and talking to her, Lauralee gently hugged him. "Father," she cried. "Oh, Father, I'm so glad you've awakened. It's been so long."

Boyd's frail hand patted her on the back. "Honey, I'm sorry I worried you," he said between raspy breaths. "I'm sorry for being such a bother."

Lauralee leaned away from him and took his hand and held it to her bosom as she sat down on the edge of the bed with him. "Father, how could you think you are a bother?" she scolded. "I'll be here for you, always."

"I wish I could have been there for *you*, Lauralee, while you were growing *up*," Boyd said, tears streaming from his eyes. "If only I would've looked harder for you."

Lauralee placed a gentle finger to his lips, silencing his regrets. "Shh," she said. "Don't waste your energy on regrets. Father, let's concentrate on now. We're together. We've found each other."

"Only to soon lose each other again," Boyd said. He turned his head to one side and coughed hard, then looked at her again. "Joe. You've got to promise me that you'll let Joe get you to the Petersons in Mattoon. They'll give you what I was robbed of. They'll give you all the loving you'd ever want."

"Father, I've told you time and again that I will go to the Petersons," Lauralee said, caressing his pale brow with her fingertips. "But now I just want to relish being with you."

Boyd turned his eyes toward the window. "Raise the shades," he pleaded. "Please let me see the sunshine."

"Father, it's midnight," Lauralee gently explained.

Boyd turned back to her. "Midnight?" he said, his eyes searching hers. "Sweetheart, you should be in bed. You need your rest for the journey to Mattoon."

"I'm not a fragile daisy." Lauralee laughed softly. "I won't wilt. And, anyhow, I'm not going to Mattoon for a long time. Just perhaps you will get up from that bed soon as good as new and we can move into our own little house. *We* can be family, Father. Not me and the Petersons."

"That's what dreams are made of," Boyd said, patting her hand. His eyes drifted closed. "I'm so tired. I'm so sleepy. Please awaken me, Lauralee, when Joe comes?"

"Yes, Father, I'll awaken you when your friend Joe arrives," she said and held his hand until he was asleep again.

Then she went to a window and raised the shade. Starlight, pale and cold, speckled the heavens. She shivered and hugged herself.

"Joe?" she whispered. "Who on earth *is* this Joe? Why is Father so insistent on his arrival?"

She had tried to get her father to tell her more about this stranger who would soon enter her life. He seemed content enough to just know the man, himself. He had just told her time and time again to trust him, that he knew a dependable man when he saw him. And Joe was the *best*.

"What is his last name?" she wondered again. She had often asked her father Joe's last name but he had ignored the question, as though knowing one's last name did not matter.

"I shall surely soon know the answers about this man of mystery," she said, sighing.

She returned to her father's bedside, her head bobbing as she fought off sleep.

4

This maiden, she lived with no other thought,
Than to love and be loved by me.

—Edgar Allan Poe

Two Weeks Later.

A soft knock on the closed door drew Lauralee from her chair in the hospital room. She stopped and glanced at her father over her shoulder, then went to the door and quietly opened it.

She took a quick step backward and gasped when she found a tall Indian standing there gazing down at her.

She nervously cleared her throat and composed herself enough to speak. "Who are you?" she asked, speaking softly so that she wouldn't awaken her father. He was resting peacefully. So often now when he was awake she could see in the depths of his eyes the suffering that he was feeling. Everyone had been amazed at how he had clung to life these past weeks.

She had been torn with how she felt about him still being alive. She knew that his suffering would be finally over when he took his last breath.

Yet she also knew that she would desperately miss him and hated to give him up.

The good Lord willing, He would do what was right for her father soon and ignore a daughter whose heart was being selfish in wanting to have him with her for as long as possible.

"I was told that Boyd Johnston was in this room,"

Dancing Cloud said in perfect English, surprising Lauralee that an Indian could speak so succinctly.

Dancing Cloud looked past Lauralee, into the gray gloom of the room where only a candle beside the bed gave off a dim, wavering light.

"Yes, this is Mr. Johnston's room," Lauralee said, relaxing more in the Indian's presence. "Who can I say is asking about him?"

Her eyes raked over him. She saw him nothing less than absolutely, strikingly handsome. His long, coal-black hair curled down over his shoulders and flowed to his waist. He was tall and strongly built. His shoulders were wide, his muscles straining against the inside of his fringed buckskin shirt. His skin had a touch of red to it, and his eyes were dark and mesmerizing.

Her heart took on a strange sort of thudding as he once again looked down at her. His smile gave away the secret that there was nothing to fear about him. He appeared to be a man of genuine kindness and gentleness.

"Tell Boyd that Joe Dancing Cloud has arrived." Once again he tried to see past her, only seeing dark-shadowed images in the room beyond.

He gazed down at Lauralee again, his eyes filled with concern. "Tell me how Boyd is feeling," he asked thickly. "Why is he in the hospital? When he sent the message for me to come to him he did not go into the details of *why*."

Lauralee's hand went to her throat. "You are Joe?" she said, her eyes widening. "You are the man my father summoned . . . the man he is counting on to . . ."

Dancing Cloud interrupted her. "You are his daughter?" he said, in awe of his discovery. "You are Lauralee?"

"Yes, I'm Lauralee," she said, still stunned over her discovery. Joe. Joe Dancing Cloud. Now she understood why her father had never told her Joe's last name. He would have then been forced to explain that he was an Indian.

Her father had surely wanted to delay telling her that until after she had already met him.

And she knew why.

The mere mention of an Indian stirred up all sorts of dreads and fears within so many people's minds.

But only these few moments with this man told her how wrong *her* misconception of Indians were. Her father had known that she would feel this way after having made his acquaintance.

"Boyd has finally found you?" Dancing Cloud said, in his mind's eye having always envisioned a young girl of five years whenever he thought about her.

He had never thought of her as grown up, and ... ravishingly beautiful! Her lovely face, where dimples deepened when she smiled, was framed by long and flowing hair the color of a coppery sunset.

Her skin was flawlessly pale, and her eyes, the color of violets in the spring along the mountainsides, were large and veiled with thick, dark eyelashes.

She wore a high-necked, yellow-flowered silk dress that clung to her bosom, revealing well-formed breasts pressing against the inside of the soft fabric, and a tiny waist, where the dress flared out in deep gathers.

She was petite in height.

To kiss her he would either have to place his hands at her waist and lift her to his lips, or she could stand on tiptoe.

Realizing where his thoughts had taken him, Dancing Cloud shook himself out of his innocently induced reverie.

"Father and I have finally found each *other*," Lauralee said, turning to gaze at the still form on the bed. Her father had taken to sleeping much too soundly, which frightened her. This past day or so she could scarcely tell when he was breathing. She was afraid that she would not even be aware of when he took his last, desperate breath of life.

"He looked *i-go-hi-dv,* forever for you," Dancing Cloud said thickly, drawing her eyes back to him when he slipped momentarily into mixing his Cherokee language with his English. "I traveled with him often to search for you. It saddened me to see his disappointment each time we parted after having not found you again."

"You have known my father way longer than I," Lauralee said wistfully. "You must know so much about him that I never shall have the opportunity of knowing. You are blessed to have known him so devotedly, Joe. So blessed."

Dancing Cloud had a strong urge to draw Lauralee into his arms and show her how happy *he* was to have finally had the pleasure of meeting her. He had carried the same disappointment in his heart along with Boyd so many times when they gave up searching for her, that now, with her standing there only an arm's length away, he could hardly refrain from lifting her into his arms to hug her to him.

He feared that if he blinked his eyes she would go away. That was how magical it seemed to be with her, actually seeing her, of actually talking *with* her.

His thoughts went quickly to Boyd again. "Your father," he said. "Tell me. Is he strong? Or is he weak? Is pneumonia the cause again for his hospital stay?"

"How could you know it was pneumonia?" Lauralee asked, taken aback by just how knowledgeable he *was* about her father.

"Many times I have sat with your father while he battled the lung disease that has wasted him away too often into skin and bone," Dancing Cloud said, again looking past her, almost afraid to see Boyd this time. It had not been all that long since his friend had been deathly ill with the same disease. Dancing Cloud had thought that his end was near then, much less to be battling the disease again, so soon.

"He came to you when he was ill?" Lauralee asked, her eyes widening.

"If he was within riding distance of my village." Dancing Cloud nodded. "He found much peace and comfort among my people. He became as one with the Cherokee."

"You are Cherokee?"

"*Ii,* yes, Cherokee."

"You fought alongside my father in the Civil War?"

"*Ii,* yes, his sorrows were my own."

"Joe, I . . ."

Joe placed a gentle finger to her lips, momentarily silencing her words. "The name Joe came from your father when he was an agent to my people all those many moons ago," he said. "The name I prefer spoken by anyone but your father is Dancing Cloud. I am called Dancing Cloud among my people. It is a name given to me at birth. Joe? It is accepted only in the presence of your father because he gave me the name when we first met to keep him from stumbling over the Cherokee way of saying Dancing Cloud."

"I'm sorry," Lauralee said as he drew his finger from her lips. "I didn't know. When Father spoke of having sent for a man named Joe, that is all he told me. I shall call you Dancing Cloud. I would not want to make you uncomfortable."

Their eyes locked and held for a moment as the magical web became more intricately weaved between them. Lauralee's knees were strangely weak. Her heart raced out of control and her face felt flushed from something deliciously sweet washing slowly and warmly through her veins.

When Dancing Cloud gazed down at Lauralee he could not help but recall his father's words—that it was time to take a wife. His father had said that one day soon Dancing Cloud would find that perfect woman to bring laughter into his lodge.

His heart, his very soul, told him that Lauralee was that woman. Everything about her seemed absolutely perfect. That she was Boyd's daughter made it even more wonderful.

"Lauralee, who is that standing in the corridor?" Boyd asked, only able to make out the shadow of a man as he peered intensely past his daughter. He leaned shakily up on an elbow and squinted his eyes. "Lauralee, who is that? Is it . . . ?"

Boyd's voice broke and his heart leapt with joy. "Joe? Is that you, Joe?" he said, his voice weak, yet filled with excitement.

Lauralee stepped aside. She smiled at Dancing Cloud, then nodded toward her father. "Go to him," she murmured. "Dancing Cloud, I swear to you that you are the sole reason my father is still alive."

Dancing Cloud gave her a lingering look that made her melt inside, then he went to Boyd. He leaned over the bed and swept Boyd's frail body within the muscled comfort of his arms.

"My *o-gi-na-li-i*, friend," Dancing Cloud said thickly, torn apart inside by how thin and bony Boyd was. He closed his eyes and remembered the days when Boyd was muscled and active, his eyes always dancing with laughter. Now he was only a skeleton of that man.

"Joe," Boyd said, his voice breaking as he clung to Dancing Cloud. "I knew you'd come."

Dancing Cloud held Boyd for a moment longer, then eased away from him and sat down in a chair beside the bed. "I regret having taken this long to reach Saint Louis," he said thickly. "I slept only half the nights of my journey. I felt your need deep inside my soul. I could hear you calling to me as though you were there with me."

"Did you see her, Joe?" Boyd asked, his eyes anxious as he peered up at Dancing Cloud. "Did you see my Lauralee?"

Dancing Cloud looked up at Lauralee as she now stood on the other side of the bed. Again their eyes locked and held. "*Ii*, yes," he said, everything within him aware of her presence. "I have made acquaintance with your Lauralee."

"Isn't she as pretty as I said she'd be?" Boyd asked,

reaching a shaky hand over to Lauralee, grabbing one of her hands with his bony fingers.

"Prettier," Dancing Cloud said before he could stop the word from rushing across his lips.

Boyd managed a chuckle between his raspy breaths. "I knew that you two would hit it off just fine," he said, looking slowly from Dancing Cloud to Lauralee, then back at Dancing Cloud. "That makes what I am going to ask of you much simpler, Joe."

"You summoned me here for what purpose other than to be with you again during your time of illness?" Dancing Cloud said, his voice having turned solemn. "Was it for me to make acquaintance with Lauralee? Or is it something else?"

"Yes, I wanted you to meet my lovely daughter," Boyd said, his voice becoming weaker with each word. "But I want something more, Joe. Something way more."

"Tell me what you want of me and it will be done," Dancing Cloud said, looking into Boyd's faded eyes. He flinched when Boyd suddenly closed them and it did not seem as though he was breathing any longer.

Dancing Cloud sighed heavily with relief when Boyd once again opened his eyes and sucked in a wild breath, then began to talk again.

"My daughter has never had a true family since my departure for the Civil War when she was five," Boyd said slowly, feeling more drained by the minute. "Her mother was murdered by the Yankees. She . . . she . . . was raised in an orphanage."

Boyd wanted to hurry on with his request, for he could feel himself slipping away. This time he felt it might finally be the last hurrah of his life.

Dancing Cloud shot Lauralee a quick look. Sympathy for how she had lived was like a sharp edge within his soul. When he had returned from the Civil War he had found many Cherokee children orphaned whose parents had been killed when the Yankees had passed through on their way to the battlefields farther south.

Seeing this had made him not wish to have children of his own. He had even considered getting married only to give some Cherokee waif a home. Perhaps more than one. Due to the ravages of the Civil War, the need was still great.

His eyes smiled into Lauralee's, thinking that she would understand the need to adopt some unfortunate Cherokee child and give them a home filled with love and understanding.

Then his attention was drawn back to Boyd when Boyd broke into a fitful bout of coughing.

Lauralee moved into quick action. She bent over her father and raised him into a half-sitting position. She stroked his perspiration-beaded brow.

The coughing finally subsided. Lauralee eased her father back down onto the bed and drew a cover up snugly beneath his chin.

"Joe, I need you to escort Lauralee to Illinois," Boyd said in an almost whisper. "You will be taking her to relatives where she will finally have a true home." He paused and inhaled a deep, trembling breath. He grabbed Joe's hand. "Will you do that for me, Joe? Will you?"

Joe glanced up at Lauralee, then back down at Boyd. "Does she agree to such an escort?" he asked thickly.

"Not entirely," Lauralee blurted out, yet wishing that she hadn't the moment she saw the wounded look in Dancing Cloud's eyes. "You see, I feel that I am old enough to care for myself. I told Father time and again that I can travel quite well on my own." She paused and sighed. "But he still insists."

"And you agreed to allow Joe, honey," Boyd said, patting her hand.

"Yes, I did, but . . ."

Boyd took her hesitance as something else, as something reflecting on the escort that he had chosen for her. In what breath that he could find, he tried to explain to her why Joe could be trusted.

"Lauralee, although Joe is Indian, he is the only man I would entrust your care," he said between shaky breaths. "Yes, he is Indian. He is a full-blooded Cherokee. Joe is of the Eastern band of Cherokee, the remnant that still clings to the woods and waters of their old home country. They are of the mountain Cherokee of North Carolina, the purest-blooded and most conservative of the Cherokee nation. He is not of the mixed bloods who are guided by shrewd mixed-blood politicians who are chiefly on the low grounds and in the railroad towns."

When Lauralee saw that this little speech had totally winded her father, she leaned into his embrace. "Hush, Father," she murmured. "You don't have to explain anything else to me. I can see the kind of man Dancing Cloud is. I, too, see that he can be trusted."

"Good," Boyd wheezed out. "Good."

Although Dancing Cloud saw traveling with Lauralee as a way to get to know her better, to give him a better understanding of this intrigue that he felt for her, he was torn again with what to do. The time it would take to get Lauralee to Illinois would be many days and nights of travel.

Could history repeat itself?

Could tragedy strike his village again in his absence?

His father!

Could he die?

Whenever Dancing Cloud thought of the possibility of his father dying before he returned to his village, he would remember what his father had said about being ready to cross over to the other side. He was anxious to join his wife, to walk hand in hand with her in the hereafter.

That comforted Dancing Cloud to know that his father thought of death as a means to be happier. When the time came that his father did pass on over to the other side Dancing Cloud's grieving would not be as

severe. He would envision his father and mother together again and smile.

Then there was Lauralee, and how troubling it was
think of being with her for the length of time it would
take them to reach Illinois. Although he did wish to
know her better, he doubted that it should be for any
reason other than just to know the daughter of his
friend Boyd! It was time for him to take a wife. He
was not sure if his people could accept a white wife for
a man who would one day be their leader.

Yet he again remembered his father's words. The
debt to Boyd would be paid once and for all if he did
this final deed for him. And it was obvious that Boyd
was dying. This made Dancing Cloud want to do this
last deed for him, no matter the cost to himself.

Dancing Cloud's silence worried Boyd. "Joe, I'll understand if you feel that you can't do this for me," he
said, his voice scarcely audible. "I feel guilty for even
putting you in the position of being away from your
people for this length of time."

Boyd's eyes widened. He attempted to rise on an elbow only to crumple back down onto the bed. "I am so
thoughtless," he said. "I did not ask about your father."

"He is not well," Dancing Cloud said solemnly. "For
some time now I have seen his health failing."

"Then you must return to him," Boyd said, reaching
a hand to Dancing Cloud, patting him on the arm. "Go.
I will understand."

"It was my father's wish and advice that I come to
you," Dancing Cloud said softly. "I will escort
Lauralee to Illinois, *then* return to my people."

Boyd looked from Dancing Cloud, to Lauralee.
Tears streamed from his eyes. "Come to me," he said
softly. "Both of you at once. Let me hug you."

Lauralee and Dancing Cloud's eyes met again, then
they both leaned down and eased into Boyd's embrace,
their shoulders touching.

"My two favorite people in the world," Boyd said, a

sob lodging in his throat. "Now when I have everything to live for, I'm not going to be able to stay around to enjoy it."

His sobs finally broke through, silencing everything else around him.

5

I love her for her smile . . .
her looks . . . her way.
—ELIZABETH BARRETT BROWNING

The state of Missouri and the Mississippi River were now behind Lauralee and Dancing Cloud. Dancing Cloud riding beside her on his magnificent steed, Lauralee rode comfortably, yet sullenly, in a covered buggy. She had purchased this with the inheritance money that Boyd had willed over to her during his last moments of life. She snapped the reins, urging the beautiful black mare that she had also purchased into a soft trot along the narrow dirt road in Illinois.

Tears sprang into her eyes as she thought of how hard it had been to give up her father to the ground after having only found him a few short weeks ago. It had been almost unbearable for her as she watched the casket being lowered into the grave.

He had been given a military funeral at Jefferson Barracks, which was located a few miles south of St. Louis. It had torn Lauralee apart inside when the guns fired off a salute to her father, followed by the mournful sound of taps being played in his honor.

It caused a shiver to race across her flesh even now at the thought of the taps and how hauntingly solemn the trumpet had sounded.

She glanced down at her lap upon which lay a wilted rose. The priest who had spoken at her father's funeral had given this to her. He had taken it from the spray of roses from the top of her father's casket, on which had been placed a red ribbon with the word daughter written in gold across it.

Wiping the tears from her face with her black-gloved hand, Lauralee peered through the black veil once again and watched the direction of the road. Up ahead was a huge mound in the ground. As she rode past it and stared at it she was reminded of Joe Dancing Cloud and that he was riding at the left side of her buggy, for this mound was the burial ground of another tribe of Indians, the Cahokia.

Lauralee turned her eyes to Dancing Cloud. She had argued briefly with him after the funeral when she had once again reminded him that she did not need an escort while traveling to Mattoon, Illinois.

He had reminded her that she had promised her father that she would accept him as her escort.

"He has just begun his long walk on the spirit path of life," Dancing Cloud had said. "He is with us now, as will he be with us always, in spirit. Do not disappoint him by disobeying his final wish."

Dancing Cloud felt her eyes on him. He turned and smiled at her. Thus far the journey had been one of silence. He with his sad thoughts of Boyd. She with hers of her father.

They were both mourning a valiant, courageous man, a man who had brought them together.

Obviously Boyd had willed himself to stay alive long enough, not only to see that Dancing Cloud was there to look after Lauralee, but also to make sure that they met so that a bond could be formed between them.

The bond was there, Dancing Cloud thought to himself. Now to nurture it into something more . . . into something everlasting.

He knew for certain now that he did not only want to escort Lauralee to Mattoon, he wanted to look after her for the rest of her life. Although she tried to put on a bold front of being independent and able to take care of herself, he could see the vulnerable side of her. He had enough love within his heart to make up for all of that which she had not known since she had been wrenched from the loving care of her parents at such a young age.

No. She was no longer just a means to repay some-one special to him. She was now way more than that to him.

Lauralee blushed beneath his steady, warm stare. She turned her eyes away, the rapid beat of her heart dizzying her.

She fought the feelings for Dancing Cloud that were nagging away at her consciousness.

She fought the strange, hungry need she felt for him.

It seemed almost impossible to her that she could even ever think of giving herself to a man. Not when the remembrances of that soldier forcing himself on her mother remained in her mind like a festering sore.

An involuntary shiver ran through her, causing her body to lurch with the intensity of it.

Dancing Cloud saw her tremor. He edged his horse closer. "You are *u-yv-tla,* cold?" he asked. "Would you be more comfortable if you had a blanket draped across your lap?"

Lauralee was never sure what he said when he mixed his Cherokee language with his English, but she was slowly learning how to interpret it by the words that followed. This time she interpreted him as having asked if she was cold.

"I'm fine," she said softly. "But the air is cooler now that the sun has slipped behind the trees. How much farther will we travel today? Will we be making camp soon?"

Lauralee somewhat dreaded stopping for the night. There were many private things to see to. Her bath, and changing from her black mourning clothes into something comfortable for sleeping.

And how would they sleep? Since her journey from

her burned-out home to St. Louis, she had not slept out of doors.

Especially not with a man who stirred her insides into feelings she had never experienced before.

She feared these feelings, but not the man. He was nothing at all like the soldier who had raped, then killed her mother. He was more like her father, gentle in every way.

"We will make camp now," Dancing Cloud said, jerking his horse's reins to guide his steed from the road. "Come. Follow me. We will find a place that will be far enough from the road so that there will be no dangers from passersby. Although the war brought peace to this country, there are still highwaymen who rob and steal from the innocent."

"I never thought to worry about that," Lauralee said, sending a wary glance over her shoulder as she followed Dancing Cloud from the road. In many ways, living in the orphanage had not prepared her for life anywhere but there. She had much to learn.

"The war left many men scarred, and not only physically, but mentally, as well," Dancing Cloud explained. "That is why it is important that no woman travels alone."

"Yes, I now see the importance of having an escort," she said quickly. "Sometimes one tends to forget how ruthless and brutal men can be to defenseless women. Yet I don't see how I could ever forget."

Dancing Cloud cast her a quick glance. He wanted to ask her what she was referring to. Had she been treated brutally? Was she scarred by it?

But he could see by the wavering of her eyes that she was uncomfortable over having revealed too many of her feelings to him. There would come a time when he would know all of her hidden secrets. He would draw them from deeply within her. Once spoken, perhaps they then could be forgotten.

They traveled onward through tall, green grass, until they came to a stream that trailed, snakelike, through the groves of oak and cottonwood trees. When the bushes and trees became too thick and impassable, Dancing Cloud drew a tight rein and dismounted.

After securing his horse's reins to a tree limb, he went to Lauralee and placed his hands at her waist to help her from her buggy. He could feel her become tense beneath his fingers.

Their eyes met.

His were full of questions.

Hers were full of apology for having shown even the slightest fear of him being so close to her, actually touching her.

She had fought off dreams of him being so close, of their lips coming together in a soft kiss. She could not help but be afraid of what this kiss might lead to. She was not sure if she could ever allow a man to take her sexually.

Not while in her mind's eye she could so quickly replay her mother's rape.

"Thank you," she murmured. She held onto her hat as he lifted her to the ground. "But please don't feel that it is necessary for you to see to my every need. I have learned to take care of myself far more than most women my age."

She knew that most women her age were married and already had children. *She* had shunned all men as though they were the plague. She had wanted a nursing career, only. She wanted to be there for others, herself finding much comfort in helping the needy.

Now, for the first time in her life, she wanted more.

"Perhaps it is time for you to allow someone to make life easier for you," Dancing Cloud said, easing his hands away from her. "There is no harm in accepting help, especially from someone who willingly gives it."

"I never want to feel obligated to anyone again," Lauralee said, lifting her hat from her head. "I paid my debt to the orphanage for caring for me through the years. I gave them half of my inheritance. That should help pay for many of the meals they fed me. The clothes I wore? They were donated to the orphanage. Most of the time those clothes were perhaps a size too small, or too big. But at least I was warmed by them. That was all that mattered."

She went to the back of her buggy and placed her hat in a box. She then lifted an embroidered travel bag from her belongings and went back to Dancing Cloud. She turned soft eyes up at him.

"I truly won't be obligated to you, either," she said, her voice drawn. "I will see to it that you are paid well for your inconvenience. You refused money from father. But I will make sure you take what I offer you." She lifted her chin defiantly. "You see, *I* won't take no for an answer."

Dancing Cloud responded only with a slow smile. This woman's show of independence was attractive to him. He could tell that she had much spirit and pride, none of which had been beaten out of her during her time without parents.

He had to be sure that nothing robbed her of those traits now. Not only because she was Boyd's daughter, but also because she was the first woman who Dancing Cloud had ever allowed himself to love.

And he did love her.

He loved her with all of his heart and soul.

He would chance even losing his rights to chieftainship to be with her for eternity.

He was afraid that the big fight would come when he tried to prove to *her* that she belonged to him, not the Petersons of Mattoon, Illinois.

Somehow he would convince her that she would receive much more in life by being his wife, than by being Abner and Nancy Petersons' daughter.

He feared that the *true*, main obstacle to his plans might not be Lauralee at all, but instead the Petersons. Judge Abner Peterson had fought for the Union during the Civil War. He might not want anyone near him or

Lauralee who had fought for the Confederacy cause, especially a Confederate Cherokee.

But Dancing Cloud had several days to gain not only Lauralee's love, but total trust. Then the Petersons would not have a say in the matter. Lauralee was old enough to make up her own mind about things, even about loving a Confederate Cherokee.

When Dancing Cloud showed no signs of arguing the point of money with her, Lauralee became unnerved. "Dancing Cloud, the money that you earn by escorting me to Mattoon is money that will buy many seeds and garden supplies for your people's planting season," she said quickly. "Isn't corn your people's staple food? The money could also buy clothes for the children of your village."

Her gaze went to his buckskins, then she looked up at him again. "Or do your women still only make clothes from the skins of deers?" she said softly. "I know the buffalo are gone. Surely that has made a hardship on your people."

"I hope to show you one day how my people *do* live. Then you will see that our lives do not vary much from the white man's."

Lauralee's eyes widened with that remark. She started to make a comment, but he turned from her and went to his horse and removed his saddlebags.

Lauralee followed him through a thick cluster of bushes, wincing when the thorns of a blackberry bush ripped the skirt of her black dress. She shielded her face with one of her arms as she bent beneath low tree limbs. She was relieved when they came to a clearing where Dancing Cloud lay his saddlebags.

When he started to walk back to his horse, to get his buckskin travel bag, she was surprised when he took a wide step around a vine of poison ivy, addressing it as he would a friend at the same time that he was avoiding it.

She realized then just how much he was a man of total mystery to her. His customs and his way of living differed so from that which she had ever known.

Yet she could not help from loving him, this man whose dark, midnight eyes sent her into a tailspin of rapture.

She worked with him to get the campsite ready. When a half-moon spilled its silver light over the sky she had already bathed in a private cove in the river and had shared a meal of roasted rabbit with him that he had cooked over a fire that was only now shimmering its faint light into the darkness.

She now lay huddled between blankets beneath the stars. She was bone-weary from the journey and felt emotionally washed out from the loss of her father.

Yet sleep would not come to her.

Perhaps she was too tired, she argued to herself.

Or perhaps being alone with Dancing Cloud was the cause.

Besides the priest who had escorted her to the orphanage, and her beloved father, she had never been alone with a man since her mother's rape. She knew that Dancing Cloud could be trusted, but she could not relax enough in his presence to go to sleep.

Deep down inside herself she knew that lack of trust was far from the reality of why she could not sleep. It was, in truth, because she wanted to snuggle into Dancing Cloud's arms. She wanted to take his offer of protection to the limits. She wanted him not only to hold her within his embrace. She wanted him to kiss her and give her the experience of wild bliss for the first time in her life.

Until she had met Dancing Cloud she had never thought it possible to have the need of a man. Now she wanted nothing less than to experience what her mother had felt when she had been held within the protective arms of Lauralee's father. Their love had been sweet and special. It had been picture-perfect.

Lauralee now saw that it was possible for her to have the same sort of sensual relationship with a man.

When Dancing Cloud rolled over on his blanket and gazed her way, Lauralee's insides melted.

She turned her back to him when she suddenly recalled her mother's rape.

How could she truly be free to love Dancing Cloud when there were so many bad memories that would not allow it? she despaired to herself.

Tears streamed from her eyes.

She closed them and stifled a sob behind a hand.

Then it was as though the arms of her father were there, enveloping her within them, whispering comforting words to her as he had done so often when she had been a child.

She recalled Dancing Cloud saying that her father's spirit would be with them always.

She smiled.

He was there now.

She could almost feel the warmth of his breath on her cheek, but realized that it was just the warmth coming from the embers of the fire.

She turned to her side and drew her legs up in a comfortable position. Finally she felt as though she could drift to sleep. She welcomed the peace that came with it.

Dancing Cloud watched Lauralee until she was asleep. Then he left his bed of blankets and went to sit by the river. As the moon spilled its light into the water his thoughts again became filled with Lauralee. It was hard to keep his feelings for her at bay, and the journey had just begun. He knew that going to sleep would not stop his thoughts. She was with him now, bonded like a second skin.

Sighing heavily, he left the river and went and stood over Lauralee. Her coppery-red hair was spread out over the blanket in a satin sheen, tempting him to run his fingers through it. Her lashes were closed over her pale cheeks like black veils, and her perfectly shaped lips were just barely parted, her breathing soft and even.

He knelt on one knee beside her and dared touch her cheek, and then her lips. Almost reverently, absolutely cautiously, he bent over and kissed her lips, then drew away when she inhaled a deep breath and flipped over to her other side.

When she turned over, the blanket was kicked away. Dancing Cloud could not help but look at the swell of her breasts that pressed against the inside of her simple cotton dress.

His gaze moved lower. Her dress was hiked up way past her knees, revealing to him the sensuous curve of her thighs.

His heart almost pounding out of control, he rose quickly away from her and returned to his blanket.

But even that did not keep him from looking at her. He would never get enough of her. She was food for his soul, this woman whose very presence threatened his future as a leader of his people!

6

What are these kissings worth,
If thou kiss not me?

—PERCY BYSSHE SHELLEY

The sound of a loud splash in water awakened
Lauralee with a start. She bolted to a sitting position
and looked wildly around her.

At first she was frightened.

She then sighed when she recalled where she was,
how she had gotten there, and with whom.

She peered toward the river. When she saw Dancing
Cloud's clothes and his rifle laying on the riverbank
she concluded that he was taking an early-morning
swim before resuming their journey to Mattoon.

Lauralee glanced up at the sky. Night was changing
into day. A glorious color of orange suffused the heavens as the sun rose slowly from beyond the beckoning
horizon.

Thoughts of her father being alone on the hillside
that overlooked the Mississippi River in Missouri sent
a keen melancholia through Lauralee. She shivered
from loneliness for her father.

But knowing that she must move on with her life she
started to leave her bed of blankets, but stopped. A
thrill shot through her when she noticed how considure-
ate Dancing Cloud continued to be. While she had
slept he had covered her with a warm buffalo robe. He
had placed fresh wood on the fire, which had revived

the flames and now swept around the logs like orange, caressing fingers. A large bowl of delicious-looking, plump purple grapes for her breakfast sat nearby.

She was so touched by his thoughtfulness she wanted to thank him now. Not later, after he returned from his early swim.

Scampering to her bare feet, and ignoring her wrinkled dress and tangled hair, she ran to the riverbank. She looked for Dancing Cloud.

Just as she found him making a bend in the river, his powerfully muscled strokes taking him swiftly through the water, her voice froze in her throat. A water moccasin was slithering its way through the water toward him. Lauralee could tell that he was unaware of the snake!

Instead, he had just caught sight of Lauralee standing there.

He smiled, then stopped with a start and eyed her with a strange wonder as he stared at the rifle that she had grabbed up from the ground and seemed to be aiming at him.

Many thoughts ran through his mind in a matter of seconds.

He knew that she had not wanted an escort to Mattoon.

But he had thought that she had accepted the fact that she would be better off in the company of a man who could offer protection.

Had he been wrong?

Did she, in truth, resent his presence so much that she would shoot him to rid herself of him?

He had even thought there was a bond, even a mutual attraction that had formed between them.

How could he have been so wrong about so many things? he despaired.

Dancing Cloud started to make a deep dive to get away from the bullets she might fire at him.

But he was not quick enough.

He heard the report of the gun.

As though in a daze, thinking that he would feel the sting of the bullet at any moment now, Dancing Cloud continued to gaze up at Lauralee.

As far as he knew, she would be the last thing that he would see before dying. . . .

Then his gaze shifted just as the bullet made a splash in the water on his right side. His insides grew cold when he now realized what she had been truly shooting at.

A water moccasin!

And she had missed!

The snake was still making its way toward him.

"Dancing Cloud!" Lauralee cried, her heart skipping a beat when she realized that her aim had not been accurate enough.

And how could she have thought that it would be?

She was not at all familiar with firearms. The people in charge of the orphanage certainly did not take the time to teach their children such things.

Dancing Cloud was filled with many emotions. Relief that Lauralee had tried to save his life, and fear that he might not be quicker than the snake this time. Often he had grabbed a snake around its head before it had struck with its fangs.

But this time he was in water.

He had nothing on which to anchor himself.

Where he was treading water the river was deeper than his height.

The only way to possibly save himself was to take a deep dive, them come up behind the creature.

Without further thought he dove deeply into the water and swam a short distance.

Just as he surfaced the snake turned and faced him.

Dancing Cloud made another deep dive and this time came up behind the water moccasin. With the speed that might be compared to a lightning strike he grabbed the snake around the scaly flesh of its neck and held onto it as it struggled to get free. He did not want to kill the creature. He just wanted it out of his way, and Lauralee's.

With the snake still struggling within the powerful grip of Dancing Cloud's hand, he swim with one arm to the opposite shore from where Lauralee awaited him.

When he reached the shore and was able to place his feet on the pebbled bottom of the river, he took a mighty swing with his arm and tossed the snake as far as he could onto the land.

Knowing that the snake might be dazed only for a moment, then might return to the river, Dancing Cloud turned and swam quickly to the other side.

When he pulled himself out of the water only then did he remember that he was nude. Lauralee's eyes were wide as she stared at him. Then she dropped his rifle to the ground and turned and ran away from him, screaming.

When Lauralee reached the campsite she struggled to regain her normal breathing. She tremored and hugged herself as she stood over the fire, staring into the dancing flames. Seeing Dancing Cloud standing there nude had sent hideous remembrances of the soldier standing nude before her mother . . . of the soldier throwing her mother to the ground . . . of the soldier mounting her mother, her mother's screams even now echoing over 'and over again within Lauralee's memory.

Warm hands gripping her shoulders made Lauralee come back to reality. Dancing Cloud turned her to face him. She was glad that he had taken the time to get dressed. Now she was a little more relaxed.

But if today was an example of how she would behave in the presence of a nude man, then her future with any man, even Dancing Cloud was bleak.

While working in the hospital, helping men who were ill, she had not reacted so strangely to their nudity. But a man who had his full strength and faculties was a different matter!

"You saved my life and then ran from me as though frightened of me," Dancing Cloud said, his voice drawn. "Did my nudity frighten you? I was so anxious to thank you for what you did that I forgot I had no clothes on."

His dark eyes searched hers. "Was my body so ugly to you?" he asked sullenly. "Is that why you reacted so strangely to it? Or is it something else? You can confide in me."

Whispers and sighs of the wind feathered through the trees. Birds were awakening with their cheerful chatter. Squirrels were scampering overhead on limbs.

Everything was beautiful and innocent this morning, except for Lauralee's memories, which clung to her like glue.

Always the steel-blue eyes of her mother's rapist appeared, reminding her of what men could do to women.

It was hard to replace in her heart those moments when she had witnessed such a sweet loving between her parents when her father had held her mother in his arms, and how he kissed her so gently.

That was what Lauralee wanted.

A sweet loving!

"Lauralee, if I frighten you this much how can we continue together?" Dancing Cloud insisted, his fingers tightening on her shoulders. He leaned down into her face. "Do you want me to leave? Although I promised your father that I would be your escort, I cannot do this if you are frightened of me."

Panic seized Lauralee. She could not bear to continue the journey without Dancing Cloud. She could hardly bear to see the hurt that she had inflicted on him because of her inability to interact with him as a normal person might do. She saw herself as less than normal because of her inability to place her past totally behind her.

She had learned to live with such a disability until

she had met Dancing Cloud. In him she had seen all that she ever wanted in a man.

Her body spoke to her in unknown ways when she was in his presence. But these natural hungers frightened her.

Yet, she could not bear to send him away. Somehow she had to find a way to overcome her past, of her fears of being with a man sexually.

Without further thought she wrenched herself free of his clasping fingers and flung herself into his arms.

"I'm sorry," she said, her body racked with sobs. "I don't want you to go."

"But, Lauralee, the way you behaved only moments ago," Dancing Cloud said, his heart throbbing over her closeness and the way she clung so desperately to him. "What was I to think?"

"I never meant to hurt you," Lauralee sobbed. "It just happened."

"Then you are not frightened of me?"

"Not you. Just of my feelings."

"Because I was nude?"

"Yes."

"Is my body unpleasant to look at?"

Lauralee eased somewhat away from him. "No," she murmured. She wiped tears from her eyes as she gazed up at him. She felt that same familiar melting sensation that came with being so near him.

And his eyes.

Oh, how they mesmerized her.

"Nothing about you is ugly," she murmured. "Please believe me when I tell you that my behavior moments ago had nothing at all to do with you."

Dancing Cloud's lips quavered into a slow smile. "That is good to know," he said, trying to make things more lighthearted between them. "I would not want to think that seeing my body caused such a reaction. The Cherokee men take much pride in their muscles and bronzed skin."

Dancing Cloud decided not to question her further. It

was obvious that something had triggered her reaction. If it was not because she found him loathsome, then it was something else. He would wait until she was ready to confide in him.

Lauralee laughed softly. "You have much to be proud of," she said, blushing when she realized how that must have sounded.

"Thank you for the buffalo robe and for picking the grapes for breakfast," she blurted, to change the subject. "And for building the fire. It helped to ward off the chill of the morning."

"Will grapes be enough for you?" Dancing Cloud asked as she swung away from him to walk beside him toward the campsite. "I felt that something lighter might be best since we have a long trip today in the hot sun."

"Thank goodness I purchased a covered buggy for my comfort," Lauralee said, smiling up at him. "And, yes, grapes will be fine until we stop for lunch. Then for supper I will show you what the cooks at the orphanage prepared for our long trip. I was too tired last night to spread a fancy cloth for our meal. Tonight, however, I shall not spread only a checkered cloth on the ground, but place many surprises upon it for you."

So relieved to see that Lauralee was behaving her normal self again, Dancing Cloud placed his arm around her waist and swung her to face him. He saw no fear in her eyes as she gazed up at him. Instead he saw a need that matched his own. He drew her close.

"Lauralee," he whispered as he lowered his lips to hers, glad that she allowed it.

He did not imagine her arms twining around his neck and the way she returned his kiss so willingly and sweetly.

He did not imagine the feelings that were soaring through him like a raging fire.

He did not imagine it when she just as quickly wrenched herself free and stared up at him again with wild, frightened eyes, then stormed away from him and stood beside her buggy, clutching the seat, her back to him.

Stunned by her sudden mood changes, Dancing Cloud looked at her, his lips parted. He knew that she enjoyed being kissed! Why then did she run away from him as though he were a rogue? A kiss was all that he had wanted from her. Nothing more. If it were more than that, then he could understand why she might be afraid, or feel incensed by his boldness.

He hung his head and shook it slowly, then knelt down beside the fire and stared into the flames. He now realized that he was in love with a complex, troubled woman. It was evident that she had been scarred from some experience in her past, but would she ever be able to overcome it? he wondered. Somehow he had to find a way to help her forget.

Lauralee was keenly aware of having once more inflicted hurt on the man she loved, yet she felt helpless in being able to stop herself. It was as though an alarm went off inside her brain, an alarm that warned her not to let a man get this close to her vulnerable self.

Yet her insides tremored sensually as she recalled the power of his kiss, the power it had *over* her. If any man could make her forget, it was Dancing Cloud.

She turned and slowly walked toward Dancing Cloud. When she reached him she knelt down beside him. "Again I apologize," she murmured.

When he turned his eyes to her, she became swallowed whole by the intensity of his gaze. She moved limply into his arms.

"Please kiss me again," she whispered against his lips. "I promise you that I shall not run from you this time."

Fearing a reenactment of what had just happened moments ago, Dancing Cloud hesitated.

But with her lips so soft and trembling against his, he could not deny her anything.

He swept her gently into his arms and kissed her softly, then eased her away from him.

As their eyes held, the feelings were there, like liquid, warm light, between them. Dancing Cloud wanted to take her into his arms and carry her to his bed of blankets and prove to her that she had no reason to fear him and that what he had for her was something special and pure.

But that would have to come later, after her full trust was gained again.

"Shall we have breakfast?" Dancing Cloud asked, taking her hand and walking her toward the bowl of grapes. "Swimming always makes me hungry."

"I hope I haven't spoiled the morning for you," Lauralee said, giving him a quick, apologetic glance.

He turned heavy eyes down at her. "You could never ruin anything for me," he said thickly. "Do you not know that I love you and would protect you with my life?"

Lauralee's eyes widened and her pulse raced. He had just confessed to loving her. She felt the same way about him but just couldn't find the words.

Yet, she knew that he wouldn't believe her even if she did reveal her true feelings for him. Not after her behavior toward him this morning. To love someone as totally as she loved Dancing Cloud, she had to find a way to prove it, without becoming frightened by her feelings.

And she would.

For now, she just smiled sweetly up at him.

When they sat down on the blanket near the fire and he fed her that first grape, she looked adoringly into his eyes, wondering what tonight might bring.

Could she fight off the tormenting memory of the blue-eyed, red-haired Yankee and allow herself to love this wonderful man without reservations? Or would that hideous creature always be there, raping her, instead of her mother?

"I wonder what the city of Mattoon is like?" she said quickly, to stop her torturous thoughts.

"Nothing like the Great Smoky Mountains where I

make my residence," Dancing Cloud said, picking up another grape. He looked intensely into her eyes. "I would much rather be taking you there, instead of Mattoon. I have for so long been looking for that special woman to bring laughter into my lodge."

"How can you want me as that woman?" Lauralee asked softly, casting her eyes downward. "Too often you have seen my tears instead of laughter."

Dancing Cloud placed a finger beneath her chin and lifted her eyes to his. "I will do everything within my power to make that change," he said thickly. "One day I hope you will never have cause to cry again. Your face is like the sunshine when you laugh. It fills my very soul with its warmth."

Moved deeply by his words, and the sincerity in which they were spoken, Lauralee felt closer to him now than she would have ever thought possible. She so badly wanted to move into his arms and kiss him.

But she feared disappointing him again. If that damnable Yankee appeared in her mind's eye again and she behaved like a crazy fool, Dancing Cloud might soon take back his wonderful loving words, thinking that she was too undeserving of them.

"Perhaps I will go with you to your beautiful mountain some day," she said, instead. "But for now I must make things right in my life in Mattoon."

He nodded, yet doubted that she could ever make things right in her life while living among the white people. Thus far her life bordered on tragedy. He blamed the white community for this. He felt that the only place that she could possibly find peace was among his people. For however long it took, he would see that she became as one *with* his people, as his *wife*.

He would erase all fears from her life and her heart.

And she *would* allow it.

He would not take no for an answer.

7

Will, when speaking well can't win her,
Saying nothing do?
Pr'y thee, why so mute?

—JOHN SUCKLING

The day had passed uneventfully along the trail. Night had come with its black umbrella sky, sequins of stars sparkling like small fires in the heavens.

The campfire built, and their private rituals seen to, Lauralee lifted a picnic basket from the back of her buggy.

Dancing Cloud became comfortable as he reclined on a blanket beside the campfire, one long leg stretched out before him. With a quiet wonder he watched Lauralee spread a checkered cloth on the ground, then placed sparkling china, as well as fancy cloth napkins and silverware on the cloth, all of which she had purchased with her inheritance.

Lauralee was being particular with how she prepared the cloth for the picnic. She had read many novels during her teen years, in which she had discovered ways to make a picnic pleasant, especially if one wanted to please a man.

While she purchased these special things for her picnic with Dancing Cloud she had not allowed her troubled thoughts to get in the way of how she wished it could be between herself and the handsome Cherokee.

She had recently discovered, however, that it was easy to fantasize.

It was another matter to actually live it.

Now with Dancing Cloud so close, watching her, she wondered if she should have not gone this far to make this picnic so alluring. With the delicious cheeses, breads, and fruits that the cooks at the orphanage had placed in her basket, and with the bottle of wine that she had purchased for this occasion, she knew that she had created an atmosphere for lovers.

"You call this that we are going to share a *picnic*?" Dancing Cloud said, unfamiliar with the word, or the ritual.

"Yes, a picnic," Lauralee said, smiling shyly over at him as she sat down opposite him. She scooted a plate in front of him, and also a napkin and silverware.

She hesitated placing a tall-stemmed wineglass beside his plate, thinking that might be going just a mite too far.

She even doubted that he drank alcoholic beverages. She had heard that most Indians turned their eyes away from such drinks, except for those whose disappointments in life led them into drinking.

"If you'd rather not have this picnic, I'd understand," Lauralee then blurted out, clasping her hands together on her lap. "It is a bit presumptuous of me to think that you'd want to sit with me like this with such fanciness."

"After you have gone to such trouble?" Dancing Cloud said, reaching to the center of the cloth to get some cheese and bread. "I would not think to turn my back to this which you offer me."

"Then you do like it?" Lauralee asked, her eyes brightening. "You don't think I'm being childish?"

"I find you, and everything you do, anything but childish," Dancing Cloud replied, his dark eyes imploring her as their eyes locked and held.

Instead of placing the food that he had chosen on his own plate, he reached over and placed it on Lauralee's. He also placed several slices of apple on her plate, then took it upon himself to remove the cork from the wine bottle and poured her a glass.

Smiling, feeling a sweet bliss flowing through her veins, Lauralee, in turn, readied his plate with food. She took the bottle of wine and poured him a glass.

They ate in silence, their eyes smiling into each other's. Dancing Cloud had developed a fondness for wine while in Boyd's company, yet he drank it sparingly because it could quickly send his head into a crazy spinning.

But tonight the wine was not the cause for him to feel giddy. The air was charged with feelings being exchanged between himself and Lauralee, and he felt that just perhaps she was getting beyond her fears of being close to him.

Still, he would not chance upsetting her again. Tonight was a perfect time for them to become more acquainted in a less sensual way. After all, they did not know that much about each other.

Through the years, when Boyd had talked about Lauralee, Dancing Cloud had grown to know her as only a small child.

This adult Lauralee was something much more than Boyd's remembrances of the child Lauralee, or of his descriptions of her.

Lauralee, as an adult, was someone fascinating, beautiful, and wonderfully gentle.

She was everything Dancing Cloud wanted in a wife—except for that dark side of her that he had yet to penetrate, and perhaps never would.

This was why he must go slowly with her. Just perhaps that side of her that she kept hidden might open up to him like the bud of a flower unfolds itself to the warming rays of the sun, and at the same time relieve herself of her burden.

"Lauralee, tell me about yourself, why you chose to enter the nursing profession," he said, breaking the silence that had fallen between them.

"For many reasons," Lauralee said, taking a sip of

wine as she gazed into the fire. "I wanted to find a way to help the unfortunate. The hospital was on the grounds of the orphanage. That gave me the opportunity to work after school, and on weekends."

She looked over at him. "I never actually went to nursing school and became a registered nurse," she murmured. "That was in my plans but I just never got around to it. I knew enough about nursing to be able to help out at the hospital. I was content with what I knew, and seemed to be able to use my skills well enough to get me by. The important thing was that I was helping someone. I needed that—to feel that I was worth something. That I was not just a forgotten person."

"Your father never forgot you," Dancing Cloud quickly corrected. "I traveled with him many times while he searched for you. He thought that someone had taken you in, to raise as their own. He did not ever mention an orphanage. I believe perhaps because he did not ever want to think of you as an orphan. The word 'orphan' means 'a child deprived.' He never wanted to think of you as deprived, or alone without family."

"And I was both," Lauralee said, her voice breaking. "It will be wonderful to be a part of a family again. The Petersons in Mattoon are generous to offer me this opportunity."

"I also offer you this opportunity," Dancing Cloud blurted out before he could stop himself. "You could be my wife. *We* could be a family."

Lauralee's eyes wavered. She looked away from him. She had intense feelings for him. Yet until she knew that she could perform duties *of* a wife, in which intimacy was shared between a man and a woman, she would not torture herself into even considering marrying Dancing Cloud.

"That would not be the same," she said, her heart sinking as she spoke the words that she did not mean. She wanted him with all of her heart and soul.

Yet not only did she fear that intimate side of a relationship, she felt that she must follow through with her promise to her father, as well as fulfill that promise to the Petersons.

They had been without a child forever.

She was going to fill that space in their lives left there from being childless.

Dancing Cloud's insides stiffened. He had never asked a woman to marry him. And now that he had the same as said the words to Lauralee and she had turned him down, it was as though a part of his heart had been cut away.

Yet he could not allow her to see disappointment, nor his wounded pride.

And he would not give up on her all that easily, either. When she placed the demons of her past behind her *he* would be there to lead her into a wonderful future of happiness.

"Tell me about yourself, Dancing Cloud," Lauralee quickly interjected, to change the subject back to something less personal, and hurtful. "I have always been fascinated by Indian culture."

Dancing Cloud bit off a piece of cheese and washed it down with wine. He then shoved the wineglass and dish away and again relaxed on the blanket. As he talked he watched the fire-thrown shadows dance across Lauralee's lovely face, wanting her no less now than before she had rejected his marriage proposal.

"My people are woodland people," he said quickly, glad to enter into small talk with her. The more serious would have to wait again until another time. "We lead the hunter's life and have always followed the path of peace. The Cherokee were never lawless savages as most have said."

He paused, leaned over and shoved another log into the fire. "Long ago a solid silver pipe from George Washington was placed on the council table of the Cherokee," he said thickly. "The same hand of Thomas Jefferson that wrote the Declaration of Independence also helped the Cherokee draft their early laws. The Cherokee takes pride in the knowledge that they are a people of respect and of law who understand when and how to use the respect in a lawful process."

"If the Cherokee thought so much of George Washington and Thomas Jefferson, why then did they choose to fight for the South, instead of the North?" Lauralee asked softly.

"My people met in council and made this decision as though we were all one mind and heart," Dancing Cloud said, in his mind's eye recalling the day that he had sat beside his father in council, his heart already knowing with whom he wanted to fight. With Boyd Johnston's regiment. How could he choose differently? He had known Boyd since he was eight. He had looked to him as a second father figure.

"Was my father among those sitting in council?" Lauralee asked, recalling the very day her father had left to travel to the mountains to meet with Dancing Cloud's chieftain father.

"Yes, Boyd was there. Your father explained many things while in council that day. We came to realize that we could not be sure how the North would treat our people during such a vicious war that had been started between the white people. The South had at least some feelings for the Cherokee's way of life."

He paused and inhaled a quavering breath, these remembrances of a time that had then seemed exciting, now like a hot brand upon his memory, so vividly remembering the bloody trail of the Civil War.

"Our people also knew that it was not a war fought for free soil or dignity of the farmer," he then said. "It was fought for things only whites ever fight for—power and profit. The Cherokee did not want to see that gained at the expense of our people!"

He paused again, then said, "On October seven in the year 1861 a treaty was concluded by which all Cherokee cast their lot with the Confederacy," he said softly. "The Cherokee nation always strives faithfully to uphold its treaty obligations."

They had been so drawn together into conversation they had not noticed that the sky had lost its lustrous stars. Thunder trembled the ground beneath them and lurid streaks of lightning flashing across the dark heavens sent Lauralee and Dancing Cloud quickly to their feet.

With the help of Dancing Cloud, Lauralee soon had everything back in the wicker basket and secured at the back of the buggy.

Just as the heavens opened up, and the rain came down in a blinding rush, Dancing Cloud led Lauralee into a cave, two blankets thrown across one of his arms.

When he noticed that Lauralee was trembling he took one of the blankets and placed it around her shoulders.

"Where on earth did this storm come from?" Lauralee asked, shivering. She peered through the sheet of rain and saw that the campfire had been quickly extinguished. "And what if it rains all night?"

Dancing Cloud lit a match and looked into the depths of the cave. He discovered that others had used it for lodging. A circle of rocks held within them a pile of cold, gray ash. Not far from where a campfire had been built, several logs had been stacked, unused.

"We shall make camp in the cave for the night," Dancing Cloud said, already laying the logs on the circle of rocks. "When I first noticed the cave I thought it might be best to sleep there, anyhow. I had just not yet had the chance to tell you about it."

Lauralee turned and looked warily around her, the campfire just now taking hold as the flames cast dancing shadows along the wall of the cave. "When I think of a cave, I think of *bats*," she said, again shivering, not from the cold, but from the thoughts of a bat suddenly swooping down on her, tangling itself into her thick hair.

"Do not fear bats," Dancing Cloud said, spreading the other blanket out beside the fire. "They fear humans. If there are any bats in this cave, they will stay hidden."

Smiling weakly, Lauralee sat down on the blanket beside Dancing Cloud. She reached her hands over the fire and absorbed the warmth into her flesh. "Dancing Cloud, I have been wondering about something," she said, glancing over at him.

"About what?" he said, nudging the blanket back into place on her shoulders when it began slipping down her arms.

"When you see poison ivy, why do you always address it as though it is your friend?"

Dancing Cloud chuckled. His eyes danced into hers. "In the old, innocent days of my youth, I was taught that poison ivy is feared by all Cherokee, and being polite to it is a way to conciliate it . . . to gain its goodwill," he explained. "I have carried that teaching into my adult life. It is a habit I shall never break, it seems."

A great crash of thunder and a fierce bolt of lightning that was so bright it lit up the entrance of the cave caused Lauralee to lurch with fright. When Dancing Cloud's arm snaked around her shoulders, she tightened inside. She feared disappointing him again.

But a kiss? she wondered desperately to herself as his lips moved toward hers. What harm is there in just one little kiss? She so badly wanted to feel his lips upon hers again. He had such beautiful lips, so soft and gentle.

Dancing Cloud framed her face between his hands and gazed down at her. "*O-ge-ye,* my woman, allow my kissing you," he said huskily. "Passion is not so much an emotion as it is a destiny. It is *our* destiny, *o-ge-ye,* to come together, as one."

Lauralee's heart pounded fiercely within her chest. Her throat was dry. Her knees were weak. She prayed to the good Lord that Dancing Cloud's kiss would not once again bring horrid memories to destroy this moment.

She wanted to enjoy the kiss.

She wanted to enjoy *him*.

All of him!

She closed her eyes and laced her fingers through his hair as she urged his lips to hers. When he kissed her, everything within her melted into a wild bliss, the urgency of wanting to be free to love giving way to a dismayed, wonderful pleasure.

And then, like those flashes of lurid lightning that were erupting along the sky outside, came the face of the blue-eyed Yankee. His laughter rushed through her like a black dread. Her mother's screams swept through her like wildfire.

Lauralee shoved Dancing Cloud away and grabbed up her blanket and rushed away from him, stopping where the light of the fire still reached and lit up the dank gloom around her. She lay down on the blanket and pulled its corners around her. She curled up on her side, trembling, her eyes wild.

Dancing Cloud sat in a stunned silence, thinking that she was lost to him, forever. Never again would he attempt to kiss her, much less anything more sensual. He was anxious now to get her to Mattoon. He would leave her there and never look back, yet knowing that his heart would remain there with her. He doubted that he could ever love again, for she would always be there in his memory, so beautiful, so gentle, so sweet.

And so totally frightened, he thought despairingly to himself.

8

All tastes, all pleasures, all desires combine,
To consecrate this sanctuary of bliss.

—CHARLES SWAIN

Lauralee fell into a fitful sleep, then awakened quickly when she heard something that sounded like the rush of wind approaching her. She turned over and noticed that the fire had died down to glowing embers. She could hear that the rain had stopped outside the cave. And Dancing Cloud was asleep on a blanket several feet away from her.

The strange sound that awakened her grew closer and louder. Lauralee clasped her blanket up tightly beneath her chin as she rose slowly to a sitting position.

A scream froze in her throat and her eyes grew wild and wide when she finally discovered what was making the sound.

Bats!

Hundreds of bats were entering the cave in a massive cluster of black. The embers of the fire gave off just enough light for her to make them out in the semi-darkness as they swept by her overhead. A dizziness overcame her when she realized that they were so close she could reach up and touch them.

Never had she been as afraid.

She could not move.

No sound would come from her throat.

The thunderous roar of the bats flying overhead

awakened Dancing Cloud. He sat up quickly and looked in awe at the flying creatures as they continued to sweep past.

Then he shifted his eyes quickly to Lauralee. Earlier she had spoken to him of her fear of bats. He could see the fear in her eyes now, the wildness, as she stared up at the rushing throng of black creatures.

Although he could see that she was stiff and pale from fear, he could not go to her. He knew the dangers of making any movement. If even one bat became alarmed and flew away from the others, that could possibly change the direction of the rest of them.

They might even be confused and fly around in a frenzy, attacking anything they might come in contact with.

Yet Dancing Cloud saw that he *must* go to Lauralee, to assure her that he would protect her. Although she had given him good cause to ignore her, his love for her sent him quickly to his feet.

He kept himself bent low as he moved slowly and stealthily around the glowing embers of the fire. When Lauralee turned her frightened eyes toward him, he gave her a look of warning. If she jumped to her feet without thought, she could alarm the bats into a wild frenzied flight of fright.

"Do not move," Dancing Cloud whispered. "I will come to you. Stay quiet, Lauralee. Just . . . stay . . . quiet."

Lauralee tremored as she waited for him to reach her. She hugged the blanket around her shoulders, her eyes again on the bats. How could there be so many? They just kept coming and coming!

Warm, comforting arms were soon around her shoulders, enveloping them. As Dancing Cloud knelt down over her, she turned to him and clung desperately to him. "Thank you for coming to me," she sobbed. "I'm so frightened."

"The bats are returning from their nightly feeding," Dancing Cloud whispered back, slowly and comfortingly stroking her back through the blanket. "The storm must have interrupted their return to their home. They seized the opportunity now since the rain has stopped."

He paused and squinted his eyes as he looked farther into the cave. "The cave is deep," he then said. "Soon we will not even be aware of their presence. They will reach their resting places."

"We must get out of here as soon as possible," Lauralee whispered shakily, gazing wild-eyed up at Dancing Cloud. "I don't want to chance them discovering us here. There are so many. They could surely kill us."

"If you wish we can leave the cave," Dancing Cloud said, gently framing her face between his hands. "But I can assure you that we are safe here. You will be much more comfortable in here out of the dampness that the rain has left in the grass, trees, and air. The embers of the fire in the cave will be enough to give us lasting warmth until morning."

Lauralee looked up at him a moment longer, then lowered her eyes when she recalled only awhile ago when she had fled from him as though he were a monster.

"How can you be so kind to me after . . . after . . . I . . ." she started to say, but was stopped when Dancing Cloud placed a finger to her lips, gently sealing them.

"Do not fret so about something that you were driven to do because of something that is troubling you," he said thickly. "No matter what you have done, we still remain friends."

Dancing Cloud having put it to her in such an impersonal way, that he now only classified himself as her *friend*, made Lauralee's insides quiver with a warning. Had she lost his love after having only gained it?

"Dancing Cloud, I'm sorry for my behavior," she said, her voice breaking. "I never wanted to hurt you. Dancing Cloud, I love you so much. I . . . I . . . *need* you. But I'm afraid of this need. How can I learn not to be afraid to show my love for you? Or is it too late? Has your love for me turned into something else?"

Dancing Cloud wove his fingers through her silken coppery-red hair and drew her lips close to his. "I shall love you forever," he said huskily. "Even if you are not there to *return* the love. A love as powerful as mine is for you can never be cast aside into the wind."

He wanted to kiss her, but he was afraid that doing so might set off something within her mind that would send her away from him again.

He uncoiled his fingers from her hair and started to lean away from her.

But her arms were there too quickly locked around his neck for him to move.

"The bats are gone," she murmured. "I feel much more relaxed now. Will you please kiss me? Will you please teach me how it feels to be loved? I want you. I need you. Please teach me how not to fear these feelings I have for you."

"You have always fled my arms when I have tried to become close to you," Dancing Cloud said, smoothing her hair back from her face. "How can you be sure you will not leave me again, as frightened? I want to make love to you. Yet I fear this want, as *you* do. I fear you denying again that which I want to share with you."

"I want you too badly now ever to run from you again," Lauralee said, her hands already slipping his fringed shirt over his shoulders. "If I start recalling the past, I shall not allow it to devastate me again."

"Your past? What happened in your past that is so ugly to you? I know of your mother's death. Was there something else? Do you carry invisible war scars in your memory that you do not even wish to share with me?" Dancing Cloud asked, his insides quavering as her fingers moved along his chest, and across his flat stomach, stopping at the waist of his buckskin breeches.

"You truly don't want to know," she murmured. Her

fingers trembled as she dared to lower his breeches. Yet she knew this was the only way to prove to herself that her feelings for him could overcome her remembrances of her ugly past.

"Did a man force himself on you?" Dancing Cloud asked, lifting her chin with a finger so that her eyes would lock with his.

"Not I," she said, swallowing hard. "My *mother.* I witnessed my mother being raped. A Yankee. During the war, a Yankee raped and killed my mother."

She could hardly believe that she had actually told someone besides her father and the priest with whom she had confided everything all of those years ago the terrible secret of her past.

And now that she had purged herself of the ugliness, she truly felt as though she might be able to leave it behind her.

"You have carried this with you since you were five?" Dancing Cloud said, then drew her gently into his arms and held her close. "No wonder you have been too frightened to allow yourself to feel anything for a man. *O-ge-ye,* my woman, I will show you how it should be between a man and a woman who mutually love each other."

"You will be gentle?" Lauralee asked, her pulse racing at the thought of actually giving herself to a man sexually. But she felt that if she didn't do this now, she might not only lose Dancing Cloud, she might never find the courage *ever* to make love to a man.

She hoped and prayed that she would not be stifled again by the thoughts of the rape.

Especially not while searching for bliss within the arms of the man she loved.

She wanted it behind her.

Once and for all!

For as long as Dancing Cloud would love her.

For forever!

"*Ii,* yes, gentle," Dancing Cloud said, his heart

pounding. "I shall show you how it should be between a man and a woman in love. Just relax. Allow it."

"Yes, I will allow it," Lauralee said, drawing a ragged breath of anticipation. "I *want* it."

Dancing Cloud's eyes swept over her with a silent, urgent message, then he tilted her chin and touched her lips wonderingly with his.

Cradling her close, he kissed her softly at first, and then his mouth seared into hers.

Lauralee moaned against his lips, a wild, exuberant passion spinning through her veins. Her hands sought out the feel of his sleek back, then moved around. She ran them over his smooth chest, her fingers lightly pinching his nipples until he groaned with pleasure.

When her hands roamed lower and she felt something hard and long pressing against the inside of his breeches, she fought off the alarm of realizing what it was. She refused to allow remembrances of another man, another time, enter her consciousness. This was Dancing Cloud. He had promised her that he would be gentle.

Wanting to prove to herself that she could continue with what had started between herself and Dancing Cloud, she shakily placed her fingers over the swell of his manhood and slowly caressed him through the thin fabric of buckskin.

She did not flinch and draw away when he began moving his body in rhythmic motion with her caressing hand.

She kissed him long and hard. She could tell that she was giving him pleasure by the way he occasionally emitted soft moans and groans against her lips. She found it hard to understand, but she was getting pleasure from giving it to him.

Her whole insides warmed to the ecstasy that was pressing forth within her. She came alive in ways never known to her before.

And then she drew her hand away. She became stiff when Dancing Cloud backed away from her and she was the reason why. He needed room between them to loosen the buttons of her white cotton blouse.

She scarcely breathed when he swept her blouse away from her shoulders, her breasts now fully exposed to him.

She felt the heat of his gaze as he looked at her breasts, aware herself of her erect rosy nipples that had stiffened from desiring his hands on them.

And when he cupped them in his hands, his thumb slowly circling the nipple, Lauralee closed her eyes, her knees almost buckling beneath her from the rapture. A kind of slow fire was beginning to lick through her body, burning where his fingers touched. The heat was tiding through her, flowing everywhere.

When he bent to flick his tongue around one of her nipples, the feeling of wild bliss came at once, startling her. And then she was aware of another new sensation after he skillfully, quickly finished disrobing her. One of his hands swept down where curls of coppery-colored hair hid the secrets of her womanhood. Lauralee sucked in a wild breath of pleasure as one of his fingers delved into her clasping, moist inner flesh.

A brief moment of pain ensued, and then the sweetest sensations followed as he caressed her where her throbbing mound was slowly awakening to unknown bounds of pleasure.

Dancing Cloud's blood spun hot and wild through his veins. He realized now that Lauralee had finally placed her fears behind her and was ready to accept the ultimate of pleasure. He drew her within his powerful arms and kissed her, freeing one of his hands so that he could shove his buckskin breeches to the floor of the cave.

When he was freed of his clothes, and nothing more stood between them, he lifted Lauralee into his arms and placed her on the blanket, then knelt over her. He parted her thighs with a knee. He smiled down at her as he again stroked the swollen cleft between her thighs.

Her hair disarrayed around her smooth and creamy shoulders had a coppery sheen that reflected the blushing glow from the embers of the fire. Her hips curved voluptuously from her slender waist. Her pale, ivory breasts were well rounded, and her soft, full thighs were open wide, an invitation for him to enter.

"Relax now and let me transport you to paradise," Dancing Cloud whispered, brushing a soft kiss across her lips, and then her breasts. "Do not stiffen. Allow your body to mesh with mine. Slowly. I shall enter you slowly."

Lauralee's eyes were wide as she gazed down at his hand as he led his hardness inside her. She scarcely breathed. When remembrances of her mother screaming tried to rob her of this moment of pleasure, she found the willpower to brush it from her mind.

Pleasure.

She would feel only pleasure.

Dancing Cloud was gentle.

Dancing Cloud loved her.

He ... was ... not taking her by force!

She was allowing it!

Dancing Cloud shoved himself fully into her and delved into the rose-red, slippery heat of her innermost sensual place. He showered her with loving kisses as he began his rhythmic strokes within her, her inner flesh warm and clinging like an embrace.

Lauralee sighed and relaxed her body. She closed her eyes and laced her fingers around Dancing Cloud's neck as between kisses she pleaded for more, her voice quivering emotionally in her excitement of the discovery of just how wonderful it was to be with a man. She swirled in a storm of passion that shook her innermost senses.

Dancing Cloud could feel the pulsing of the blood through his body. Lauralee's answering heat and excitement was wonderful to behold as she strained her hips upward. He buried himself deeply inside her. He kissed her hungrily. There was only the world of feeling, sliding, touching, throbbing.

He cupped her swelling breasts. They pulsed warmly beneath his fingers. His hands moved downward and cupped her buttocks in a sensual ecstasy. He forced her hips in at his, smooth and hard, as he crushed her against him.

He fought to go slowly, but there was a tingling sensation in his toes that worked its way upward. And then a great flood of sensations swept raggedly through him as their bodies jolted and quivered together.

Great waves of pleasure swept through Lauralee. Ecstasy raged and washed over her in great splashes, drenching her with warmth. She clung to Dancing Cloud and rocked and swayed with him.

And then their bodies stilled against each other. Tilting her head up, her fingers locked around his neck, she brought his mouth down hard upon hers. She moaned against his lips, their naked bodies still fused, flesh against flesh in gentle pleasure.

Sighing, Lauralee released her hold on Dancing Cloud. He slid away from her and lay at her side. They lay there for some time with her stroking his neck gently.

And then they turned and smiled at each other.

"Never shall I be afraid again," she murmured. "You sent my demons away tonight, my darling."

"I never shall allow them to return," Dancing Cloud promised. His hands moved over the glossy-textured skin of her breasts, and down over her ribs. He leaned over her and his lips brushed against the nipple of a breast. He kissed the nipple, sucking it.

Lauralee drew in her breath sharply and gave a little cry. A slow breeze of renewed excitement began like the deep rumblings of a volcano before its eruption.

Dancing Cloud stretched out on his back and lifted Lauralee so that she straddled him. When he entered her again, her hair spilled over her shoulders as she held her head back in ecstasy.

Dancing Cloud pressed himself endlessly deeper inside her. Lauralee moved with him, shocked at her intensity of feelings, of her ability to love so openly and so freely after having feared being with a man for so long.

A sudden curling of heat tightened inside her belly when his hands gently cupped her breasts. Everything but now, but *him,* and the pleasure, was cast from her mind.

In Mattoon, Illinois, the inside of Brian's Place Saloon was enveloped in a foggy haze of smoke. A piano tinkled out a jolly tune in a corner. Several men played billiards at a table swathed in green felt in the center of the room, a kerosene lamp hanging low over it.

Clint McCloud sat on a stool at the bar, enjoying a glass of whiskey and a good, fat cigar after a long day's labor supervising the replacement of tracks along the Illinois Central Railroad.

An unsociable sort, he did not join in the conversation at the bar. But his ears perked up at what was being said about Abner Peterson's niece arriving to Mattoon soon from St. Louis.

It was not so much the mention of Abner's niece that caused Clint to lean closer to listen more intently to the conversation. It was the mention of her *escort* that made Clint's eyebrows fork.

An Indian was her escort.

And not just any Indian.

A damn rebel Cherokee who had fought against the North during the Civil War.

From what was being said, he now knew that this Indian had fought for the same regiment that Clint had ambushed that day along the road near the Great Smoky Mountains.

He knew this to be true at the mention of Boyd Johnston's name. Johnston had been the leader of that Cherokee regiment . . . the very ones responsible for Clint's wooden leg.

An Indian had done the actual maiming. That Indian's face had been captured inside Clint's memory for posterity, like a leaf is fossilized into stone. If this was the same Cherokee, Clint would finally get his revenge. It had been obvious that Boyd Johnston and the Indian who had shot Clint were close friends. It only made sense that if this Boyd Johnston asked an Indian to escort Peterson's niece to Illinois, then it would more than likely be the Indian who had maimed Clint for life!

Grumbling, Clint slammed a coin on the counter of the bar. Limping, he left the saloon and stepped out on the boardwalk on Broadway Avenue. He stood there for a while as his mind swirled with plans.

He would find this Indian.

He would stalk him.

He would kill him at his first opportunity.

9

We parted in silence—our cheeks were wet
With the tears that were past controlling.
                                                —MRS. CRAWFORD

Lauralee and Dancing Cloud had traveled for several more days. They had entered Coles County long ago, which made Lauralee realize that Mattoon could not be that far away. Roads and trails had been made by earlier red men, those paths or "tracers" easily identified by their thick cover of blue grass, and by the presence of saplings whose branches had been twisted to point the way.

The road that Lauralee and Dancing Cloud had traveled on for some time was called the Cumberland Road, often referred to by some as the National Road.

But now they were going north on a highway called The Highway of Ebenezer Noyes.

Lauralee had enjoyed her journey through Illinois. A mixture of vast sea of tall prairie grass and trees covered the land. In some places the treeless terrain seemed endless.

In other places, prairies were smaller, with islands of groves dotting their surfaces, bordered and bisected by strong stands of hardwood trees.

Lauralee gazed around her now and sighed at the pleasant sight. A mosaic of wondrous color met her eyes. Blue stem, dock, Indian grass, and Canadian rye, some as high as a horseman's head, rippled in the sum-

mer wind. Wild vines rioted in the lower places. And
across the long ridges, nodding stems of ox-eye daisies
and sunflowers mingled with purple ironweed and
snake root.

Dancing Cloud enjoyed the journey as well. He had
seen enough to know that this land of Illinois was a
hunter's paradise. The wide fields of blue stem sheltered large numbers of deer, elk, raccoons, and foxes.
Rabbits, opossum, and squirrels were also plentiful.

He had also seen a good number of wild turkeys,
prairie chickens, and quail.

But what he disliked were the vicious green-headed
flies and gnats that could come in swarms without notice. He was also aware of the presence of malaria-
carrying mosquitoes.

The long, haunting whistle of a train a short distance
away made a keen excitement flow through Lauralee's
veins. Trains. The presence of trains meant that they
were most certainly nearing Mattoon. The town had
been established because two railroads crossed at mid-
point. The railroads had created the city. They had determined the character of its people and had brought
Mattoon prosperity, and made it a major hub in Central
Illinois.

Lauralee smiled when she recalled her father telling
her about Mattoon and the Petersons while they had
awaited Joe Dancing Cloud's arrival. Her father had
been to Mattoon only a few times, but knew that those
who lived there called themselves "Mattooners."

Boyd had told Lauralee that the city had been named
after the chief construction officer of the Terre Haute
and Alton Railroad, William B. Mattoon. She remembered how he had spoken with such fondness the tale
of how the name Mattoon had been chosen.

As tracks drew closer to the crossing point at
Mattoon, he had told her that Bill Mattoon challenged
Roswell Mason, engineer-in-chief of the Illinois Cen-
tral Railroad, to a track-laying contest.

Since Roswell Mason was not a gambling man he

refused the wager, but agreed that the crew that crossed the point first would have the honor of naming the future train station.

Roswell Mason's men won the race, and in gratitude of his opponent who had provided the incentive for his men's fast work, he named the station "Mattoon."

Lauralee sighed at the remembrance of her father, often gasping for breath, telling her so many other things about Mattoon. He had explained that mainly open prairie framed Mattoon on the east by the timbers of the Embarrass River and its tributaries, and on the west, by the Okaw and Little Wabash woodlands, with fingers or points of forest projecting into the open spaces.

Confused by the terrain now, and wondering which road she should take so that she could go directly into Mattoon, Lauralee brought her horse and buggy to a halt. She unfolded a map that her father had drawn for her. The rainstorm that had dampened her belongings in the buggy had smeared some of directions.

"Why do you stop?" Dancing Cloud asked, edging his horse closer to her buggy.

"I'm not sure which way to go." Lauralee gazed from side to side, at a road that looked more traveled than the one that she was on. She stared at a post in the road, upon which had been painted its name.

"Old State Road," she said, forking an eyebrow. "We are now on Old State Road."

She cast Dancing Cloud a questioning look. "I can no longer tell by the map which way to go, though," she said, refolding the map in fours. As several horsemen and horse-drawn wagons went past her on Old State Road, she could not help but think that this was the main artery through the city of Mattoon.

"I think we should go *that* way," she finally said, nodding to the right.

"I am not familiar with these roads, so I will follow you whichever way you go," Dancing Cloud said, giving her a shrug.

He was not at all anxious to reach Mattoon. Even though he had shown Lauralee that his love was intensely true for her, she still insisted that she must stay with the Petersons.

"At least for a while," she had said, to be sure that her promise to her father was kept.

Then later, she had promised, she would go to him. She would be his wife.

He was afraid that should he leave her behind, something might change her mind. Namely the Petersons. Surely to the Petersons Dancing Cloud would be an outcast. And not only because his skin was not white. But also because he fought for the South during the war.

He even felt as though he was entering enemy territory by *going* to Mattoon.

One thing for sure. He most certainly did not look forward to meeting Abner Peterson whose heart could still be filled with venom for those he had fought against.

Dancing Cloud was guilty of the same sorts of resentments. It was the Yankees who had ravaged his village during the war. Now it would be especially hard for him to come face to face with *any* staunch Union supporter!

But for the moment, for Lauralee and Boyd, he would place those feelings aside.

And he would leave Mattoon as soon as he saw that Lauralee was safely with the Petersons.

There was no need in tempting resentments to flair up into something ugly between himself and Abner Peterson; or anyone *else* whose heart lay with the Union during the war, for that matter.

They rode awhile longer on Old State Road, then through a break in the trees at Lauralee's left she got a glimpse of houses in the distance. If she stayed on this road she would bypass the city. She might even reach the town of Charleston.

After explaining to Dancing Cloud about the mistaken road on which they were traveling, they moved onto a narrow trail and went onward until they came to the edge of Mattoon. They turned onto a street named Broadway and soon found themselves directly in front of the Peterson House, seemingly the last house on the main street of Mattoon, on the east side.

Lauralee rode into the circular driveway and stopped when she reached the front of the house. She stared in awe at the grand, Italianate two-storied house. It was made of brick. Three tall windows looked down from the second floor at her, and a door flanked by two windows were on the first floor where a wide porch reached out across most of the front.

The house was landscaped beautifully with tall-timbered trees, a combination of oaks, elms, and maples. Flowers brightened circular gardens in the front lawn with their riots of color. Behind the house stretched a massive piece of land.

Her father had said that Abner Peterson had told him that one day he wished to see a park established on that land, with ponds, water fountains, and swings for children.

Abner had said that he wished to make sure picnic tables were placed throughout the park for family gatherings on Sunday.

She could envision such a place as that in her mind's eye and hoped that one day his dream could become a reality.

But for now, she was anxious to meet Abner and Nancy, so much that she could hardly wait to leave her buggy.

Dancing Cloud dismounted, secured his horse's reins on a hitching rail, then went and assisted Lauralee from her buggy.

"My heart is fluttering so," Lauralee said, beaming up at Dancing Cloud. In preparation for her arrival today she had dressed in a lovely pale blue travel suit, the skirt flared at the hem, the waist tight.

She wore a straw bonnet with a blue satin bow tied

beneath her chin, fine leather gloves on her hands, and glistening black slippers on her feet.

"Do I look presentable enough?" she asked, turning to gaze anxiously up at Dancing Cloud. "Do you think they will like me?"

"Perhaps too much," Dancing Cloud said before he could stop the words from passing across his lips.

Lauralee's smile faded. "Please understand why I must stay for a while with the Petersons," she softly pleaded. "Just remember that I love you. It will not be long until we will be together forever."

"That will seem forever," Dancing Cloud said. He stiffened when the front door of the Peterson House opened.

He then gazed down at Lauralee again. "I will leave now," he said, his voice drawn. "But I will return for you after I return home to see to my father's welfare."

"Aren't you staying to meet the Petersons?" Lauralee asked as he turned to walk away from her. She lifted the hem of her skirt and followed him to his horse. "Aren't you going to even kiss me goodbye?"

He turned to face her, then looked quickly up at the woman standing on the porch. He then gazed down at Lauralee again. "I do not think Mrs. Peterson would understand a red man kissing her niece," he said tightly.

Lauralee turned on a heel and her eyes brightened when she discovered a woman standing on the porch, who from her father's description, fit Nancy Peterson. She gave Nancy a soft smile, then turned to Dancing Cloud again. "Please stay," she pleaded. "Please let me introduce you to Aunt Nancy and Uncle Abner."

"Abner would not appreciate offering me, a rebel, a hand of friendship," Dancing Cloud said, swinging himself into his saddle. "As for Mrs. Peterson? She has the appearance of a sweet and caring woman. But I am sure she would share the feelings of her husband for someone who wore the uniform of a Confederate during the war. To them I may still be the *ha-ma-ma*, enemy."

He gazed longingly down at Lauralee. "*O-ge-ye*, my woman, may the *A-da-nv-do, Wah-kon-tah*, Great Spirit, follow you in my absence and keep you safe from all harm," he said thickly. "*A-qua-da-nv-do*, my heart stays with you, so that you will not forget this Cherokee who loves you."

Tears streamed from Lauralee's eyes. "I fear we may never see each other again," she said, stifling a sob behind a hand. "Promise you will return for me. *Promise*."

"Sometimes promises are foolish," Dancing Cloud said, his voice grim. "Had you not promised your father you would come to the Petersons, would you have not then felt free to come with Dancing Cloud, *instead*?"

At this moment, Lauralee felt torn between two worlds. That which would reunite her forever with true family, and that which would unite her with the man she loved.

"If you don't promise me, you might change your mind," she blurted. "Give me your word, Dancing Cloud, that you will return for me. I doubt you would want me to travel alone to come to *you*, when you were so adamant to escort me from Saint Louis to Mattoon."

"I will come for you," Dancing Cloud reassured. He gestured toward the sky with a hand. "When the moon is full again I will be here for you."

"God be with you," Lauralee said softly.

Watching him ride away sent a wave of melancholia through her.

But when Nancy spoke from behind her, Lauralee turned around and stared up at a most beautiful woman, whose dark eyes matched the darkest of all midnights. Although quite fleshy, Nancy's face was beautifully sculpted. Her brown hair was tied up in a tight chignon. She was short and heavyset, her large breasts straining against the inside of her dress.

"Nancy!" Lauralee cried, breaking into a run until she reached the porch. "Aunt Nancy!"

Lifting her skirt, Lauralee went up the three wooden steps, then stood eye to eye with Nancy Peterson on the porch. She soaked in the wonder of being with Nancy as though she were being reunited with her true mother.

"Lauralee?" Nancy said, reaching a thick, short hand to Lauralee's face, gently touching it. "You are Lauralee?"

"Yes, Aunt Nancy, I am your niece Lauralee," she said, then found herself engulfed within soft, thick arms. She returned the hug, the fragrance of her aunt's perfume pleasantly flaring her nostrils. The perfume was surely from France!

And, ah, the clothes that Nancy wore, Lauralee marveled to herself. Her dress was pure silk, pale yellow flowers dotting across a white backdrop of the expensive fabric.

"I'm so glad that you made it safely from Saint Louis," Nancy said, then took a step away from Lauralee and held her by the hands at arm's length, studying her. "And look at you. You are beautiful and such a picture of health."

She looked past Lauralee, only barely able to see Dancing Cloud as he rode on away from them. "And your escort?" she said softly. "He was an Indian. I wish Boyd had not assigned the Indian to escort you to Mattoon. It has stirred up much gossip."

Nancy sighed and placed a hand to her brow. "Abner was so anxious to tell everyone that you were coming, he did not think about how telling everybody who your escort was going to be would get so many tongues to wagging."

She sighed again. "And I am certain you drew much attention along the roads as you traveled them with the savage," she said solemnly.

Lauralee blanched of color and gasped. "Aunt Nancy, Dancing Cloud isn't a savage," she quickly corrected. "He's one of the most gentle men I have ever met. In fact, I . . ."

She started to blurt out that she was going to marry Dancing Cloud soon, yet felt this was not the time. It was obvious that her aunt had different feelings toward Indians than Lauralee. Nancy's feelings mirrored most white people's.

Lauralee was glad that her father had not been among them!

"You were about to say?" Nancy said, taking Lauralee by an elbow. She took her inside the house where they entered a foyer that led to a room on the right and left sides. A kitchen was at the end of the long corridor. A grand, oak staircase to the upstairs rooms was to the left of the door that led into the parlor.

"I was going to say how wonderful it is to see you, Aunt Nancy," Lauralee said, smiling over at her. "My father spoke so highly of both you and Uncle Abner."

"After receiving Boyd's wire, requesting that Abner and I make room in our lives for you, I have counted the days until you arrived," Nancy said. She suddenly grabbed for the staircase banister and steadied herself. She closed her eyes and breathed hard, frightening Lauralee.

"Aunt Nancy, what is it?" Lauralee asked, placing a hand on her aunt's arm to support her. "You are so suddenly pale. Are you dizzy? Do you have these spells often?"

"It's nothing," Nancy said, breathing hard. "Just a slight heart problem."

"Your heart?" Lauralee said, her eyes widening. "Aunt Nancy, that's *serious*. While working at the hospital in Saint Louis I became acquainted with many heart patients. Please don't take your illness too lightly. You must take precautions not to have a heart attack."

"You are making too much of this," Nancy said,

laughing softly. She straightened her back. "I'll be fine. Just fine."

"I will make certain of it," Lauralee said, lifting her chin proudly. "I am here now to see that nothing happens to you."

"Abner is in his study upstairs," Nancy said, looking up the stairs. "I will show you the rest of the house, and then we shall see if he can be disturbed."

Nancy ushered Lauralee into the dining room to the left. "You see, Lauralee, Abner is a powerful judge," she said, almost too wistfully. "He is not content to keep his work at his office. He often brings it home and works by lamplight into the wee hours of the morning. Too often he does this. I get quite lonesome."

"You shan't be lonesome anymore," Lauralee reassured, yet even as she said this to Nancy she knew that nothing she promised could last for long. When Dancing Cloud returned for her, she *would* say her goodbyes to the Petersons.

As she toured the house, Lauralee became in awe of everything. The beautifully wallpapered walls of the dining room where a huge oak table sat beneath a chandelier that displayed at least a hundred candles ready to be lighted. The china and crystal in the hutch were illuminated by a beam of sun that splashed through a lacy froth of curtains at the window.

They left the dining room and went across the hall into the parlor. Lauralee stared disbelievingly around the elegant room. The walls were painted creamy white, embellished with hand-painted ivy motifs. More ivy circled the edges of the ceiling, creating a wonderful false domed effect.

Jewel hues—ruby, jade, green, topaz, and honey amber—were embodied in the silk stripes of the very traditional down-filled sofa and chairs. It looked like furniture you wanted to sink into and fall asleep in. An oversize leather ottoman topped with a lap rug was an inviting place to prop one's feet.

Lauralee looked further around the room, at the soft,

stuffed armchairs upholstered in silk brocade, and at an enormous gilt mirror that hung beside one of the tall windows that were ornamented by looped and corded drapes.

Other various chairs, and tables upon which sat beautiful figurines, were artfully arranged around the room.

Upon one wall hung two gilt, oval-framed portraits. One oil painting was of Nancy, when she was younger and very petite in build.

She studied the other portrait. She knew that it must be her uncle Abner and found him handsome and dignified, and surely much younger than now.

"We shall leave the kitchen till later," Nancy said, sweeping Lauralee back out into the corridor. "I shall now show you your room." She paused, then said, "And then you will meet your uncle Abner."

Her own room, Lauralee thought excitedly as she climbed the stairs beside Nancy. At the orphanage she had always been forced to share a room with several other girls. Even when she had reached her teen years she had not had any privacy.

And now?

To have a room all her own?

Her heart thundered as she reached the second-floor landing. A hallway led to four doors. One of those would be the room that Nancy and Abner had chosen for her.

Nancy walked down the hall just a short distance and opened a door.

"Tell me how you like your room," Nancy said softly. "Come on, Lauralee. I've prepared it just for you. I so enjoyed doing it. I have always wanted a daughter."

Her knees weak, her eyes wide, Lauralee looked upon a room that could charm the cockles of any young woman's heart. She slipped past Nancy into the room. Her breath was taken clean away. A huge white-lacquered four-poster bed centered the room, the spread trimmed in frilly lace to match the lacy drapes at the two long windows and a wall covering festooned with vines, birds, and butterflies and flight-of-fancy paint treatments. A carpet, as soft and plush as balls of freshly picked cotton sank with her weight as she walked across it.

She stepped into a small alcove off the bedroom and found herself standing in a small powder room. On the walls, periwinkle-blue moire, backed with knit fabric, provided a rich backdrop for the furnishings. A porcelain basin sat on a commode, a gilded French mirror placed in the center echoing the beauty of the room beyond.

A dressing table, upon which sat a gilded mirror that reflected many bottles of perfume in it, as well as a gilt-trimmed hairbrush, made her gasp from utter delight.

She went to the bed and pressed her fingers into the plush feather mattress, and then the plump pillows. The Peterson House meant many things to her. Security, family, and now that she was there and saw its grandness, she could hardly think of anything else—eiderdowns, smooth, clear sheets, soft down pillows.

Lauralee turned to Nancy and gave her a soft smile, then gave her a gentle hug. "It's more beautiful than I had ever dreamed," she said. "Thank you. Thank you."

Nancy patted Lauralee's back. "Thank you for coming to be a part of our lives," she said, her voice breaking. "I gave up long ago thinking about children. I had to accept what God gave me. A good husband. A beautiful home. I learned to accept my lot in life without regrets. Then came the wire from your father. That changed everything for me and Abner. You are a blessing, child. A blessing."

Knowing that she would soon disappoint Nancy, Lauralee swallowed hard. She was a lovely woman. And ill?

Lauralee blocked the worry from her mind. She wanted to savor this moment, when she had finally become a part of a family. She would live every second of it as though it were the last. Then when the time truly came to leave, it would surely not be as hard.

"Shall we now go and introduce you to your uncle Abner?" Nancy asked as she swung herself away from Lauralee. She took Lauralee's hand. "Just across the hall. When we had this house built, Abner made sure he had a large study. It also serves as our library."

They left the bedroom and stepped out into the hallway. Nancy led Lauralee to another door. There they stopped long enough for Nancy to tap lightly on the closed door. When a voice said to enter, Nancy opened the door slowly, then stepped aside so that Lauralee could enter ahead of her.

Again Lauralee was amazed at what she saw. The mahogany and green damask study had walls lined with shelves filled with books and photographs and memories. It was surely a place to go and feel good about one's family and one's life.

A needlepoint rug filled the center of the room in Chinese lacquer red with a floral pattern in creams, beiges, and greens. The strong red lent a masculine feel even with the flowery motif. Both the crown molding in Chinese red and the yellow tone-on-tone wallpaper tied in with the colors of the rug, as did the richly upholstered seating pieces.

To soften the windows but not cover them completely, floral glazed chintz were swagged over black lacquer rods with an undercurtain of white lace edged with red ribbon.

A grand old mahogany desk sat at the far end of the room where she found her uncle sitting behind it in a sumptuous chair. He was edging middle age but his muscled body gave the impression of competence. His clean-shaven face was broad and long. His features were heavy in a cushioned, boneless way. He had a mild expression and wore a half smile as he stared back at her.

When he rose from behind the desk and spoke to

her, his voice was soft with courtesy. He was dressed in well-fitted dark trousers and a frock coat where a cravat displayed a diamond stickpin in its folds.

"And you are Lauralee?" Abner said, taking long, wide strides as he walked toward her. "If I didn't know better I'd think I was in the presence of your mother. You are the very mirroring *of* Carolyn."

He swept Lauralee into his muscled arms and she suddenly felt that she belonged there. If she closed her eyes and pretended, she could very well think that she was in the arms of her father when he had been well and as muscled. She now wondered how she could ever leave this place, where there was so much love, where there was so much security.

Dancing Cloud, she thought desperately. Oh, Dancing Cloud, what am I to do?

She knew that she could not be two people living in two places.

She went with her aunt and uncle to the downstairs parlor. As Lauralee's aunt served a delectable orange poppy seed bread that was stuffed with sweet fillings, she tried to enjoy it, yet could not deny the emptiness within her that Dancing Cloud's absence made.

Feeling downhearted, with an emptiness within him that Lauralee's absence made, Dancing Cloud forged ahead through a thick stand of trees. He made his way along a narrow trail left there by others who had veered away from the main, more-traveled roads.

Wanting to take advantage of the last light of the fading sun, he sank his moccasined heels into the flanks of his horse.

His horse bolted with alarm when a man on horseback was suddenly there, blocking the way. Dancing Cloud patted his steed to steady him, his eyes narrowing on the pistol aimed at him.

Then his eyes shifted upward. A hate he had felt all those years ago, when Boyd had been shot by the red-haired, blue-eyed Yankee, came to him in a heated rush. It was as though he was reliving that day, when the Yankees had ambushed what had been left of Colonel Boyd Johnston's regiment.

The same man, with the same leering, cynical smile, and the same red hair and blue eyes, was there now. It was obvious that the Yankee wanted to finish what he had started all those years ago.

Dancing Cloud made a quick movement for his rifle in the gun boot at the side of his horse. . . .

10

Parting is all we know of Heaven,
And all we need of hell.

—EMILY DICKINSON

Even though the Yankee's pistol was aimed at him, Dancing Cloud could not allow himself to be shot without a fight.

But his hand had no chance to get even near his rifle. The bullet, as it entered his right shoulder, was so forceful, it threw him from his horse.

Dazed from the fall, Dancing Cloud lay there for a moment.

Then when he came to enough to realize that he was losing much blood from his wound, he covered it with his hand and tried to get up.

But his shoulder seemed to weigh ten times what was normal. And he felt himself drifting away again, a dizziness sweeping through his consciousness that threatened to make him pass out.

Suddenly a foot kicked him over onto his back. Through hazy eyes Dancing Cloud looked up at the face that he had seen in many of his midnight nightmares.

Clint McCloud.

Dancing Cloud had never thought that he would see him again.

But when he had come north and had entered territory occupied by those who had fought on the Union's side, Dancing Cloud should have known there was always the chance of coming face to face with this heartless villain.

"Die, you son of a bitch Cherokee," Clint McCloud hissed out between his narrow, clenched lips. "Fate brought us face to face again so that I could finish what I started at the end of the war." He laughed throatily. "Just look at you groveling in the dirt. You were a mere kid when I last saw you. Now you're a man. Die like a man. Get it over with so I can be on my way. I don't dare shoot you again. Someone might hear."

Dancing Cloud fought against the waves of unconsciousness that were washing through his brain. He only half heard what Clint was saying.

But it was enough to know there was no way that this Yankee would allow a Confederate Cherokee to get out of this skirmish alive.

Again Dancing Cloud struggled to get to his feet.

Each time he managed to get partially to his knees, Clint kicked him back down into the pool of blood that was spreading on the ground beneath him.

The sound of an approaching wagon on the narrow trail made Clint jump with a start. He turned his back to Dancing Cloud and lifted his pistol in the direction of the sound and waited for the wagon to make the slight turn in the road.

And when the driver of the buckboard wagon made the turn and his face became visible to Clint, he lowered his pistol and met the wagon's approach.

"Noah Brown, I didn't expect you to come this way," Clint said, stopping beside the wagon as Noah drew his one horse to a halt. He glowered up at the man in overalls. "Your farm lies yonder. What brings you this far from your farm grounds?"

"I just purchased this acreage today," Noah said, peering past Clint, his face ashen at what he saw lying in the road a short distance away. "I intend to farm it, as well."

"Come back another time, Noah," Clint said. He took the reins to Noah's wagon in an effort to get the horse turned around. "I've business on this road. Don't go stickin' your nose in it. I wouldn't want to be forced into doin' somethin' I might regret later."

Being a strong-willed man, who took orders from no one, Noah grabbed his reins back from Clint. "Clint McCloud, don't try tellin' me what to do," he said gruffly. "As I see it, you're trespassin'. I'll have you locked up if you force my hand."

"Not if I shoot you first," Clint said, slowly raising his pistol again. "Don't force *my* hand, Noah. I've grown to like you durin' my stay in Mattoon. And remember. Your son Brad fought side by side with me durin' the war."

"And my Brad is dead and you're alive," Noah said, stepping down from the buggy. He leaned his face into Clint's.

"And that can change mighty quick," Noah said, slipping a derringer from his rear pocket. He thrust it against Clint's abdomen. "Now step aside, sonny boy. Let me see to that gent in the road. Seems you've not left your warrin' days behind you. It's a pity that someone as smart as you can in the same breath be so dumb. Do you think shootin' that Cherokee is goin' to solve any problems for you? It's just one more thing that'll keep you awake nights."

"Because of that damn Cherokee and those who fought with him on the Confederate side, I'm forced to walk with a wooden leg the rest of my life," Clint growled. "I've not thought of much else but gettin' my revenge one way or the other for being disabled."

"You can still ride a horse," Noah argued. "You can still make love. And by George you're one of the best railroad men in these parts. So don't whine like a baby over a wooden leg." He leaned into Clint's face. "At least you're still alive." He gave the derringer a shove. "But I can change that pretty quicklike, Clint. If you don't get on your horse and ride away and leave me to see to that wounded Cherokee, I swear I'll shoot you right here on the spot."

"He's a damn gray coat Confederate," Clint whined. "He don't deserve to live."

"The war's been over for years, Clint," Noah said tersely. "So I suggest you put down your arms and be on your way."

"What are you going to do about him?" Clint asked, gazing over at Dancing Cloud.

"What I'd do for anyone I'd find bleedin' in the road," Noah said, himself glancing over at Dancing Cloud. "And as I see it, he won't have a chance in hell if I don't get him to Dr. Kemper, and *fast.*"

"You're takin' him to be mended up?" Clint said, his voice almost a shrill cry. "I went to all this trouble for nothin'? Ever since I heard that this Confederate Cherokee was arriving to town, I watched for him, and then I've stalked him. I just waited for him to be alone away from Judge Peterson's niece. And by damn I took advantage of it. Let him die, Noah. For God's sake, let him die."

"I don't like Rebels any more than you," Noah said thickly. "They killed my eldest son. But I'm a Christian. I don't believe in vengeance. Now, Clint, get on your horse and get the hell out of here so I can see to the wounded man."

"I can't let you," Clint said, his eyes narrowing.

"I don't see how you can stop me, unless you shoot me once I place my derringer back in my pocket to see to the Indian," Noah said, narrowing his blue eyes into Clint's. "Can you truly shoot me, Clint? You're sure as hell going to get the chance."

Clint backed away. He raised his hands in the air as he edged himself backward, his horse only a few feet away. When he reached Dancing Cloud he stepped around him. "Go ahead and do what your religion guides you into doing," he said angrily. "There'll be another time when I'll get my chance to make sure this Rebel never takes another breath."

"It might be sooner than you think if I don't get him to Dr. Kemper's house," Noah said, slipping his derringer in the rear pocket of his overalls.

"Noah, if you tell the authorities that it was me who shot this Cherokee I'll come for you," Clint threatened. "I'll not stop at killin' just *you*. I'll also kill your wife, June, and your son, Paul. You'd better forget your religion long enough to tell a lie that will be convincin' enough when you are questioned about findin' this Rebel on your land."

Noah gave Clint a sour look. "I believe you *would* kill my family," he said, his eyes narrowing. "I truly believe you would."

Then ignoring Clint as he mounted his horse, Noah went and knelt down beside Dancing Cloud. He took a pocket knife from his front breeches pocket, opened it, and cut the buckskin shirt away from the wound.

He winced. "Terrible, terrible," he said, closing his knife and placing it back inside his pocket. He gazed down at Dancing Cloud whose eyes lazily opened and closed, his body limp. "Young man, you may not make it until morning."

Dancing Cloud still drifted in and out of consciousness. He had partially heard the discussion between the two men. He now understood that Clint McCloud had lost a leg due to the gunshot wound that Dancing Cloud had inflicted on him during the war.

He also knew from the conversation that Clint was a railroad man, and that this kind man leaning over him, caring for him, was a farmer.

Through his hazed-over eyes Dancing Cloud could see a man with a lean face that had been bronzed over by the sun, smooth features, a long, straight nose, and kind, blue eyes that mirrored the sky. He wore baggy overalls and a long-sleeved denim shirt. His hands were large and comforting, his voice soft and gentle.

"Young man, there ain't much I can do for you way out here away from the city," Noah said, taking a handkerchief from his rear pocket. It was fresh and clean, directly off the clothesline in his backyard. He placed the handkerchief over the wound. "It's going to hurt like hell when I lift you and take you to my wagon. Just grit your teeth, young man. I'll be as gentle as I can."

Noah gathered Dancing Cloud into his powerfully muscled arms. He slowly lifted him from the ground and held him there for a moment as he peered down at him. "You see, Cherokee, although the Rebels killed my eldest son during the war, I hold no grudge," he said, his voice breaking. "I'm sure you lost someone as close, yourself, during that damnable war."

The pain of his body being shifted as he was lifted from the ground was so intense Dancing Cloud drifted instantly into a black void, welcoming it.

Seeing that the Cherokee had slipped into what might be a coma, Noah hurried him to his wagon. As gently as he could, worrying about the blood that Dancing Cloud was still losing from the wound, he laid him in the back of his wagon.

He covered Dancing Cloud with a blanket that he always carried with him for those times when his wife June came out into the fields and surprised him with a picnic lunch. Many a time he had stopped his planting to have time with her. She had not yet totally gotten over the loss of their eldest son. Perhaps she never would.

He patted Dancing Cloud on the leg, then went to his wagon and climbed onto it. Making a wide turn on the narrow trail, he headed back toward town.

When he reached the house that Dr. Kemper had turned into a temporary hospital on Western Avenue, the doctor took immediate charge.

Even after Noah told Dr. Kemper that this Cherokee had sided with the South during the war, the doctor who had been a captain in the Fifth Illinois Cavalry, still did not hesitate to care for Dancing Cloud. He took him immediately into surgery to remove the bullet, and to repair the damage inflicted by it. He had been born to sustain life, not to take it!

While Noah sat in an outer room and waited to hear the results of the surgery, Sheriff Wes Decker came into the room.

"Noah, I hear you found a man on that property you just bought today," the sheriff said, lifting a wide-brimmed hat from his head, revealing brown hair that was trimmed neatly to his shirt collar. He was dressed in black from head to toe, his ruddy-featured face solemn. "Want to tell me about it, Noah? How you found the man? Who might have shot him?"

Noah rose from the chair. He straightened his back and lifted his chin as he looked square into the pale gray eyes of the sheriff. "Not much to tell 'cept that I found him layin' in the road all bloodied up and shot," he said, not taking a chance in telling the total truth. He was afraid that Clint might follow up on his threats and go to his farm and kill his family while Noah was tending business in the fields.

"I did my Christian duty, Wes," Noah quickly added. "I brought him here for patching up."

"Gossip spread fast about this man," Sheriff Decker said, tossing his hat onto a chair. He took a half-smoked cigar from his front shirt pocket. He slipped it between his thick lips and lit it with a match.

"Yes, I heard the same gossip," Noah said, slipping his hands down the front of his overalls, locking his thumbs over the sides of its bib. "He's an Indian. He's a Cherokee, and he's a Rebel. But that don't mean that I was to leave him to die on my land."

"See who did it?" Sheriff Decker asked, puffing on his cigar. He took his hat from the chair and circled it slowly around between his fingers.

"Can't say that I did," Noah said, trying to make the lie as white as possible.

"Did you hear the gunfire?" the sheriff continued. "Is that how you came upon the scene of the crime?"

"Yes, I heard the gunfire," Noah said, nodding.

"But still you can't tell me who did the shootin'?"

"Are you deaf, Wes? I already answered that question."

"All right, all right," Sheriff Decker said, plopping the hat back on his head. "I may never know who did it. Damn that Rebel. Why'd he have to come north, anyhow?"

"I guess Judge Peterson had no idea the turmoil it would make once news spread that an Indian was escorting his niece to Mattoon," Noah said, sighing deeply. "The judge is usually a quiet man. Keeps to himself. But I guess he was so happy about his niece comin' to be a part of his life he couldn't help but talk about it."

"I only hope that once the news spreads that the Indian is still in town, there won't be a mob formed to lynch the guy," Sheriff Decker sighed out as he slowly shook his head back and forth. "One thing for sure, though. Nothin' else bad will happen to this Indian while he's in my jurisdiction. I'll threaten everyone with a jailin', perhaps even a *hangin'*, if they try anything."

Noah looked over at Sheriff Decker and chuckled. "Then I'm certain this young man's life is in no danger," he said. "Who'd go against *you*, Wes?"

Wes laughed boisterously. "I guess I've got my work cut out for me," he said, sauntering toward the door. "Leavin' now, Noah? Or are you going to stick around?"

"I think I'll wait and see if the Cherokee makes it," Noah said, walking Wes to the door.

"Tell your pretty June I said hello when you arrive home," Sheriff Decker said, swinging the door open. "Tell her I'd love a piece of her cherry pie the next time she makes one."

"Same as done, Wes," Noah laughed after him. "Same as done."

He watched Sheriff Decker mount his horse and ride

away. The sound of footsteps behind him drew him quickly around.

When he saw Dr. Kemper standing there, bloodstains on his clothes, and his eyes heavy, his insides quavered uneasily.

"Well, Doc?" Noah asked, searching the doctor's face for answers. "Did he make it, or not?"

Doctor Kemper inhaled a deep, shaky breath.

11

Doubt that the stars are fine;
Doubt that the sun doth move;
Doubt truth to be a liar,
But never doubt I love.
—WILLIAM SHAKESPEARE

Lauralee looked proudly at her bedroom again, this time feeling even *more* wonderful that it was all hers. Abner had carried the last of her travel bags into the room and she had already arranged her clothes and toilet articles where they belonged.

She was overwhelmed at how lovely it was. Everything smelled so clean, fresh, and new.

And the view from the window was so different from the one at the orphanage where she saw only the dull, brick wall of the hospital next door.

Now she could see miles of beautiful trees and lawn that stretched out from the Peterson House.

"I've a present for you, as a welcome, my dear, to our household," Nancy Peterson said as she stepped into the room.

Lauralee turned around, her face flushed from the excitement of the day.

Her eyes widened when she gazed at the package wrapped in beautiful pink tissue paper, a white satin bow tied around it. "What *is* it?" she asked, thrilled at the thought of receiving a special gift from a special person. During her long stay at the orphanage she had never received any gifts except at Christmas.

Even *then* it had only been something used that had

been donated by those who felt sorry for the children who lived there.

Today there were no other children grabbing for her gift.

It was hers, alone.

Lauralee's fingers trembled as Nancy brought the wrapped package to her.

"My dear, take it and *open* it," Nancy said, smiling sweetly at Lauralee as she gently shoved the gift in her hands. "Before your arrival, Abner and I went shopping together and picked this out for you. We hope you like it."

Lauralee sat down on the edge of the bed and gently removed the satin bow and laid it aside.

Then, breathless, she unfolded the tissue paper until a small box was revealed. A wonderful fragrance wafted from it, similar to the one worn by her aunt.

Lauralee's eyes widened and she smiled up at Nancy. "Oh, but surely it isn't," she said, guessing what her gift was, without actually seeing it. "It surely cost so much."

Nancy sat down beside her. "My dear, go ahead and open the box," she said, her dark eyes gleaming happily.

Feeling almost giddy, Lauralee raised the lid and saw a bottle of perfume cradled in a bed of maroon velvet. She sighed and took the bottle into her trembling fingers. After unscrewing the lid she splashed some of it on her fingers. Placing her fingers to her nose, she inhaled. The fragrance was so tantalizingly sweet she closed her eyes and sighed.

"There is something more." Nancy gently took the perfume from Lauralee and gave her another beautifully wrapped gift.

Bubbling over with excitement Lauralee smiled at Nancy, then quickly opened the second box. She found a tin of talcum powder with the same fragrance as the perfume in the box, and some soft pink balls the size of marbles.

"Those are bath oil beads," Nancy explained when she saw the question in Lauralee's eyes. "When your water is warm enough you place these beads in it. They will melt and spread such a *wonderful* oil through the water. Your skin will be soft, beautiful, and fragranced."

"I have never seen anything like it," Lauralee said, rolling the small beads around in the palm of one of her hands. "How can these melt . . ."

Her words were stolen when Nancy suddenly dropped the bottle of perfume and grabbed at her chest. When the bottle hit the floor, not even the soft cushion of the carpet could stop it from breaking. Perfume splashed and spread everywhere, the scent overpowering.

But Lauralee's concern was not over the broken bottle, the ruined carpet and bedskirt of her bed, nor the spilled perfume that she had momentarily cherished as hers. She was totally stunned and frightened over Nancy's condition.

Nancy lurched, gasped, and clawed at her blouse where her heart lay beneath it, then swayed and fell back onto the bed, unconscious.

"Oh, my Lord!" Lauralee cried, the perfumed bath oil beads rolling out of her hand. She stared at Nancy for a moment, aghast.

Then knowing from her nurse's training that her aunt had experienced a heart attack, she shoved the gifts aside on the bed and ran from her room.

"Uncle Abner!" she screamed as she rushed down the hallway, toward his study. "Uncle Abner, it's Aunt Nancy! I truly believe she's had a heart attack!"

When she entered his office he was already away from his desk and running toward her.

"Go and see that the horse and buggy are readied!" Abner cried, panic in his voice. "You'll find James at the stable. Tell him to get a horse hitched to my buggy. Hurry, Lauralee. We've no time to waste. We must get Nancy to Dr. Kemper's."

Lauralee ran down the steps and rushed through the house until she reached the back porch.

Night had fallen in its vast crown of black. The moon was full and bright. Panting, Lauralee went down the steps and ran toward the stable.

She was relieved to find James there. He was spreading fresh straw on the floor. A kerosene lamp hung from a hook inside the stable emitting a soft, glimmering light.

"James!" Lauralee ran to the tall, thin stable hand. Frantically, desperately, she grabbed his arm. "Ready the Petersons' buggy. Quick. Mrs. Peterson is ill. She has to be taken to Dr. Kemper's."

James, all legs and arms, dressed in fawn breeches and a long-sleeved white shirt, rushed around, Lauralee assisting him. Just as he led the horse and buggy out of the barn, Abner came running toward him with Nancy laying limply within his powerful arms.

Lauralee scurried onto the buggy seat. Abner laid Nancy on the seat beside her so that Nancy's head could rest comfortably on Lauralee's lap.

Abner rushed around and stepped into the buggy beside Nancy. He looked with a concerned longing down at her as he spread a blanket over her.

Then he nodded to James who released the reins to him.

Abner swung the horse away from the stable.

He slapped the reins.

The horse moved into a quick gallop up the small gravel drive that led to the larger circular drive in front of the house.

Lauralee ran a comforting hand over Nancy's pale, ashen face as Abner sent the horse and buggy down Broadway Avenue, dust spraying out from beneath the wooden wheels.

Lauralee looked around her as the horse and buggy flew down the street. One- and two-storied homes lined both sides of the street, lamplight splashing softly from lacy curtains at the windows.

These homes multiplied as the horse and buggy fled on down the avenue, until larger buildings came into sight a short distance away.

Although used to the large buildings in St. Louis, Lauralee saw this city as no less lovely with its long row of two- and three-storied brick establishments, as well as a few four-storied.

The Petersons' horse and buggy continued to travel until it reached Western Avenue. Lauralee quickly grabbed for Nancy with one hand and the edge of the seat with her other hand as the buggy came to a lurching stop.

Everything after that happened so quickly it was all that Lauralee could do to keep up with Abner.

He had whisked Nancy into his arms, running toward the large, two-storied house. He shouted at Lauralee to open the door.

She did as he asked, then entered a large room where chairs were lined against the wall, magazines and newspapers spread neatly on tables beside them.

"Doc Kemper!" Abner shouted as he ran down a narrow corridor, leaving Lauralee tailing along behind him, winded.

Lauralee gazed at a distinguished-looking man, with kind, warm eyes, as he hurried from a room toward Abner. He removed his eye spectacles and shoved them in his vest pocket, then took Nancy from Abner and carried her into one of the many rooms that lined the corridor.

Lauralee stopped and caught her breath, then looked slowly around her. If this was a hospital, it was nothing like the one in which she had learned the art of nursing. It was a house transformed into a hospital. She could smell the aroma of ether, rubbing alcohol, and other various medicinal smells. Sheeted tables lined the walls. Lamps fueled by kerosene flared their shimmering light from several wall sconces along the corridor and in the outer waiting room.

Lauralee fidgeted with the gathers of the skirt of her dress as she waited for Abner to return.

She stared at the closed door, then allowed her gaze to move slowly down the corridor again. This time something at the far end of the passageway drew her attention. A man sat in the shadows outside a room, a gun heavy in a holster at his left hip, a badge reflecting the light of a lamp in it. It was a lawman.

Curiosity getting the best of Lauralee, she walked slowly toward the man. She couldn't help but wonder if a criminal was locked up in this room. If so, what sort of crime had he committed?

From outward appearances Mattoon did not seem to be the kind of city that would allow criminals to run loose. It looked like a beautifully clean and respectable place.

But she also knew that the railroads had caused many saloons to be built in the city, which in turn attracted all sorts of men. Even criminals.

Lauralee tiptoed up to the lawman. When he gave her a hard look, his eyes squinting up at her, a shiver soared through her.

Yet she refused to be intimidated.

"Sir, it seems that you are perhaps guarding someone in that room," she said stiffly. "Is it a hardened criminal? What might he have done?"

"His biggest mistake was comin' to Mattoon," the lawman said. He scooted his chair back as he stood up, towering over Lauralee with his six-foot-four height. "I killed the likes of him in the war. Damn shame I've been given orders to protect him now from someone like me who'd like to see him hangin' from a noose."

Lauralee paled and placed a hand to her throat. She knew that his lawman had fought for the Union. The one he was guarding had to have been a Rebel. Panic grabbed her insides. She was keenly aware of one man in particular who was from the South and had just recently come to Mattoon, enemy territory in his mind, heart, and soul.

"Sir, are you saying that this man you are guarding is not a criminal?" she asked, her heart pounding, afraid to hear the answer.

"Naw, not exactly," he said, raking his long, lean fingers through his shoulder-length brassy-colored hair. "Just got himself into a bit of trouble. If he'd stayed south, he'd not be fightin' for his life. As it is, he escorted some dumb broad from Saint Louis to Mattoon and got himself into a peck of trouble 'cause of it."

Lauralee felt faint. She grabbed for the wall, to steady herself. She looked wild-eyed up at the lawman. "Is by chance that man Cherokee?" she asked, her voice breaking.

"How'd you guess *that*?" the lawman said, idly scratching his brow.

"Because, sir, I have a feeling that *I* am that dumb broad from Saint Louis who you so callously referred to," Lauralee said, her voice trembling.

She shoved past him and opened the door. She then died a slow death inside when her gaze sought and found Dancing Cloud lying still on the bed, a sheet drawn up to his waist, his chest totally bandaged.

"Ma'am, you ain't s'posed to be in here," the lawman said as he stepped up to Lauralee and grabbed her by an elbow. "Come on, ma'am. I've been given strict orders not to let this Injun be disturbed."

Lauralee wrenched herself free. She turned and glared icily up at the lawman. "Didn't you hear what I said?" she said, her voice tight with anger. "*I* am that woman who was escorted to Mattoon by this man. Don't you dare lay a hand on me again. I'm staying with Dancing Cloud."

"Dancing Cloud?" the lawman said, peering over at him. "So that's what his Indian name is." He shrugged. "I was told that his name was Joe. Should've known that an Injun would have to have an Injun name."

Lauralee gave the lawman a shove. "Get out of here," she cried. "Take your insults with you."

The lawman shrugged and turned to leave, then

Lauralee rushed to him and grabbed his arm. "Who did this to Dancing Cloud?" she asked, pleading up at him as he turned cold, angry eyes down at her. "Who brought him to the hospital?"

"Noah Brown found him on his land," the lawman said, resting a hand on his holstered pistol. "Seems someone who still carries the same grudge as me against Rebels took a shot at 'im." He smiled slowly and smugly. "I doubt this rebel Injun's goin' to ever see the light of day again. The shoulder wound was bad. *Bad.*"

Shivers of dread ran up and down Lauralee's spine. Tears spread across her cheeks as she turned and gazed at Dancing Cloud. "No," she whispered, a sob lodging in her throat. "He *can't* die. He just can't die."

The lawman left and closed the door behind him. Lauralee went to Dancing Cloud's bedside and searched beneath the sheet for one of his hands.

When she found the one that lay at his right side, the one closest to her, she slipped her fingers through his and stared down at him.

So beautifully sculpted, so beautifully bronzed, but yet so deeply unconscious! she thought to herself, sighing heavily.

Footsteps entering the room behind her caused her to flinch. She slipped her hand from Dancing Cloud's and turned around, then realized that in her despair over Dancing Cloud's condition, she had forgotten about Nancy. Abner was standing there, his eyes heavy, his face gaunt.

"How is she?" Lauralee asked, going to him. She splayed her fingers across his massive chest. "Please tell me that she's going to be all right."

"It was a slight heart attack," Abner said, drawing her into his embrace, his eyes locked on Dancing Cloud. "She'll be all right. But she'll be delicate as a flower for the rest of her life, Lauralee. We'll have to treat her thusly."

"I'll do everything I can for her," Lauralee murmured, then slipped from his arms and followed his gaze as she again looked at Dancing Cloud.

"I only heard a moment ago about Joe Dancing Cloud," Abner said, moving slowly toward the bed. "Lord, what's this world coming to when a man can't ride along the trail without being ambushed?"

"Who did it, Uncle Abner?" Lauralee asked, moving to touch Dancing Cloud's face.

"Noah Brown found him. That's all I know," Abner said thickly. "I'm not at all surprised that Noah brought Joe to the hospital. Although Noah lost his son Brad in the war, he's not the kind of person who'd allow a man to die of gunshot wounds, especially during these times of peace. Not even *if* the man who's shot is known to have fought for the South."

He kneaded his chin and looked over at Lauralee. "But as for who *did* this," he said, his voice drawn. "Your guess is as good as mine. Noah said he heard shots. He found Joe Dancing Cloud. That's all he had to say about it."

Dancing Cloud moaned and his head turned to one side.

Lauralee dropped to her knees beside the bed, her heart beating anxiously. "I'm here, darling," she murmured, again slipping her hand beneath the sheet, to intertwine with his. "Darling, oh, darling, please wake up."

Abner's insides splashed cold when he saw Lauralee's devotion to the Cherokee. Now her legal guardian, Abner would never want to see her aligned with an Indian, especially one who fought against the northern cause during the war. He wanted better for her. There were many young, unmarried men in Mattoon who would make Lauralee a deserving husband.

Noah's son Paul!

Now that was a man who was hardworking on the farm, and whose dedications to the northern cause had been the same as his brother's.

Abner tapped Lauralee on the shoulder. "Lauralee, can you step outside in the corridor for a moment?" he asked stiffly.

Lauralee looked up at him guardedly, knowing why he wanted her to leave Dancing Cloud's room. He had just witnessed her true feelings for the Cherokee. It was obvious that he did not approve.

"Uncle Abner, I can't leave just yet," she murmured. "Dancing Cloud is showing signs of awakening."

Abner's upper lip stiffened. His eyes narrowed, then he left the room in a dignified, slow stance.

Lauralee gazed down at Dancing Cloud again. "He'll never understand, darling," she whispered. She leaned down and gave him a soft, lingering kiss. She ached inside over his lack of response.

Tears flowing down her cheeks, Lauralee scooted a chair beside the bed and waited . . . and . . . watched. . . .

12

Dancing Cloud felt pressure on his hand. A sweet, soft pressure. He felt the black fuzziness floating away. A dim, golden light was beckoning his eyes to open.

But the more aware he became of things, the more he realized the depths of the pain in his right shoulder. He groaned as he fluttered his eyelashes.

Lauralee stifled a cry of relief behind a hand when she heard Dancing Cloud make a sound and saw his eyes slowly opening. She rose to her feet and leaned low over him, her hands framing his face. She smiled down at him as his eyes locked with hers.

"Darling?" Lauralee said, tears warm against her cheeks. "Dancing Cloud, I'm here. Once I knew that you were here I haven't left your bedside."

She so badly wanted to hug him, but the bandages around his chest and up over his right shoulder gave her reason not to. She was afraid of hurting him.

"Lauralee?" Dancing Cloud said, his voice weak. "*O-ge-ye?* Where am I? How did I get here?"

Lauralee dreaded telling him about the ambush. It made her feel sick inside to know that someone could resent him this much. She was not sure if the resentment centered on him being a southern Rebel, or an Indian.

Either way, she regretted that he had been a target for someone's prejudices.

"Do you remember anything about the shooting?" Lauralee asked, easing down on the bed beside him. She gently stroked his brow. "You didn't get far from Mattoon. A farmer . . . a Noah Brown found you."

Remembrances then came to Dancing Cloud in flashes. He had been aware enough of things going on around him after he had been shot by Clint McCloud to recall a kind man coming to his rescue.

If he recalled accurately enough, the man had said something to Dancing Cloud's assailant about having lost a son in the Civil War, himself.

But that had not stopped the flow of this man's compassion for an injured man from the South.

Dancing Cloud had passed out before he had actually been transported to the city.

Yet he would never forget the very instant that he was shot, nor by whom.

"Dancing Cloud, can't you remember how this happened?" Lauralee pleaded. "Can you describe the man who shot you?"

"I remember most of it," Dancing Cloud said, wincing when a fresh rush of pain flowed through his wound. He looked slowly around. "Where am I? Who cared for my wound?"

"A Dr. Kemper cared for you and performed the operation," Lauralee murmured. She stroked his cheek. "To date, Mattoon has no true hospital. Dr. Kemper has turned his private home into a medical center. It seems to me that thus far it is serving the community adequately enough. The proof is in how the doctor was able to operate on you to remove the bullet, and to repair the damage the bullet caused."

Footsteps entering the room caused Lauralee's eyes to shift upward. She gave Dr. Kemper a sincere smile as he walked toward the bed.

"I see our patient has awakened," the doctor said, stopping to stand beside the bed. Everything became quiet as he leaned over and listened to Dancing Cloud's heartbeat with a stethoscope, while with his free hand he felt the rhythm of his pulse.

Lauralee looked adoringly at Dancing Cloud. She was grateful that he had finally awakened. She now even believed that he would have a full recovery. Soon Dancing Cloud would be well enough to leave the hospital.

She would make sure that he did not take off right away for his home in the mountains. He needed adequate time for total recovery. She would enjoy doting over him.

Her only concern was that the Petersons might resent her asking them to allow him to stay at their house. She had seen how her uncle felt about Dancing Cloud the instant he had seen her attentiveness toward him.

She had to chance going against their wishes.

For Dancing Cloud, she would chance any and everything.

Her love for him was total.

"Seems you're farin' well enough," Dr. Kemper said, slipping the stethoscope into his front suit pocket. "Ready for some food, young man? It's way past suppertime but I made sure some broth was kept steamin' on the stove for you."

"I appreciate your kindness," Dancing Cloud said, his throat dry, his lips parched.

"And I shall get much delight in feeding him," Lauralee said, smiling up at the doctor.

"Then, young lady, once he has had his fill of broth, I recommend that you go on home with Abner and get yourself a good night's sleep," the doctor softly urged. "Your aunt is awake now and farin' well enough."

Lauralee was relieved to hear the news about her aunt. She felt guilty for having given more attention to Dancing Cloud than to her aunt Nancy.

But her aunt had Abner.

While Dancing Cloud was so far from his home and family, he had no one but Lauralee.

"I'm so glad that Aunt Nancy is all right," she said. "She will be well soon, Dr. Kemper?"

"With a heart condition, no one is ever totally well again," the doctor said, slipping his hands into his front suit pocket. "She'll require plenty of tender lovin' care."

"I'll be sure she doesn't want for a thing," Lauralee said softly.

"Remember now, after you see that this young man is fed, I advise you to leave," Dr. Kemper said bluntly. "Your uncle has been given the same advice. Your aunt and this young man need a full night's rest. You can come tomorrow at the break of dawn, if you wish, and feed him some more solid food for his breakfast."

"I would love to." Lauralee smiled. She then gave Dancing Cloud a soft, wondrous gaze.

"A nurse will bring the broth soon," the doctor said, turning to leave. He gave Dancing Cloud a lingering gaze over his shoulder, then left the room.

"There goes a dedicated man," Lauralee said. "This city of Mattoon is lucky to have him. He not only gives up his *home* to the ailing people of the community, but gives his undivided attention to those who are ill."

"The doctor said something about your aunt having a heart attack?" Dancing Cloud said, reaching a shaky hand to touch Lauralee's face.

"Shortly after you left," Lauralee said, leaning against his hand, melting inside at his mere touch.

Then a thought came to her that made her grow cold inside. She drew his hand away and held it on her lap. "Lord, Dancing Cloud, had I not had cause to come to the hospital, I may have never known you were here," she said, her eyes wavering into his. "You would have been here among total strangers."

Another thought sent shivers up and down her spine. "The man who shot you," she said, her voice drawn. "I wonder if he knows that you were brought to the hospital?"

Then she sighed when another thought came to her. "But you are protected from him," she said. "A man of law has been placed outside your door."

"A lawman?" Dancing Cloud said, trying to lean up on an elbow as he looked toward the door. He groaned when the pain forced him to lay flat on his back again. "He is guarding someone he surely sees as an enemy?"

"It's not entirely that. But yes, it is mainly to protect you from those who *do* still hold deep feelings against those who they fought against during the war," Lauralee said. She once again stroked his perspiration-laced brow. "But there are only a few heartless cads who would act on their resentments. You just ran into one of those men today while leaving Mattoon."

Dancing Cloud's jaw stiffened as he recalled having come face to face with his wartime *ha-ma-ma,* enemy again. It was obvious that the man's mind was twisted and might do anything to avenge his wooden leg.

"I do know the man. My bullet wounded him during the war," he said, giving Lauralee a sudden look. "I am almost certain that one of his legs is gone and that a wooden one has replaced it. I could tell by the way he sat on his horse and by the way he held the leg out away from him so stiffly. This is how deep his resentment lays over having lost his leg—that he would perhaps go to any lengths to see me dead."

"You know the man?" Lauralee gasped. "His name, Dancing Cloud. Tell me his name. I will go to the authorities so they can hunt him down and arrest him."

"Clint McCloud," Dancing Cloud said solemnly. "I have remembered that name with much anger in my heart since the war. I have remembered the *face* of the man."

"Describe him to me," Lauralee said anxiously. "That should help the sheriff. A posse can be sent out to look for him."

"I am certain that many a man fits the description of my assailant," Dancing Cloud said tersely. "I would be the only one who knows for certain that it is he. In time we shall meet face to face again. I then shall make sure he does not harm anyone else again."

Lauralee's heart ached to realize now just exactly what had driven the man to shoot Dancing Cloud. And if he knew that Dancing Cloud was not dead . . .

"I shan't leave you tonight or any other night until you are safely out of this hospital and with me and the Petersons," she blurted.

"You heard the doctor," Dancing Cloud said, taking her hand. "You will got to the Petersons and get a full night of rest, as I shall get mine here. *O-ge-ye,* do not fret so over this Cherokee who allowed himself to get too careless."

He looked slowly around the room. His gaze stopped on his clothes that were slung over a chair, as well as his saddlebags. His eyes locked on his rifle.

Then he shifted his gaze and caught sight of his sheathed knife where it lay among his moccasins and other articles of clothing on the chair.

"I see that someone brought my belongings to me," he said, his voice revealing his fatigue. "Among them are my weapons."

"I imagine Noah Brown found your horse and belongings," Lauralee said softly. "Your belongings are safely with you now. I will find out where your horse is being lodged and will see that it is taken to my uncle's stables."

A young woman, wearing a floor-length white dress and apron, entered the room with a tray. She smiled over at Lauralee, then Dancing Cloud, as she set the tray on a table beside the bed. "Ma'am, Dr. Kemper said that you would be feeding the gentleman?" she asked as she poured a glass of water from a pitcher.

"It would be my pleasure." Lauralee smiled down at Dancing Cloud. Then she gazed over at the nurse. "And thank you for bringing the broth for Dancing Cloud."

She could see the nurse's eyes waver at Lauralee's mention of Dancing Cloud's Cherokee name.

But Lauralee ignored this and went to the other side of the bed. She scooted a chair close and smiled another thank you to the nurse before she left.

She plumped a pillow beneath Dancing Cloud's head in an effort to position him higher so that he would not choke on the liquids that she would feed him.

"You frightened me when you were asleep for so long," Lauralee said, lifting the spoon of broth to his lips. "The ether. I am sure the ether was the cause. Some doctors use more than others to be assured their patients don't awaken during surgery."

Dancing Cloud felt the flow of the warm broth move down his throat and into his stomach and heartily welcomed it. It was not so much that he was hungry. He knew what was required to get his strength back.

Food, *and* exercise.

He would get out of bed as soon as his knees would hold him up. He had to be able to defend himself should the red-haired Yankee show up again.

Dancing Cloud had been alert enough after the ambush to know that Noah Brown had told the Yankee that he could not allow Dancing Cloud to die.

He also recalled the Yankee's threats about what he would do if Noah revealed that it was *he* who had fired the shot.

That made Dancing Cloud even more grateful to the farmer for having saved his life. He was taking his own life in his hands by doing it, as well as those of his entire family.

Dancing Cloud managed to empty the bowl of broth, then drank down slow gulps of water.

As Lauralee eased his head back down on the pillow, he closed his eyes and sighed.

"It's wonderful that you were able to take so much nourishment," she murmured as she kissed his brow. "But I can tell, darling, that you do need your rest. Although I hate having to, I will leave you now. But I shall be here again early in the morning."

Dancing Cloud eased an arm around her shoulders.

He drew her lips to his. He gave her a kiss that left her shaken with desire.

Her face was flushed as she rose away from him. She smiled, then left the room, feeling that the promise of her future was bright again. Although she enjoyed her beautiful room at the Peterson House, she would willingly leave it behind to be with Dancing Cloud.

This time when he left Mattoon she *would* be with him.

She met Abner in the corridor. He gave her an affectionate hug, then placed an arm around her waist and ushered her toward the front waiting room.

"I wanted to see Nancy," Lauralee said, giving an anxious look over her shoulder at the closed door of Nancy's room.

"She's asleep and resting comfortably," Abner said, walking her on outside, to the horse and buggy. "She knows your thoughts are with her. You can sit with her tomorrow."

"Would you mind if I gathered some flowers from your garden to take to Nancy tomorrow?" Lauralee asked. She smoothed the wrinkles from her skirt as she sat down on the cushioned seat of the buggy. Abner soon flicked the horse's reins and rode away from the hospital.

"Yes, Nancy would like that," Abner said, nodding. "Snapdragons. They are her favorite."

They rode awhile in silence. Both were lost in their own thoughts.

But when Abner took a swing away from the Peterson House when they reached it, and traveled down a road away from it, Lauralee looked over at him with surprise.

"Uncle Abner, where are we going?" she asked softly. "You've gone past your house."

"There's someone who needs to be thanked," Abner said, casting Lauralee a quick glance.

"Oh?" Lauralee said. An eyebrow raised quizzically. "Who? It's getting quite late."

"It's never too late to say a polite thank you," Abner said, laughing softly. "And who might we both be saying a thank you to, Lauralee? Noah Brown. That's who."

Lauralee looked quickly over at him.

"My dear, Noah saved your young man's life today," he said. He smiled at her. "I am taking you there to give you the opportunity to thank him yourself."

Stunned, Lauralee looked away from him. Of course she knew that Noah Brown should be thanked. She *wanted* to oblige him with a heartfelt thanks. But having seen her uncle's coolness toward Dancing Cloud, she had to wonder what his true motive was for taking her to the farmer's residence.

"Noah has a son, Lauralee," Abner said, eyeing her speculatively as she gave him another quick, questioning glance. "I think you might enjoy meeting him. He'd make some lucky woman an excellent husband."

Lauralee's spine stiffened. *Now* she understood. She understood that Abner was not truly concerned about taking "thank you's" to Noah. Her uncle wanted to push another man on her in hopes that she would forget all about Dancing Cloud.

"Lauralee?" Abner turned quizzical eyes her way. "Aren't you anxious to meet the son of such an honorable man as Noah Brown?"

Lauralee frowned at him and refused to answer. She most certainly was not going to play this matching game with him.

When Abner drew his horse and buggy into a narrow drive that led to a small farmhouse, Lauralee's pulse raced.

She felt trapped.

Totally trapped.

And without even having met Noah's son yet, she felt as though she was a part of the betrayal that Abner was forcing upon her.

13

Henceforth I will not set my love
on other than the country lass,
For in the court I see and prove
Fancy is brittle as the glass.
                    —SIR ARTHUR GORGES

A huge collie met the horse and buggy, barking and
hopping up on Lauralee's side. She recoiled and
scooted closer to Abner.

Then her eyes were averted elsewhere when a young
man opened the front door of the small farmhouse and
stepped out onto the porch, a kerosene lantern held out
before him.

Abner drew tight rein directly in front of the porch.
"Good evening, Paul," he said, leaving the buggy in
one hop. "Will you go and tell your mom and pop that
Abner Peterson and his lovely niece have come calling?"

"Yes, sir," Paul said. "I'll go and tell them. It's nice
of you to drop by. You should come more often."

Paul paused long enough to hold the lantern farther
away from himself so that he could get a better look at
Lauralee. He whistled at his dog when he realized it
was frightening her. The dog followed him into the
house.

Abner circled his reins around a hitching rail, then
went to Lauralee and held his arms up for her.

She had no choice but to oblige and allowed him to
help her from the buggy. It was obvious that he was

not going to settle for anything less than her meeting a young man of *his* choosing tonight.

It took no fortune-teller's crystal ball to understand what was behind this late call to the Browns, especially now that Lauralee had seen their son. She could tell that he was not that much older than herself.

And there was no denying how handsome he was. Even in the dim light of the lantern she had noticed. If not for loving Dancing Cloud so much, she could say that she might have even allowed herself to enjoy her uncle's ploy.

But she *did* love Dancing Cloud.

Nothing or no one could change that.

In overalls, Noah came outside and gestured with a hand. "Come on inside and sit a spell," he said, his voice filled with a pleasant warmth. "June just brewed a fresh pot of coffee. She made a cake earlier in the day. Have some refreshments with us while you tell us what brings you out to our farm so late at night."

"I think I'll pass on the coffee, Noah," Abner said, laughing softly as he ushered Lauralee up the steps. "I only drink coffee past suppertime if I plan to work all night in my study."

"And so this is your niece who you've talked about these past weeks?" Noah said. He stepped aside and held the screen door open for Abner as he escorted Lauralee on inside the house. "She's a pretty one, Abner. I'm sure she'll have all of the Mattoon men wantin' to escort her to various functions."

Lauralee looked quickly around the room. It was lit by two kerosene lamps. She could see that it was comfortably furnished. Flowered wallpaper graced the parlor walls, clean, sparkling white sheer curtains hung at the windows, and a roaring fire on the grate of the fireplace filled the room with warmth and light. The aroma of bread baking wafted from the kitchen.

Noah gazed over at Paul. He could see his son's interest in Lauralee. "I have a son who just might beat all of the other gents to the punch," he said, chuckling. "What do you say, Paul? Ain't she somethin'?"

Lauralee blushed from the close scrutiny, herself now even more taken by Paul since she was close enough to get a true look at his handsomeness.

She could see why her uncle had tried this ploy to avert her attention and feelings away from Dancing Cloud.

Tall and square-shouldered, his golden hair cut straight just above his shirt collar, Paul Brown was a breathtakingly handsome man whose blue eyes seemed to pierce the very heart and soul of Lauralee.

Then she recalled other blue eyes.

Those of the damn Yankee.

The Yankee's eyes had been cold and evil.

Paul's were warm and friendly as was his smile as he gazed at her.

Lauralee's eyes shifted and took in the rest of his facial features after having already seen how virile and muscled he was in his skin-tight black breeches and pale blue denim shirt. He had a long, straight nose, a set jawline, and lips that seemed way too sensual to be a man's. She wondered how it might feel to be kissed by them.

Then she shook herself out of her reverie when she realized where her thoughts had taken her. Now she felt for certain that she was betraying Dancing Cloud's love for her. Allowing another man to cause her insides to grow weak was wrong.

She could *not* feel anything for this man.

She could not allow her uncle's scheme to work!

She *would* marry Dancing Cloud one day. She adored the thought of living with him forever as his wife.

She was relieved when someone else came into the room, her very presence breaking the tension. Lauralee looked over at the middle-aged woman, instantly liking her. A gentle warmth radiated from her, her blue eyes dancing, her perfectly shaped lips smiling.

Dressed in a fully gathered cotton dress, her golden hair tied in a bun atop her head, she was tall and statuesque.

"Abner, how nice it is to see you again," June said, rushing toward him with an extended hand of welcome. She clasped onto his hand and shook it, then turned wondering eyes to Lauralee. "And this must be Lauralee."

Lauralee was not at all surprised when June came to her with a warm hug. She found herself returning the hug.

Then Lauralee blushed uneasily when June stepped away from her and looked over at her son with a twinkle in her eyes, then gazed at Lauralee again.

"I'm sure you two young people have other things you'd rather do besides stay in the house," June said, again smiling from Paul, back to Lauralee. "Son, why don't you take Lauralee and show her our pond? Get acquainted."

Lauralee gave a panicked look at Abner. She then sighed resolutely when Paul was suddenly there, his hand at her elbow, ushering her outside.

She walked stiffly with him down the steps, and across the wide stretch of lawn. Neither of them spoke until the pond was reached, where the moon made a path along the water and crickets sang love songs.

"You'll have to pardon my parents," Paul said almost bashfully as he gave Lauralee a half glance. "I think they are worrying about this bachelor son of theirs *way* too much."

"I noticed," Lauralee said, laughing loosely. "And I imagine you may have noticed that my uncle has the same thing on his mind about his *niece*."

"I heard talk about you coming to town to live with the Petersons," Paul said, giving Lauralee another shy glance. "You staying long?"

"That was my father's intentions when he wired my uncle and aunt from his deathbed," Lauralee said. She flinched when he took her hand and led her to the ground beside the pond, then sat down beside her.

Lauralee eased her hand away from his and rearranged her skirt beneath her on the grass. She then primly folded her hands on her lap as she coiled her feet beneath her.

"I'm sorry about your father," Paul said, drawing his long, lean legs up before him, to hug them. "It must be rough to have lost both parents."

"It's the worst feeling in the world," Lauralee said solemnly. "It's all because of the war. But I'm not the only one whose life was altered by it." She gave him a soft look. "I was told that you lost a brother. I'm sorry."

"It's been hard to live with the knowledge that I'll never see Brad again," Paul said, his voice breaking. "But I keep busy on the farm. That helps me forget. At least for a while."

"It was kind of your father to take Dancing Cloud to Dr. Kemper's," Lauralee said. She inhaled a quavering breath as she envisioned Dancing Cloud in bed now, trusting her as he slept.

"The reason my uncle and I paid your family such a late visit tonight was to thank your father for what he did for Dancing Cloud," she quickly added. "Also, I would like to ask about Dancing Cloud's horse. Is it in your stable?"

"Yes, Pop brought it home but planned to take it to Abner's tomorrow," Paul said. "If it's all right, I'd like to bring the horse. Perhaps you and I could talk some more?"

"If you wish," Lauralee said, without thinking. Then she felt guilty again over Dancing Cloud because of her easiness with Paul.

Torn with feelings she did not understand, Lauralee tried to convince herself that it was only out of kindness that she was behaving this way with another man. How could she feel anything for him, when the most wonderful man in the world loved her?

"I truly must go," she blurted, rushing to her feet. "I'm sure my uncle has said his thank you's by now. I am bone-weary. I need to get home."

"I understand," Paul said. He rose to his full height, towering over Lauralee.

Lauralee started to walk back toward the house, but Paul's warm hand in hers stopped her.

She was all eyes and breathless when he swung her around to face him.

She went numb inside when he swept his arms around her waist and drew her close.

"Don't misunderstand what I'm about to do," he said. "I've never wanted to kiss anyone ever, as badly as I want to kiss you."

She grew weak in the knees when his full lips covered hers in a warm, passionate kiss. When she began experiencing something akin to rapture, she became frightened and shoved at his chest.

When she finally wrenched herself away, she stared up at him. "Please don't ever do that *again*," she said, her voice trembling. "Now I am forced to decline your invitation of coming to talk with me tomorrow when you bring Dancing Cloud's horse to the Petersons' stable. I'm afraid you have more in mind than mere conversation."

She stiffened her back and stamped away, but gasped when once again his warm hand was there in hers, stopping her.

"I apologize," he said as he urged her around to face him again. "I shouldn't have."

"Never shall you *again*," Lauralee said, her whole insides trembling from confusion.

"I would still like the opportunity of seeing you again." Paul's voice was soft and convincing.

"Only long enough for you to give me the reins to Dancing Cloud's horse," Lauralee said stubbornly. She wrenched her hand away from his. "I would expect you to leave quickly then."

"I can't make such a promise," Paul said, frowning down at her.

"Then don't bother coming," Lauralee persisted. She placed her hands on her hips. "Send someone else with Dancing Cloud's horse. If not, I shall make sure only the Petersons' stable hand is there to accept the horse."

"Why are you being so stubborn?" Paul insisted. "I felt you respond to my kiss. Why would you want to deny your feelings? Is it because there is someone else?"

Lauralee paled.

Her eyes wavered.

That was all it took for Paul to know the answers.

"Is it the Cherokee?" he asked thickly.

"I'd truly rather not continue this conversation," Lauralee replied. She whirled her skirt around to walk away from him again. She gave him an aggravated look when he caught up with her and walked beside her in a lazy but most intriguing saunter.

"Lauralee, I would truly like the opportunity to court you and change your mind about anyone else you may think you have feelings for," Paul said, not giving her up all that easily.

She thought back to the orphanage. Living like that, she had never had the opportunity to have men come calling, as women do who lived in normal homes, with normal families. It gave her a strange sort of thrill to think of having a man come calling on her at a front door, of having a man escort her to a fancy carriage, of having the man possibly taking her to a fancy ball where she would whirl around the floor from night to dawn.

She wanted to experience all of these things.

But she still did not want to have a life with anyone but Dancing Cloud.

And she knew that he would not be the courting kind, who would come calling in a fancy carriage, or who would even know how to dance!

To go with him to his village to be his wife would be paradise.

Yet she just wished that she could experience what she had missed at least *once*.

"If I would allow you to come courting, would it be understood between us that I am only accepting your company for the fun of it, not to be seriously considering becoming your wife?" Lauralee blurted out, giving him a guarded glance.

"It would be understood." Paul nodded. "But would you also understand that you just might enjoy my company enough to want more of it?"

"I imagine that is a gamble we both shall be taking," Lauralee said, smiling as their eyes locked.

Again he swept her into his arms and kissed her.

This time she did not shove him away. For now it was all right to experience things that she had been denied as a young girl blossoming into a woman.

Surely Dancing Cloud would understand if he ever found out!

She continued returning his kiss with a wild abandon. . . .

14

Love me for love's sake, that evermore
Thou mays't love on through love's eternity.
— Elizabeth Barrett Browning

The bed on which Dancing Cloud lay asleep was illumined by a beam of morning sun. Having arrived before dawn, Lauralee sat beside his bed, deep in thought.

The night had been a long and restless one for her. She had not been able to forget how foolish she had been to allow herself to feel anything for Paul Brown. She truly realized now that she had only been swept away by the idea of courting a man like most women whose lives were normal. If she had not been deprived of so many things while growing up in the orphanage she would not be swayed as easily by smooth-talking men today.

On the other hand, there was Dancing Cloud. Although she had been as swept away by him and his night-black eyes and his finely chiseled features, she knew from the depths of her heart that her feelings for him were nothing less than genuine.

And after tossing and turning and thinking the long night through in her soft feather bed at the Peterson House, she now knew for certain that in her heart there was room only for one man.

That man was Dancing Cloud.

She sighed heavily. She now had the unpleasant

chore of telling Paul Brown that she could no longer
see him. She hoped they might remain friends. He was
a sweet man; he would have no trouble finding a
woman who would fall under the spell of his deep,
mesmerizing blue eyes. Lauralee gazed lovingly at
Dancing Cloud. She so badly wanted to wake him up
and tell him that she loved him. Although he could not
be aware of her one small infidelity to him, she carried
the burden for them both. She knew that this burden
would not be lifted until she met with Paul and revealed her feelings to him.

"Today," she whispered to herself. "I must find a
way to break away long enough to go to Paul and tell
him before tonight."

When Dancing Cloud stirred in his sleep Lauralee
leaned closer to him. She wanted to be the first thing
he saw when he awakened. She felt she owed him so
much because of her behavior with Paul Brown.

She most definitely owed him a lifetime of loving.

When he did not awaken, Lauralee eased back in the
chair. She continued watching him, never getting
enough of looking at his lean, bronzed, and handsome
face.

Hungering for his kiss, she gazed at his lips.

She shifted her gaze lower and looked at his powerful hands as they rested beside him on the bed, a blanket covering him only past his waist.

She shivered with rapture when she recalled how he
knew so well the skills of teasing and stroking the supple lines of her body. When he had touched her that
first time between her thighs, everything wonderfully
sweet had been awakened inside her.

She was glad that no one else was in the room with
her and Dancing Cloud. They would see her blushing
while thinking such brazen thoughts so early in the
morning at the bedside of a man who had nearly lost
his life.

She cleared her throat and squirmed in the seat, then
stiffened and again leaned closer to Dancing Cloud. He

was not waking up. Instead, he seemed to be dreaming. His closed eyelids were twitching. For a moment he grimaced, then *smiled*.

Puzzled, Lauralee continued to watch him. She wondered what the dream could be about that it could cause him to react so?

Dancing Cloud felt himself being drawn into a hazy world of white light. As he seemed to float through a long, swirling tunnel of white he heard soft voices on all sides of him, as though whispers in the night.

The farther he traveled into the vastness of the swirling tunnel, as though some unseen force was pulling him, the voices became louder and more distinct. They were familiar voices of his past.

Dancing Cloud realized now that his wound was healed. The bandages were gone!

He reached out his hands in a beckoning gesture. And in a response to the voices, he found himself speaking his mother's name, then his sister's and brother's, and so many more of his loved ones whom had passed on to the afterlife before him.

When he finally reached the end of this strange, misty-white tunnel he found himself in a large meadow of wildflowers. In the distance were a widespread range of mountains. Bordering the mountains were vast forests. Overhead, birds of all kinds soared, their wings shadowing the land beneath them.

The feeling that overcame Dancing Cloud was that of total peace. He no longer felt any pain; only a serenity never known to him before.

And then suddenly before him, in a film of white, glorious light, came his beloved family who had died during the war at the hands of the enemy Yankees.

"*E-tsi*, Mother?" he said.

His eyes widened as she stepped forth in her beautiful doeskin dress decorated with beads in designs of flowers.

Then his younger ten-year-old brother, Young Elk,

came and stood at his mother's side, his breech clout softly flapping in the wind.

And then he gazed with a total serenity and happiness at Little Firefly, his sister of five winters, when she stepped forth and took his mother's hand.

"How can this be?" Dancing Cloud said, looking incredulously from one to the other.

"For a short time you are in the spirit world, the hereafter, because *Wah-kon-tah* has bid you here," his mother said, reaching a hand out for Dancing Cloud. "Come and let me embrace you, my son. Your time with us will be gone quickly."

Dancing Cloud went to his mother and drew her into his powerful embrace. He trembled with happiness as he sank his nose into the depths of her black hair, enjoying the familiar fragrance of his mother who he remembered so well.

"*E-tsi,* I have missed you so," Dancing Cloud said, clinging to her. "I do not understand why I have been allowed to be with you again, but I give thanks to *Wah-kon-tah* because of it."

"Your sister and brother have also missed you," his mother said, easing away from Dancing Cloud. "Give them an embrace also, my son. They have missed their older brother."

Dancing Cloud hugged them each, savoring the moments, then again turned to his mother. "Mother, I have carried guilt with me for so long because I was not there for you when the Yankees came and ravaged our village," he said thickly. "Had I been there . . ."

She placed a soft hand over his mouth to silence his worried words. "My son, your father was there," she said gently. "Was he not a powerful warrior chief?"

"*Ii,* yes, that is so," Dancing Cloud said, nodding as she slipped her hand away.

"Had anyone been able to stop the Yankees that day your father would have seen that it was done," his mother softly explained. "It was beyond his power to stop the many soldiers with their blazing guns. He was not slain *only* because the soldiers saw how much losing his loved ones affected him. They thought it was more cruel to allow him to live, than to kill him. My spirit hovered above your father as the soldiers mocked and mimicked him. My son, I witnessed *your* recent ambush. The man who did this to you is also the same man who laughed at your father and led the attack against our people."

Another voice spoke up.

Dancing Cloud turned and stared at the swirling white shadow, where the voice originated.

"What she says is true, my son," James Talking Bear said, slowly materializing for Dancing Cloud to see. Instead of walking with the aid of his tall staff, he walked on his own, his shoulders squared, his back straight. "You see, my spirit also witnessed your ambush. I have watched over you, since, as you have lain in the white man's bed, healing."

Dancing Cloud was stunned to see his father now among the other spirits of his past. He would only be there had his spirit passed on from earth!

It meant only one thing.

In Dancing Cloud's absence his father had passed onto the land of the hereafter.

His father was dead!

Yet Dancing Cloud felt no remorse. While among his loved ones in this spirit world he could not experience regrets or remorse. He felt blessed to have been given the chance to be with them at least one more time.

"*E-do-do*, Father?" Dancing Cloud said, reaching a hand out for him.

"It is too soon for me in this spirit world for you to physically touch me," James Talking Bear said, nobly squaring his shoulders. "It is enough, is it not, that *Wah-kon-tah,* the Great Spirit, has granted this one last reunion with family?"

"*Ii*, yes, it is a wonderful thing that *Wah-kon-tah* has done for us," Dancing Cloud said. "But why? Is it because I lay perhaps between life and death in my bed? Is that why I have been beckoned here? To prepare me for what is to come? If so, I welcome it. I welcome being with my family again. Except . . ."

"Except that the woman of your heart is not among us?" James Talking Bear said, completing his son's sentence. "My son, you will be with your white woman again soon. But not in the spirit world. You will return to her after I prepare you for your future. You are now chief of our Wolf Clan of Cherokee. Rule our people with a firm hand, but with much love and from the heart. Keep peace, my son. At all cost keep peace so that our people can multiply in number. Not dwindle away from warring with the whites."

"I am chief, yet I am not with our people," Dancing Cloud said. "And I will not be there for some sunsets to come. My body needs time to heal before taking the long ride on horseback to the mountains."

"Our people are faring well enough under the direction of the elder statesmen of our village," James Talking Bear said. "They know you will return. They know that your heart is with your people."

"My heart is also with Lauralee," Dancing Cloud said. "She will sit at my right side as my wife during future councils."

"It would be best if you choose a woman of our own culture, but I have watched you from the spirit world while you have been with this woman named Lauralee," James Talking Bear said. "And I see that you have chosen well. She will blend well enough with our people. But your children, Dancing Cloud? Had you considered children by this woman? What if you bring a white-skinned child into the life of the Cherokee? Thus far we are all full-blooded and are proud that we are."

Dancing Cloud did not have a chance to respond. Another figure was emerging from the bright light of the tunnel behind him. He turned and shadowed his eyes with his hands.

He then sucked in a wild breath of surprise when he saw a massive figure of a man whose buckskins were the whitest white, and whose face was the noblest of all.

"*Wah-kon-tah?*" Dancing Cloud said softly.

"*Ii,* it is I," the Great Spirit said, his voice gentle as all spring breezes. "I allowed you to come to the spirit world to be with your family so that your father could ease your sadness when you discover back on earth that he has passed on to the other side. I allow you to return to earth, to lead your people. But I promise you, Dancing Cloud, that I will call you again at a later time, to be with your family forever in the hereafter spirit world."

A hand reached out from *Wah-kon-tah* and placed it on Dancing Cloud's shoulder. "Go now," he said. "Return to your other life. Lead your people well."

Dancing Cloud turned and gazed at his loved ones one last time and felt no sadness in leaving them. He now knew that he would be reunited with them one day. They would walk these beautiful meadows, mountains, and forests together. They would be as one until the end of time.

Suddenly he felt himself being drawn again into that vast vacuum of white, swirling light.

He felt no pain.

He felt no regrets.

He felt no remorse.

Only total peace, and very blessed.

He awakened. He found Lauralee there, leaning over him, her eyes questioning.

"What were you dreaming about?" she asked, gently stroking his brow. "Darling, I could tell that you were dreaming about something that disturbed you."

"I was not disturbed," Dancing Cloud said, in awe of what he had just experienced. "I was with *family.*"

"With family?" Lauralee asked, easing her hand from him. "How could you be?" Then she laughed lightly. "Oh, I see. You were dreaming of your family."

"No. I was *with* them," Dancing Cloud insisted. He forced himself to a sitting position, fighting off the pain that this caused him. He looked down. The bandages were there again. His wound was not healed as it had been in the land on the other side.

"And my *father* was among them," he said as he looked up at Lauralee. "My father has passed on to the other life. I must return to my people. I must gain my strength back quickly so that I can make the journey back to my mountain. I am now chief. My people need my leadership."

Lauralee's head was spinning from what he was saying. She was also amazed at how determined he was to leave the bed. "I don't understand," she murmured. She took him by the arm and helped him as he insistently swung his legs over the side of the bed. "Darling, how could you know that your father is dead? How could anyone know how to find you to tell you here in Mattoon? When *did* they tell you?"

"No one came here. Although I do not understand myself *how,* I crossed over to the spirit world today," Dancing Cloud said, sweat pearling his brow in his effort to place his feet solidly on the floor. "But I was. I met with my family who died during the war. Also my father was there. He has passed on to the spirit world. I was there momentarily. I saw. I talked with him. I talked with my whole family. I talked with the Great Spirit. Now I must get my strength back so that I can return to my people."

"Do you mean you were actually separated from your body?" Lauralee asked, rising from the chair as Dancing Cloud rose slowly and shakily from the bed. "I have heard of people who have spoken of such a rare thing as that. Until today I thought it was a hoax. But, Dancing Cloud, you are not the sort to play games of the mind with people. I believe you. Oh, Lord, I believe you."

"Help me pace the floor," Dancing Cloud said,

wrapping and tying a blanket around himself so that he would not be totally nude.

"Dancing Cloud, it's too soon," Lauralee pleaded, yet saw his determination.

Still in awe of what he had told her, she allowed him to sling his left arm around her shoulder. He leaned against her as he slowly began to walk across the floor, then back again.

"It was good to see my family again," Dancing Cloud said, panting as he continued walking back and forth. "Although I mourn my father's death, I feel no deep remorse, for I know, I have *seen* his happiness. It is complete. And his body is mended. He is a strong and vital man again."

The pain in his shoulder was excruciating. But the need to return to his people was far more overwhelming to him.

"Oh, if I could but just once see my mother and father again," Lauralee said, sighing as tears sprang to her eyes. "But at least I now know that they are together, hand in hand, waiting for *me,* when I die."

"It is a place of paradise," Dancing Cloud said, giving her a soft smile. "We shall be there together, my love, after we have walked a full and happy life on this side of the spirit world."

Lauralee suddenly remembered with much pain and guilt her fleeting moments with Paul Brown. Most certainly she had something that needed done to make things right in her world again.

15

Many waters cannot quench love,
Neither can the floods drown it.

—KING SOLOMON

Lauralee glanced over at the window. It was growing
dusk. She had wanted to leave and go to Paul's farm
before now and break the news to him that she did not
wish for him to call on her this evening. She would tell
him, then get Dancing Cloud's horse and take it back
to the Petersons' stable.

But she had felt that Dancing Cloud needed her with
him for a while longer. He was driven to get his
strength back. He felt a strong need to return to his
people, which had to mean that she would also be saying a much earlier goodbye to her aunt and uncle than
what she had expected.

Lauralee's promise that she would look after Nancy
in her weakened condition came to her in a flash. A
deep feeling of melancholia swept through her knowing that she wouldn't be able to keep her word to her
aunt.

And it was sad that they had been allowed only a
brief acquaintance. Had things been different there
could have been such a long, lasting, and wonderful relationship between herself and the Petersons.

Lauralee only hoped now that Abner and Nancy
would not hate her. It was never her intention to play
with their affections.

Fate, her *destiny,* had changed everything.

"You are in such deep thought," Dancing Cloud said, shifting his weight on the bed to get more comfortable. His legs ached from the persistent pacing.

And that wasn't all that he planned to do to heal his body. Tonight he was going to escape from the hospital long enough to go to a small pond that he had seen at the edge of town on his and Lauralee's arrival to Mattoon. He would seek the healing powers of water, that which was practiced by all Cherokee warriors.

The heroic treatment of the plunge bath in the water healed wounds more quickly than any of the white man's medicines.

He had not shared this plan of escape with Lauralee knowing that she wouldn't approve. She would say that it was risking his health by doing it.

In time, everything about the Cherokee would be understood by her, he thought warmly to himself. When she became as one with him as his wife she would by then know most of the customs of his people.

He would gladly teach her.

Something nagged at his consciousness that his father had said to him in the hereafter about marrying Lauralee. But no matter how hard he tried to remember it would not come to him. As each moment passed, things experienced in the afterworld were becoming vague to him.

But never would he forget the happiness of being with his family again.

Never would he forget how blessed he had been to have been granted such an experience.

Whenever he thought about his father no longer being alive, he would recall his father's smile and his strong body as he stood with his family somewhere high above in the vast realm of the heavens. It made losing his father easier.

"I feel as though I've neglected Aunt Nancy," Lauralee quickly blurted. She couldn't tell him her true reason for being so quiet and pensive—that another man was on her mind.

She took one of his hands and gently held it. "Darling, would you understand if I went now and spent time with Aunt Nancy?" she murmured. "You see, I feel I owe her so much that I shall never be able to repay."

Although she was going to spend *some* time with Nancy, it was not going to be now.

And, oh, how she hated lying to Dancing Cloud.

But this lie was necessary. It was being told to help further along their future, unhampered.

"Go," Dancing Cloud said, leaning up on an elbow, reaching his lips to hers. "It has been a tiring day. This Cherokee needs some rest."

Although he *did* need to rest, it wasn't going to be at this very moment, he thought to himself. And, oh, how he hated lying to Lauralee.

But he felt that this lie was necessary. It was told to help further along their future, unhampered. The more quickly his body healed, the more quickly he could return to his people.

Lauralee did not know it yet, but he would insist on taking her with him this time when he left Mattoon. The altercation with McCloud had taught him that life could be way shorter than one plans.

"I feel that I should stay to feed you your supper," Lauralee said, melting inside when he kissed her.

Fighting the need for her, Dancing Cloud eased away from her. "Did you not see me feed myself adequately enough today?" he said, still resting his weight on his one elbow. "I believe I can take care of myself well enough during the evening meal."

Lauralee's eyes widened. She couldn't help but wonder why Dancing Cloud was trying to get rid of her, but she felt it was best not to question him about it. She had things to do. The longer she delayed, the harder it would be to tell Paul her true feelings.

"All right, if you truly feel you don't need me, then

I shall come shortly after supper," she said, still questioning him with her eyes as she rose from the chair.

"You haven't spent much time with Nancy, that's for certain," Dancing Cloud quickly interjected. "To make up for it, stay the entire evening with her. I will get my rest. Today has been tiring."

"You truly don't want me to return this evening?" she asked, stunned by his insistence to be alone.

"I always want you with me," Dancing Cloud said softly. "But I must learn to share you with others. Tonight I share you with your aunt."

Still unsure about his willingness to be apart from her for the rest of the day, *and* evening, Lauralee stared down at him for a moment longer.

But knowing that this made her plans even more easier to carry out, she questioned him no further about it.

As she sat up from the chair, her silk dress wrapped provocatively around her legs, revealing their shape to Dancing Cloud. She could feel Dancing Cloud's eyes raking over her. She was delighted with his response. She had dressed as beautifully as she could this morning just for him.

It worried her to realize that she would be seeing Paul Brown later and that he might think she was wearing her best clothes to encourage his attentions. This was an impression she didn't want to convey at all.

"This Cherokee's eyes cannot get enough of you today," Dancing Cloud said, reaching to grab her hand. He drew her down onto the bed beside him. He moved his fingers over the swell of her breasts, wishing the barrier of silk was not there to impede the touch of her soft, sweet flesh against his fingertips.

Lauralee sucked in a quavering breath and closed her eyes as she leaned her breast into his hand. "I have so missed our private moments together," she whispered, her body trembling with need of him. "Have you also missed me as badly?"

Dancing Cloud slid his hand upward and cupped her chin within its palm. He drew her mouth to his. "I hunger for you, always," he whispered. He crushed his lips against hers, the flames of desire lapping at his loins.

Footsteps entering the room caused Lauralee's heart to skip a beat. Fearing that it might be her uncle Abner, she yanked herself free of Dancing Cloud and rose shakily to her feet.

Her face hot with a blush, she turned slowly. She sighed with relief when she found herself gazing wide-eyed at Dr. Kemper instead of her uncle.

The doctor's jaw tightened and his eyes narrowed as he looked from Lauralee, to Dancing Cloud, and then back at Lauralee.

"Lauralee, I've come to say that should he feel up to it, Dancing Cloud can leave the hospital as early as tomorrow morning," he said, his voice drawn and tight. "That is, if Dancing Cloud has somewhere to go. He must not travel yet as far as his home in the mountains. The Petersons. Lauralee, do you think the Petersons will allow Dancing Cloud to stay at their house for the short time he needs for further recuperation?"

"Yes, I believe the Petersons will allow him to stay at their home until he is able to travel," Lauralee said, yet truly not certain at *all* how her uncle would take this news. No one knew as much as Lauralee how her uncle felt about Dancing Cloud. His resentment seemed to lay way deeper than was even *decent*.

It was up to her to change all of this for Dancing Cloud. It was important that her aunt and uncle grow to like him as much as Lauralee *loved* him.

"Then that's settled," Dr. Kemper said, coming on into the room.

Lauralee stepped aside and stood breathlessly watching as Dr. Kemper slowly unwrapped the bandage from around Dancing Cloud's chest and shoulder.

When the bullet wound was revealed to her, a sick feeling engulfed her. She hadn't been aware of how much surgery had been required to remove the bullet.

There was a wide, puckering scar across his right shoulder, reaching down across his chest.

Dancing Cloud winced and gritted his teeth as the doctor pressed and pushed on the skin around the wound. Dancing Cloud glanced down at it and saw it for the first time.

Hate swelled inside his heart against the one responsible for not only this infliction upon his body, but so much hurt inflicted inside his heart. He now knew, from the short time with his mother in the hereafter, that the very same Yankee who had ravaged his village and had killed many innocent Cherokee, had also shot Boyd!

He thanked the Good Spirit for allowing him to remember some of what had been said between himself and his loved ones amid that peaceful, swirling white light.

Dancing Cloud vowed again to himself that he would find Clint McCloud. He would end the Yankee's days of murder and plundering.

Ii, yes, somehow their paths would cross again.

Dancing Cloud looked toward the window. When night fell in its cloak of black and the lawman was asleep outside the door in the corridor, Dancing Cloud would flee from this room and get the healing powers from the water.

So much depended on his total recovery . . . his people's future, and his and Lauralee's lifetime together.

"Joe Dancing Cloud, I'm going to leave the bandage off now," Dr. Kemper said, dropping the soiled bandage in a wastebasket. "Ofttimes the air can help the healing process better than leaving a wound covered. We'll see how you do today. If I feel you should be bandaged again, I'll do it tomorrow before you leave the hospital."

Dr. Kemper gazed in silence down at his patient a moment longer, then turned to Lauralee. "He looks tired," he said dryly. "I'd suggest you go home so that he can get some rest."

"I was just leaving," Lauralee said, smiling awkwardly at the doctor.

Dr. Kemper nodded, gave Dancing Cloud another glance over his shoulder, then left the room.

Lauralee knelt down beside the bed and gently stroked Dancing Cloud's cheeks with her hands. "Darling, are you going to be all right?" she murmured. "If you insist that I stay, I shall."

"You heard the doctor," Dancing Cloud said, taking one her hands, kissing its palm. "It is best that you leave."

"And you don't want me to come again until tomorrow?" Lauralee asked, searching his eyes for the truth in his response.

"*Ii*, yes, that would be best," Dancing Cloud said softly. "Then tomorrow I shall leave this place. We shall never be apart again."

"You do understand, don't you, that you won't be able to leave Mattoon until you are truly better?"

"I would not rush into anything that might in the end harm my people. I will not plan my lengthy travel to the mountains until my body is strong and able."

His eyes widened. He leaned quickly up on an elbow again. "My *so-qui-li*, horse," he gasped. "My horse is lost to me!"

"No, darling," Lauralee said, gently placing a hand on his cheek. "Don't you remember me telling you? Noah Brown. The man who brought you to the hospital? He also rescued your horse." She swallowed hard at the thought again of what lay ahead of her. Her meeting with Paul. "Your horse will be waiting for you at the Petersons' whenever you have a need for it."

Dancing Cloud eased back down on the bed. "My mind is not as clear and as alert as it normally is," he said, sighing heavily. "This Noah Brown is a man of good heart. I owe him much. So very much."

Lauralee nodded. When she realized that he had drifted off into a sound sleep, she tiptoed from the room.

As she stepped out into the corridor she glanced over at Nancy's closed door. She was torn between needs.

A need to go and sit with Nancy.

And a need to go and end this thing with Paul Brown!

She went and placed her hand at the doorknob of Nancy's room, to at least tell her that she loved her. She stopped when she heard Abner's voice wafting from the room.

Realizing that Nancy had Abner for the moment to keep her company, Lauralee turned and fled down the corridor.

When she reached the front door and opened it she stood frozen in place when she found herself face to face with the very man of her many midnight nightmares.

The damn Yankee from the Civil War!

The man who raped and killed her mother!

The sight of him made Lauralee's knees grow limp as a dizziness swept through her.

Clint stared disbelievingly back at her. He had come to Dr. Kemper's to see if it was true that Sheriff Decker had actually placed a guard outside the Indian's door to protect him. Never had he expected to come face to face with Abner Peterson's niece! And he knew for certain this woman *was* Lauralee Johnston. He had stalked Dancing Cloud while she was still with him.

As she stood in a strange sort of trance, as though she knew him enough to be frightened of him, a plan came quickly to his mind. He would abduct Lauralee. This was one way to lure Dancing Cloud into his clutches. Then Clint would finally end this vengeance that gnawed at his insides like a sore.

And *this* time, Noah Brown wouldn't get a chance to interfere! This would be between only Dancing Cloud and himself.

And to hell with Judge Peterson, Clint thought bitterly to himself. After hearing that the judge was in on actually protecting the life of a Rebel, Clint saw him as no better than a gray coat himself!

Another thing. Clint needed to get this damn thing over with. He had other pressing matters, both personal and business, that needed tended to in North Carolina. His wife should have had her baby by now. He was anxious to see if the baby resembled him, or her. If it took after her, he'd yank it from her arms and get rid of it so fast her head would swim.

But Clint sure as hell had to take care of Dancing Cloud before he left Mattoon. The opportunity might never be there again to kill the Cherokee.

Clint looked quickly around and made sure that no one was in the corridor or waiting room.

He glanced over his shoulder to make sure no one was coming up the steps.

Then when he realized that the coast was clear, he grabbed Lauralee around the waist.

This made Lauralee come quickly out of her stunned state. She slapped and kicked at Clint. She tried to scream, but he quickly clamped one of his hands over her mouth.

With his one arm anchoring her to him, her back against his left hip, Clint dragged Lauralee down the steps. The shadows of evening gave him the cover he needed to get her to his horse and make his escape.

"I hope to find out why you looked as though you saw a ghost when you saw me," Clint grumbled as his eyes watched around him. "I'd say that was strange behavior for someone you've never laid eyes on before."

Her eyes wide over his hand, Lauralee yanked and tugged at his arm, and then the hand that was held across her mouth.

But nothing could budge either his hand or his arm. They seemed glued to her.

There was one thing in her favor. The man had a wooden leg. She could see that his movements down the steps were hampered by it. As he struggled to get her down the steps, the wooden leg dragged heavily behind him.

Lauralee's eyes widened even more as she suddenly recalled Dancing Cloud saying that his assailant had a wooden leg.

Could this man be the one and the same?

Clint McCloud.

She remembered Dancing Cloud saying that his assailant's name was Clint McCloud!

She was then aware of something else. Of the feel of a pistol grinding into her back as Clint walked her toward his horse.

The pistol.

It was in a holster.

It was so very, very temptingly close.

If she could just reach behind her . . .

When he finally got to his horse and began untying his reins, Lauralee gave his good leg a swift, backward kick.

Clint yelped with pain and loosened his grip on her enough for her to get a solid hold on the handle of his pistol.

As he reached for her, to force her onto his horse, she swung the pistol from his holster and aimed it at him. "You no good damn Yankee," she hissed, holding a steady aim on him. "Now you're going to pay for all of the evil you have done in your lifetime."

Clint went pale. Not so much over Lauralee having for the moment got the best of him. He remembered another lady of his past and how she had drawn a pistol on him, her exact words—"You no good damn Yankee"—having haunted him through the years. It had been only moments later when one of his soldiers had disarmed her.

Clint had enjoyed raping and killing her for having humiliated him in front of his regiment of soldiers that day.

This woman standing before him today was an exact

replica of that lady those many years ago, as though she had come back to life to haunt him.

His heart pounding, he fitted his good foot in the stirrup, and as he had been forced to learn long ago, he swung his wooden leg over the horse.

Quickly in the saddle, and taking the chance that this lady's aim would not be accurate enough, he gave her one last stare, then snapped his reins and rode away.

"Stop!" Lauralee cried. Her hand trembled as she held her aim on him, yet knew the chances were good that he would escape.

She knew nothing about firearms.

She even feared them.

When he did not stop, she closed her eyes, held her face sideways back from the pistol, and pulled the trigger. . . .

16

Her eyes were deeper than
the depth of waters still'd at evening.
—DANTE GABRIEL ROSSETTI

Nothing came from the pistol but a noise hardly as loud as a firecracker. Lauralee stared down at the firearm, stunned. It had misfired. When she had finally been given the opportunity to avenge her mother's death, the damn Yankee's pistol hadn't worked!

She looked quickly up and watched the man disappear around a street corner on his horse. She threw the pistol down and stamped a foot, then turned and ran back inside the hospital.

When she reached Nancy's room she didn't stop to knock. She ran on inside.

Her sudden noisy entrance caused Abner to rise quickly from his chair at Nancy's bedside. He went to Lauralee and placed gentle hands on her arms and gazed down at her questioningly. She seemed desperate about something. She was breathless. She was flushed. Her eyes were wildly pleading up at him.

"Whatever has happened?" Abner said, searching her face. "Is it the Cherokee? Has he worsened?"

"No," she blurted out. She pointed toward the door. "Uncle Abner. I saw him. I saw him."

"You saw Dancing Cloud?" Abner said, arching an eyebrow.

"No," Lauralee cried. "I saw the man ... who ...

raped and killed my mother. I'm certain it was he. I've carried that man's face around with me since I was five. Uncle Abner, he was here. He was entering the hospital. When he saw me it was as though he knew *me*. He grabbed me. He was abducting me."

She had to stop to get her breath.

"Abduct you?" Abner said, dropping his hands to his sides. "Your mother was raped? The same man killed your mother? He's here now?"

Afraid that she was going to upset Nancy, Lauralee looked past Abner and found Nancy's soft, brown eyes on her.

But she had to place her worries about Nancy behind her. She had to get her uncle to go after the man. If he got away, Lauralee would never find him again.

"And, Uncle Abner, I believe this was the same man who also shot Dancing Cloud!" she blurted out. "Dancing Cloud said that his assailant had a wooden leg. *This* man had a wooden leg!"

She grabbed her uncle's hand before he had a chance to respond to what she had just disclosed. "Let's go after him, Uncle Abner," Lauralee pleaded, yanking on his hand. "Please? Now? If we wait longer we'll never be able to catch up with him."

"Whoa, slow down a minute," Abner said, leading Lauralee to a chair.

By no choice of her own she sat down. Her fingers dug into the arms of the chair so hard her knuckles were white.

Abner knelt on a knee before her. "Now tell me about the man," he said softly. "Describe him to me. *Then* we'll go to the sheriff and let *him* take care of this for you. We'll talk about your mother later. Your aunt and I want to know everything."

"He'll get away if we wait any time at all," Lauralee said, her voice breaking. "Please, Uncle Abner. I know which way he went. Please let us go after him."

"Describe him to me," Abner said, ignoring her insistence to do otherwise.

Lauralee inhaled a quavering, frustrated breath. "He has bright red hair and cold blue eyes," she said. "He was a man with much standing during the war. He led a regiment of men. He was in charge of everything that happened at my parents' plantation. He made sure nothing was left behind ... except me. And that was only because I knew to hide from the Yankees."

Abner rose to his full height. He stared down at Nancy. "You know who fits that description?" he said, his voice drawn, as though in total of awe of such a discovery. "That damn son of a bitch."

"That railroad man from North Carolina. Clint McCloud," Nancy offered softly. "Surely she has described Clint McCloud."

"The one and only," Abner said, turning to gaze down at Lauralee again.

"Yes," Lauralee said excitedly. "I'm sure it was Clint McCloud. Dancing Cloud said that was his assailant's name!"

"Come on, honey," Abner said, slipping his hand from hers. "I think I *will* oblige you the opportunity to meet up with this fella again. We shall surprise him at his hotel before he gets the chance to pack up and leave town."

"You aren't going to the sheriff?" Lauralee asked, scrambling to her feet.

"No, like you, I doubt if we have the time," Abner said, placing a hand to Lauralee's elbow. "Although I'm sure Clint doesn't know that you know his name, he knows you'll be able to describe him. If we take the time to go to the sheriff, the damn railroad man will have already skipped town."

Abner looked over his shoulder at Nancy as he ushered Lauralee toward the door. "Darling, I'll be back as soon as I get this ugly business over with," he said.

Lauralee also looked over at Nancy. "I'm sorry for having disturbed your evening, but I had to tell Uncle Abner."

"I understand," Nancy said. "Get along with you. I

hope you catch him. I never did like the looks of Clint McCloud. By his shifty behavior I always thought he had a skeleton or two hidden in his closet."

Lauralee and Abner went outside to his horse and buggy. They were soon riding away from the hospital, the horse moving in a fast trot along Western Avenue, toward Broadway.

"Besides him being a railroad man, do you know this Clint McCloud, otherwise?" Lauralee asked. "Please don't tell me you were in his regiment during the war."

"Honey, I had more control of my destiny during the Civil War than being ordered around by the likes of Clint McCloud," Abner said, laughing throatily. He slapped his horse's reins, rode over the railroad tracks, then turned left onto Broadway. "I knew of his regiment and heard tell of some of the horrendous acts they pulled. But I came to know him better by his association with the railroads here in town. He has quite an influence on any improvements that are voted on for the railroad."

The horse and buggy swung to a quick stop before the Byers Hotel, one of Mattoon's finest hotels, where General Ulysses S. Grant had stayed for a short time during the war, and also President Abraham Lincoln.

Abner jumped from the buggy and wrapped the reins around a hitching rail. Lauralee left the buggy and hurried to his side.

Breathless, and with a thumping heart, she looked up at the tall brick building, where many windows looked out onto the thoroughfare.

"Do you think he's here?" she asked as Abner took her by the elbow and whisked her toward the double doors that led inside the grandly furnished hotel.

"This is where he's made his residence during his stay in Mattoon," Abner said, nodding a hello to the desk clerk as he headed on toward the steep staircase that led to the upstairs rooms. "His job would be finished here soon. He was supposed to go back to North

Carolina then. He has a wife and child waiting for him there."

"If he fought for the North, why does he live in the South?" Lauralee asked, arching an eyebrow.

"Normally he is from somewhere up north. Some years ago he went south to Tennessee and the Carolinas to work on the railroads," Abner explained. "He met his wife there. He makes his residence somewhere in North Carolina, and for the most part, his job keeps him there. He only came to Mattoon to help out with instructing building the new spur west of town. He's been here most of the summer."

Lauralee's eyes were anxious and her throat was dry as they came to the second-floor landing, and then the third. Abner placed a hand on the holstered pistol at his right side. Lauralee had not known the firearm was there. The coattail kept it hidden from sight.

Slipping the pistol from the holster, Abner took stealthy steps down the corridor until they came to one room in particular.

Abner nodded to Lauralee to step aside.

Her pulse racing, she did as he said.

Then she jumped with alarm when her uncle kicked the door open and stepped hurriedly inside.

It was almost completely dark outside now as night fell in its black silence. The room held dim shadows and was quiet.

Lauralee inched her way inside and found that her uncle was the only one there. His pistol was holstered again and he was going through drawers, and then the chifferobe.

"He's gone, isn't he?" Lauralee said, disappointment heavy on her heart.

"Seems he is," Abner said, sighing disconsolately.

"I knew it." Lauralee stifled an angry sob behind her hand. "Now I'll never be able to see that he's put behind bars, or better yet—hung."

Abner went to Lauralee and drew her into his arms. "I could have the sheriff send a posse after him, but because of his association with the railroad, Clint knows this countryside well," he said solemnly. "I doubt he'd be caught. He'd be like the field mice, quicker than the eye, and much more clever."

Downhearted and ready to cry, Lauralee eased from Abner's arms. She went to the window and stared down at the activity on Broadway, a man just now lighting the gaslights. She had never been as disappointed as now. She had come so close to making things right for her mother, *and* Dancing Cloud.

But now?

She doubted she ever would.

A sudden thought sprang to her mind as she watched the sky darkening overhead. "Oh, no," she cried, recalling her plans to go to Paul to explain things to him.

She turned wide eyes to Abner. "Uncle Abner, are you planning to go to the hospital and stay with Nancy for the rest of the evening?" she asked guardedly, not wanting him to suspect anything.

"Yes, I expect so," Abner said, forking an eyebrow when he saw something in her expression that seemed amiss. Only moments ago she was disappointed. Now she seemed anxious about something.

"Can I drive you there, then borrow your horse and buggy?" Lauralee asked, pleading up at him with her violet eyes.

"Honey, you don't plan to try and find Clint McCloud, do you?" he said, placing a gentle hand to her cheek. "It's obvious that he's dangerous where you are concerned."

"You said yourself that he's more than likely left town," Lauralee said softly. "I'm sure I'll be safe. Please allow me to use your buggy for a while tonight, Uncle Abner?"

"I'm not sure," Abner said, kneading his chin. "I just don't know. I imagine Nancy would jump all over me if I allowed you to go out wandering the streets, unescorted."

"You said yourself that this city of Mattoon is for

the most part genteel and trusting," Lauralee persisted. "And you could give me the loan of your pistol while I'm gone. Please, Uncle Abner? Please?"

"Where on earth do you want to go so badly?" Abner asked, taken aback by her persistence.

"To see Paul Brown," Lauralee blurted out without thinking.

Abner's eyes lit up. "*Well*, now," he said, smiling slowly. "Why didn't you say so earlier? Honey, I'd not mind at all lending you my horse and buggy if you plan to travel out to become better acquainted with Paul Brown. That'd please me greatly, Lauralee. I *thought* you'd see much in that man that you would take a liking to."

Lauralee felt guilty for misleading her uncle. But she felt that this little deceit was the only way to correct the larger deceit of the previous night. Her uncle would be disappointed when he discovered the full truth about her flight to the Brown farm tonight.

But he would get over it. When he saw just how exceedingly happy Dancing Cloud made her, how could he argue that?

Their short jaunt back to Dr. Kemper's was done in an awkward silence. Lauralee was afraid to say anything that might bring to light what she truly had planned for tonight.

And she could not help but dwell on Clint McCloud having gotten away so spotlessly clean again from the law.

Oh, if only his pistol had not misfired!

The man would be lying in the morgue even now with a bullet through his back!

Lauralee pulled the buggy to a halt before Dr. Kemper's. So afraid that her uncle would change his mind, she scarcely breathed when he departed the buggy. She smiled clumsily at him when he slipped his pistol onto her lap.

"You do know how to *use* a weapon, don't you?" Abner said, nervously slipping his hands in his rear pants' pockets. "I wouldn't want you to come to the hospital with a blown-off toe, or anything *else*, for *that* matter."

"Don't worry," Lauralee said, laying the pistol beside her on the seat. "If I'd come face to face with that damn Yankee again, you'd better believe I'd know enough about this firearm to shoot him dead."

Abner stood there for a moment. His eyes closely scrutinized her. There was still something amiss in her behavior tonight. But he shrugged and gave her a wave.

"Get on with you and don't you and Paul do anything *too* romantic," he said, laughing.

"We won't, I assure you," Lauralee said, for certain her uncle had nothing to worry about in *that* department. When she got through telling Paul what she had on her mind, he would never see her as someone to romance again. He might even hate her.

She gave her uncle a wave, then rode down Western Avenue again. She cast her eyes heavenward, worrying about the time of night. If Paul was already on his way to the Peterson House, then she would be put in a position of doing more convincing than she had wished to do.

If she could find him still at his home she could tell him quickly why she was there, take Dancing Cloud's horse, and put that foolish part of her life behind her.

One thing for certain. She couldn't allow Paul to lure her down to the pond again. There was something romantic about being with a man by a body of water in the moonlight.

The only man with whom she wanted to share such a romantic interlude was Dancing Cloud.

The wheels of her buggy clattered as she rode over the tracks. Her heart pounding, she then turned left and rode down Broadway Avenue again.

Dancing Cloud slipped into his fringed breeches and his moccasins. He picked up his shirt and studied it, the bloodstains and the bullet hole having ruined it.

"I will meet up with you some day," he said, his thoughts on Clint McCloud. "You will pay. For sure you will pay."

Tossing the shirt aside, Dancing Cloud went to the door bare-chested and inched it open. His eyebrows lifted with surprise. The lawman was gone.

The smell of food wafted down the corridor. He had to believe that the lawman had gone to eat.

The smell of food also made Dancing Cloud know that some would soon be brought to his room. He had to escape before that happened. By the time they found him gone he would be on his way to the pond at the far edge of town. He worried about the house that sat not all that far from the pond. If he was discovered there he might be mistaken for an intruder, and shot.

Or perhaps the one who caught him might have a generous, caring heart like Noah Brown, Dancing Cloud hoped to himself.

Dancing Cloud tiptoed down the empty, dimly lit corridor, then on outside. When he reached the road, he limped along, then forced himself into a soft trot. He groaned. The pain in his chest was so severe every inch of the way seemed his last.

"Water," he kept whispering to himself. "I must reach the healing water."

He spied a lone horse hitched to a rail alongside the road. Without any further thought he went and pulled himself into the saddle. Holding one hand over his throbbing wound, and bending low over the horse, he guided the steed off onto a fairly deserted side street, then rode on through the city.

The pond.

He had to find the pond.

17

I shall not hear his voice complain,
But who shall stop the patient rain?

—ALICE MEYNELL

Instead of turning off the road in the direction of Paul
Brown's house Lauralee swung her uncle's horse and
buggy from Broadway Avenue into the circular drive
of the Peterson House. Although she was anxious to
get to Paul and get this over with, and knowing that
she was taking chances that he might arrive at the
Petersons' before she left to go to his, it was a chance
she must take.

She felt the need to change into something less pro-
vocative before seeing him.

She would even tie her hair up in a tight bun atop
her head and make sure her face was pale without
makeup.

She wished to make him change his mind about her.
That would make telling him that she no longer wished
to see him easier.

Drawing tight rein before the front porch of the
Peterson House she left the buggy quickly and secured
the reins.

She looked guardedly up and down Broadway Avenue. When she saw no signs of Paul or Clint McCloud
she turned and fled inside the house.

She scrambled up the stairs and went to her room
and sorted through her clothes. When she found a drab

cotton dress that had been worn many times at the orphanage and had been washed repeatedly in strong lye soap and bleach, she smiled mischievously.

"This should do just fine," she whispered to herself. "I never *ever* felt attractive in *this* terrible rag."

Seeing the pond shimmering beneath the soft rays of the moon a short distance away, Dancing Cloud sighed with relief.

He had found it.

And none too soon.

He was about to drop from the horse from exhaustion and pain.

Glancing down at his wound he found a small trickle of blood flowing from one end where the stitches had been torn open from the jerky ride on the stolen horse. This steed was not as gentle as his.

Seeing soft lamplight in the windows of the farmhouse that sat a short distance from the pond, Dancing Cloud drew tight rein and dismounted the feisty steed. His shoulders hunched, giving into the pain, he led the horse amid a thick stand of bushes, then went the rest of the way to the pond on foot.

When he reached the water he did not take the time to remove his fringed buckskin breeches or his moccasins. He was too anxious to get in the water and allow the true healing process to begin.

The breeze was cool and the water was cold and penetrating as he walked into the pond until he was hip-high.

Then knowing how painful it would be, but seeing it as necessary, he dove downward into the water and swam beneath the surface for a while.

Then he bobbed to the surface again and began taking his powerful strokes. He swam from one side of the pond to the other, the pain intense with each and every movement.

Thoughts of his father stayed with him as he swam,

as though his father were there, taking each stroke and bearing the pain with him.

His thoughts shifted to his time in the spirit world where he had been with his beloved family. He thanked *Wah-kon-tah* again for that opportunity.

His thoughts then strayed to his mountain home where his people awaited him and his leadership. There was no time for mourning the death of his father yet. When he returned and was among his people they could gather around him and mourn with him.

Now he must focus on getting well and on being able to make the long journey to his home. He understood that it might take several more days.

He would also spend time loving Lauralee so that leaving her newfound family would not be so painful for her.

He could see it in her eyes every time she spoke of leaving them that it was not going to be an easy task for her.

He would see to it that he would help his *o-ge-ye* get her through all of her sorrows and misgivings about leaving the Petersons.

He would make every wrong right for her!

The sound of an approaching horse and buggy on the small dirt lane that led to the farmhouse made Dancing Cloud swim quickly to the side closest to the farmhouse. He placed his feet on the graveled bottom of the pond. He stooped over and huddled close to the land, hoping that whoever was arriving in the horse and buggy had not caught sight of him swimming beneath the light of the moon.

His heart thudded wildly within his chest as he waited for the horse and buggy to stop. When it finally came to a halt, he listened for footsteps, and then voices as the visitor was met on the small porch of the farmhouse.

His eyebrows forked when he thought he recognized the soft voice of the woman.

"Lauralee?" he whispered, straightening his back in order to see over the embankment toward the house.

He could see the outline of a woman standing in the shadows, but he could not see the face.

He listened more intensely, the breeze only occasionally wafting the woman's soft voice his way.

Still he could not be sure.

And if it was Lauralee?

What did it mean except that she had made acquaintance with perhaps some of the Petersons' friends?

He hunkered low again when he heard the voices get somewhat louder.

Were they coming to the pond?

No.

It seemed that they might be arguing about something.

Then the voices got softer again.

Only the man was speaking.

The woman had gone quiet.

"Did I not tell you that I would bring Dancing Cloud's horse to you tonight?" Paul demanded again. "I thought that we were going to spend some time together, talking."

"I've thought things over, Paul," Lauralee said, nervously and tensely clasping and unclasping her hands behind her. "I will be leaving Mattoon soon. I . . . will . . . be marrying another man."

"You'll *what*?" Paul said in an almost shout.

Frustrated, he raked his long, lean fingers through his golden hair. "You only arrived at the Petersons'," he said, his voice drawn. "You will leave again, so soon? Do you not enjoy their company? Is mine so unbearable? How could you be considering marriage?"

He frowned. "It's the damn Cherokee, isn't it?" he grumbled. "He's coerced you into leaving town with him, hasn't he?"

Lauralee squared her shoulders angrily. "No man forces me to do anything that I don't wish to do," she said, her voice drawn. "Especially not *you*, Paul

Brown. You have some nerve to think that you mean so much to me."

Paul stepped from the porch.

Lauralee slowly backed away from him.

"When I kissed you last night I felt you respond *to* the kiss," Paul said, reaching a hand to her cheek.

Lauralee jerked away. "Paul, don't," she said warily. "Don't do anything you might be sorry for later."

"All I want is to kiss you again to prove a point," Paul insisted, his arms reaching around her waist, drawing her tightly against him. "Lauralee, I've waited a lifetime for someone like you. I could so very easily love you."

She glanced over and saw Dancing Cloud's horse reined to a hitching post on the far side of the Browns' house. If she had arrived at the farm only moments later, Paul would have left for the Peterson House. The horse was there, saddled and ready to be taken.

Thank God, she sighed to herself. She had arrived before he had left, but for other reasons than why she had planned it that way. If she had been alone at the Peterson House, then ...

The Browns were inside their house should Paul get out of hand and unreasonable. It was already getting close to that.

She tried to shove him away, then had no choice but to give in when his powerful arms anchored her against him as he kissed her long and hard.

Dancing Cloud's eyes widened and his mouth went agape.

Lauralee.

He now knew that the woman *was* Lauralee!

She had stepped into the reflection of the moonlight.

He was able to see her face.

And she was being kissed by a man!

From this vantage point he saw that she was willingly returning the kiss!

Anger filled Dancing Cloud's veins and heart. He

started to pull himself out of the water but stopped when a low growling sound came close.

A collie suddenly bounded into sight and ran toward the pond, barking.

Dancing Cloud stayed still, then lifted a hand to the collie when it reached the embankment. He had always had a way with animals of the forest, as well as dogs of all breeds. There was something magical that flowed between himself and animals.

Even this dog that was only moments ago looking so wild and vicious was now spread out on its belly, licking Dancing Cloud's hand as though the Cherokee had been a friend, forever.

Paul released Lauralee and gazed toward the pond. His dog had not barked at Lauralee because Paul had been on the porch waiting for her. He had comforted his collie into realizing that Lauralee was a friend, then his dog had leaped away and had ran into the woods.

It seemed by the behavior of the animal only seconds ago that he may have trapped something besides a raccoon or 'possum. His dog had behaved as he was taught to when a prowler came snooping down the road.

Paul stepped up onto his porch and leaned inside his front door long enough to get a rifle.

Then he went outside again and walked past Lauralee. "I'll go and see who's trespassin' on my land," he said over his shoulder.

Lauralee followed him a step or two, her eyes searching for Clint McCloud.

He had surely followed her.

Her heart pounded frighteningly as she peered more intensely past Paul.

Then her heart seemed to skip a beat and her insides quavered strangely as she watched Dancing Cloud suddenly emerge from the pond, his body wet and shiny with water, his eyes looking past Paul at her, as though he hated her.

Puzzled and confused by his presence, wondering

why, and how, he had gotten there, Lauralee could not find the power to make her feet move.

She was also stunned speechless.

Then she emitted a small cry behind her hand when Dancing Cloud yanked the rifle from Paul and threw it in the water, then knocked Paul to the ground.

She expected Dancing Cloud to come to her.

Instead he disappeared among tall brush, then just as quickly rode into view on a horse.

He gave Lauralee a lingering, questioning stare, then rode toward the road.

Panic seized Lauralee.

She now knew that he had seen her being kissed.

He had misinterpreted it!

He did not know, and obviously had not heard, the true reason she was at the Brown farm.

To say a final goodbye to Paul!

And placing aside her wonder of how and why Dancing Cloud could be there, Lauralee saw no other choice than to go after him.

She looked at the horse and buggy, then at Dancing Cloud's horse.

To catch up with Dancing Cloud she chose the horse.

So thankful that at least she had learned the art of horseback riding at the orphanage, when she had been deprived of all other outdoor activities, she ran to Dancing Cloud's horse, quickly untied the reins, then swung herself into the saddle.

Paul ran after her. "Don't go after him, Lauralee!" he shouted. "He's a madman. Stop, Lauralee. Stop!"

She ignored Paul and rode onward. She leaned over the horse and sank her heels into his flanks, glad now that she had Dancing Cloud in sight. He did not seem to be riding as quickly as she would have thought.

Then she remembered his wound. That surely was hampering his riding ability. Every bounce had to cause him renewed pain.

Again she puzzled over how and why he was at the Brown farm.

Had he discovered her misguided liaison with Paul?

Had he come to spy on her?

If so, why did he have the need to hide in the pond? That, above all else that was confusing to her, was the most outlandish of all.

She rode onward, gaining on Dancing Cloud, her mind drifting back momentarily to the time when she had learned the art of riding a horse.

The owner of the orphanage in St. Louis had discovered a new breed of horse, a heavy draft-horse breed that originated in Clydesdale, Scotland.

The Clydesdale.

Scott Hopper, the owner of the orphanage, had begun breeding Clydesdale horses.

After learning the art of riding a horse after the Clydesdales had been brought to the stables at the orphanage, Lauralee had fallen in love with them; one in particular. She had named him Buddy. He was dark brown in coloring, with prominent white markings.

As discovered with all Clydesdale horses, Buddy became noted for his high leg action while walking or trotting. He had feathery long hair on his legs, an attractive head, and well-formed legs and feet.

But as with everything and everyone else in her life that she loved, Buddy had been taken away from her and sold to another breeder in New York.

She could let nothing take Dancing Cloud away from her. She would fight tooth and nail for him. He had to understand that what he had seen tonight was not of her own choosing.

He had to believe that she had gone to the Browns' not only to get his horse for him, but also to tell Paul that she was going to marry Dancing Cloud!

Her heart sank, realizing now that she would also have to reveal some small truths that she had wanted to keep hidden from him—that she had for a moment or two been taken by this farmer whose eyes were so blue one could get lost in them.

Of course she would not tell Dancing Cloud *that*,

about how she felt about Paul, *or* Paul's *eyes*. But she would tell him that because of her deprivations as a child, she almost allowed herself to be taken in by a man she could never love.

Now only a few feet behind Dancing Cloud's horse, Lauralee shouted at him to stop.

Dancing Cloud looked over his shoulder at her, his eyes widening when he realized whose horse she was riding. *His own!* Had Noah Brown brought the horse to the Petersons'? Is that why she was riding him?

No. He now recalled that she had arrived at the farm in a buggy. That had to mean that the farm, where he had taken his moonlight swim, was the Browns'. She had surely gone to get his horse.

But who was that man he had seen kissing her?

It came to him in a flash. Noah had mentioned two sons. One had died during the war. The other was still alive.

His surviving son had seen Lauralee and had become attracted to her!

But then he recalled how she seemed to be returning his kiss.

Wanting answers, tired of speculating, he wheeled his horse to a stop and turned it around and waited for Lauralee.

Lauralee drew rein beside him. Her eyes wavered as she gazed at him.

"Why were you at the farm kissing that man?" Dancing Cloud asked tightly, the first one to demand answers.

"Why were *you* there, swimming in the Browns' pond?" she demanded equally as adamantly.

They both then started to talk at once.

She with her explanations.

He with his.

When it was all over and done with, they both broke into laughter.

Lauralee leaned over and gave Dancing Cloud a hug. "Darling, don't you know that you have my heart—

lock, stock, and barrel?" she whispered. She sighed and went weak inside when he gave her that much-needed kiss of understanding.

When he groaned, she knew that it was not from passion. It seemed borne of pain.

She drew away and gazed at his wound. "Lord, you're bleeding," she gasped. She looked wildly into his eyes. "You should be off that horse and in a bed."

She glanced over her shoulder, stunned to see that they had unknowingly stopped directly in front of the Peterson House.

She then took Dancing Cloud's reins and urged his horse into a trot beside hers as she headed into the driveway of the stately house. "The doctor said that you were going to be released tomorrow from the hospital," she said flatly. "Well, we'll just not wait that long. You're going to stay here and take my bed *tonight*. I'm going to see to the wound personally, darling. I see no need in you having to ride clear across town to go to Dr. Kemper's, when I am here, to see to your every want and need."

Dancing Cloud hunched over, breathing hard. "The Petersons," he said thickly. "They may not approve of my being in their house, much less in your bed, Lauralee."

"They will just have to accept my decision to do this," Lauralee said stubbornly. "I have already tested the softness of the bed. It will work perfectly for you as you recover. I shall move into the other bedroom down the hall from you. I do know there is one spare bedroom not being used."

"*O-ge-ye*, do you know how much I truly love you?" Dancing Cloud said.

"I'm so glad," Lauralee murmured.

The sound of an approaching horse and buggy made Lauralee stiffen. She drew tight rein, then turned and watched Paul Brown come into the driveway in the Petersons' horse and buggy, his horse trailing on a rope behind it.

Paul stopped and came to Lauralee. "I believe you forgot something," he said tersely. He frowned over at Dancing Cloud, then at Lauralee. "The horse and buggy. I don't think I have a need for them, Lauralee."

A quiet panic seized her.

Lord. Her uncle was stranded without the buggy.

Then she looked past Paul and saw another horse and buggy approaching. Dr. Kemper was driving it, her uncle on the seat beside him. It seemed she did not have to go after her uncle after all. He had surely realized that something had happened for her not to have arrived back at the hospital as expected. The doctor had delivered him to his doorstep.

Dr. Kemper and Abner left the buggy. They stood side by side as Lauralee rushed into explanations.

Everything was quiet for a while after she was through.

Then to her relief her uncle and the doctor went and helped Dancing Cloud from the horse and up the front steps. Her uncle had given Dancing Cloud permission to stay at his house. The doctor saw no harm in Dancing Cloud completing his recuperation period there.

And even though she knew her uncle's resentment toward Dancing Cloud over being a Rebel, and perhaps even over being an Indian, he had pushed that resentment aside in favor of pleasing Lauralee.

Lauralee went to Paul. She took the reins to the horse and buggy. As they gazed silently at each other she could feel the tension between them. It was as tight as a rope.

She started to apologize but he didn't give her a chance. He gave her a mock salute and rode away.

Sighing, then taking a deep breath, Lauralee gathered the reins of all of the horses but Dr. Kemper's into her hand and led them to the stables.

She looked around and heaved another sigh. James wasn't there to ready them for the night. It was all up to her.

She stared at the horse that Dancing Cloud had stolen. She would see to it that it got returned. She didn't want Dancing Cloud to be arrested for horse-stealing. He could tell her approximately where he had found the horse. She would tie it at a hitching rail and the owner would surely soon find it.

Lauralee lit a kerosene lamp. As she worked with the horses in the semidarkness she kept peering over her shoulder. She would never be able to feel safe. Not as long as Clint McCloud was out there somewhere, a threat to her well-being.

But at least everything *else* seemed on the right track again.

But she could not feel comfortable with it. She still felt like that young girl at the orphanage who loved and lost more often, than not.

18

The angels not half so happy in heaven,
Went envying her and me.

—EDGAR ALLAN POE

It was way past the midnight hour. Everything was
quiet and serene in the Peterson House, yet it thrilled
Lauralee to know that just down the hall from where
she lay was the sound of someone else's breathing besides her own and her uncle Abner's.

Dancing Cloud.

He was in her bed.

She ached to be there with him. Sometime ago she
had heard Uncle Abner retire to his own bedroom.

Breathless with anticipation of going to Dancing
Cloud, Lauralee slipped from the bed and crept quietly
to the door.

She held her breath as she slowly opened it, glad
that it made no squeaking sounds that her uncle might
hear. If he caught her with Dancing Cloud he would
get the wrong impression. She certainly did not intend
to have a sexual encounter with Dancing Cloud.

No. She just wanted to cuddle next to her beloved
and whisper sweet nothings to him, hopefully erasing
all thoughts of Paul from his mind.

Seeing no lamplight spilling beneath her uncle's
closed bedroom door, Lauralee lifted the hem of her
frilly silk chemise into her arms. She tiptoed, bare-
footed, down the carpeted hallway, the light of the

moon reflecting through the window at the end of the hall paving her way.

Her pulse racing, she stopped outside her bedroom door and wove her fingers through her hair. She had taken pains tonight with her bath. She had washed her hair with a fragranced piece of soap. Her skin smelled sweetly from the tiny perfumed bath beads that had evaporated into a silky oil through her bath water. She smiled when she smelled the sweetness of the talcum powder that she had patted across her flesh.

Lauralee inhaled a quavering breath, then slowly opened the door and peeked inside.

Her heart melted as her eyes found Dancing Cloud lying on his side, the moonlight shining through the lacy, sheer curtains at her window caressing his long, lean body.

Lauralee's face flushed crimson when she saw that Dancing Cloud was nude.

Then she recalled her uncle having taken Dancing Cloud's wet fringed breeches and moccasins, to let them dry on the back porch rail.

Dr. Kemper had sent a young man to the Peterson House with Dancing Cloud's belongings. Lauralee had, in turn, asked the young man to return the horse that Dancing Cloud had borrowed, glad to be rid of it.

Dancing Cloud's saddlebag lay on the floor beside the bed. She could see that he had sorted through it. He had taken from it fresh clothes that now lay neatly across the back of a chair.

Her gaze held on a beautifully beaded pair of moccasins beside his bed. They seemed new. Had some pretty Cherokee maiden sewn them for him? she wondered.

That thought sent a painful, jealous ache through her, to think that somewhere in his past were other women with whom he had shared intimate moments.

Brushing the thought aside she stepped into the bedroom. She turned and eased the door closed, then almost screamed with alarm when she felt strong arms encircle her waist.

When she realized whose arms, and whose body was pressing into hers from behind, she closed her eyes with ecstasy.

The frilly chemise was thin enough for her to feel the full outline of his body, especially what was most defined to her at the juncture of his thighs.

He drew her back more securely against him.

Her heart pounded.

She was dizzy with need of him.

Yet she had to force herself to deny this that he might be offering her tonight. She could not be this disrespectful to her aunt and uncle by giving herself fully to a man beneath their roof.

"Dancing Cloud, please," Lauralee whispered, her voice trembling. When his hands slipped up and cupped her breasts through her chemise, she sucked in a wild breath of pleasure. Her knees almost buckled from the rapture that was taking hold of her senses.

"You said please?" Dancing Cloud whispered into her ear.

"Please *don't*," Lauralee forced out, wishing she did not have to deny him anything, *anytime*.

Dancing Cloud slipped his hands back down to her waist and drew her around to face him. "You do not wish to make love?" he said, searching her eyes.

"With all of my heart I do," Lauralee whispered, reaching a hand to his cheek. "But we mustn't. Darling, you are not well enough. And we must remember where we are. My uncle. He is only across the hall. What if he would discover us . . . ?"

"You are right," Dancing Cloud said, wincing when straightening his shoulder. "But you came to the room. If not to make love . . ."

She placed a finger to his lips. "Shh," she whispered. "I came to be with you. To lay beside you. To tell you how much I love you. And to tell you how anxious I am for us to make love again. I have so missed being with you in that way. Am I a hussy for hungering for that part of our relationship? Before I met you I so feared it."

"You are a woman with womanly needs. Never allow yourself to feel that is wrong," Dancing Cloud said. He took her by the hand and led her to the bed. "Lie down with me. Let me hold you. Soon we will go farther with our feelings again. It is good to know that your hungers match my own."

When he stretched out beside Lauralee, she turned to him. She leaned up on her knees and her hair tumbled over her shoulders as she gently kissed him near his wound. She could hear him take a quick intake of breath and could feel his heart throbbing hard as she continued giving him kisses across his massive chest.

When she felt something warm and hard against her thigh she scarcely breathed. It was obvious that she had stirred feelings within him that could hardly be denied.

Dancing Cloud reached his hands to her breasts and stroked them. His thumbs circled her nipples, causing them to harden. He leaned up on an elbow and led one of them between his lips. His tongue swirled around it, his lips nipping.

"I didn't mean to cause this," Lauralee whispered, her face blushed hot with want. She held her head back and sighed when she felt his fingers caressing her throbbing center.

When she could take no more, she drew away from him. "We truly mustn't," she whispered. "Dancing Cloud, you can't be strong enough. And my uncle . . ."

He yanked her down beside him and turned to her. His lips sealed any more denials as he kissed her with a frenzy of kisses. His hand led his hardness to where she opened so willingly and quickly to him.

She sank into a chasm of desire, his kiss stealing all quarrel and reason from her.

Feverishly, she raked her fingers down his spine and along his hips. When he entered her she shuddered pleasurably and gripped his hips lightly, abandoning herself to the torrent of feelings that swam through her.

Dancing Cloud ignored the pain that was gripping his insides, his mind escaping in the pleasure that he was receiving from his *o-ge-ye*. He made love to Lauralee slowly, in a long and leisurely fashion. His lips brushed her throat, then again went to her lips.

Their embrace was long and sweet as one kiss blended into another, the slow thrusting of his pelvis bringing them closer and closer to that wondrous brink of wild abandon.

Lost in a reverie of need, Lauralee moved her hips with his, her blood quickening. Her senses swam as she felt a drugged passion seize her. She was soon gripped in an intense pleasure that spread through her in a delicious tingling heat. She moaned throatily against his lips, his own groan of pleasure revealing to her that he had reached the same summit of pleasure as she.

Their bodies quaked.

Her hips moved and rocked. Her pelvis was pressed hard against his, gyrating, pulling him even more deeply into the velvet warm walls of her femininity.

And when their bodies subsided, and the pleasure was spent, Dancing Cloud drew away from her. He pushed her hair from her face. Her eyes were sheened by moonlight as she peered with intense love at him.

Then when he grabbed suddenly at his shoulder and rolled quickly onto his back, panting, Lauralee became frightened and moved to her knees beside him. She clearly saw the pain in his eyes as he looked up at her.

"Dancing Cloud, we truly shouldn't have," she whispered, her eyes wavering into his. "Oh, darling, look now how you are in pain. It's all my fault. I should've stayed in my bed."

"*I* am in your bed," Dancing Cloud said, taking her hand, drawing her down beside him. "And what a lovely bed and room it is. Are you certain you wish to go and live in a log cabin in the mountains? Will that be enough for you?"

"Wherever you are, that is where I want to be," Lauralee said, cuddling close. "Whether it is in a cabin, or in a castle, if you are there, that is where you will find me."

"When I leave Mattoon again I insist that you go with me," Dancing Cloud said, turning to face her.

"As I plan to do," she said matter-of-factly. She smiled at him. "Darling, do you think I would let you go on that journey without me after what has happened to you? You might be ambushed again. I want to be there for you."

"And what if that Yankee should kill us both in the ambush?" Dancing Cloud said thickly.

"Then that is what fate has planned for us," Lauralee said, moving closer. "Remember how you described being in the spirit world with your family? The next time you go, I want to be there with you, hand in hand."

"It is destiny for us to be as one with each other," Dancing Cloud said. He paused, then said, "Tell me again about this man named Paul Brown. I saw you kissing him. Are you certain your feelings are nothing for him?"

"You saw me kissing him because he forced me to," she murmured. "You were too far away to see me shoving at his chest."

"Then you have no feelings for the man?"

"How could you ask that? After what we just shared, surely you realize the depths of my feelings for you."

He placed a finger to her chin and lifted her eyes to him. "We will leave Mattoon as soon as I am able to travel," he said thickly. "That may take days, perhaps weeks. Will the Petersons tolerate my presence that long? Or should I go in the woods and make camp?"

"Heaven forbid!" Lauralee said, sitting up quickly. "I wouldn't allow it. The Yankee. He's surely out there somewhere, just waiting for the next opportunity to shoot you."

Then she raised an eyebrow. "Except that when my uncle took me to the Byers Hotel with him to check on the man, we found that his clothes and belongings were missing," she said.

Dancing Cloud moved as quickly to an elbow as his shoulder allowed and stared at her. "What are you talking about?"

She just now remembered that he did not know about what had happened at Dr. Kemper's, that the Yankee of his past was most surely the same Yankee of *hers*. Ironic as it may seem, it was no less true.

She told him everything, about all of her discoveries, and about the man trying to abduct her. She could see a seething hatred enter his midnight-dark eyes.

"Please don't upset yourself," she begged. "Darling, Clint McCloud must be long gone by now. Surely he fears what my uncle could have done with him should he be caught after having tried to abduct me. A trial would not be wasted on him. He would hang as quickly as one could blink their eye."

"But he is still out there, somewhere," Dancing Cloud said. "More the reason you will leave with me when I leave Mattoon. I want to be the one protecting you from this evil white man."

Lauralee cuddled closer, her eyes wide. She had never thought that her nightmare when she was five would follow her the rest of her life. She now recalled her uncle having said that Clint McCloud lived in North Carolina. If so, that was perhaps his destination even *now*.

That was also hers and Dancing Cloud's destination, where Dancing Cloud made his home in the North Carolina mountains.

That thought totally terrified her.

19

The passion of the fire, love,
What'er it finds, destroys.

—R. W. RAYMOND

Several days had passed and except for the constant
fear of Clint McCloud jumping out at her, continuing
his reign of terror, Lauralee felt that everything was finally right in her little world.

Her aunt had recovered as best that could be expected when someone had a heart condition.

She was able to leave her bed now and resume most
of her normal activities.

Best of all was that her aunt was able to putter
around in her flower garden and have tea with her lady
friends at her favorite tea room and inn—Tomaso's.
She had even accepted that Lauralee was going to be
leaving soon.

Lauralee's Uncle Abner was embroiled in a new
case, proving once again to the communities of
Charleston and Mattoon that he was the best judge in
Coles County. He had not said much about Lauralee's
decision to leave. But she had seen it in his eyes each
time he looked at Dancing Cloud that his resentments
for him still lay heavy on his heart.

Putting aside further thoughts of her uncle's resentments, Lauralee was happy that Dancing Cloud was almost as good as new. She had encouraged him not to
ride his horse again just yet. Today he rode beside her

in her horse and buggy. He was at the reins. She was
enjoying the outing with him as they took in the city of
Mattoon.

"Isn't it just a wondrous, glorious day?" Lauralee
said. She repositioned her straw hat on her head, then
retied the satin bow beneath her chin. "The sky is so
brilliantly blue. The sun is so bright."

Dancing Cloud shifted his gaze to her. "The true vision sits beside me," he said, smiling.

His eyes raked slowly over her. The fully gathered
silk dress that she wore complemented her thin waist
and the gentle curve of her breasts where they swelled
slightly above the low-swept bodice.

"I do want to look special for you, always,"
Lauralee said, giving him a winsome smile. "Tell me
about the dresses that I shall wear when I become as
one with the women of your village. Are they beautifully beaded as are your moccasins? Are they soft?
Your buckskin clothes feel like the petal of a rose to
my fingertips. Will I also be wearing buckskin?"

"My clothes are like the petal of a rose?" Dancing
Cloud asked, chuckling.

"Well, perhaps that is not the best of comparisons,"
Lauralee said, laughing softly. "I am just anxious to
know what to expect when I reach your village. What
I will wear. What my duties as a wife will be." She
blushed and lowered her eyes, then looked slowly up at
him again. "I mean besides that which I will enjoy
with you each night."

"Each morning I will take you into my arms and
give you a special loving," Dancing Cloud said, his
eyes dancing into hers. "The same as I will give you
each night."

Lauralee's eyes brightened and she giggled. "And so
that is all that we shall do, both you and I, the long day
and night through?" she teased.

"That could be arranged, *o-ge-ye*," he said, his eyes
slowly raking over her again. "When I look at you to-

day, I see no dress. I feel your body with my eyes as though my fingers are there, caressing you."

"Dancing Cloud, *hush*." Lauralee squirmed uneasily on the seat of the buggy. "We are sightseeing today. We are supposed to be seeing the city of Mattoon. If you continue to talk like that, exciting me so, I shall want to bypass the city and go to a country road where you and I can . . .

"Lord," Lauralee said, after pausing for a moment. "Where is my mind taking me this morning?" She gave him a laughing smile. "You are the cause. You and your ways of making me come alive inside. Please, Dancing Cloud. Please let's not stray from the subject at hand. I need to know everything about your people and what I will be doing each day to allow me to become a part of their daily activities."

"The clothes that you will wear?" Dancing Cloud said, shifting his gaze back to the street. He frowned when he found himself now amid the city where the buildings soared overhead on each side.

He looked uneasily from side to side, at the men walking along the thoroughfare on walks made of wood, or corncobs. When they saw him at the reins of the buggy, most stopped and gawked.

He tried to ignore their rudeness.

"If you wish, you can wear the types of dresses that you normally wear each day," Dancing Cloud said. "Or you can wear what is normally the Cherokee women's attire."

He stiffened when a man on horseback rode past and looked him square in the eye as he called him a savage Rebel.

Dancing Cloud's jaw tightened with anger and humiliation. "Sometimes the women's clothes are made of the softest of doeskins," he continued, trying not to make Lauralee uncomfortable by showing his humiliation over the man's comments. "Or they might choose to wear cotton skirts and blouses. It will be of your own personal choice, *o-ge-ye*. You can wear what will make you the most comfortable."

Lauralee half heard what he was saying. She had heard the man's comments. It took all of her willpower not to have Dancing Cloud stop the carriage so that she could run after that man and tell him a thing or two about her Cherokee fiancé.

But she knew that those who might see Dancing Cloud as the enemy surely also saw *her* as the enemy, for she was also from the South, a Rebel in her own right.

She had surely only received a more pleasant treatment because of her uncle's reputation in the city. Everyone knew that he would not stand for his niece suffering any verbal abuse.

Even *if* her father had fought against the North during the war.

Dancing Cloud was in deep thought now. He knew that he could do nothing about protecting his pride while he was among the white community. He was one man against a whole city. One false move on his part and they would have a reason to imprison him. Until he left Mattoon he must walk lightly and speak carefully.

The important thing, above defending his pride and proud name of Cherokee, was to return to his people, to lead them.

"We shall leave on the morrow," he blurted out. "When the sun rises along the horizon we shall already be gone from this city."

Although it came as no surprise to Lauralee that he made this quick decision, she was taken aback by the actual suddenness of it. "Tomorrow?" she murmured, thinking about her aunt and uncle.

In truth, she hated having to say a goodbye not only to her aunt Nancy and uncle Abner, but all that they offered her. They lived a grand life in Mattoon. Had she decided to stay, she would have been part of that life and finally be accepted in the eyes of the community as someone with something more than the title of "orphan."

She reminded herself that by leaving them she would have even more than all of those things put together.

Dancing Cloud. He was more to her than the sky, stars, and heavens! So she could most certainly do without the menial things that she at one time thought were most important to a person.

And she would cast aside her title of "orphan" while around his people. She would live each day to the fullest with her beloved Cherokee and only hope that the hurt that she may have inflicted on the Petersons might be replaced by something else their wealth could bring into their lives. They had gotten along quite well before she had come along. They would most certainly get along without her.

"The time has come for me to return to my people and for me to mourn for my father with them," Dancing Cloud said thickly. "I would leave now except that this one more day of building my strength will guarantee that I am bodily able to take the long journey to my mountain."

Lauralee pointed the way. She led Dancing Cloud past Brian's Place Saloon, then down Western Avenue.

They rode past the magnificent Trinity Episcopal Church, then onward, past the lovely houses that lined Western Avenue.

They traveled at a leisurely pace until the houses lessened along the street. Lauralee motioned for Dancing Cloud to turn left and urged him to stop the horse and buggy at the corner of Western Avenue and 32nd Street.

As she stared up at the tall elm, she recalled the many stories that her father had told her about the "Lone Elm" in Mattoon, Illinois. She repeated the tale to Dancing Cloud.

She said that her father had told her that this tree had served the traveling pioneers well, not only as a landmark, but as a symbol of the strength and self-sufficiency of the many families crossing the prairie who stopped to rest in its shade.

As the elm had grown in size it was a memorable sight, standing alone in the midst of tall, waving blue stem grass.

After telling Dancing Cloud about the Lone Elm, they rode onward down 32nd Street and past several smaller houses. They stopped at a railroad track and waited for a "ballooning" smokestacked locomotive to go past.

They continued for only a few feet past the tracks when Lauralee motioned for Dancing Cloud to make a right on a small dirt road. They rode toward a great white fenced-in pasture in which several beautiful horses grazed and pranced. She had heard her uncle refer to this place as "The Stables," where prized show horses were kept and sired.

Recalling her love of the Clydesdales in St. Louis, she wanted to see these horses up close so that she could pet them.

"There," Lauralee said, pointing to the horses. "Let's ride over there, Dancing Cloud. Oh, but I do love horses."

Dancing Cloud's own love of horses caused his eyes to search through those that were grazing amid an abundance of tall, green grass. His heart skipped a beat when his gaze locked on one horse in particular.

It was a white stallion with a flowing mane, handsome tail, and bold, dark eyes.

As he grew a tight rein beside the fence the horse's eyes locked with his and there was an immediate bonding.

"I have never seen such a magnificent steed," he said. He stepped from the buggy as Lauralee slipped down from the seat on the other side. He tied the reins, then walked with Lauralee to the fence.

The horse came to Dancing Cloud as though a silent bidding had sent him there. He thrust his nose through the slats in the fence and nuzzled Dancing Cloud's hand as he offered it to him.

Lauralee's heart melted at the sight of the horse and Dancing Cloud's bonding. She immediately knew that Dancing Cloud must have the horse, but she would not speak that aloud to him. She knew that he had no money for which to buy it, nor did he have anything to trade for it—except perhaps his own horse?

Then she cast that thought aside. Although his horse was beautiful and obedient to Dancing Cloud, to someone else who knew horseflesh well might think it was trivial. Most certainly his horse did not compare with this white stallion and no equal exchange could be possibly made.

She smiled to herself. She would use some of her inheritance money to purchase the handsome steed as a special gift for Dancing Cloud.

Her uncle! she thought. Just perhaps he might help her with this surprise. He was surely quite skilled at making purchases. She could give him the money. He could come and buy this horse for her while she was with Dancing Cloud elsewhere. Oh, how surprised Dancing Cloud would be if she presented this horse to him before they began their journey to his Great Smoky Mountains!

Yes, it was worth a try, she finally decided. She so badly wanted to see Dancing Cloud on this horse, the two seemingly meant for each other. And her uncle surely would not resent Dancing Cloud so much that he would refuse to help Lauralee in this little scheme. He knew by now that nothing he said or did would change her mind about him.

"He is truly beautiful." Lauralee sighed, reaching a hand to the stallion's mane, gently stroking it. "Wouldn't you love to ride him, Dancing Cloud?"

She turned. A tall, thin man was approaching at a brisk clip. He wore denim breeches and shirt, high-heeled cowboy boots, and a fancy leather belt to match the boots. A large diamond ring flashing on a finger of his right hand revealed to Lauralee that he was a wealthy man.

"I don't take to strangers hangin' around my horses," Kevin Banks said in a snarl, ignoring Lauralee's show of friendship. His thick, black eyebrows fused as he frowned from Lauralee to Dancing Cloud. "Go on. Scat. The both of you. Get outta here."

Lauralee was shocked almost speechless by his attitude, then she stubbornly lifted her chin. "You are quite rude, sir," she said, placing her hands on her hips. "We were only admiring your horses, not stealing them."

"One usually admires just prior to stealin'," Kevin said in a low snarl. He turned slow eyes to Dancing Cloud and gazed intensely at him. "Injuns are clever at stealin' horses." He motioned with a nod of his head toward Dancing Cloud. "Get him outta here."

"Sir, I am certain that Dancing Cloud is used to being insulted by cads like yourself," Lauralee said, anger firing her eyes. "And he is being a gentleman for not taking a swing at you. But as for me? I have never been as insulted, as now."

She paused and breathed in a deep gulp of air. "I shall tell my Uncle Abner about this," she warned. "He won't appreciate you treating me, or my fiancé, so callously."

"Abner?" Kevin said, arching an eyebrow. He straightened his back and shuffled his feet nervously. "Are you speakin' of Abner Peterson? You're the niece I've been hearin' about? This is the Injun? The Cherokee? And . . . you . . . refer to him as your . . . fiancé . . . ?"

"Yes, my uncle is Abner Peterson, and yes, Dancing Cloud is my fiancé," Lauralee said, smiling smugly up at him. "And I don't think you or anyone would want to fall out of grace with my uncle. He wields much power in this city. Should you ever give him cause to meet face to face with him in court, I pity you."

Kevin stared down at Lauralee for a moment longer,

then shifted a quick glance Dancing Cloud's way, then hurried to the white stallion and patted him.

"So you'd like to ride this grand beast, eh?" he said, giving Dancing Cloud a guarded, sidewise glance.

Dancing Cloud's jaw was clenched and his lips were pressed tightly together. His eyes were filled with a loathing he dared not act out. "The horse intrigues this Cherokee, but no, I do not wish to ride it," he said, his heart not agreeing with his words.

In truth, he wanted to feel the power of this horse beneath him.

He wanted to share this bonding that had been there at the first meeting of their eyes.

But to do so would leave him wanting the stallion. He had nothing to trade for the horse. Even if he did he would not make trade with this man, a man whose tongue was too loose and filled with venom toward himself, a Cherokee.

Lauralee understood why Dancing Cloud had refused the chance to ride the beautiful horse. She held her chin high as she walked back to the horse and buggy with Dancing Cloud, Kevin Banks gaping after them.

Just as Dancing Cloud started to swing away from The Stables in the buggy, Lauralee saw another place that her aunt had talked about often.

Tomaso's.

It was the inn and tearoom that sat not that far from The Stables, where her aunt met her friends and had tea and cake.

An Italian man by the name of Tony Collodi owned the inn.

There had been some rumors that one of Mr. Collodi's close relatives, who still lived in Italy, had written a children's book that he had titled *The Adventures of Pinocchio*. It was about a little puppet boy whose wooden nose grew longer each time he told a lie, and after many adventures, Pinocchio's ambition to become a real, live boy, was fulfilled.

The book had not yet been published, but there was much excitement about it. Some said that the book would one day reach America and be a classic!

As in the book, Lauralee's life seemed to correlate somewhat with that small puppet Pinnochio who wanted to become a real, live person. She had always wanted to feel like a normal person, real in every sense.

And she had achieved the goal, thanks to her father for having come into her life again. Even if for only a short while. And also to the Petersons. But mostly Dancing Cloud. When she joined him as his wife, everything that she had wanted in her life would have come true.

She gazed at him. She ached inside over the constant humiliation that he had to endure because he differed from others in the color of his skin, and culture. A sudden fear came to her. What if *her* peace of mind and feeling of belonging were premature? What if Dancing Cloud's people treated *her* as an outcast and wrought humiliation after humiliation upon her when she went to live among them?

What if they did not share Dancing Cloud's feelings for her?

She was afraid they might even cause him to change his mind about her and send her away. She was not sure if she could stand another rejection, another deprival.

She scooted over on the seat and slipped an arm through Dancing Cloud's and clung to him. When he cast her a look void of expression, a chill soared through her. What if he was thinking the same thing that had troubled her only moments ago? She might not even get as far as his village to be tested *by* his people!

"You do love me, don't you?" she murmured. "You do still want me, don't you?"

His silence caused her insides to run cold.

20

Shall I compare thee to a summer's day?
Thou art more lovely and more temperate.
—WILLIAM SHAKESPEARE

They rode on through the hustle and bustle of the business area of Mattoon, then farther down Broadway. Lauralee felt as though her insides were being torn asunder when Dancing Cloud still refused to speak with her. He just sat there with an angry set jaw and narrowed eyes as he stared straight ahead, never casting her another glance since the last heated one that she had received just after they had left The Stables.

Still she did not question him as to why he was behaving so coldly toward her. Although she had done nothing but defend him, the mere fact that she had been forced to seemed to be the reason behind his behavior now.

He just might be thinking through marrying a white woman, perhaps thinking that down deep inside herself she had her own deep-seated bad feelings for Indians.

Lauralee did not see how she could convince him otherwise if he did not already know enough about her to realize that she was not a person of prejudice. She saw no one's skin as cause to see them as different from herself.

If he did not understand that about her now, perhaps she, herself, had to reconsider marrying *him.*

Tears burned at the corners of her eyes but she

willed herself not to cry. She just kept wondering what the next moments would bring.

Oh, but she had already battled so many tumultuous feelings over so many things. Could she bear to fight the worst battle of all? That of losing the man she would die for?

Her breath quickened when Dancing Cloud made a wide swing with the horse and buggy and traveled down a narrow road where corn stood shoulder tall on each side. Afraid to hear the answer, she did not ask him why he had taken a road that traveled away from the Peterson House. Was he going to leave for his home in the mountains now?

But no. That couldn't be it. He was going north instead of south. And there was his horse and belongings at the Peterson House. He would not leave without them.

They left the cornfield behind and now traveled beside a thick stand of oak, elm, and maple trees. Lauralee grabbed for the seat and steadied herself when Dancing Cloud swung left into a narrow road that took them beneath the sheltering of trees and to a small, winding creek.

Lauralee questioned Dancing Cloud with her eyes when he finally came to an abrupt halt. The horse whinnied and shimmied as it steadied itself and got a more solid footing.

Dancing Cloud jumped from the buggy and secured the reins on a tree limb, then went in wide, determined steps to Lauralee. He momentarily peered up at her with his midnight-dark eyes, then placed his hands at her waist and lifted her from the seat.

Lauralee clung to her straw bonnet as Dancing Cloud set her to the ground, his fingers still at her waist. Her breath was stolen away when he yanked her against his muscled body and kissed her long and hard.

Her head spun with questions when he released her. Her eyes were wide as he grabbed her up into his arms and carried her through the trees until they reached the banks of the creek.

Holding her steady, he pressed her down with his weight onto the ground, then knelt over her, his hands gently on each side of her face.

"How could you ever question my love for you?" he said thickly. "My anger that you have witnessed these past minutes? It was more toward you than the crass white man. You questioned my love for you so easily. Do you not know that nothing anyone says or does to me, red or white, could make me love *you* less?"

"But you looked at me as though you hated me," Lauralee said, her eyes wavering into his. "And when I tried to get you to talk to me, you *wouldn't.*"

"That is because of what you chose to say *to* me," he said, brushing a soft kiss across her lips. "My *o-ge-ye,* it was your doubts voiced in your question that lay hurt upon hurt inside my heart. Do you truly doubt my love for you? Is one angry look that I gave you enough for you to doubt me?"

"I'm sorry, oh, so sorry," Lauralee said, twining her arms around his neck. "All that I can say is that in my life I have never had much to hope for. And to have your love seems so very impossible. You are everything I would ever want in a man. How could *I,* someone who has never had anything to call my own, or to cling to, have *you*? So you see, my darling, how I could doubt so easily?"

"How can I make you know never to doubt my love for you again?" he said thickly. "I thought I already had."

"You have, oh, but you have, but because of my insecurities, I forget so easily," she murmured. "I shall try to place those insecurities behind me. I vow to you that I shall try my very hardest."

"I shall help you do this, always," Dancing Cloud said. "I should have known the cause. I should never forget those long years you were forced to live in an orphanage away from family and the security that family brings into a child's life."

"I am no longer a child," Lauralee whispered, her hands at his fringed shirt, smoothing it upward, across his hairless chest. "Let me prove to you once again that I am a *woman*."

They slowly undressed each other.

Dancing Cloud led Lauralee to a thick bed of moss that grew spongy and green beside the creek. He lay her down onto it. He leaned over her. Their eyes met, locked in an unspoken understanding, promising ecstasy. The air was heavy with the inevitability of pleasure.

And when Dancing Cloud led himself into her warm, moist and tight place, she felt a soft, melting energy warming her insides. Desire raged and washed over her as he shoved into her, her hips responding as she thrust her pelvis toward him.

Although her senses were swimming with delicious sensations, she had enough rational thought to worry about his shoulder. "Darling," she whispered, placing a gentle hand over the puckered skin of his wound. "I always fear hurting you while we make love. Are you certain . . . ?"

"Do not question *anything* at this time," Dancing Cloud said. "Take. Enjoy what I give so willingly. In turn, I shall take what you so willingly give to *me*. That is all that should be on your mind now. Being together. Freely loving each other."

"Oh, I do love you, Dancing Cloud," Lauralee whispered, feverishly moving her fingers over his face. "Oh, my love, kiss me. Hold me. Take me to paradise with you."

His lips came to hers in an explosive kiss. Only half aware of making whimpering sounds, she clung to him. She rocked with him. Caught in his embrace, all of her senses yearned for the promise of what they sought—the ultimate of giving, of sharing, of enjoying.

She ran her trembling hands down his back, savoring

the feel of his sleek, copper body. She could never get enough of him. The touch of him. The feel. His pleasant manly aroma. His hands. His *lips*. Everything about him was wonderful . . . was perfect.

Dancing Cloud pressed endlessly deeper. He gathered her into his arms and sculpted himself to her body. Feeling as though a great fire was burning within him with a fierce heat, he inhaled a quavering breath. The pain of need that was building inside his loins was both agony and bliss. He felt it growing, growing, almost to the bursting point.

Wanting to delay the pleasure, to the limits of his endurance, knowing that it would be twofold if he waited, he fought to go slowly within her. He willed himself to wait.

He paused and leaned away from her so that he could take in her loveliness with his feasting eyes . . . the slimness of her body below her breasts, the supple broadening that led to her hips, the muff of hair that lay between her long, smooth thighs.

"Why have you stopped?" Lauralee questioned, her heart pounding, her body aching for that final fulfillment. She tremored when he reached his hands to her breasts and cupped them, his thumbs circling the nipples.

"To delay the pleasure so that it will be enhanced," Dancing Cloud said, softly kneading her breasts.

Then he shifted his position. She rolled her head and closed her eyes when he began loving her body with his mouth and tongue. She abandoned herself to the pleasure that was swimming through her like sunshine spreading its warmth over a newborn day.

He made love to her slowly, finding every part of her body to delight and pleasure her. Each lazy caress, each exploratory sweep of his eager tongue over her warm flesh, brought her ecstasy.

"Darling, I am so close," she murmured. "Please?"

His eyes dark and knowing, he rose above her. Without hesitation he came to her, thrusting hard into the rose-red slippery heat of her body.

She shuddered and gripped him lightly.

Their bodies strained together hungrily as his mouth covered hers with a fierce, fevered kiss.

The urgency then gave way to total pleasure. He kissed her long and deep. He thrust powerfully into her, bringing her to a wild abandon that matched his own.

Spent, his shoulder aching, Dancing Cloud rolled away from Lauralee and stretched out on his back. Panting, he closed his eyes.

"Darling, you're in *pain*," Lauralee said, her eyes wide as she moved to her knees beside him. She bent low over him and gently kissed his wound. His fingers laced through her hair and drew her lips to his.

A curling warmth spread through her again. She stretched out beside him, thankful for his muscular arms that swept around her, and the wonders of his kiss. They made love again, then both lay side by side, breathing hard.

"Let us leave now for my home in the mountains," Dancing Cloud suddenly blurted, drawing Lauralee out of her pleasant reverie. He turned and faced her, his hands gently stroking her face. "We shall go to the Peterson House and pack our belongings, then leave. Why delay it? Have I not just proved that I am strong enough to travel?"

"You have just proven *many* things to me," Lauralee said, laughing softly. Then her smile faded. "But, darling. I've promised the Petersons that we will spend one more night with them. What can it matter? I have already inflicted hurt on them. Why make it worse by leaving earlier?"

And she wanted to have time to talk her uncle into going and purchasing the stallion for her so that she could surprise Dancing Cloud with it early in the morning. How handsome he would look on such a magnificent steed as that! They were meant for each other, it seemed, as though it were their destiny.

"It would mean so much to you to spend this one more night with your blood kin?" Dancing Cloud asked, running his hands up and down the velvet smoothness of her body.

"So very much," she whispered, sucking in a breath of pleasure as he again stroked her where she still throbbed from the aftermath of their lovemaking.

Again they made love.

The sun sent its slanted rays through the trees overhead, warning Lauralee that soon it would be evening. She did not want to worry Aunt Nancy. And she wanted to have a private talk with Uncle Abner about the stallion.

Feeling deliciously drained from making love, Lauralee rose shakily to her feet. Laughing softly, she began dressing. "If you had the energy to last through making love three times today, I am positive that you can endure a day's travel on horseback," she teased as Dancing Cloud moved into his own clothes. His shoulder was stiff and painful as he raised it to slip on his shirt.

"Tomorrow," he said thickly. "We shall leave tomorrow. Nothing will stop us from starting our journey to my home tomorrow, my *o-ge-ye*. My people beckon me home. They grow weary of not having a chief to lean on for true leadership."

Completely dressed, her hair thrown over her shoulders, Lauralee leaned into Dancing Cloud and clasped her arms around his neck. "No," she said, smiling up at him. "Nothing or no one will stop us, darling. Yes, I feel sad leaving my aunt and uncle, but I am anxious to travel to your village to make an acquaintance with your people. Do you truly think they will approve of me? Or will they see me as an interference in your life, and also theirs?"

"When they see you and get to know you how could they not see the goodness and sweetness that I see in you?" he said, drawing her into his tight embrace. "Do not worry over such things. Enjoy life. Together, life is filled with much meaning, hope, and promise."

Lauralee closed her eyes, blocking out her fears and doubts, at least for now. Dancing Cloud had a way to make her forget.

He was good for her.

He was her promise of all tomorrows.

Supper had been eaten. Lauralee had helped her aunt with the dishes. Her uncle was in his office, going over the day's events in his mind. Dancing Cloud had taken a walk to commune with the Great Spirit.

Laying her apron aside, Lauralee hugged Nancy, then stepped back and gave her a pensive smile. "Is it truly all right if I go and knock on Uncle Abner's door?" she asked softly. "I do so badly want to talk over something of importance with him."

"Honey, Abner will welcome your interference tonight," Nancy said, patting Lauralee on the arm. "Go on. Talk to him. He'll enjoy having a few private moments with you." Tears sprang into Nancy's eyes. "We're both going to miss you so, Lauralee."

"I will miss you, as well." Lauralee flicked tears from her eyes. "But I shall return and see you from time to time. I promise."

"Honey, don't make promises so quickly that might be hard to keep," Nancy said, wiping her eyes with a lacy handkerchief that she had taken from her dress pocket. "The Great Smoky Mountains is far from Mattoon, like a foreign country across the ocean, to me."

"But I truly shall try to come back and see you as often as I can," Lauralee persisted.

Nancy took Lauralee by an elbow and led her out of the kitchen, down the dimly lit corridor, and to the foot of the staircase. She nodded toward the stairs. "Go on," she murmured. "Go and have that talk with your uncle. I'll wait in the parlor. I have some embroidery to do."

Lauralee gave Nancy a warm hug, then scurried up the steps. When she got outside her uncle's study, she stopped and inhaled deeply.

Then she knocked softly on the door.

"Come on in," Abner said, smiling at Lauralee as she stepped into the room and closed the door behind her. "Lauralee. I hoped you'd come. I'd like some private time with you."

"Oh?" Lauralee said, raising an eyebrow.

Abner gestured with a hand toward a chair that sat opposite his desk. "Come," he said, his voice drawn. "Sit. Tell me what's on your mind."

Lauralee's heart beat rapidly as she eased into the leather chair. She placed her hands demurely on her lap, her back straight, her knees weak. "Sir, today, while Dancing Cloud and I were sightseeing, we found the most beautiful horse at The Stables," she said softly.

She continued to recount the experience of the day, and how rudely Dancing Cloud and she had been treated by the owner.

She proceeded to tell him her wishes to have the white stallion for a special gift for Dancing Cloud.

"Please do this for me, Uncle Abner," she pleaded. "You are a man who is surely quite practiced at making business dealings. If I give you the money, will you please go and purchase the white stallion for me? I would so appreciate it."

"You say that Kevin Banks was quite brash to you and your Cherokee, eh?" Abner said, as he placed his fingertips together before him. "Seems I'll have to have a talk with that man."

He frowned over at Lauralee. "Do you still insist on leaving tomorrow with Dancing Cloud?" he asked, his voice breaking.

"I love him," she said, lifting her chin proudly. "I

plan to marry him. So, yes, Uncle Abner, I plan to leave with him."

"Then, dear, knowing that my arguments would be in vain, I give you my blessing," Abner said, inhaling a quavering breath. "And I will do as you ask. I will go and purchase the stallion for you. It's too late tonight to take care of the transaction, but I'll be up at the crack of dawn to see that it's done."

"But Dancing Cloud said that he will be leaving that early," Lauralee fretted aloud.

"Just tell him that you have reasons to wait for me to return once he sees that I am gone," Abner said, smiling over at her. "He would not deprive you of a last farewell to your uncle, now would he?"

"No, I'm sure he wouldn't," Lauralee said, laughing softly. She left the chair and went around the desk and bent to her knees before her uncle. She flung herself into his arms. "Thank you for everything. Oh, so much for everything."

Tears pooling in his eyes, he patted her back, then embraced her long and hard.

With the sweet fragrance of flowers all around him, Dancing Cloud was on his knees, looking heavenward. "Oh, Great Spirit, *Wah-kon-tah,* whose voice I hear in the winds, and whose breath gives life to all the world, hear me," Dancing Cloud pleaded to the stars, the moon, the sky. "I need your strength and wisdom these coming weeks. Please guide me safely home. I seek strength. Make me always ready to come to you with clean hands and straight eyes. Help me lead my woman into a world unknown to her . . . the world of my people."

When he was through he bowed his head and listened. He soon felt the wind blow gently around and over him. He had been heard. He felt at peace with the days that lay ahead.

21

When two mutual hearts are sighing
For the knot there's no untying.
                    —THOMAS CAMPBELL

The sky was streaked with crimson ribbons as the sun rose slowly from behind the horizon. Feeling that it was important to keep his promise to Lauralee, Abner guided his horse onto the small street that led to The Stables. He wanted her to remember him and Nancy with pleasant memories. Even after she was gone, he wanted her to still consider them as her family. He had visions of her returning with her children to spend Christmas each year in the Peterson House.

Of course he knew the chances were small of this ever happening. The Smoky Mountains were quite far from Mattoon. And once Lauralee arrived there, she would be thrust into a world very separate from any that she had ever known. She would have much to learn. She would have to become Cherokee, herself, heart and soul, to survive among them. She might soon forget that the Petersons ever existed.

Abner set his jaw and his eyes narrowed angrily. He was still not able to understand why Boyd had asked an Indian to escort his daughter to Mattoon. But there was no sense laboring over the if's and why's of things any longer. Lauralee's mind was made up. There was no way around the fact that she had chosen Dancing Cloud over living with her aunt and uncle.

Abner's thoughts shifted elsewhere when he saw a group of men standing beside The Stable's tall white fence. His gaze went from man to man, recognizing them all.

Then he stared at one in particular. Sheriff Wes Decker. He was a tall and well-built man, who stood eye to eye with Kevin Banks, seemingly involved in a serious discussion. One of the other men was Sheriff Decker's deputy. The other was Kevin's stable hand.

They all turned and looked toward Abner as he swung his horse and buggy beside the fence. They sauntered over to him and before he had the chance to leave the buggy, Sheriff Decker was there, his gray eyes fixed on him.

"Is that Cherokee still stayin' at your place, Abner?" the sheriff asked, slipping his massive hands inside the front pocket of his dark breeches.

"He's leaving this morning," Abner said, guardedly looking from man to man as they came and stood beside Sheriff Decker. "Why do you ask? What's this small gathering about, anyhow, this time of morning?"

Kevin edged in close beside Sheriff Decker. "Abner, seems you've been housin' a horse thief these past few days," he said, peering angrily up at him.

"What's that you say?" Abner said, his spine stiffening. He looked slowly from man to man again as they all edged closer.

"The Cherokee?" Kevin said flatly. "That damn gray-back scum Cherokee was here admirin' my white stallion yesterday with your niece. Well, seems he wanted to do more than just look. Abner, the stallion was gone this mornin'. Everything points to the Cherokee being guilty of horse stealin'."

"And what proof do you have of his guilt?" Abner asked tersely. "Dancing Cloud is housing only one horse in my stable. *His.*"

"I heard that he stole another horse here in Mattoon. He's a smart Injun," Kevin said, laughing sarcastically.

"He wouldn't take the stallion where you could see it. He has surely hid it."

"Kevin, first of all the horse that Dancing Cloud took the night he left the hospital has been returned to the rightful owner. He never intended to keep it. It was a means by which he could get to what he called in his Cherokee beliefs as 'healing water'," Abner said, his voice smooth and even. "And as for you. Why do you think that anyone would believe anything you say?"

Abner left his buggy and went and stood eye to eye with Kevin. "As I see it, if someone could be so quick at humiliating my niece, they could be as quick to make up a lie."

Kevin shuffled his feet nervously, his eyes wavering. "So you know, then, that she was here with the Cherokee," he said tightly. "That's proof enough that the Injun had the chance to admire and want the stallion. He was surely making plans on how to steal it the minute he saw it. I lived out west for a spell. I learned damn quick that Injuns cain't be trusted. Especially one who wore gray during the war."

"The war is long over, Kevin," Abner grumbled. "You'd best put it behind you. I'd say there's been enough commotion around here since the Cherokee was ambushed by someone whose opinions of the Indian match your own. Why, Kevin, I might just accuse you of shooting Dancing Cloud."

Of course Abner knew that Kevin didn't. But making him uneasy about perhaps being accused of such a heinous crime seemed the right thing to do. Kevin deserved taking down a notch or two over having treated Lauralee in such a callous manner.

"I'd be the first to confess that I hold no love for *any* Rebel in my heart," Kevin stammered out. "But to accuse me of ambushin' a gray coat ain't right, Abner. All I want to do this morning is get back my stallion and see that the man who stole it gets thrown in jail."

"Seems as though we have enough to go on to make an arrest," Sheriff Decker said, patting a heavy pistol holstered at his right hip. "Abner, you'll probably be the judge to hand down the Cherokee's sentencing. So don't you think it's best to cooperate with me and accompany me to your house to arrest the Indian?"

Although Abner wanted a way to keep Lauralee in Mattoon, he sure as hell didn't want to see Dancing Cloud jailed, which would, indeed, keep Lauralee with him and Nancy for some time to come. Abner knew that if an Indian was accused of *anything* and jailed, there was hardly a chance in hell of him getting off without being hanged.

Especially a gray-coat Indian.

"Wes, the evidence is way too weak to make the arrest, and you know it," Abner said, placing his fists on his hips. "And you know as well as *I* that Kevin's word isn't worth spit."

"I've got a witness," Kevin said, his eyes gleaming as Abner looked quickly his way. "If I have to I'll go and get him now. It's Jason Pratt. The little boy that lives yonder? He told me that he saw the Indian lurking around the stables after dark. Ain't that enough proof of the Indian's guilt?"

Abner scratched his brow idly as he thought back to the previous night. He *couldn't* account for all of Dancing Cloud's time. The Cherokee had excused himself after dark so that he could go into the woods and commune with his Great Spirit.

Did Dancing Cloud, instead, go to The Stables and steal the stallion? Abner wondered.

Abner had been too intent on searching through law books to help him with his decisions in court to notice much of anything, especially when Dancing Cloud came into the house. The law books had been studied way into the night after Lauralee had come to him, to ask his assistance in purchasing the stallion.

He narrowed angry eyes at Kevin. "You'd better be telling the truth and that young man who you said was a witness to the crime had better be able to testify in court that he saw Dancing Cloud take the horse, or by

God, Kevin, I'll throw the book at you. You'll wish you never messed with Judge Abner Peterson."

Worrying about Lauralee's reaction to Dancing Cloud's arrest, yet knowing that for now there was nothing more he could do to stop it, Abner climbed back into his buggy. With the sheriff and his deputy riding on each side of the buggy, they made their way through the town, down Broadway, then swung into Abner's circular drive.

Lauralee was placing her last satchel in her buggy when she heard the clatter and commotion of approaching horses. Dancing Cloud came from the house and down the steps of the back porch when he also heard the horses. He moved to Lauralee's side and watched the approach of Abner and the two lawmen.

"What could they want?" Lauralee asked, giving Dancing Cloud a quick glance. "What are the lawmen doing with my uncle?"

Dancing Cloud did not respond. He stiffened, his eyes looking suspiciously from one lawman to the other.

Then his gaze shifted to Abner. Dancing Cloud's insides froze when he saw the look on Lauralee's uncle's face. He was solemn. His eyes were filled with a strange sort of apology as he stared back at Dancing Cloud.

Abner drew his horse and buggy to a stop. He dropped the reins into the seat and stepped to the ground, the sheriff and his deputy dismounting at the same time.

"Uncle Abner, what's the matter?" Lauralee asked weakly. Her heart thumped wildly over the strange behavior of her uncle and the two lawmen as they walked toward her and Dancing Cloud.

"Step aside, miss," Sheriff Decker said, slipping a pair of handcuffs from his rear pocket. "I've my duties to perform."

Lauralee's eyes widened and she became dizzy with

fear as she watched the sheriff reach out for Dancing
Cloud with his free hand.

"Hold your wrists together, Cherokee," Sheriff
Decker said thickly, his eyes never leaving Dancing
Cloud's face. "Don't give me no fight. You wouldn't
have a chance in hell of escaping."

"Why are you doing this?" Lauralee cried, going to
grab the sheriff's arm. "What are you arresting Dancing Cloud *for*? It's a mistake. It has to be a mistake!"

"Horse stealin' is a serious crime, miss," the sheriff
said, frowning down at Lauralee.

"The horse I borrowed has been returned to its rightful owner," Dancing Cloud finally said after somewhat
getting over the initial shock of what was happening.

"Don't play dumb with me," Sheriff Decker grumbled. "There's a witness that said you stole Kevin
Bank's white stallion last night. I'd say that calls for an
arrest, wouldn't you?"

"I did not take the white stallion," Dancing Cloud
said, his jaw tight, his throat dry.

Sheriff Decker nodded toward his deputy. Deputy
Dobbs came in a rush to the sheriff's side.

"Watch him," the sheriff growled. "Draw your gun
on him if he even looks like he's going to resist arrest."

Knowing that he had no other choice but to do as he
was ordered, yet knowing himself who had framed
him, Dancing Cloud held out his hands, his wrists
quickly in the handcuffs.

"Get his horse, Dobbs," Sheriff Decker said. "Bring
the horse to the Indian." He narrowed his eyes at
Dancing Cloud. "I'm helpin' you onto your horse.
Don't try any funny business, do you hear? Hand-
cuffed, you can't get far."

Lauralee ran to Abner. She clutched his arms frantically. "Do something," she cried. "Tell them they are
arresting the wrong man. Dancing Cloud didn't steal
that horse. You and I both know it. They are arresting
an innocent man."

"Honey, I'll see that justice is done," Abner said, easing Lauralee's fingers away.

"Justice?" she cried. "You call this justice? Lord, Uncle Abner, just how much more humiliation do you think Dancing Cloud can take? Why can't you stop this? Let us be on our way. Please, Uncle Abner. Please stop this. You are a man of power in the community. One word spoken and he'd be released."

Abner clutched his fingers to her shoulders. "Lauralee, it's not that simple," he said hoarsely. "Now settle down. We'll get this straightened out. You'll see."

"He shouldn't have to spend one minute behind bars!" Lauralee screamed. She ran after Dancing Cloud as he rode away, the sheriff holding the reins of his prisoner's horse. "Let him go!"

She stumbled, then jerked away from her uncle when he came and tried to comfort her.

She turned and ran to the stable. She took one of her uncle's horses from a stall, saddled it, then swung herself into the saddle. "By damn I shall stop this if I have to shoot that damn sheriff and deputy!" she screamed at her uncle, then rode away, getting only a slight glimpse of her aunt at the door, her face drawn and pale from the commotion at hand.

Nancy left the house and stood on the front porch. She welcomed Abner's strong, comforting arms as he came to her and drew her into his embrace.

"Abner, Abner," Nancy murmured. She eased away from him and gazed into his eyes. "You know you could have stopped this thing. Did you allow it to happen, hoping that might prevent Dancing Cloud from marrying Lauralee? Could you truly stand by and see that man hang only because you don't want to give up Lauralee?"

Abner took Nancy's hands. "You know me better than anyone else and yet you can think that of me?" he asked, his voice breaking. "Nancy, trust me. I'll make all wrongs right."

"Will you, truly?" Nancy asked, tears spilling from her eyes. Her shoulders slouched, her head hung, she went back inside the house and closed the door between herself and her husband.

Abner sighed heavily. He kneaded his chin.

Then he went to his horse and buggy and headed back in the direction of the city again. He was truly torn with what he should, or could do. Quite possibly if he did not make things right for Lauralee, his wife as well as Lauralee would hate him for eternity.

Frowning, he drove down Broadway.

He had much to think about.

He had decisions to make.

Lauralee paced the floor inside the jail, the keys rattling in the sheriff's hand as he came from the back room where the cells were lined against opposite walls.

"And so do you feel like a much bigger man today since you have incarcerated a savage, Confederate Cherokee?" she asked, glaring at him. She lifted a chin haughtily. "I wish to see my future husband. If you don't give me permission, I shall do it, anyhow."

"You're a goddamned spitfire, ain't you?" Sheriff Decker said, slamming the keys onto his desk. "And you're plannin' on marrying' that son of a bitch Indian?" He laughed raucously. "I wouldn't count on it."

Lauralee stamped away from him and went to the back room. The small barred windows in each cell allowed only a fraction of light to shine through them. But Lauralee had no trouble finding Dancing Cloud. He was the only prisoner.

An empty, gnawing ache at the pit of her stomach came with seeing her beloved behind bars. She stepped up to the cell and circled her fingers around the cold bars, glad that at least the handcuffs had been released from Dancing Cloud's wrists.

"Dancing Cloud, oh, Dancing Cloud, what can I say to make up for what is being done to you?" Lauralee sobbed, melting inside when his fingers covered hers.

"Darling, I swear to you, I will find a way to get you out of here. You won't have to spend an entire night behind bars. I will come for you. After it is dark, expect me to find a way to get you out of here. Then we shall leave immediately for your home in the mountains."

"Do not do anything that will endanger yourself," Dancing Cloud said thickly. "I will be released soon. I am innocent. An innocent man does not stay behind bars for long."

She looked over at him. Tears burned her eyes. Doesn't he know that he is not just any man who will go before a judge and jury? she thought. He is an Indian! And he fought for the South during the war, not the North. Those two things alone would cause enough prejudice among the jurors to make sure that he would hang for a crime that he did not commit.

"It's all Kevin Bank's fault," Lauralee hissed out. "He hated you the minute he saw you."

"Men like him do not live with peace in their hearts," Dancing Cloud said, his voice drawn. "He is a tormented man, filled with much hate. He only used me, a Cherokee, to focus the hate on this time. Tomorrow? It will be someone else, perhaps white."

"Darling, I must go now," Lauralee murmured. "I owe it to Nancy to go to her. I saw how distraught she was. I worry about her having another heart attack. But I will leave when she is asleep tonight. I *will* come for you. You shall not be here for long."

They kissed. She gave him a lingering, soft look, then turned on a heel and left. She walked past the sheriff without a word. When she got outside and found her Uncle Abner leaving his buggy, she looked at him for a moment, then started to move past him.

She stopped when he reached out and grabbed her by the arm and turned her toward him.

"Don't blame me for any of this," he said thickly. "You must remember my standing in the community. I am a judge. I can't take sides. But I will see that Dancing Cloud is treated well while he is incarcerated, and that he gets a fair trial."

"Why not spend your precious time finding the one who *truly* stole the stallion?" Lauralee said, her voice breaking. "Uncle Abner, please do right by Dancing Cloud. He is the world to me."

She yanked herself free and ran to the horse. Sobbing, she wheeled her horse around and headed back for the Peterson House. She had to make things right with Nancy now, for tonight would be too late. Lauralee would not even be there for a final, melancholy farewell.

22

With long eyes I wait,
Expectant of her.
My lady comes at last.
—WILLIAM MAKEPEACE THACKERAY

Her valises packed and placed snuggly at the back of her buggy along with Dancing Cloud's belongings and his saddle and saddlebags, Lauralee paced the floor, waiting to see that Abner and Nancy were asleep.

When the clock below her in the parlor began chiming off each separate hour, she mentally counted them to herself, then said the time aloud in a soft whisper as it came closer to the midnight hour.

"Nine . . . ten . . . eleven . . . twelve," she said, clasping her hands before her.

Her eyes widened with a mixture of excitement and fear for what she had planned. It would be the most daring thing that she had ever done in her life.

But she had to do it.

She must!

She would not leave Dancing Cloud at the mercy of *any* man.

Not even her beloved Uncle Abner.

Although Judge Peterson would have the final word that would decide Dancing Cloud's fate, Lauralee couldn't chance that he might even, himself, go against her beloved Cherokee. Her uncle might use this opportunity to separate her and Dancing Cloud forever by sending Dancing Cloud to a prison for a lengthy sentence.

She could not chance that.

Come hell or high water she was going to break Dancing Cloud out of jail tonight.

Tying a shawl around her shoulders, Lauralee stepped out into the quiet hallway. Her heart thudded inside her chest as she peered toward her aunt and uncle's door. She breathed a sigh of relief when she did not see lamplight at the crack beneath the door.

She tiptoed to their door and leaned an ear to it. She heard absolutely nothing. That had to mean they were asleep.

Unsure of how soundly her aunt and uncle slept, she feared what she had to do next. While leading her horse and buggy from the stable, would she be heard? She knew that she had grown used to sleeping through all sorts of noises at the orphanage.

But here on the outskirts of Mattoon everything was so quiet. The sound of wagon wheels and horse's hooves could sound like thunder to someone who was trying to get a peaceful night of sleep.

Knowing that she would have to take that chance, Lauralee clutched the shawl more tightly around her shoulders and tiptoed to the staircase, and then down the steps. There was no lamplight or candles to light her way. Just one slip of the foot and she would be caught.

Nervous perspiration beading her brow, she finally reached the first-floor landing. She felt her way down the long corridor, through the kitchen, and then to the door that led to the back porch.

She held her breath as she slowly inched the door open. She eyed the outdoors and the shadows of the night. The moon was only a slight sliver in the sky now and gave off scarcely any light.

Seeing Dancing Cloud's freedom only a short time away should she succeed with her ploy to draw attention from the jail, Lauralee ran down the steps. She lifted her travel skirt from the dew of the night and ran toward the stable. She cast a look over her shoulder toward the Petersons' bedroom window. Thus far they had not been awakened. But the true test was soon to come.

Breathless, Lauralee patted her horse and smoothed her gloved hand down its withers. She then stared into the buggy at one bag in particular at the back. Inside this bag were rolled-up pieces of paper that she had taken from her uncle's wastebasket, and small pieces of kindling she had taken from a bucket beside the front parlor stove.

She reached inside the pocket of her skirt and circled her fingers around several matches. She prayed that she had stolen enough to get a good fire going across the street from the jail.

Smiling *and* trembling, Lauralee quickly stepped up into the carriage and plopped down. Picking up the reins, she lightly snapped them.

As the horse and buggy left the stable, Lauralee kept her eyes on the Petersons' bedroom window. If she saw a stirring of the sheer, lacy curtains, then she would know that her plan had failed and that Dancing Cloud would have to stand trial after all.

Careful just to inch the horse and buggy along, Lauralee watched as she came directly below her aunt and uncle's bedroom window.

Her pulse raced.

Her throat went dry.

Her eyes misted. This was not the way she would have liked having said her final goodbye to two very special people. By leaving them, she knew that she was leaving behind many opportunities.

But there were boundless opportunities offered her by going with Dancing Cloud. While with him, every day would be filled with many blessings.

Only if his people accepted *her,* she again fretted to herself.

She sighed heavily when the circular drive was left

behind her as well as the Peterson House. Her eyes were intent now on all sides of her, watching for any sudden movements, any signs of life. She rode in an elusive manner, watching over her shoulder to see if she was being followed.

Clint McCloud.

He was always on her mind, especially when she was alone. Although she had her small derringer slipped into the pocket of her skirt, it did not give her much peace of mind.

Her aim was no better than a toad's!

Feeling more confident by the minute, and satisfied that no one trailed her, Lauralee slapped her reins and sent her horse into a harder gallop. She wanted to get this over with. Not only to get Dancing Cloud released to freedom, but to get her insides settled down into something akin to being normal again.

She was queasy.

She was tense.

She was strangely cold all over, yet still perspired.

The gaslights up ahead along the street alerted Lauralee that she was almost to her destination. She swung the horse and buggy into a small side street, then up again toward Broadway. She had missed the jail by one block. She would go by foot back a half block and get the fire started across the street from the jail.

Then she would swing around again in her horse and buggy and go to the rear of the jail. She would find Dancing Cloud's horse tethered there. She would saddle it.

After Deputy Dobbs ran from the jail to see about the fire, it would be easy for Lauralee to sneak into the front door. She would release Dancing Cloud. They would flee into the night while the fire wagon bells clanged noisily as they arrived at the scene of the fire.

She frowned at the thought of having to set fire to the small wooden building that sat squeezed between two brick establishments.

But there was one thing in her favor.

It was unoccupied.

And it was going to be torn down soon so that a brick building could be built in its place.

The irony of her having chosen to set fire to this building was that it had just recently been purchased by her Uncle Abner. He planned to lease the new brick building out to bring in more business to Mattoon.

"I shall just hurry the process along," Lauralee whispered to herself, smiling. "Uncle Abner, if the fire wagons don't arrive quickly enough you will not have to pay for the demolition of the squat, ugly wooden building."

She shivered at the thought of being caught and labeled an "arsonist." Her aunt and uncle would be disgraced for life for having brought her into their lives.

Knowing that she had to chance even that, Lauralee climbed from her buggy and secured her reins on a low tree limb. She then grabbed the heavy bag of kindling and paper. Keeping in the shadows as much as possible, she inched her way along in front of the buildings.

Her heart hammering hard, Lauralee stopped and leaned her back against the wall of the wooden building long enough to get her breath. Her eyes studied the jail. There was only a faint lamplight shining from the windows at the front.

Then she smiled when she saw the shadow of Deputy Dobbs walk past one of the windows. He would surely see the fire as it progressed into something raging and brilliant in the darkness of the night. After he left the jail unguarded to run and check on the fire . . .

As planned, Lauralee methodically placed the bits of kindling and paper around the foot of the wooden structure. Her fingers trembled as she struck one match and then another, setting small fires along the bottom of the building. There was one thing that she had forgot about. The sidewalks. They were made of wood and corncobs. If they began burning, a path of fire would make its way down Broadway Avenue.

"Lord, please just let burn what I want to burn," she whispered, peering into the dark heavens. "You know that what I am doing is right. Dancing Cloud's life depends on it."

She dropped the last burned-out match. Not turning to see whether or not the building was going up in flames yet, she ran hurriedly to her wagon, climbed aboard, slapped the reins, and soon found herself behind the jail.

Sliding from the seat, her eyes wide, Lauralee went and looked around the corner of the building. The fire quickly caught her eye. The flames were lapping up the front of the building. She jumped with a start when the glass in the window exploded and sprayed in all directions.

Then she placed a hand to her throat when Deputy Dobbs ran from the jail, stopping only momentarily to stare at the blazing inferno halfway down the street from the jail.

As she had hoped, he did not look back with concern at the jail, his worries for his one prisoner gone the instant he had seen the fire.

Running down the middle of the dirt road, he waved his hands in the air, shouting "Fire."

Having not expected the deputy to make such a racket, Lauralee frowned and died a slow death inside. Before long the whole town would be awake! Now she had to work twice as fast or she would be caught.

Breathless, her heart beating anxiously, Lauralee saddled Dancing Cloud's horse. She then swept the hem of her travel skirt up into her arms. Her knees weak, yet filled with determination and spirit, she ran into the jail.

She recalled the sheriff having slung the keys idly on top of the desk earlier in the day. That was where she expected to find them.

Her heart seemed to drop to her feet when she stared at the clutter on top of the desk, the keys nowhere among it.

Then recalling novels that she had read about the West, and where the sheriff in the books usually kept their keys, she ran to the door that led to the back room. She swung it open and just as she had hoped, to the right, on a nail in the wall, hung the huge circle of keys.

"O-ge-ye?" Dancing Cloud said, rising up from his bunk, the lamplight in the outer room illumining Lauralee's face as she turned to him.

Seeing Dancing Cloud behind the bars, his hands clutched to them, made Lauralee know that she would go to the ends of the world, if needed, to set him free. Never had she loved him more than at this moment.

The love that soared through her gave her the strength to move on to the jail cell. She smiled weakly up at Dancing Cloud, then with trembling fingers, slipped the key into the lock. She wanted to shout "hooray" when the lock sprang free.

Dancing Cloud shoved the door open. For a moment he engulfed Lauralee within his powerful arms. "I told you not to take chances," he said, his voice drawn.

"I had to," Lauralee said, clinging.

Then she wrenched herself away from him and grabbed his hand. "Come on," she said, her eyes looking guardedly around her as she and Dancing Cloud moved out into the outer room. "If we move quickly we won't get caught."

The sound of the fire bells and the thundering of hooves as the fire wagon rode down Broadway Avenue toward the raging fire caused Dancing Cloud's eyes to move quickly to one side. "There is a fire," he said, momentarily pausing as he stepped outside the front door.

He shifted his gaze down at Lauralee. "Did you . . . ?" he questioned, raising an eyebrow.

She smiled sheepishly up at him and nodded her head, then jerked on his hand. "We must leave," she said. "Now. Thus far, no one is suspicious over the nature or origin of the fire. How could they think it was set to create a diversion so that someone could escape from their jail?"

Together they ran around the corner of the building, then stopped with a start when they came face to face with Paul Brown.

Lauralee stiffened.

Her eyes wavered into Paul's.

Paul gazed slowly from Lauralee to Dancing Cloud, then at Lauralee again.

Lauralee's first thoughts were to draw her derringer on Paul. But she knew that he would be much quicker. The heavy pistol hanging at his right hip caused her not to chance that.

"Lauralee, how did Dancing Cloud get free?" Paul asked, idly scratching his brow.

"Why are *you* here this time of night?" Lauralee questioned guardedly, her chin lifted stubbornly. "Did the fire bring you from the farm? I do not see how you could have seen it from that distance."

"No, I didn't see the fire. I'm not here for that reason," Paul said. He rested a hand on his holstered pistol as he cast Dancing Cloud a frown. "I'm here to relieve Deputy Dobbs of his duties for the night." He turned slow eyes to Lauralee again. "You see, I was deputized, myself, yesterday. It's always been my ambition to become sheriff some day."

"Lord," Lauralee said, paling when she realized how she had alienated the very man who might have the power to seize Dancing Cloud again and be certain that he hanged. And not because he was a guilty man. Because Paul would be rid of the one obstacle standing in the way of having Lauralee.

But how was she to know? she despaired to herself. When she had been making plans to help Dancing Cloud, Paul Brown had been the last person on her mind.

Recalling the goodness of Paul's father, how kind and generous he had been to Dancing Cloud, Lauralee saw the only recourse here was to get on that better side of *Paul*. She had often heard the phrase "like father, like son."

Now she would give that saying a true test.

"Paul?" Lauralee said, stepping up to him. She rested a hand on his arm. "You're a good man. An *honest* man. Do you wish to see someone as honest as you done wrong? Paul, I beg of you, let us pass. Dancing Cloud is innocent. He didn't steal Kevin's white stallion."

She gestured with her free hand toward Dancing Cloud's horse. "Don't you see?" she said. "Dancing Cloud owns only one horse. If he was guilty of having stolen the white stallion and I went along with that theft, don't you think the stallion would be tied to the wagon so that Dancing Cloud could take it with him now to his home in the mountains?"

"That's where you're headed tonight?" Paul asked, his voice guarded. "After helpin' the Indian escape, you are going with him?"

"Yes, that's my plan," Lauralee said, worrying now about how long it was taking to convince Paul that Dancing Cloud should not be taken back into the jail. She also realized that someone besides herself and Dancing Cloud now knew the direction of their travel should Paul allow them to leave.

"Paul, I give my word that Dancing Cloud is innocent," Lauralee blurted. "Please believe me. And stop and think about what might happen if he stays here after everyone finds out that he's in jail. The word about town that he's a Rebel *and* an Indian horse thief could stir up a lynch mob. He might not even live long enough to have a trial."

The sound of people shouting and seeing the great reflection of the fire against the dark heavens made Lauralee grow even more tense. "We're leaving, Paul," she said, firming her jaw. "If you shoot Dancing Cloud you might as well turn the same firearm on me. I would rather die than live without Dancing Cloud."

"Lauralee, I'm the law," Paul said, shuffling his feet

nervously. "I can't just let you ride away. I must abide by my duties as a lawman."

"Like I said, Paul, the only way you can stop me and Dancing Cloud is to shoot us," she said. She took Dancing Cloud's hand and walked with him toward the horse and buggy, his horse standing obediently beside it.

She held her breath and prayed over and over again that Paul Brown was not the sort to want glory over capturing an escaped criminal as well as capture the one who was guilty of helping with the escape.

She hoped that he cared enough for her to let her go.

If not, there was not much more she could do about it. Stopping short of getting on her knees and begging Paul she had said all that she could.

Her knees weak, her breathing shallow, and her fingers trembling, she eased her hand from Dancing Cloud's. She watched him swing into his saddle.

Then she stepped up into her buggy, plopped down on the seat, and grabbed her reins.

Her eyes locked with Paul's.

They stared at each other for a moment longer.

When he nodded to her and clasped his hands behind himself, away from his firearms, tears streamed from her eyes.

"Thank you," she whispered. "Oh, Paul, thank you."

"God be with you on your long journey," Paul said thickly.

Lauralee flicked tears from her eyes, smiled at him, then looked over her shoulder at Dancing Cloud. "Follow me," she whispered. She had already mapped out the plans for her escape out of the city, where she and Dancing Cloud would be less apt to meet up with anyone else.

As she swung her wagon around and headed it south through a narrow alley, she turned and gave Paul a last lingering look.

When he gave her a mock salute, then walked on around the building so that she could no longer see

him, she inhaled a shaky breath and snapped her reins
and rode away.

When she got to the far edge of Mattoon she took
another look over her shoulder. The orange spray of
the fire's reflection in the sky drew her eyes upward.

"Uncle Abner, you'll never know who saved you the
cost of demolishing your new-bought structure, will
you?" she whispered, then laughed softly and rode onward, Dancing Cloud riding ahead of her. He had taken
his rifle from its gun boot at the side of the horse. The
faint rays of the moon reflected in its barrel.

23

Each star is to me a sealed book,
Some tale of that loved one keeping.
                                    —MRS. CRAWFORD

"Do you think it is truly safe enough now to make camp?" Lauralee asked as Dancing Cloud made her a bed of green boughs, upon which he spread a blanket. She hugged herself, chilled and cramped by the coolness of the night air.

"As long as we do not make a campfire I feel that should a posse be after us, we will be safe enough for you to get some rest," Dancing Cloud said, drawing her into his embrace. He held her against him, touched to the very core of himself at the lengths she had gone to save him. "We have far to go, *o-ge-ye*. To survive the journey, you must get adequate rest."

Lauralee leaned limply against him. The warmth of his body melding into hers through her clothes made her feel better already. She closed her eyes and found herself drifting off. Then Dancing Cloud carried her to the bed of boughs and lay her gently upon it.

Smiling down at her peaceful sweetness, he drew another blanket over her and tucked it lovingly beneath her chin, and then snuggled it closer to her body on all sides.

He ran a hand over one of her cheeks, leaned down and kissed her, then rose slowly to his full height. He stretched his arms and yawned, but fought off sleep.

That would be a luxury he must wait for later. He could not be all that certain that Paul Brown could be trusted not to tell about Lauralee helping him escape. And how *was* Paul going to explain Dancing Cloud's absence unless he knew well the art of lying?

Because of his mistrust of all Yankees Dancing Cloud grabbed his rifle. He walked determinedly toward a rise in the land a few yards from where Lauralee trustingly slept. From that vantage point he could see for miles where a meadow stretched out before him, a thick forest at his back.

He sat down beside a cedar tree that was warped by the wind of centuries. It was bent and hunched into the shape of a crone, an eerie chanting old woman of the rain, wind, snow, and sun.

Laying his rifle across his lap, Dancing Cloud leaned his back against the bent cedar tree. Reaching inside his fringed jacket pocket he gathered up several juniper berries into the palm of his hand. He had accumulated a good supply of these berries from evergreen shrubs in the forest and had placed them in his pocket.

One by one he chewed on the berries, six to ten each day recommended. The berry was good for digestion. It also warded off sickness and weakness, and kept the mind awake and clear, which was essential now that they were running from the law. He could not see Sheriff Decker allowing him to escape that easily from his jail.

And it was up to Dancing Cloud to make sure that Sheriff Decker never caught up with him and Lauralee. Lauralee would be incarcerated like a common criminal, herself.

Dancing Cloud would never allow that to happen.

Even if he was forced to shoot and kill her Uncle Abner should he be among those who were a part of a posse.

Fighting off sleep as his eyelids grew heavy and his eyes burned, Dancing Cloud gave himself a shake, then looked slowly around him. They had just passed into Indiana a short while ago. It was daylight enough now to enjoy the beauty of the land.

Green. The wide stretch of the green meadow reaching out to the horizon was beautiful and serene.

Green. The symbol of everlasting life.

Dancing Cloud closed his eyes and thought of his home, missing his people and his home in his mountains with every fiber of his being. The sprigs of green, the whir of a rattle, the shush-shush of ankle bells, the lift and stamp of feet. . . .

A sound in the distance drew him from his reverie. His eyes quickly opened and he jumped to his feet. He listened again for the sound that had come to him like muffled, distant thunder.

Clutching the rifle in one hand, he cupped his other hand over his eyes and surveyed the horizon before him. His heartbeat quickened and he went numbly cold inside when he saw several horsemen approaching. They were far enough away so that they looked just like dots on the horizon.

But still they were there and Dancing Cloud did not have to think about who it might be.

He knew.

Sheriff Decker and a posse had managed to find the route of Dancing Cloud and Lauralee's travel!

Thoughts of Paul Brown came quickly to his mind again. He had surely allowed Dancing Cloud and Lauralee to leave Mattoon so that he could lead the posse to them and take on the appearance of a white man's "hero."

But for now he cast all blame aside. He and Lauralee had no time to waste.

He broke into a run down the slight incline. He hoped that neither Sheriff Decker, nor those men who made up the posse, had the ability to sniff out an actual trail made by Dancing Cloud and Lauralee's horses.

He hoped that it had only been a good guess that had led them *this* close.

If it was the latter, Dancing Cloud still felt hopeful

that he and Lauralee could elude Sheriff Decker and his men long enough so that they would tire of the search and return to Mattoon empty-handed.

"Lauralee," Dancing Cloud whispered harshly, bending over to give her a slight shake. "*O-ge-ye,* wake up. We must leave. I have spied Sheriff Decker in the distance. He brings with him many men."

The name Sheriff Decker drew Lauralee instantly awake. She rubbed her eyes and jumped to her feet.

Disoriented by having been awakened so suddenly, she moved in one direction, stopped, then moved in another.

Wild-eyed, she gazed up at Dancing Cloud as he came and steadied her by placing a hand on her shoulder.

"I'm frightened," she cried. "They will surely catch up with us now, Dancing Cloud. What will they do to us?"

Angry over Lauralee having been put in the position to be this afraid, Dancing Cloud's fingers gripped more tightly to the rifle, so tight that his knuckles were rendered white.

"Always before you have shown such strength and bravery in the face of danger," he said thickly. "Reach inside yourself and find the same strength now. To escape these men we must keep a level head."

Lauralee straightened her shoulders. She wiped the tears from her cheeks. "I'm sorry," she said as she looked into Dancing Cloud's dark, troubled eyes. "I'm all right now. I'll gather my things. I'll place them in my buggy. I shall be ready to go in a minute."

"Now is the time that your buggy must be left behind," Dancing Cloud said, seeing the shock register in her eyes. "To travel more quickly and to be able to ride to a higher plateau to give us better cover, we both must travel on horseback."

Lauralee glanced over her shoulder at her buggy. Should she leave it behind she must also leave most of her precious clothes that she had only recently pur-

chased. She could carry only one valise on her horse.
And there was only so much room in one embroidered
valise. She might not even have time to search through
her things for those belongings that meant more to her.

Seeing her disappointment and how troubled she was
over what was required of her, Dancing Cloud placed
a finger to her chin and turned her face around so that
she was looking sadly up at him.

"*O-ge-ye*, we would have been forced to leave your
buggy behind soon, anyhow," he said softly. "When we
neared my mountains, you would have soon seen how
impossible it would be to travel up the steep mountainside."

Her eyes searching his face, Lauralee said nothing
for a moment, then nodded. "I understand," she murmured. Then she sucked in a wild breath. "But there is
no extra saddle. I ... I ... would be forced to ride
bareback. I'm not sure that I *can*. I will be slipping and
sliding all the time. That would make it impossible for
a quick flight from the sheriff."

"You shall ride in my saddle on my horse," Dancing
Cloud said. "I shall ride yours bareback." He walked
away from her in a rush and set his rifle aside only
long enough to detach her horse from the buggy.

Lauralee looked into the distance and went limp
with fright when she saw that the men were no longer
just a dot along the horizon. She could make out their
shape. She knew for certain to expect Sheriff Decker
and Deputy Dobbs among those making up the posse.
More than likely Paul Brown was riding with him. He
had probably been the first one to even suggest forming the posse so that he could look big in the eyes of
the community if she and Dancing Cloud were brought
back to stand trial.

She gasped. She was almost certain that she could
make out her Uncle Abner riding tall in a saddle! It
made a keen melancholia sweep through her to think
that he would go along with such a thing as a posse,

when in the end it might mean that she would hang beside Dancing Cloud on a hangman's noose.

Exhaling a quavering, frightened breath, she ran to her buggy and dumped all of her belongings from her valises. Her fingers trembling, she sorted through it all and finally had one of her valises filled with those things that she felt she would need the most. Especially her toilet articles and dresses and skirts and blouses that would travel easier.

Grabbing up the valise, she ran to Dancing Cloud's horse. After tying it in with the other things that were secured to the saddlebags, she gazed with a longing at her buggy again, then at the bed that Dancing Cloud had made for her on the ground.

She then swung herself into the saddle just as Dancing Cloud mounted her horse. He edged the horse next to his own, his eyes steady with Lauralee's. "Keep up with me," he said flatly. "Never lag behind. We will be riding through the dense forest. You could be lost to me quickly."

Lauralee looked at the buggy and bed again. "They will for certain know that we were here," she said worriedly.

"As long as we have a good head start on them, it does not matter that they realize they have come close to catching us."

"But won't that make them more determined than ever to keep on coming after us?"

"Yes, that is so. But there is not much we can do about that except put many more miles between us today and keep far enough ahead so that they will soon tire of looking for us."

"Dancing Cloud, did you get any sleep at all?" Lauralee asked as they nudged their horses and rode away.

"Sleep will come later. During tests of endurance at my village I learned as a child the art of going days and nights without sleep."

Knowing that she was not as trained in the art of

staying awake, or of riding for hours on horseback, *or* of surviving in the wilderness, Lauralee wasn't sure if she could withstand all that now faced her before reaching Dancing Cloud's village.

At least for now, though, she felt that she no longer had to be afraid of Clint McCloud causing her harm. He would not be among those who were after her and Dancing Cloud. He would most definitely steer clear of them. He was, himself, a fugitive from justice!

She leaned low over Dancing Cloud's horse, wondering where Clint McCloud *might* be at this moment, where he might have gone to elude the law. . . .

His shoulders slumped, exhausted from the long ride from Mattoon, Clint McCloud drew a tight rein beside a log cabin. He had built this cabin with his very own hands amid a thick forest in North Carolina to hide his choice of wives, and especially the son who had come from his union with the Cherokee squaw.

Fog laying like a heavy-laden band of steel over the treetops reminded Clint of the Great Smoky Mountains. The mountains were only a half-day's ride from his cabin, a place that jarred his memory of the war every time he gazed upon the mysterious haze that could lay like puffs of smoke over the mountains for days.

The massacre.

The massacre had been his show of power over the damn redskins.

His wooden leg seeming to be even more heavy than usual, Clint moaned as he lifted it over the saddle.

Finally standing, he swayed and groaned again and held onto the saddle horn to steady himself.

Reeking with perspiration, his dark suit dust-laden, Clint stood there for a moment longer, then secured his horse's reins to a hitching rail.

He limped slowly around to the front of the cabin. The slow spiral of smoke rising from the chimney indicated that his wife, Soft Wind, was out of bed, preparing herself for her daily chores.

"She always rises with the sun," he grumbled to himself, recalling the many times that he had grabbed her back down onto the bed with him.

A wicked smile fluttered across his lips at the thought of her silken, copper body next to his. When she had been sixteen he had found her at an orphanage in Kentucky and had taken her away, with promises that if she married him, she would never want for another thing.

Soft Wind had been so grateful to him for having rescued her from a life where she had lacked identity that she had done everything to make him a perfect wife. And she had succeeded. He had been content with her.

Until she was with child. He had silently hoped throughout her pregnancy that the child would reflect his heritage. Not hers.

When their son had been born and every inch of him was Indian, Clint had not been able to openly love the child. Each time he looked at Brian Brave Walker he would be haunted by the Cherokee children whom he and his regiment had so viciously slaughtered that day in the Great Smoky Mountains during the Civil War. Killing had come so easy to him, no matter were they children or adults. He had joined the Union to kill anyone whose beliefs differed from his.

The Smoky Mountain Cherokee were among those who had not seen eye to eye with Clint's.

He had made them pay for those differences.

Now *he* was paying for what he had done to those people by not being free to love and embrace his very own son.

His thoughts returned to Mattoon and how ironic it had been that he had come face to face again with another Cherokee of his past.

Dancing Cloud.

Seeing the Cherokee, stalking him just outside Mattoon before Dancing Cloud arrived there with Lauralee, had convinced Clint that he *was* the Cherokee who filled his very soul with hate; the Cherokee who made his heart cry out for vengeance.

Grumbling to himself, half dragging his wooden leg behind him, Clint shoved the front door open. Upon first glance into the small cabin he found his wife and ten-year-old son cowering against the far wall, their eyes filled with fear at the mere sight of him.

"Is this the kind of reception I can always expect from my wife?" Clint said, glowering at Soft Wind. His eyes softened as he raked his eyes over her. Her sleek, black hair hung long and beautiful across her shoulders and down her back. Her tiny waist and her large bosom were revealed to him and made his heart skip a hungry beat as the buckskin fabric of her dress clung sensually to her curves.

He had missed her.

He never stopped hungering for her.

His gaze shifted to his son. It took him aback somewhat to see the look of defiance in Brian Brave Walker's eyes. At first glance it had looked as though he was cowering.

In truth, it was his mother who held Brian Brave Walker in place so that he would not be able to display his disobedience to his father openly.

Clint went across the room, past the fancy, overstuffed chairs that he had brought to Soft Wind in an effort to please her after realizing that she not only feared him, but hated him as well. Clint stopped in front of her and gathered a handful of her hair in his fingers and gave it a yank, causing her to cry out with pain and stumble toward him.

"The baby," he said thinly. "Where's the baby?"

Soft Wind nodded toward a small cradle in the shadows.

Clint released Soft Wind's hair and lumbered over to the cradle. Leaning over, he unfolded a blanket from around the small baby, then slung his hands into the air in a fit of fury.

"It's a girl and her skin is not white!" he shouted.

"She is Indian! Just like her brother, she is Indian through and through."

"Please do not be angry," Soft Wind sobbed. "She is a beautiful child no matter what color her skin is. Please do not harm her!"

Clint went to Soft Wind and grabbed her by the shoulders. He shook her as he leered down at her. "I told you what I'd do if that brat was Indian!" he shouted. "I'm going to take her away!"

"No!" Soft Wind cried. "Do not take my baby away!"

"Shut up, squaw," Clint said, giving her another rough shake. He then shoved her down onto the bed and stood with his fists on his hips over her. "She won't stay another night beneath my roof. Do you hear? I'll never lay claim to her. Never!"

"Leave my mother alone," Brian Brave Walker said, taking a bold step toward his father. "I told her she should leave with my baby sister when she had the chance. She should not have to give in to your abuse only because you rescued her so long ago from an orphanage." Brian Brave Walker thrust his bare chest out proudly above his fringed buckskin breeches. "I told Mother that I could care for her *and* my baby sister."

Clint backhanded Brian Brave Walker in the mouth, causing a trickle of blood to spill down his chin. "You shut your mouth, savage brat," he snarled. "You'd best keep your suggestions to yourself as far as your mother and sister are concerned. You know that I told her if she ever left I'd hunt her down and kill her. I don't want no other man pawin' her. She's mine. All mine. So you see, *brat,* she ain't goin' nowhere. As far as *you* are concerned, I'd welcome your absence in my home. I ain't never had no use for you, nor have you for *me.* There'd be no love lost if you'd just walk away and not set foot on my property again."

Clint went and stood over Brian Brave Walker, his eyes narrowed. "Go," he said darkly. "But don't bring anyone back here thinkin' you're going to rescue your mother and sister. I'll shoot anyone who gets near my property. Even *you*."

Soft Wind rose shakily from the bed. Clint saw her and went and held her back as she tried to reach for Brian Brave Walker.

"No!" she cried. "Son, do not listen to him. Do not leave your mother!"

Brian Brave Walker wiped the blood from his mouth on the back of a hand, his eyes wavering into his mother's. Then he spun around on a moccasined heel and went and stood over the cradle and took a lingering, last look at his sister. He stifled a sob as she gazed up at him with her trusting dark eyes. Never would he see her again!

Turning his eyes away from her he left the cabin in a mad run. He trembled inside as he heard his mother yelling his name over and over again—and then she became quiet.

He closed his eyes and doubled his hands into tight fists at his sides as he envisioned what was now happening to his mother. His father had surely thrown her on the bed and was using her as though she were no better than an animal.

Then his father would take the child away!

"*Aieee!*" he cried in Cherokee as he broke into a hard run away from the cabin.

Brian Brave Walker had thought of leaving many times. But his concern for his mother had kept him there, with her.

Now it was just too much for him.

He was ten winters of age.

If he was among his true people he would be classified as a brave!

"I must search until I find my mother's true people," he whispered. "She has told me often that they are not far away."

Fearing that Brian Brave Walker would leave her, she had never told him exactly which village she had

fled from during the war, having found a refuge in the
orphanage when she had been near to starving to death.

But he knew that it could not be too far away. He
would find it. He would go there.

But how could he tell the elders about his mother?
How could he tell them about his baby sister?

His father's warnings consumed him. He knew that
Clint McCloud would follow through with his threats.
He was capable of doing anything.

No. Brian Brave Walker could not endanger his
mother by telling the truth of her captivity.

Not now, anyhow. But somehow he would find a
way to end his father's tyranny! His mother had to be
rescued from a life of cruel treatment wrought upon
her by an evil husband.

He ran even harder at the thought of searching the
mountains and finally becoming as one with his mother's people. He would never think again about having
blood of that vile, insane white man flowing through
his veins. This man had never been a true father.

To Brian Brave Walker, this man was nothing.

24

For all my world is in your arms,
My sun and stars are you.

—Sara Teasdale

The hot August sun was slowly burning away the blue
haze of morning. Fearing the posse, and saddened over
her uncle being among those men who were after
Dancing Cloud, and even herself, Lauralee fought hard
to keep up with Dancing Cloud.

But oh, how she missed the comforts of her buggy.
She had never stayed on a horse for so long. Her thighs
ached. Her bottom was numb and seemed glued to the
saddle.

Yet she still forced her steed into a hard gallop now
that the forest and the slight mountain ridge had been
left behind. They had come out on a smooth meadow.
The grass was green and high. A stream of cold, clear
water ran along one edge, watering the valley.

Lauralee's eyes feasted on the water as she rode
alongside the stream. Her throat was parched. Her lips
burned. Dirt seemed plastered to her face.

"Dancing Cloud," she cried. "Please, darling. I need
a drink. I need to stretch my weary, aching bones.
Can't we please stop for at least a few moments? The
water. I can hardly pass it up. I'm so thirsty. I have
never been as thirsty."

Dancing Cloud wheeled his horse to a quick stop.
Sighing with relief, Lauralee followed his lead.

He rode up to Lauralee and reached a gentle hand to her cheek. "Yes, *o-ge-ye*, we will stop for water," he said thickly. "We have left the posse far behind us."

He yawned and stretched his arms high above his head. "I do not like confessing to how my body needs rest," he said.

"Dancing Cloud, you have just cause to be tired," Lauralee said softly. "You were recently wounded. You have not fully regained your strength."

Her gaze lowered and she gaped openly with alarm when she saw blood spreading on his buckskin shirt, over his shoulder wound. "Lord, Dancing Cloud," she gasped. "The stitches may have broken loose. We *must* stop now. You have pushed yourself much more than your body can tolerate. I will bathe your wound. I will get a petticoat from my valise and rip it into strips for a bandage."

Dancing Cloud looked down at the seepage of blood through his shirt. He reached a hand there and slightly pressed his fingers against it, wincing when pain shot through his wound.

Lauralee saw Dancing Cloud's discomfort. "See?" she said, her jaw tight with determination. She tried to hide her own discomfort when sliding from the saddle made her aches worsen. She could hardly stand placing her full weight on her feet. There was not one inch of her body that did not ache worse than any toothache that she had ever experienced.

Forcing herself not to react to her discomfort, Lauralee secured her horse's reins to a low limb of a tree, then took Dancing Cloud's reins and secured them with her own.

She turned to Dancing Cloud. She frowned with worry as she slowly pushed his fringed buckskin shirt over his head.

She dropped the shirt with alarm when she realized the seriousness of what the hard travel had caused. Several threads were hanging bloody and twisted from his wound, his skin open and raw as blood trickled in a tiny stream from it.

"Damn them," she said, hating the posse, even her uncle. "Damn them all. Why couldn't they leave us alone?"

She gazed sadly into Dancing Cloud's eyes. "Why couldn't they have believed us?" she murmured. "Especially my Uncle Abner. He saw the sort of man you were. It seems impossible that he could truly believe you are guilty of having stolen that stallion."

"White men believe what they wish about men with red skin," Dancing Cloud said, his voice drawn. "Your uncle's skin is white. Why should he be different from the others?"

He clasped gentle hands to her shoulders. "And remember this, my *o-ge-ye*," he said softly. "I am not only Indian. I am also labeled a Rebel. So you see? There are too many things about me that brought anger into the heart and eyes of those who call me a horse thief. Do you not see that this Cherokee need not do anything to be accused? In the white man's hearts, this Cherokee is already guilty."

"It's so unfair," Lauralee said, tears pooling in the corners of her eyes.

"Many things in life are not fair," Dancing Cloud said thickly. "You live. You die. That is the way it has been from the beginning of time. What you do between those two certainties is up to each individual. Whether they leave a life they can be proud of? Or whether they choose to be heathenlike. I chose to walk with a proud chin and heart. Those who chase me down now as though I'm no better than a dog? They are of the breed of man whose life is filled with hate and vengeance."

"I hate to think that of my uncle," Lauralee said, her voice breaking. "During the short time I was with my aunt and uncle I grew fond of them. I wish that I were wrong about how I am feeling about my uncle now. I see him as . . . as . . . a *cad*."

She looked at his wound again, then grabbed his

hand and led him to the stream. "Sit, please," she murmured. "Let me bathe your wound."

"First I will find a tassel flower plant," he said softly. "From its dry-powdered leaf I will make a poultice that will draw the blood from my wound."

After gathering up several of the dry-powdered leaves, Dancing Cloud eased down on the ground, welcoming this moment of reprieve off his horse. He folded his legs beneath him and watched and smiled at Lauralee's attentiveness to him, in how she cupped the water into her hands, and how she leaned her hands over his wound and allowed the water to trickle freely and slowly across it.

"Are you certain it is all right to place the poultice on the wound?"

"Do you not know that the Indian ofttimes knows more about the property of plants and the cure of diseases than does the trained white botanist or physician?" he said matter-of-factly. "Living as we do in the open air in close communion with nature, we know well the knowledge of properties of plants."

"I would do anything to see that you are well," Lauralee said, applying the herbal poultice to his flesh.

"The plant world is friendly to the human species and constantly at the willing service of those in need of their services," Dancing Cloud said softly.

Lauralee smiled at him, then went to her valise and removed a cotton petticoat from it. She rushed back to Dancing Cloud, surprised when she found him stretched out on his back, asleep. So quickly he had gone to sleep. So easily.

But then why wouldn't he, she thought to herself. While she had gotten a moment's sleep back at their campsite, he had kept a lookout. Had he not, the posse would have swept down upon them like a swarm of hornets.

The trees whispered peacefully overhead as the breeze sighed through them. Lauralee found that she was suddenly drowsy, yet she shook off the need of sleep and continued with the task at hand. She ripped long strips of cloth from her petticoat. She bent low over Dancing Cloud. She had a hard time lifting his right shoulder to wrap the bandage around it and beneath his arm. His muscled body seemed the weight of lead as he slept.

But after a while she had the wound comfortably covered. When he awakened she would take a few turns with the bandage across his massive, muscled chest and secure it at his back with a knot.

Lauralee moved to her knees and gazed down at Dancing Cloud with an intense love. She drew a ragged breath. How could anyone accuse him of anything vile?

There was such a gentleness in his expression as he slept. She dared to touch his lips, their sensual fullness. She ran her fingers then across the lean line of his jaw, a jaw that showed strength.

Her pulse racing, she then ran her fingers over his fine-boned frame, across his sleek, copper chest, and then along his broad shoulders.

Again she ran her fingers across his cheeks, along features that were sharply chiseled and masculine.

"Oh, how I love you," she whispered. She leaned over him and gave him a soft kiss on his lips. "How I adore you."

Realizing that she needed rest now, she sighed languorously. She crawled to the water. Bending low over it she cupped her hands into it and brought the fresh, cold liquid to her mouth and drank it. She smiled over at the horses. They had wandered to the water and were lapping up long drinks.

Her eyes burned with the need of sleep. She crawled back to Dancing Cloud. She gazed down at him again, then turned her eyes to peer into the distance. Slowly she raked the horizon with them, looking for riders. Dare she give in to her need to sleep?

But dare she not? If she did not get adequate rest how could she go on? Her body was not conditioned to such punishments as riding a horse for long hours, or lack of sleep and rest.

And although her stomach growled with her need of food, sleep and rest seemed more important at this moment. When Dancing Cloud awakened they would take time to eat some more of the provisions that she had taken from her aunt's pantry.

"Now the sheriff can add 'thief' to my itinerary while posting wanted posters on me for helping a prisoner escape," she said.

Too weary to think further on the present mishaps of her life, Lauralee sank to the ground and folded herself against Dancing Cloud's side. She snuggled close, her one arm thrown over his chest. The drifting off to sleep felt so soft and delicious.

Lauralee and Dancing Cloud awakened with a start at the same moment when the sound of approaching horses drew closer. They had no chance to rise to their feet. Too soon the posse was there, circled around them on three sides.

Feeling trapped and breathless, Lauralee grabbed for Dancing Cloud's hand. Her eyes locked with her uncle's as he dismounted his horse. She gulped hard when he came to her and Dancing Cloud and stood over them, his hands on his hips just above his low-slung Colts.

Her gaze then shifted to Sheriff Decker as he slid out of his saddle and came and stood beside Abner. And then to Deputy Dobbs who sauntered to Sheriff Decker's other side.

Dancing Cloud eyed his rifle. He had been careless to have left it in its gun boot at the side of his horse. But being so tired and sleepy, his logic had not been as sharp as it should have been.

He slipped an arm around Lauralee. Easily and guardedly he eased her up from the ground with him. His gaze searched slowly from man to man as they stood cold-silent and stiff before him and Lauralee.

Then his attention shifted back to Abner Peterson when he took Lauralee's hand and urged her forward, away from Dancing Cloud. His insides tightened as he waited to see what Peterson's next moves might be, and what he decided to do about Lauralee. Could he forgive her for having helped Dancing Cloud escape? Or was she a criminal now in the white man's eyes?

"Uncle Abner, please don't take us back to Mattoon," Lauralee pleaded.

"Lauralee, you assisted in an escape," Abner said. "Don't you know the extent of that crime? How you might be sentenced to life imprisonment? Or worse yet—to a hanging?"

Lauralee paled. Her throat constricted, making it impossible for her to speak to her uncle. She wanted to scream at her uncle—ask him how he could treat her this way? If her father were alive, he would come and make Abner Peterson pay for what he was doing, not only to his daughter, but to his close, loyal friend.

But she could not find the words. She was filled with an angry despair only known by her one other time in her life—when her mother had been assaulted.

Dancing Cloud stepped up beside Lauralee. "I go willingly back with you to stand trial," he said, holding his wrists out for handcuffs. "But spare your niece of such humiliation. She does not deserve to be treated as a common criminal. She released an innocent man. She is as innocent, herself."

Lauralee's eyes pooled with tears as she looked up at Dancing Cloud. Then she gasped and grew weak in the knees when Paul Brown rode up. He had apparently lagged behind the others. With him, tied by a rope into his reins, was the beautiful, sleek white stallion that was the cause for all of these misunderstandings.

Her thoughts became scrambled.

Where had Paul gotten the horse?

Why had he brought it *here*?

"Paul, bring the stallion to me," Abner said, turning to smile at Paul as he dismounted.

Dancing Cloud's heart raced at the sight of the horse and what it might mean. If they had the stallion, then they surely had the true criminal!

But if so, why had the posse been so hell-bent on trailing him and Lauralee?

They had been unmerciful in their pursuit!

Lauralee's eyes widened in disbelief when Paul brought the horse to her uncle, who in turn, placed the reins in Dancing Cloud's hands.

"He's yours, Dancing Cloud," Abner said, his eyes wavering over at Lauralee. He then looked at Dancing Cloud. "Damn it, Dancing Cloud, you deserve the horse. And there'll be nobody questioning your owner-ship. He's bought and paid for. *I* paid for him."

Lauralee's head was spinning. "Uncle Abner, I don't understand any of this," she said, watching how proudly Dancing Cloud stroked the stallion's sleek mane. "Does this mean that you found the true crimi-nal?"

"Sure as hell did," Abner said in a low, tight growl. "The very man who owned him is the guilty party."

"Kevin Banks?" Lauralee gasped. "How? Why?"

"To make it look bad for Dancing Cloud," Abner said. He took Lauralee's hands and drew her into his embrace. "Honey, Kevin hid the horse. He said that Dancing Cloud stole it. He made up the lie about the Pratt boy having seen Dancing Cloud snooping around the corral that night, near the stallion. Kevin hoped that Dancing Cloud would hang for the crime."

Lauralee's eyes searched Abner's. "But why would he do such a thing?" she said, her voice soft and drawn.

"You know the answer already. Dancing Cloud is an Indian and he fought against the North, and . . ." Abner said, pausing to glance over at Dancing Cloud.

Then he turned back to Lauralee. "And because Kevin did not see it fit for a white woman to be cavort-ing with an Indian."

Lauralee blushed and quickly lowered her eyes.

Then she just as quickly and stubbornly gazed up at Abner again. "Kevin Banks is an evil, vile man," she said, jerking her hands from her uncle's. She clenched them into fists at her sides. "I hope that he's behind bars now."

"Yes," Abner said, sighing. "He's incarcerated. Thanks to my snooping *around,* he's behind bars, Lauralee. I just couldn't rest easy with Dancing Cloud being accused of stealing that horse. It came to me that night of the fire. I awakened with a start that Kevin might be lying. By damn, Lauralee, I found the stallion locked up in a shed on property only a few feet away from The Stables."

Lauralee's eyes wavered as she smiled wanly up at her uncle. "The fire," she murmured. "Did it totally destroy your building?"

Now beginning to relax with the whole situation, Abner laughed loosely. "Yes, by damn, to the ground," he said, nodding. "And arson is suspected. But I tell you, honey, if I ever caught up with the son of a gun that set fire to that shack, I'd not place him behind bars. I'd offer him a handshake for having gotten rid of the place for me."

Lauralee started to blurt out that she had done it, then decided not to. If the sheriff had a mind to, he could arrest her for aiding and abetting in the release of a prisoner; stealing from her aunt; and setting fire to her uncle's building. One thing had led to another until she had a string of crimes lined up behind her.

"During the commotion of the fire you helped Dancing Cloud escape?" Abner said, frowning down at her, as though he had just read her thoughts. "Didn't you know the dangers, Lauralee, of setting a man free from jail?"

"I'd do it all over again if Dancing Cloud was arrested a second time," Lauralee said with a lifted chin. Then her eyes softened into her uncle's. "He *is* free now to go on to his village, isn't he? You don't plan to arrest *me,* do you, for my criminal act tonight?"

"You're both free to go," Abner said, stepping around Lauralee. He placed a hand on Dancing Cloud's shoulder. "Son, I know I'd be wasting my time asking Lauralee to return to Mattoon with me. Any woman who'd put her life on the line for a man like she did proves just how much she loves the man. She'll be going on with you to your mountain home. Take care of her. Guard her with your life. She's precious, Dancing Cloud. Precious."

Tears flowed from Lauralee's eyes. She flung herself into her uncle's arms. "Thank you," she murmured. "Thank you so much."

She looked over her shoulder at Paul Brown. They exchanged warm smiles.

25

My love is such that rivers cannot quench,
Nor ought but love from thee give recompence.
—ANNE BRADSTREET

Stunned at how things had turned out, Lauralee leaned
against Dancing Cloud as they watched the posse ride
away.

When Abner turned and gave Lauralee a final wave
of goodbye, she choked on a sob and returned the
wave. With him went what she had always prayed for
when she was a child.

A chance to be a family again, with a mother and father.

If she could have looked into the future all of those
long years ago and had seen herself turning her back
on this opportunity, she would have never thought it
possible.

"Are you certain you do not wish to go with him?"
Dancing Cloud asked, drawing Lauralee's eyes suddenly to his.

"You always seem to be able to read my thoughts,"
she stammered.

"You were thinking about wishing to go to your uncle?" Dancing Cloud's eyes filled with a sudden hurt.

"No, no," Lauralee said, laughing lightly. "It's not
that. It's that you seemed to know what I was *thinking*
about, not that I regretted not going with my uncle."

She turned and faced him. She gently framed his

face between her hands. "Darling, I was thinking also of long ago, when I was a little girl, wishing to be a part of a family," she murmured. "I had thought that family could mean only having a mother and father. I had not ventured as far as to think about when I would find a man with whom I would start my own family."

"And you have found that man?" Dancing Cloud asked, his frown fading into a warm smile.

"Oh, yes, yes," Lauralee said, leaning against him as he circled his arms around her waist.

"And, darling, don't you see?" she whispered, looking adoringly up at him. "It is all now possible and we may do as we wish without any interference from anyone. Our world is now the most perfect world of all."

She did not let on that she still feared Clint McCloud with every ounce of her being, that *he* might be the one to spoil their happiness, to possibly even *kill* any chances of them having a beautiful future together.

No. She would not say that man's name again in a whisper to herself, or aloud to Dancing Cloud. She would try and force him from her mind again. She had almost managed to after having fallen in love with Dancing Cloud.

But seeing the Yankee fiend again in Mattoon had started the cycle all over again in her mind . . . the remembrance of her mother being raped . . . of her mother being murdered. . . .

"We are free now to fulfill our intertwined destinies," Dancing Cloud said, brushing a soft kiss across her lips. "Once my mourning for my father is behind me after we reach my village, *then* I can agree with you that everything is right in our world."

The sound of powerful wings overhead, like a vast rush of wind, drew their thoughts elsewhere. Eyes wide, and standing arm and arm, they looked upward.

Lauralee sucked in a wild breath of wonder as she watched two eagles overhead doing a kind of mating dance in midair, oblivious of an audience. First they were two birds on the wing, then they merged as one

Then as one tilted up in the down draft of the evening breeze, the other went down, soaring . . . soaring, the deep blue of evening and the orange of the sunset mingling and captured gloriously in the sheen of the feathers.

As the eagles met again and swept across the sky so effortlessly, their feathers wrapped around their sandy faces like human hair over a goddess's cheek.

And then they soared on away and got lost to Dancing Cloud and Lauralee's sight high in a puff of white clouds, only then to reemerge as only two dots far away in the darkening heaven.

"I've never seen anything as beautiful," Lauralee said, still touched deeply by the sight.

Dancing Cloud took Lauralee's hand and turned her to face him again. "We are like the eagles, free to love, free to mate," he said huskily.

"I want you so badly," Lauralee said. Her hands moved gently over his bare chest, savoring the touch of his smooth, copper flesh.

Her fingers gingerly touched the bandage that she had tied over his wound. "Perhaps we should wait?" she murmured. "Aren't you in pain?"

"There is much pain in my body now, *ii*, yes," Dancing Cloud said, his eyes flared with hungry intent.

"Then, darling, we have time now to lie down so that you can rest without the fear of being overcome by lawmen," Lauralee said, easing away from him.

His hands held her in place as they locked around her waist.

She stared up at him. "Dancing Cloud, you are looking at me as though . . . as though . . . rest is the last thing *on* your mind," she said, smiling slowly.

She trembled sensually when he took one of her hands and led it to the place on his body that throbbed and ached with need of her.

"You are feeling my pain, my need," he said throatily.

A hot flush rose from her neck to her cheeks when

she felt the most identifiable shape of his manhood straining against the inside buckskin fabric of his breeches.

"How can I ease your pain, my darling?" she teased, her hands already stroking him through the soft fabric.

Dancing Cloud leaned his head back. He closed his eyes and moaned as her fingers stirred a fire within him. The flames grew higher, licking their way through him. His whole body quivered with the pleasure.

Wanting more, needing more, he placed his thumbs at the waist of his breeches on each side and slowly lowered them past his hips, then kicked them away.

He spread his legs and again enjoyed her caresses, her hands soft, sweet, and warm.

But when he felt that the pleasure was building to an intensity that threatened sharing it with her, he gently eased her hand away.

Lauralee's heart throbbed as Dancing Cloud removed her blouse, her skirt, and her underthings. Her body tingled with pleasure each time the flesh of his fingers brushed against her body while disrobing her.

When he grazed a breast, she sucked in a breath of pleasure.

When his fingers brushed against her thigh, she trembled and closed her eyes.

After she was fully nude he stepped away from her, his dark, stormy eyes feeding on the sweetness of her flesh. His gaze burned along her bare skin as his eyes swept over her with a silent, urgent message.

In turn, her eyes moved over the sleekness of his body, his muscular thighs, his narrow hips, his long, lean torso.

When she gazed down at the full length of his manhood remembrances of how he so magnificently made love made her shoulders sway with unleashed passion.

Dancing Cloud placed his hands to Lauralee's waist and led her to a blanket on the ground. As night fell over the valley, a faint silvery mist appeared above the water. The frogs began to boom and croak. The forest behind them became alive with the call of insects.

Dancing Cloud knelt down over Lauralee and silently gazed upon her loveliness again.

Her coppery red hair lay disarrayed around her smooth, creamy shoulders. Her hips curving voluptuously from her waist framed the triangle of hair beneath which lay the secrets of her desire. It was a hot, moist place where he would again find escape and intense pleasure.

Unable to wait any longer for that paradise that he always found in Lauralee's arms, Dancing Cloud blanketed her with his body.

Lauralee's soft, full thighs opened as Dancing Cloud's loins surged forth. He entered her with one deep thrust. His lean, sinewy buttocks moved rhythmically within her, plunging into her, reaching deeply for her innermost part.

Feeling the quickening of her senses, Lauralee clung to Dancing Cloud with a rapturous intensity. Soft moans repeatedly surfaced from inside her as his lips came to her in a grinding, fierce and fevered kiss.

He kissed her long and deep, his hand cupping a breast, his thumb rolling the nipple. He squeezed the breast gently, pulling and rotating the stiff, resilient nipple.

Her hips moved and rocked.

She pressed her pelvis into his.

Dancing Cloud felt the nerves in his body tensing, the wild abandon near. His hand moved over her creamy flesh, then held her in a torrid embrace as he shoved more deeply into her.

He lay his cheek against hers and closed his eyes. He anchored her fiercely still for a moment, then again plunged into her.

The blood was spinning hot through his veins.

Lauralee tremored sensually when Dancing Cloud pressed his lips to her throat, then swept his tongue down her flesh, soon lapping one of her nipples to an even more taut tightness. The golden web of magic was spinning around them, capturing them as their other world slowly melted away.

Then the warmth spread, bringing them together as though one, their bodies quaking, throbbing, and shuddering.

Lauralee arched and cried out and clung to Dancing Cloud with a wildness and desperation as that most wondrous of feelings overwhelmed her. She could tell that he had reached that same pinnacle of pleasure, for he was plunging over and over again inside her. His grip was tight, as though she were being held within a vise.

When their bodies subsided and Dancing Cloud rolled away from Lauralee, he knelt over her and lifted her head from the ground, raining kisses on her lids, and on her hair.

"I so adore you," Lauralee whispered. Her hands traveled over him, never tiring of feeling his wonderfully muscled copper body. She rediscovered the contours of his sculpted face as he leaned only a fraction away from her, his eyes filled with a loving warmth and peace.

Dancing Cloud suddenly laughed softly as his stomach growled, filling the night air with the sound. "More of myself now needs fed," he said. "My desires have been fed. Now I must see to the needs of my stomach."

The night breeze had turned cool. Lauralee sat up and drew the blanket around her shoulders. "If you build a fire I shall prepare our evening meal," she said, her eyes twinkling into his.

"I believe that is an easy enough bargain to make," Dancing Cloud said, pulling on his breeches. He slipped his shirt over his head, again aware of the pain in his shoulder. While making love, he had been oblivious of everything but Lauralee.

Lauralee hurried into her own clothes and set about spreading a tablecloth on the ground, and then sliced an apple, peeled a banana, and placed these with a hunk of cheese on a platter.

Unwrapping a checkered table napkin, she withdrew a loaf of bread, surprising Dancing Cloud that she seemed to have thought of everything.

Soon the aroma of coffee filled the air.

Crickets chirped musically.

An owl hooted in the distance.

Lauralee playfully fed Dancing Cloud small slices of banana. "I feel wicked I am so happy," she murmured. "But I have waited so long for such a happiness, I shan't allow anything to spoil it."

She paused.

"How much longer will it take us to reach your home in the mountains?"

Dancing Cloud's smile faded as he gazed into the leaping flames of the fire. "Many more days," he said dryly. "Then duties to my father must be paid."

He looked slowly over at her. "Do not feel neglected when I begin mourning my father's death with my people," he said softly. "Although I spoke with my father in the spirit world, his spirit is not wholly there until the proper mourning has been seen to. I could not do that until I was among my people. We all mourn together our greater losses."

"I shall mourn with you," Lauralee said, moving to sit beside him. She melted against him when he swung his arm around her shoulders.

"My people might feel uncomfortable about that," he said thickly. "Until they grow to know you better, I would think that it would be best for you not to join the mourning rituals for my father. In time, though, you will be a part of everything I and my people do."

Lauralee felt hurt by the rejection, then thought more about it and understood. He had his private times to see to. She would not interfere.

She rested against him. What he had just said pulled her into worrisome thoughts again about things that had concerned her when she discovered they were in love. She had heard Dancing Cloud say more than once that his clan of Cherokee were full bloods. She could not help but worry again about whether or not his people would tolerate her breaking this practice? Or even Dancing Cloud, for being the one to bring her into their fold?

It gave her a deep, dark feeling of apprehension to think that possibly they would look to her as one might look upon an alien.

A shadow moved through the darkness, silencing the night creatures in its wake. Brian Brave Walker's eyes were wild and wide as he ventured on through the dense forest. His father, who had never been a father at all in the true sense of the word, hadn't prepared him to know how to fend for one's self. He had never taught his son how to shoot a gun, or how to ride a horse, or *anything*.

Brian Brave Walker had been an object to his father, an object for loathing, nothing more. He had not guided him into ways of other children Brian Brave Walker's age. He had never been alone with his father.

In truth, Clint McCloud was Brian Brave Walker's father by blood only. Not by emotions and bonds of loving and parental guiding.

Brian Brave Walker wanted desperately to live up to the name that his mother had given him when he had been born. Brave. He had to be brave! Or he might not survive living alone without the guidance and loving of a mother.

Tonight the air was cool, causing goose bumps to rise on his flesh. He hugged himself as he fought the dense thickets of briars and creeping vines. He flinched when a sound behind him made him think that perhaps his father might have decided to come for him after all.

"He sent me away. He *will* be glad to be rid of me," Brian Brave Walker said in a harsh whisper. "I do not have to worry about him coming for me. My mother's pleas for him to come and search for me will fall on deaf ears."

His spine stiffened and his jaw tightened when he thought of what his father was perhaps even now still forcing on his mother. McCloud would always be gone for several weeks or months, but when he returned to his cabin he would wreak sexual havoc on Soft Wind's body for endless days!

"I wish to release her from her life of slavery to that man," Brian Brave Walker whispered as he stepped high over a slender fallen tree. "But I do not dare try."

He would never forget his father's threats.

"And he means everything he says," Brian Brave Walker said, his voice breaking.

Determined to get farther and farther away from the home that was never a haven, the young Cherokee broke into a mad run. He knocked limbs away overhead as they bumped into his face. He groaned when briars pierced his flesh through his buckskin breeches.

Then he crumpled to the ground, panting, exhaustion overcoming him.

He curled up on his side on the dried-up fallen leaves of last autumn.

Sobbing, he fell into a restless sleep.

In his dreams, a Cherokee warrior came to him out of the clouds in the sky. The warrior rode a magnificent white stallion. His horse had beautiful, translucent wings. Ah, but how majestically it moved its legs as it traveled down to earth.

The warrior swept Brian Brave Walker upon his saddle with him. The Cherokee warrior held him within his powerful arms as he rode away, Brian Brave Walker finally feeling some semblance of peace, and of being protected. . . .

He awakened with a start and rose quickly to a sitting position. His eyes darted around him, his heart pounding.

A dream?

Oh, surely it had not been only a dream.

It had seemed so real.

He could even now feel the strength of that warrior's arms around his waist. He could feel the protectiveness that those arms had given him. He had belonged on that magnificent white steed with that noble warrior!

Sudden sobs racked Brian Brave Walker's body. It *had* been only a dream.

He was still alone.

The night was dark and filled with mystery.

A sudden owl's call a short distance away was hauntingly real.

He lay back down and pulled himself into a fetal position. Feeling way less brave than what he wished, and more lonesome than he ever thought possible, he sobbed himself to sleep again.

26

The bond of nature draws me to my own,
My own in thee, for what thou art is mine.

—JOHN MILTON

The air was crisp and fresh as a sweet breeze swept down over the pine-covered hills. Dancing Cloud led the way up the steep incline on his white stallion, his other horse straying behind on a rope, Lauralee following. They had left the meadowland below them sometime ago and had entered the enchantment of cool, green pines where a film of haze hung low over them.

Having entered into an existence that was beyond her wildest imagination, Lauralee clung to her reins as she took everything in. "The Great Smoky Mountains," she whispered to herself as she continued studying the quiet landscape.

The path led upward, winding through trees and around rushing streams and beautiful waterfalls. She had read books about these mountains and their sheer majestic beauty and mystique. They were a range of the southern Appalachian highlands that stretched from North Carolina into Tennessee.

She was witnessing this grandeur today, the mountainside containing spectacular scenery. The summits and ridges were crowned with giant forests of red spruces.

At the lower elevations Lauralee had seen many flowering dogwood, redbud, and the serviceberry. She had felt that she might have died and gone to heaven when she had ridden past dense stands of mountain laurel, white-blossomed rhododendron and azaleas, which had formed almost impenetrable thickets.

She tensed when through a break in the trees she saw a black bear standing on a ledge far to the right side of where she was traveling. In only the short time she had been riding up the mountainside she had seen much wild life. Not only black bears, but also white-tailed deer, foxes, bobcats, raccoons, ruffed rouse, turkeys, and a variety of beautifully colored songbirds.

Dancing Cloud looked over his shoulder at Lauralee. "Do you not see now what, besides my people, has drawn me back to these mountains?" he asked, his voice echoing into many voices as it spun into the clear, quiet air around them.

The path was wide enough for him to edge over slightly, to give Lauralee room to catch up with him. When she reached him, she sidled her horse beside his.

"Is not my mountain paradise, my *o-ge-ye?*" he said thickly.

"I've never seen anything as beautiful," Lauralee said softly. "When I was a small girl in Tennessee I could see this stretch of mountains from my bedroom. I often gazed upon the mystical haze that hung over them, wondering what lay beneath it. I always thought that the mountains were smoking. I am so thrilled now to finally know what truly lies here breathlessly beautiful beneath the haze."

"Your father traveled this path often when you were a child," Dancing Cloud said. "He was an Indian agent who cared for those he served. That is why, at eight winters of age, I grew so fond of, and so admired, your father. He and my father became as close as any brothers who share their lives."

"And now both of our fathers are gone," Lauralee said, a sob catching in her throat. "Wouldn't it have been wonderful for them to have seen the depths of our love for each other? And to see that their bonding continues on now, even though they have passed on to the other side?"

"They *are* with us now," Dancing Cloud said. He reached a hand heavenward, then swung it slowly from one side to the other, encompassing everything around him. "Do you not feel their presence in the breeze and in the warm touch of the sun upon your flesh? Do you not see them in the flowers? Their spirit path will always be ours to follow. They embrace us as we move into our future as one heart and soul, my *o-ge-ye*."

"You always have such a beautiful way of expressing yourself," she said, sighing.

"You bring forth from deeply within me feelings that normally I would not express aloud," Dancing Cloud said. "With you, I feel such inner peace and happiness."

"As I feel the same because of you." She paused and enjoyed the call of the birds and the hum of the bees. She inhaled the sweet fragrance of the flowers that clung to the mountainside. She again absorbed the glories of her surroundings.

"How long now until we reach your village?" she finally blurted, anxious, yet afraid, to arrive there. If it were possible, she would postpone ever leaving this beautiful place where it seemed no other people existed except for herself and her beloved.

She could not stop being afraid of Dancing Cloud's people's reaction to her. Her heart thumped wildly at the thought of moving among them, their eyes intent on her, perhaps hating her. . . .

"My village lays beyond that rise yonder," Dancing Cloud said, pointing. "Long ago my Wolf Clan of Cherokee settled in a valley where they were sheltered from the worst harshness of winter and the intrusion of those who might be our enemy."

"Yet even that did not stop the damn Yankees as they wreaked their treachery during the war," Lauralee said solemnly. "No one could escape their plundering, it seems. Both of our lives were altered because of the Yankees' hunger for blood and power."

She hung her head as thoughts of her Uncle Abner swam through her consciousness. He had been a Yankee and he and Nancy were precious to her. It seemed impossible that she could separate her feelings for them from those she had always felt for anyone who lived in the Union states, yet she *had*.

And she could not help but recall the kindness of Noah Brown and his son Paul, nor the doctor who had saved Dancing Cloud's life. They were all Yankees and she had warm feelings for them all.

The war, she despaired to herself.

The Civil War had not only left confusion in its wake all those years ago.

It did so even now.

A sound, like the small, faint cry of a child, drew Lauralee's head up. She looked quickly over at Dancing Cloud. She could tell by his guarded expression and wandering eyes as he peered slowly around him that he had also heard the sound.

"Dancing Cloud, could that . . ."

She got no more words out. Suddenly before them was a small child stumbling in a drunken stupor toward them. Although his skin was copper, it was ashen in color, and his eyes were sunken. He was gaunt and thin, as though he hadn't eaten for days.

Lauralee and Dancing Cloud slid quickly from their saddles. Lauralee took the horse's reins and secured them beneath a boulder on the graveled path, then ran to Dancing Cloud and knelt down with him before the boy.

Dancing Cloud gently steadied the small child between his strong hands as he clasped them onto his frail shoulders.

Brian Brave Walker blinked his eyes as he stared up at Dancing Cloud, then over at his white stallion. This warrior! This horse! He had seen them both in his dreams!

Then he looked questionably at the white woman. This was not the way it was supposed to be. She had never appeared to him in his dreams. She was not supposed to be with the noble warrior on the white stallion.

For sure this was not a dream.

This was real!

Brian Brave Walker's dark eyes widened with fear. Again he looked quickly from Lauralee to Dancing Cloud, then tried to wrench himself free.

Lauralee wanted so badly to go and draw the child into her arms and comfort him. It was plain to see that he perhaps trusted no one.

"We are friends," Dancing Cloud reassured, releasing one of his hands to talk in sign language with the boy in case he could not understand English. He pointed to himself with his right thumb, then pointed to Lauralee in the same way, meaning "we." He then clasped his hands together and shook them, meaning "friends."

"My name is Chief Dancing Cloud." He motioned toward himself with a hand. Then he gestured toward Lauralee. "Her name is Lauralee. What is *your* name?"

Deep inside himself Brian Brave Walker was glad to have finally found someone who might give him directions to *any* Indian village. He had given up hoping that he would find the one in which his mother had lived as a child before the Civil War. As he had wandered, searching, he seemed to have gone in circles.

Until now, until he had come across these two people, he had begun to think that he might die on this mountain. He had fled from more than one bear. Now he was too weak to flee from anything, or anyone.

He was glad to know that this brave whose skin color matched his own was declaring himself a friend.

He looked guardedly over at the woman. She was most beautiful! Yet her skin was white. He hated all whites. In them he always saw his father! He could not look at a white-skinned person and at the same time think "friend." His very own father was his enemy and he was white-skinned!

"My name is Brian Brave Walker. I speak English well," he said, giving Lauralee another insolent stare. Then he gazed up at Dancing Cloud. "But I also speak in Cherokee. Do you know the Cherokee language?"

Dancing Cloud's eyes lit up. "I *am* Cherokee," he said proudly. "You are also Cherokee?"

"Partly," Brian Brave Walker said, lowering his eyes with shame to ever have to admit to being part white. His little, thin legs gave way beneath him. He sucked in a quavering breath when Dancing Cloud caught him, preventing the fall.

"How long has it been since you have eaten?" Lauralee asked, reaching a hand to the child's face to smooth a fallen lock of coal-black hair back from his eyes.

She gasped when he flinched at her touch, wondering how he could hate her so quickly?

"I have fed off berries," Brian Brave Walker said, looking up at Dancing Cloud as though *he* had asked the question. He wanted to ignore Lauralee as though she were not there. "My stomach hurts from the berries. I . . . I . . ."

He jerked himself away from Dancing Cloud and stumbled behind some bushes.

Dancing Cloud and Lauralee exchanged quick glances when they realized what the child was doing in private. The single diet of berries had caused him to have a bad bout of dysentery.

Lauralee's heart went out to the child when she heard him groan with pain as he continued to stay behind the bushes.

Dancing Cloud was torn with what to do. He wanted to go to the boy and comfort him. Yet he did not want to embarrass him while he was in such a terrible state.

Then they heard no more noises. Everything had become stone quiet. The boy no longer groaned and

moaned. There was no more sounds of his overactive
bowels. There was a sudden strained silence.

"Child?" Lauralee said, trying to get the boy's response. "Are you all right, child?"

When he did not respond nor reappear, Dancing
Cloud and Lauralee ran behind the bushes.

Lauralee felt faint at what she saw.

Dancing Cloud saw the danger of the boy's condition.

"He's unconscious," Lauralee cried, placing her
hands to her throat at the sight of the small child lying
in the filthy mess, his breeches wrapped around his ankles.

"We must see to him quickly," Dancing Cloud said,
grabbing the boy up into his arms. He looked around,
searching with his eyes. Through a break in the trees a
short distance away the shine of a rushing stream
caught his quick attention.

"*O-ge-ye,* get one of my shirts from my saddlebag,"
he said in a rush of words. "The child will wear that
once he is bathed. You will bathe him while I search
the forest for the skullcap herbal plant that can be used
to better his condition."

"Dancing Cloud, I'm afraid that he is already too de-
hydrated to . . . to . . . possibly survive," Lauralee
cried.

Breathless and fear gripping her heart for the child,
she ran to Dancing Cloud's stallion and grabbed a shirt
from the saddlebag. She also yanked a blanket out of
the bag.

Then she ran and caught up with Dancing Cloud just
as he broke through the denseness of the trees and
reached the stream. She was glad that the ground leveled off somewhat beside the water. She would be able
to minister to the child more easily.

Dancing Cloud lay Brian Brave Walker beside the
stream, then turned and left without saying another
word.

Lauralee removed the child's soiled clothes and

pitched them into the weeds. She recalled the inner strength that she had learned to grasp onto when she had taken care of the men at the veterans hospital, and drew from it today as she bathed the child and dressed him.

She scooted away from Brian Brave Walker when Dancing Cloud returned and managed to force some of the herbs that he had smashed into a fine powder down the boy's throat. He followed that with small trickles of water, stopping when the child coughed or sputtered.

Lauralee's heart skipped a beat when Brian Brave Walker began coughing more earnestly, his arms flailing wildly in the air. "Oh, Lord, he's choking," she cried.

She went to him and lay him over her lap and hit his back with the palm of her hand. When he began crying and speaking incoherently to her, she knew that at least he was finally awake and that the herbal mixture had made its way on down to his stomach.

"Help," Brian Brave Walker cried weakly, dizzying even more as he tried to open his eyes. "Help me."

Dancing Cloud placed his hands beneath the young brave's arms and drew him over onto his lap. "You are going to be all right," he said, slowly rocking Brian Brave Walker back and forth. "We will make you well. Then you can tell us where you came from and where your parents are."

Lauralee jumped with a start when the mention of his parents caused the child's eyes to open wide and wild.

"No," Brian Brave Walker cried. "I do not talk ... about ... parents ... ever to you."

Brian Brave Walker was still afraid to draw any attention to his mother. He always had to remember that her life was in danger so long as the threat of his father was there.

He glowered over at Lauralee. "Especially to *her*," he said, his voice weak, yet noticeably filled with a venomous hate. "She . . . is . . . white. I . . . trust . . . no whites."

"Her skin is white, yes," Dancing Cloud said, glancing over at Lauralee. "But never equate her with those who are evil. Lauralee's heart is pure and sweet. She is loved by me, a Cherokee *chief*. So, Brian Brave Walker, you must see that she is deserving of more than hate. And know this, young brave. She is to be my *wife*."

Brian Brave Walker's lips parted in a disbelieving gasp.

Then he drifted off again, finding peace in the black void of sleep.

"Let us move onward and get him to my village," Dancing Cloud said, rising to his feet. "I will carry him in my arms."

When Lauralee said nothing back to him, Dancing Cloud kissed her softly. "Do not fret over this young brave's misguided feelings for you. Once he is awake and lucid for clear thinking, he will learn quickly the sweetness of your heart."

"I wonder what has happened in his past that makes him hate white people so quickly and easily?" Lauralee said, walking beside Dancing Cloud back to their horses. "His hate seems to run way deeper than anyone else I have ever known."

She stopped and paused, then looked quickly up at Dancing Cloud. "Except for the hate *I* feel for a man, I should say, I have never witnessed such total hate," she said, her voice drawn. "Clint McCloud. The Yankee with the red hair and blue eyes."

"And wooden leg," Dancing Cloud said, proud to be the one who caused the man such discomfort for the rest of his life.

"Yes, and wooden leg." Lauralee nodded.

She shoved the rock aside that had kept the horse's reins in place. She waited for Dancing Cloud to get secure in his saddle with Brian Brave Walker on his lap, then handed his reins to him.

Watching the child, to see if he was still asleep, Lauralee swung herself into her saddle.

They resumed their journey up the mountainside. Brian Brave Walker awakened for a while, then would drift off to sleep again.

"Once we get him to my cabin he can eat proper foods that will make his strength return," Dancing Cloud said, gazing over at Lauralee.

"It must be done slowly, though. He apparently has been without solid food for quite a while now. He has to adjust to it gradually or his body will continue to rebel against it."

Dancing Cloud nodded. "You bring your teachings of the white man's hospital to my mountains?" he said, smiling over at her. "That is good. Like your father you will share with the Wolf Clan Cherokee."

"I only hope that your people will accept me as they did my father," Lauralee said warily. "You see, Dancing Cloud, I am arriving to your village in a much different capacity than my father. I will remain among your people as one *with* them. My father came to your people, brought them supplies, smoked their peace pipe and shared talk and knowledge with them, then he *left*. He returned to *his* own life, leaving your people to live theirs apart from his."

"The difference also is that you are coming to my village as my future *wife*," Dancing Cloud quickly interjected. "Who dares question that since I am their chief, their spokesperson?"

Lauralee smiled, yet did not share his confidence.

She looked straight ahead again, her spine stiff, her heart pounding when the first signs of the village came in sight as the ground leveled off into a wide valley beyond.

As they came closer to the village, Lauralee was stunned to see that it was so nearly like the smaller white communities in their manner of living, that a stranger could rarely distinguish an Indian's cabin or little cove farm from that of a white man. The cabins were made of logs and roofed with the bark of chestnut trees. Each cabin had its own garden, corn, and various other vegetables maturing in them.

She looked past the village at the many orchards, manure evenly spread around the fruit trees. She could tell by the trunk and leaves of the trees that during the harvest season the Cherokee had an abundance of apples, peaches, and plums.

She looked elsewhere. Although there were some cows grazing in small plots behind the cabins, it seemed that pork was highly esteemed by the Cherokee. A considerable amount of hogs were fenced in beside the cabins, as well as some that ran wild and untended throughout the village.

As they came closer to the village and Lauralee could see some of the people outside their lodges doing various chores, she could tell that the primitive costumes had most certainly been long obsolete. Just like Dancing Cloud had told her, she saw that his people's dress was like that of the white people, except that for the most part moccasins took the place of shoes.

And noticeably also were the men who still wore buckskins along with those who wore the breeches and shirts of the white man.

Her gaze was drawn to women sitting outside their cabins at spinning wheels and looms. It was obvious they manufactured their own clothes.

Dancing Cloud was observing, himself, things of his people and village. The Great Spirit had given them the land. And what a beautiful land it was. The sky was dark blue, the trees casting shadows. The arched backs of the hills beyond served as a sturdy backdrop for the thriving village.

He saw that the horses and ponies of his people were tethered in their usual places. Many dugout canoes, hollowed out of poplar logs with ax and fire, were beached along the banks of the river. Toddlers were busy at games that he had once played. Some women were fleshing yesterday's kill for tonight's dinner. Fresh meat hung from drying rocks, blood red; white sheets of buck fat were spread out to dry beneath the hot rays of the sun.

Dancing Cloud's gaze stopped on one woman in particular. Susan Sweet Bird, his father's sister. She was sitting solemnly outside his father's lodge on a buffalo robe. She stared blindly ahead as she poked a steel needle into a newly cured skin.

Dancing Cloud could see her frustration as she continued to jab at the buffalo skin with her needle, her eyesight not there to assist in this chore that she was determined to do for herself.

Blind since birth, she had learned well to live with her affliction. Her senses guided her into her every movement.

And for the most part she functioned as well as one whose eyes were bright and alive.

But today it seemed that something was keeping her from her skills of sewing. He did not have to be told what. She was still mourning the death of her beloved chieftain brother.

And she surely wondered when her nephew was going to return to assume the duties of chief.

Suddenly Susan Sweet Bird jerked her sightless eyes in Dancing Cloud's direction. She stiffened and leaned her ear toward the sound of the approaching horses. She dropped her sewing and pushed herself up from the buffalo robe. Her hands groping before her, she came toward Dancing Cloud, a soft smile quavering on her lips.

"Dancing Cloud?" she shouted. She broke into a run. "It *is* you, isn't it, Dancing Cloud? You have come home to us."

Her reaction to the sounds that she had heard at the far edge of the village caused everyone else to respond and see what had caused Susan Sweet Bird's sudden anxiousness. Gasps wafted through the crowd when they caught their first sight of Dancing Cloud.

Then everyone broke into a run. Two women went to Susan Sweet Bird and gently led her onward toward her nephew.

"It *is* Dancing Cloud," they told Susan Sweet Bird. "He is home."

Susan Sweet Bird listened again, her senses telling her that three horses were arriving instead of one. "Who is with my nephew?" she asked the women.

"A white woman and it seems that Chief Dancing Cloud carries a child in his arms," one of them replied.

"A white woman and a . . . baby . . . child?" Susan Sweet Bird said, her voice drawn. "Does it appear to be a child that could belong to my nephew . . . and . . . the white woman?"

"The child appears to be nine or ten winters of age," one of them told her back.

Susan Sweet Bird sucked in a breath of relief. "That is good," she murmured. "I did not think my nephew would have brought home a white wife and child."

"The child is not white from what I can tell from this distance," one of the other women said, stretching her neck to get a better look as Dancing Cloud still approached on his horse. "It is a young man and he is as copper-skinned as you and I."

"Truly?" Susan Sweet Bird said, then frowned. "Then who is the woman?"

There was a strained silence. Susan Sweet Bird stopped when she realized that the horses were near enough for her to wait for Dancing Cloud to dismount and come to her.

When strong arms suddenly enveloped her, she clung to Dancing Cloud and sobbed out his father's name. "*I-go-no-tli*, is gone. My brother is gone."

"*Ii*, yes, my *e-do-da* is gone from this earth," Dancing Cloud said, caressing her back through her buckskin dress. "But never gone from the *a-qua-do-no-do*, heart. His spirit is here even now as my arms and voice give you comfort. In part, I *am* my *e-do-da*, father."

Susan Sweet Bird leaned away from him and placed

her hands on each side of his face. "You speak and act as if you knew of your father's passing before I told you," she said softly. "How is it that you knew? We sent no messenger to tell you. Saint Louis is far from our mountains. We knew you would return soon to us to hear of your father's passing."

"In a vision I saw my father in the spirit world," Dancing Cloud began explaining, drawing a quiet gasp deeply from within Susan Sweet Bird's soul.

Touched deeply by Dancing Cloud's gentleness with his aunt, Lauralee placed a hand over her mouth and stifled a sob. Time and time again she realized just how lucky she was to be loved by this man!

27

The night bird song and the stars above,
Told many a touching story.

—MRS. CRAWFORD

Two weeks had passed. Lauralee had tried to accept
Dancing Cloud's absence as he mourned his father's
death. The time of mourning with his people had
passed. He now mourned alone somewhere in the
mountains, the Great Spirit his only companion.

Lauralee had also tried to accept that Brian Brave
Walker had not grown close to her. Although she had
nursed him back to health, he still wouldn't talk to her.

Susan Sweet Bird had her mourning behind her and
had been assigned to keep Lauralee company in Dancing Cloud's absence.

In turn, Brian Brave Walker had chosen Susan Sweet
Bird with whom to ally himself while Dancing Cloud
was elsewhere.

Each day, Lauralee had sat back and achingly
watched Brian Brave Walker and Susan Sweet Bird
laugh and talk beside the fire in Dancing Cloud's
cabin.

Yet there was one thing that she was at least thankful
for. Susan Sweet Bird had grown close to her. She
treated Lauralee like a daughter.

But Lauralee had to wonder if that was because Susan Sweet Bird could not see the color of her skin.

If she could, *would* that make a difference? Lauralee wondered.

She paused from her sewing to gaze once again at Susan Sweet Bird. Dancing Cloud's aunt was telling Brian Brave Walker a story as they sat close to each other on the floor on a buffalo robe in front of the fireplace.

Her gaze moving slowly over Susan Sweet Bird, Lauralee admired her. She was a stately woman. Her face was long and narrow, the wrinkles at the corners of her eyes and slanting from her lips revealing that she was no longer young. Contrasting vividly against her copper face, her hair, from which she had clipped only the very tips during her mourning, was as white as snow.

Lauralee could tell that Susan Sweet Bird always took much pains with her hair. As today, it was combed smooth and close, then folded into a club at the back of the head. It was tied very tight with a piece of dried eel skin, which was said to make the hair grow long. She wore the traditional dress of fringed buckskin and an ancient collar of wampum, which were beads cut out of clam shells.

Still being left out of the conversation, Lauralee sighed heavily, her shoulders bending and giving in to her feelings. She had finally stopped trying to get Brian Brave Walker to include her in his conversations.

Even when Susan Sweet Bird tried to draw her into the happy times, Lauralee shook her head and resumed her sewing, for she could see in the boy's eyes that he did not wish for her to.

As now. Lauralee tried to position herself more comfortably in the overstuffed chair as she pushed her needle through the deer leather, to make her moccasins more beautiful. Susan Sweet Bird had taught her how to make the moccasins. Lauralee had cut them from newly cured deer leather with a hook knife. When finished, she had soaked the moccasins in water, and while wet, she had put them on her feet.

As instructed by Susan Sweet Bird, Lauralee had walked the moccasins dry until they fitted her, soft and giving and light as air. She smiled at her accomplishment.

She paused again from her sewing and looked around the cabin. She had wanted to feel a part of Dancing Cloud's life. She had wanted to be able to look at his cabin and everything in it and feel all warm inside by knowing that she shared it with him.

But because he had been in mourning these past two weeks and had not shared anything at all with her, she felt nothing but a keen loneliness.

She glanced over at Brian Brave Walker again. She had hoped that his presence would help lift her loneliness. But his ignoring her had made her feel even more alone, more sad.

She had hoped for more here, in Dancing Cloud's world.

Lauralee turned her eyes from the boy. Her gaze took in everything around her. The cabin was brightened inside by rugs woven from hemp, then painted in gay colors with bird, animal, and flower motifs. There were buffalo hide chests and cane seats and baskets of every size and shape in the room.

She looked up at the small loft overhead. It had originally been built for storage, but had only recently been renovated to be used as Lauralee's and Dancing Cloud's private bedroom. Dancing Cloud had carried his bedstead to the loft along with blankets, warm animal pelts, and quilts, and a feather mattress in which she had sank deeply the first night she had slept on it.

One of Dancing Cloud's friends had brought a bed to the cabin for Brian Brave Walker as a special gift for the young brave. It had been placed along a far wall beneath the loft. Comfortable blankets and pelts were spread atop it.

Her gaze shifted. On the end wall of the cabin opposite the wall where Brian Brave Walker's bed sat, a massive stone fireplace was set into a wall of sweet smelling logs, firelight gilding all within.

The furniture in the room was simple and handmade except for the one overstuffed chair on which Lauralee sat this early afternoon. Dancing Cloud had told her that this had been bought for his mother long ago. Now that his mother and father had passed on to the other side, the chair was now Lauralee's.

She moved her eyes more quickly over the rest of the belongings. An iron pot hung over the fire, in which bubbled a rabbit stew that she had prepared early in the morning.

A small wooden table and three chairs sat near one wall, where near it hung shelves that held a bake kettle, coffeepot and mill, a few cups, knives and spoons.

The door of the Cherokee log cabin was always open except at night and on colder days of winter. There were no windows, the open door furnishing the only means by which light was admitted to the interior.

Kerosene lamps sat on the kitchen table and on a small table beside the overstuffed chair. They emitted soft, warm light throughout the cabin.

Lauralee had learned that the Cherokee people provided for their simple wants by their own industry without asking or expecting outside assistance. Their fields, orchards, and fish traps, with their domestic animals and occasional hunting, supplied them with food.

By the sale of ginseng and other medicinal plants gathered in the mountains, with fruit and honey of their own raising, they procured what additional supplies they needed from a nearby trading post on the Soho River.

Susan Sweet Bird had told Lauralee that the usual food for the Cherokee was beans, bread, corn, and coffee. In autumn, chestnut bread was quite popular.

Lauralee was suddenly drawn from her reverie as Dancing Cloud came into the cabin, his chest wet from a swim in the river, his wet buckskin breeches hugging his legs like a second skin.

He slung his sleek, wet hair back from his shoulders as he knelt onto a knee before Lauralee. He took her hands within his, his dark eyes smiling into hers.

"It is over," he said thickly. "My outward mourning is now behind me. Inside I shall forever mourn the parting of both my mother and father. But I am relieved of my burden of mourning on this earth now when I know that my father's spirit path has led him at long last to join my mother, forever. Their spirits at this moment are standing hand in hand smiling down at us, my *o-ge-ye*. Let us now move forward with our own lives."

So relieved, so jubilant, over knowing that finally she was going to be able to be with Dancing Cloud, Lauralee wrenched her hands from his and drifted into his arms.

"I have missed you so," she murmured, oblivious of eyes on her as Brian Brave Walker glared at her. "Please tell me I was not selfish, darling, for wanting so badly to be with you. I . . . I . . . have been so lonely these past two weeks."

"It is not selfishness that causes such despair inside your heart," Dancing Cloud said, hugging her to him. "You were thrust into a different world so quickly and I was not there to help you in your adjustment. I wish it could have been different."

He looked over her shoulder at Brian Brave Walker. His insides recoiled to see such a loathing in the young brave's eyes as he gazed at Lauralee. Dancing Cloud realized now that the young brave had not adjusted well, either.

Dancing Cloud knew that he had a double duty now to make things right for his woman who he wished soon to make his wife, and for this boy he wished to make his son.

He wanted them to be *family*.

Yet he knew that he must first search and delve into this child's background to see where he had came from, and from whose lives. He had only speculation to go on. He had to believe that he had been orphaned recently by some tragic incident. Surely the boy had blocked it out of his memory. Why else would he not talk about it?

But realizing that Lauralee should be his prime concern at this moment, he held her away from him and wiped tears from her eyes with the flesh of his thumbs. "Shall we walk and talk?" he said, glad to see the suggestion bring a smile on her lovely face.

"*Ii,* yes, let's," Lauralee said, rising and taking his hand, to leave.

A sudden commotion outside the cabin drew them apart. Dancing Cloud went to the door and stepped outside. Lauralee's heart beat loudly as she listened to the muted conversation. She crept closer to the door to try and listen better.

She jumped with alarm when Dancing Cloud came back in the cabin in haste. Her insides cried out, "No!" when he gave her an apologetic look as he gazed down at her. She knew without him even telling her that he had to leave again!

"A delegation from the Cherokee Nation has arrived," he said solemnly. "I must meet with them in council. They have brought an urgent invitation to our Wolf Clan of Cherokee to remove and incorporate upon equal terms with the Cherokee Nation in the Indian Territory. I must meet with them to give them my adamant response."

He clasped his hands to her shoulders when he saw the despair and an almost desperation in her eyes. "It will not take me long to tell them that my full-blood Cherokee will remain to live apart from those who have chosen a different sort of life," he said thickly. "It will not take long for me to tell them that my people are safer from aggressions among our rocks and mountains than they would ever be in a land shared with the white man. I must make them understand that my people can be happy only in the country where nature has planted them."

Seeing the importance of what he said, and had to do, and having to put her selfishness aside again after only having thought that she was to be reunited with Dancing Cloud again, Lauralee placed a gentle hand to his cheek.

"Go," she murmured. "You are chief. You have your duties to your people."

"*You* are also my people now," he said thickly. "I do this for *you*, as well. We want a future that is free of white man interferences. The only way we can achieve that is by staying on my mountain."

He paused, then felt compelled to give her further explanations. "It is important that you know that although I disagree with my mixed blood Cherokee brothers and sisters, a common ancestry promotes an understanding between the Cherokee full bloods and mixed bloods," he said. "We are poles apart in many respects, but under the skin we are still brothers. We have Cherokee traditions in common and no amount of white blood can dilute the remembrance of what happened in centuries past to the Cherokee people."

"I truly understand," Lauralee said, fighting back tears that threatened to make her look selfish and childish again. "Please do go on."

Susan Sweet Bird came to them. She moved to Lauralee's side. "I will walk with Lauralee and Brian Brave Walker," she said softly. "I will fill their time while you must be away again."

Dancing Cloud swept Susan Sweet Bird into his arms and gave her a hug, then stepped away and gave Lauralee one last lingering look. He then left the cabin, his shoulders squared proudly.

"Come, let us walk away your sadness," Susan Sweet Bird said as she took Lauralee's hand. She turned her sightless eyes Brian Brave Walker's way. "Come, child. Walk with us. Acquaint yourself more with my people and the ways in which we live. Perhaps in turn you will want to tell us about your own people and home."

Lauralee watched Brian Brave Walker move slowly to his feet, his eyes half cast downward. As he inched his way toward her and Susan Sweet Bird, Lauralee's heart slowed its beats. She so feared that he would again walk on the far side of her, beside Susan Sweet Bird, instead.

And when he did just that, lacing his fingers through Susan Sweet Bird's, Lauralee looked quickly away and swallowed back her pride and hurt. Somehow, some day she would find a way to make him accept her. For certain it was the color of her skin that made the difference! She had to find a way to make him look past that and see the love that she offered him.

The evening shadows were lengthening and the September air was much cooler as they began their leisurely walk through the village. Everyone smiled and spoke to Susan Sweet Bird. Some stopped them and made over Brian Brave Walker.

Yet there were still obvious reservations on how the people felt about Lauralee.

But she tried to understand by thinking that she had not been seen enough with Dancing Cloud to prove that she was his woman and worthy of their acquaintance.

Hopefully after this council today everything would change.

He would finally be with her.

As they wandered, Lauralee saw women pounding corn as they made flour outside their cabins. Young girls came from the forest carrying baskets they had woven, filled with hickory nuts, walnuts, and pecans. Some women came from the direction of the river carrying pottery jars filled with fresh water.

She looked past the cabins and saw the plots of gardens more closely than when she had ridden into the village on the day of her arrival. Now she could see pumpkins that lay in orange globes across the land. The cornstalks had browned, the harvest near.

"Do the women or men gather the harvest?" she

blurted, trying to start a small conversation between herself and Susan Sweet Bird.

"The men harvest, the women make food from that which is harvested," Susan Sweet Bird said, her voice always sounding musical in its softness. "Next to corn, the bean is the most important food plant of the Cherokee. Beans that crack open in cooking are sometimes rubbed by mothers on the lips of their children in order to make them look smiling and good-tempered. They are called laughing beans."

"Laughing beans," Brian Brave Walker said, more to himself, than aloud, as he thought of his very own mother telling stories of the "laughing beans." His insides ached with a keen loneliness for his mother.

But he feared his father more than anything else on this earth, so much that he had to place his mother from his mind whenever she crept into his heart.

He . . . had . . . to . . . forget.

Lauralee looked past Susan Sweet Bird. "Brian Brave Walker, did you say something?" she asked softly, flinching when his only response was to glare back at her.

"Lauralee, the child will take to you soon, and then he will talk endlessly to you," Susan Sweet Bird said, in an effort to apologize for Brian's behavior. "Give him time. Who could not love you? My chief, my nephew, has chosen wisely for a wife."

"Thank you," Lauralee murmured. "I'm so glad to have your friendship. Without it, I don't know what I would do."

"My people as a whole will soon accept you, as I have," Susan Sweet Bird said, turning to reach a searching hand for Lauralee's face. When she found it she lay her palm against her cheek. "These things take time. Just have faith in Dancing Cloud. Then it will happen as though by magic one day that my people will look to you as one *of* us, instead of white."

They walked onward.

"Is that tobacco I see in the fields?" Lauralee asked,

seeing the large-leafed plants swaying in the evening breeze.

"Yes, tobacco is our people's sacred incense," Susan Sweet Bird said, nodding. "It is being used even now in council. It is a guarantee of a solemn oath in nearly every important function of my people—in binding the warrior to take up against the enemy; in ratifying peace treaties; in driving away witches and evil spirits. It is either smoked in a pipe, or sprinkled upon the fire. *Tsala*, tobacco, means 'fire to hold in the mouth.'"

They had reached the center of the village. Lauralee stared at a larger log lodge that had been built on elevated land so that it looked down upon those who passed by it. The outside of the house had the appearance of a small mountain, its roof covered with earth.

"Is that the council house?" Lauralee asked softly. She tried to gaze into the door when she noticed that an inward fire illuminated the room.

"Yes, that is our Wolf Clan Town House where religious meetings, social gatherings, and councils are held," Susan Sweet Bird said, nodding. "A sacred fire constantly burns in the center of this edifice. The fire is kindled atop a cone-shaped mound of earth."

"A sacred fire?" Lauralee said, again gazing at the door, seeing nothing more than the glow from the fire. She could hear men talking. She could make out their shadows. She knew that Dancing Cloud was one of them from his virile, muscled body.

"The Cherokee are people of fire," Susan Sweet Bird said as they passed on by the Wolf Clan Town House. "Some believed this was truly our origin. According to ancient legend we were given an eternal fire. The creator of life, this sacred fire, is the exclusive property of the Cherokee people. As long as the flames of the sacred fire burns, the Cherokee people will survive. Seven varieties of wood are burned in the sacred fire, symbolizing the Cherokee's seven clans."

"During the Civil War, did the fire burn even then?" Lauralee asked, looking at the Wolf Clan Town House over her right shoulder, wishing she were there, joining council with Dancing Cloud. She could not help but feel left out.

Again she brushed her selfish thoughts aside. She had to adjust to this, as well as many more things. She knew that she had surely only just begun to see the difference in hers and Dancing Cloud's worlds . . . in their cultures!

His was filled with mystique.

Hers?

She did not want to think back to what hers had been for her before she had met Dancing Cloud.

"During the white man's war of greed and power the sacred flames at times smoldered, appearing to be extinguished, but again burst forth with still a brighter blaze." Susan Sweet Bird sighed heavily. "The ceremonial fire of full-blood Cherokee now burns brightly. Those who have come into our village today in an attempt to disrupt our lives will see that the word of our chief is final in that the Wolf Clan Cherokee will not leave their mountain, *ever*."

The sound of low, angry words behind them drew Lauralee around. Her lips parted in a slight gasp when those who had come for council today were leaving in a huff. It was obvious they were disgruntled with Dancing Cloud for having rejected their offer. They surely knew him well enough to know that he walked in the same footsteps of his father and his grandfather before him and that his word was final in all things among the Wolf Clan Cherokee.

Lauralee watched the men who were dressed in neat suits that white businessmen wore as they mounted their horses quickly and rode away in a gallop from the village. She turned slow eyes to Dancing Cloud and found him walking toward her, a grim expression on his face, his dark eyes heavy with an agitated determination.

When he reached her he silently framed her face between his hands. Their eyes momentarily held. He then

stepped to her side and smiled down at Brian Brave
Walker, then turned to Susan Sweet Bird.

"Thank you for helping today, Susan Sweet Bird,"
he said softly. "Would you care to join us for the evening meal?"

Susan Sweet Bird slowly shook her head back and
forth. "It is time for your family gathering," she said,
reaching a hand out toward Dancing Cloud before she
found his arm to pat it. "You have been missed, my
nephew chief."

"I want to go with you," Brian Brave Walker blurted
out to Susan Sweet Bird, grabbing her free hand. He
clung to it almost desperately. "Please take me with
you."

He gazed spitefully up at Lauralee, then turned
softer eyes to Dancing Cloud. "Susan Sweet Bird tells
good stories," he murmured. "And she would be lonely
without me. May I go and spend the night with Susan
Sweet Bird? May I?"

Those words came like a stab wound in Lauralee's
heart. She had so badly wanted to be accepted by this
young boy. And not only because it was obvious that
Dancing Cloud adored the child. She also adored him.
She wanted to be the one who reached inside the child
and discovered what had caused him to be wandering
on the mountainside alone. She wanted to heal those
inward wounds, as she had his physical self.

If she discovered that he had no parents, then she
wanted to take on the duties of mothering him. She
knew so deeply how it felt to be orphaned.

She would bring every orphan in the world under her
protective wing if it were possible.

At least here was one child who she could help, if he
would only allow it.

Torn with what to say, or do, knowing how desperately Lauralee wanted this child's acceptance, Dancing
Cloud inhaled a shaky breath. The only way the boy
would learn to accept Lauralee into his life was to be
around her, to learn by watching her and being with

her, that she was everything good on this earth. The color of her skin blinded the child of the truth now. But soon it would be as though he had never noticed that she was white and that he was copper.

"Tonight, you may go with Susan Sweet Bird," Dancing Cloud said, rearranging his thoughts for the betterment of Lauralee and himself for the moment. They had not been alone since they had arrived at his village. Tonight he would reacquaint her with why she had chosen his world over her own. Tonight he would give her a loving she would never forget.

"Only tonight," Dancing Cloud hurriedly added. "Then we will spend time together under my roof the rest of our nights so that we can all learn to love and trust one another."

Brian Brave Walker clung to Susan Sweet Bird, his dark eyes sullen. "How can you love and trust her?" he said, nodding toward Lauralee. "She is white. All whites are evil."

Lauralee gasped as she turned her eyes from Brian Brave Walker. She wanted to cry out at him that, yes, *some* white people were evil. She knew one man in particular who Brian Brave Walker would definitely hate should they ever come face to face!

But how could she convince the child that just because one white person may have placed this hate for all white people into his heart, it did not mean that all were of the same character.

She said nothing. She knew that whatever she chose to say would fall on the boy's ears as though he were deaf. She had a long way to go to convince him that he had no cause to hate her.

She slipped an arm through Dancing Cloud's. She leaned up closer to his ear. "It's all right," she whispered. "Please say nothing more to him. Let him go and spend the night with Susan Sweet Bird. Perhaps tomorrow we can talk with him some more. But for tonight, let's not say any more to him."

"Tomorrow I must leave again," Dancing Cloud said matter-of-factly.

Lauralee paled. "What?" she said, her voice weak. "Again, so *soon*, you will leave me?"

"If you wish to go with me, you are welcome," he said, seeing how distraught she was over possibly being left behind.

"Where? Where are you going?"

"To the trading post on the Soho River."

They heard Brian Brave Walker emit a low, sudden gasp. As they looked at him they saw the fear in his eyes.

"I not go with you," Brian Brave Walker said in a rush of words. "I will stay *here*."

Neither one questioned him why. His fear was too real to ask.

"You can stay with Susan Sweet Bird," Dancing Cloud said, patting the boy on the shoulder. "But one day your fears must be faced and lost."

Brian Brave Walker nodded and lowered his eyes.

Dancing Cloud slipped a hand over Lauralee's fingers that lay over the flesh of his arm. He squeezed them affectionately, smiled down at her, then turned back to the child. "Go," he said thickly. "Listen to stories. Be happy. When Lauralee and I return from our journey to the trading post, then you will be expected to spend the night here with us. Is that understood?"

Brian Brave Walker hesitated, then again nodded.

Susan Sweet Bird took Brian Brave Walker by the hand and walked away with him, already busy with another folk tale of the Cherokee.

Lauralee turned with Dancing Cloud and walked with him toward his cabin. They were silent about Brian Brave Walker or their concerns. They had been apart for too long to allow anything to spoil these moments together.

When they reached the cabin they stopped before entering and looked heavenward. The moon was full, casting its glorious light across the village.

Lauralee looked quickly over at Dancing Cloud when he began singing a song, his voice beautiful and resonant.

"New moon, new moon, here I am in your presence," he sang. "Here I am in your presence. Make it so that only I may occupy my woman's heart tonight. My heart is like a rose tonight, opening its petals to embrace my woman. Let it be so."

When he was finished and he turned his dark eyes down to Lauralee, she smiled through a haze of tears up at him. "That was so beautiful," she murmured, then trembled sensually when he whisked her up into his arms and carried her into his cabin.

With a foot, he closed the door. His eyes never leaving hers, he carried Lauralee to the buffalo robe spread on the floor in front of the fireplace.

Without words, their eyes saying everything they were feeling about each other, they undressed and threw their clothes aside.

Vibrant and glowing, Lauralee drifted into Dancing Cloud's arms, his hard body like velvet and steel against hers.

A kind of slow heat began licking through Lauralee's body as Dancing Cloud crushed her lips with a fevered kiss, his palms moving seductively down her body, teasing, stroking her fiery flesh.

Feeling the heat of his passion pressed against her abdomen made Lauralee reel with the onslaught of pleasure. When his hands stroked her slim, white thighs, she lifted one of her legs around him.

She gasped with ecstasy when he came to her in one bold thrust. She locked her arms around his neck as her body absorbed how it felt to be with him again. She felt a drugged passion overwhelm her as his kisses became more demanding. He tantalized and loved her, his powerful hands caressing and stroking her silken flesh.

She abandoned herself to the torrent of feelings that washed over her. She clung to him around the neck and kissed him long and hard as his hands kneaded her breasts. Her hips moved rhythmically with his.

When that maddening rush of rapture was near again, she tried to hold back so that she could share the ultimate of pleasure with him. She could tell that he was nearing that point of wonder by how his body had stiffened and his chest was heaving. She could tell by how frenzied he was kissing her now. His fingers bit into her as he lifted her closer to him.

Then he pressed his lips against the slender column of her throat. She wove her fingers lovingly through his hair as he reverently breathed her name against her flesh.

And then he kissed her lips again as their bodies quavered and shook and quaked. They spoke in quiet, spasmodic gasps against each others' lips. They clung hard as the stars in the heavens reached into their hearts and the winds became their breaths as their climax went on and on in a wild, dizzying rhythm, and then tapered off, leaving them shaken and spent once it ended.

Wet with perspiration, her breathing erratic, Lauralee rolled from beneath Dancing Cloud.

He moved to his side, his eyes never leaving her. "My *o-ge-ye,* I had no true life before you," he said, smoothing his hand down the flat plane of her stomach. "You fulfill my every want as a man."

"The days, especially the nights, seemed so long without you," Lauralee murmured. She moved next to him, so that his hard body encompassed hers. "I missed you so."

"There will be times when we will be apart," Dancing Cloud said, his fingers weaving through her silken hair. "But only physically. In spirit, I am always with you. Remember that when you are lonely for me. If you allow yourself, you will feel me with you, though you cannot see me. You will reach out into the darkness of night and my hand will be touching yours."

"I shall try and remember that," Lauralee said, smiling over at him.

He drew her lips to his. "Let us not talk anymore," he said huskily. "Let us make love again."

"Shouldn't we discuss Brian Brave Walker?" Lauralee said, her heart racing as his hands swept over her in a slow caress.

"This child is not feeling everything that he pretends," Dancing Cloud said, kissing her eyes closed. "Deep down inside his heart he knows the goodness in you. Did you not nurse him back to health? Did you not sit with him day and night while he was so ill? He cannot forget who was so kind to him. It is just something in his past that causes him to hate whites so much. In time we will find out who. Then pity the man or woman of his past who has mistreated him. This Cherokee warrior will make them wish they had never put such a dread in the child's heart."

"And if we never find out who did this to him?" Lauralee asked, slowly losing her senses to his caresses.

"We truly do not need to know *who,* to make him forget," Dancing Cloud said, brushing soft kisses across her throat. "He will learn to love just as a child learns how to talk, run, and laugh. Who could have a better teacher than you?"

"You have such faith in me." Lauralee sighed. "But I . . ."

He sealed her lips with a kiss, stopping her worries and her fears, again propelling her to a place where all question and doubt was left behind, to a place of flaming passion.

28

Our love, it was stronger by far than
the love of those who were older than we.

—EDGAR ALLAN POE

The region in which Dancing Cloud and Lauralee were traveling was beautiful with its myriad bright-tinted blossoms and sweet wild fruits.

Lauralee clung to her horse's reins as she guided her steed down a narrow path beneath the towering trees, ducking now and then so that a low limb would not knock her from her horse.

The sounds were soft and quiet in the forest, as though the birds were distant, instead of overhead. Squirrels scampered up the trees, some seeming to take wing as they jumped from limb to limb, tree to tree.

"I'm so glad that you allowed me to come with you today," Lauralee said, smiling over at Dancing Cloud. "I just wish Brian Brave Walker could have joined us. I feel that this length of time away from him will erase perhaps what closeness that may have begun to form between us. I would hate to think that I would have to begin all over again trying to draw him into liking me."

She paused. "Yet I truly see that it is best that he not accompany us," she said contemplatingly. "His fear of traveling to the trading post seemed so intense. What do you think he fears there? When asked, he always shies away from answering."

Dancing Cloud's eyes narrowed with thought, then he turned to Lauralee. "It is *someone* he fears, not something," he said thickly. "I gather from this that perhaps the person or persons he has fled from trades also at this trading post. If so, and this person came to trade at the same moment we were there, and he saw Brian Brave Walker, the child's life might have that quickly been put in danger."

He sighed heavily. "We must protect this child from all harm, especially those who have filled his life with hate and fear," he said, leaning over to pat his stallion when it gave off a nervous whinny.

Lauralee sensed something might be wrong. Her own horse reacted to it. She turned halfway around in her saddle as did Dancing Cloud. She looked slowly through the tangled underbrush and trees.

When she saw nothing, she gazed at Dancing Cloud. "I'll be glad when we get to the trading post," she murmured. "Although beautiful, there is something eerie about how everything is kept so shadowed from the lack of the sun's ability to penetrate the thick foliage overhead. Anyone or anything could be lurking in those shadows. Perhaps even the very person Brian Brave Walker fears."

"Do not allow your imagination to work overtime," Dancing Cloud said, chuckling. "I have traveled this very path many times before. Never have I been accosted."

"I would have thought there would have been others traveling with us today," Lauralee said, taking another nervous glance over her shoulder.

She could not shake the feeling of being stalked. She blamed her insecurities on Clint McCloud. It was not all that foolish of her to worry about him, much less think that he was possibly there, stalking her and Dancing Cloud. Her Uncle Abner had told her that Clint McCloud now made his permanent residence in North Carolina. She prayed that his home was far from these mountains.

If not . . . ?

She was glad when Dancing Cloud interrupted her troubled thoughts.

"The others made trade while I was gone," Dancing Cloud said. "What I trade today is what I had accumulated before I received word from your father, requesting my presence at his bedside. It has kept well in my absence. I need supplies now. So now I make trade."

"What do you plan to get today for your trade?" she asked, herself having made a list of household goods that she needed for cooking.

"Many things," he said, his eyes dancing into hers. "And what do you plan to take from the shelves at the trading post?"

"Many things," Lauralee teased back, envisioning herself making pies and other surprises for Dancing Cloud. While she had lived at the orphanage she had been assigned several days in the kitchen to assist the cooks. She had learned at age ten how to make her first pie. "I think it will be fun to gather kitchen supplies for special meals that I plan to make for you, my handsome Cherokee."

"And so you also cook as well as you make love?" he teased.

Lauralee blushed and laughed softly.

Dancing Cloud chuckled at her innocent bashfulness. He then gazed around him, his eyes feasting on the beauty of the mountainside. "The mountain has been good to me this trading period," he said, his horse stepping high over a fallen tree branch. Lauralee's horse followed his lead. "I have much ginseng and other medicinal herbs this time to trade."

"I am surprised that ginseng is found in these mountains, and that this very ginseng will go as far as China for use by the Chinese," Lauralee said.

"'Sang,' as it is called by some, or referred to also as *atali-guli*, 'the mountain climber,' is very profitable for the Cherokee," Dancing Cloud explained. "It brings ten cents per pound for the green, aromatic root.

In China it is worth its weight in silver to their people. This medicinal root is also referred to by the Cherokee as 'Little man, most powerful magician.' "

"Why do the Cherokee refer to the root as a man and a magician?" Lauralee asked, arching an eyebrow.

"Because the root resembles and has the shape *of* the body of a man," Dancing Cloud explained. "This root is looked to as a sentient being. It is able to make itself invisible to those unworthy of gathering it. But to those who are worthy of having it for trade, while hunting it, the first three plants found are passed by. The fourth is taken after a preliminary prayer. It is then addressed as the great *atali-guli,* and humbly asked permission to take a small piece of its flesh. After I dig it from the ground, I always drop a bead into the hole and cover it over, as payment to the plant spirit. After that, I take them as they come without further ceremony."

Lauralee looked blankly at him.

Dancing Cloud recognized the puzzlement in her eyes. "You will learn in time everything about my people's beliefs that for now puzzles you," he said. "The white man looks simply at things. The red man sees the mystery about life and learns from it. The white man seems not to care. They just take and rarely give back."

"I care about every living thing," Lauralee said softly. "My feelings run deep for everything and everyone. And I am eager to learn, Dancing Cloud. Please teach me that which I never learned while I was packed like a sardine among a countless number of other orphans at the orphanage. No individual time was taken. I am free now not only to love, but to learn."

"See the cedar trees?" Dancing Cloud said, gesturing toward a grove of trees at his right side. "It is held sacred above other trees. Its small green twigs are thrown upon the fire as incense in certain ceremonies, to counteract the effect of harmful dreams. It is believed that malevolent ghosts cannot endure the smell, but the wood itself is considered too sacred to be used as fuel. According to myth, the red color comes originally from the blood of a wicked magician whose severed head was hung at the top of a tall cedar tree."

He gestured toward another tree, where strips of bark lay feathered on the ground at the base of its trunk, leaving long stretches of the tree bare. "Lightning has struck that tree," he said solemnly. "Mysterious properties attach to the wood of a tree that has been struck by lightning. Especially when the tree does not die from the strike. In preparing the Cherokee ball player for the contest, the medicine man of our village sometimes burns splinters of a tree that has been struck by lightning. The coals from these burned splinters are given to the ball players to paint themselves with in order that they may be able to strike their opponent with all the force of a thunderbolt."

Lauralee smiled at the innocence of these practices, then turned her eyes straight ahead when the barking of a dog a short distance away made her horse jerk its head with a start. She yanked on her reins to steady her horse.

"It is only the dog that belongs to Pierre, the owner of the trading post," Dancing Cloud said, as he steadied his own steed. "It is a way to let Pierre know someone is advancing on his cabin. It is good that he is cautious. The pelts and the ginseng at his trading post, if stolen, could make a white man wealthy in the way white men measure wealth."

"How can the dog know if whoever is approaching the cabin is friend or foe?" Lauralee said, her eyes wide as she watched the large German shepherd run toward them.

"You will soon see," Dancing Cloud said, drawing his steed to a halt. He dismounted and settled on his haunches as the German shepherd came to him, his tail wagging, his tongue searching out Dancing Cloud's hand, licking it.

"Good dog," Dancing Cloud said, smiling up at

Lauralee. "He can tell by smell and attitude if he is among foe or friend." He gestured with a hand for Lauralee to come to him. "Come. Pet him. You will have a friend for life."

Remembering another day, another time, another dog, a beautiful *collie,* brought Paul Brown to mind. She would always remember Paul Brown with much affection. If she had not already met Dancing Cloud she could have felt so much more for Paul.

Deep down inside her heart she knew that she had for a brief moment allowed herself to love him. She would never forget his mesmerizingly blue eyes nor his gentle kindness.

She wished everything good on this earth for him.

Casting thoughts of another man from her mind, not wanting guilt for having thought of Paul Brown to ruin this day for her, Lauralee slid from her saddle to the ground. She went and knelt down beside Dancing Cloud, giggling when the large dog's tongue soon found her cheek and eagerly licked it. She wrapped her arms around its neck and gave it a hug.

"I've always wanted a dog," she murmured. "A dog all my own. There was one at the orphanage. Only one for so many people to love and hug. I scarcely ever got my turn before the dog was taken back outside to its pen."

"You will no longer be deprived of anything," Dancing Cloud said, swinging himself back in his saddle. "Stay. Enjoy the dog's company. But don't wait long. Come to the trading post soon. I'll go on to Pierre's cabin and start unloading my horse."

Lauralee nodded. She watched him ride away, then hugged the dog and played with it, laughing.

Then recalling her fears earlier of feeling watched, she pushed herself to her feet, grabbed her reins, and walked toward the cabin that she now saw in the clearing up ahead.

She paused again to pat the dog's head, then gave it another hug.

But she drew sharply away from the German shepherd when it suddenly bared its teeth and growled low and menacingly.

"I thought we were friends," Lauralee said, slowly backing away from him.

The dog made a lunge.

Thinking it was toward her, a scream froze in Lauralee's throat.

She was surprised when it jumped on past her in several wide bounces.

Just as she turned to see what it might be after, thinking perhaps it was a squirrel or some such forest animal, Lauralee felt faint when the dog was stopped in midair by a knife as it came whizzing through the air.

"No!" Lauralee cried, as the German shepherd fell heavily to the ground, the knife lodged in its right shoulder.

She moved to her knees beside the dog as he lay panting, its eyes hazed over with pain. She started to touch him, to try and comfort him.

Lauralee sucked in a wild breath of terror when the one who had done this to the dog stepped out into the clearing, his blue eyes almost hypnotizing her.

She didn't have time to get up and run.

Nor did she have time to scream.

Clint McCloud was there too quickly.

Leering down at her, he lifted his rifle and brought the butt end of it down across the back of her head.

Lauralee's body lurched from the blow. She grabbed at her head, then sank to the ground, unconscious.

"Got'cha!" Clint snarled.

He gagged Lauralee with his handkerchief and tied her hands together behind her, tied her ankles together, then grabbed her up into his arms. He carried her through the thick underbrush until he reached his tethered horse.

After tying Lauralee behind the saddle, he mounted his horse and rode away.

Laughing to himself, he couldn't get over being this lucky! He had built his cabin not that far from the mountains upon which he had left a massacre during the Civil War.

But never would he have guessed that the Indian of his past, the Indian who had wounded him during the Civil War, lived among those Indians.

He had not realized this until today—until he had seen Dancing Cloud and Lauralee come from the path that led down from the mountain.

He laughed into the air. He now had a way to finally get back at the damn Injun. This woman. She would be the way to repay the Injun for burdening him with a wooden leg for the rest of his life.

"He'll never see her again," Clint grumbled to himself.

He rode hard through the forest, ignoring Lauralee's moans behind him.

Pierre kept Dancing Cloud occupied by talking in his rapid way of speaking in his mixed language of French, English, and Cherokee, while Dancing Cloud unloaded his bags on the Frenchman's counter. The cabin was rich with the smell of leather, bear skins, and raccoon pelts, and countless other items that had been brought to the Frenchman for trade. A lone lantern lit the dark cabin, a cat snoozed near the fireplace where a lazy fire sent off a soft glow.

"Did you say you had a lady with you today?" Pierre asked, raising his eyebrows and peering toward the door. He twisted the ends of his narrow black mustache as he looked back at Dancing Cloud. "Where *is* she, this woman?"

Dancing Cloud's eyes widened. A warning shot through him as he turned on a heel and looked toward the door.

He saw nothing.

He heard nothing.

The dog?

Lauralee?

Where *were* they?

He ran from the cabin. He stopped and gazed around him, his right hand going to the pistol holstered at his waist.

"She is where?" Pierre asked, coming from the cabin. He scratched his brow. "And my dog? He is gone also."

Now knowing for certain that something had happened to Lauralee, Dancing Cloud mounted his horse in one leap. His pistol held poised in one hand, he flicked his reins with the other and backtracked.

When he saw the dog lying in the path, lifeless, with a knife in its shoulder, his insides ran cold. Someone had knifed the dog. Someone had abducted Lauralee!

The heavy Frenchman came huffing and puffing on his horse, then emitted a loud shriek when he discovered his dog. He dismounted and fell to his knees beside the German shepherd. He cradled the dog's head on his lap.

"He is not dead," Dancing Cloud said, shouting over his shoulder as he rode away. "Remove the knife. See to the wound. He will be all right."

"But what of your woman?" Pierre cried after Dancing Cloud.

Not knowing the answer, and hell-bent on finding Lauralee, Dancing Cloud's jaw tightened. He knew that he could not follow any tracks that would lead him to Lauralee. There were too many tracks going in too many directions. His only hope was that he had not waited too long to discover her gone.

Clint wheeled his horse to a shuddering halt before his cabin. He slid clumsily out of his saddle, cursing his wooden leg as it again failed to cooperate with him, then looped his horse's reins around a hitching rail. He could feel the eyes of his wife on him as she stood at the door. He ignored her presence.

With trembling, eager fingers he untied Lauralee

from the horse. She was awake now. He smiled into her wide, fearful eyes as he carried her toward the cabin.

"What have you done?" Soft Wind asked, her voice shrill and afraid. "Who is that? Why have you brought her here?"

Clint brushed brusquely past her. He carried Lauralee to his bed and threw her on it.

Soft Wind ran to him and clutched at his arm. "Why are you doing this?" she cried. "Why would you bring this woman to our house? You have never done this before. Please let her go."

Clint raised his hand and backhanded Soft Wind across the face. "Shut up, squaw," he grumbled as he untied the ropes around Lauralee's ankles. "Mind your business. This has nothing to do with you."

Soft Wind rubbed her aching jaw as she backed away from Clint. She eyed the woman again, then Clint, then without further thought, ran from the cabin.

Clint ran to the door. "Come back here, you bitch!" he shouted, then fell facedown halfway in and out of the door when Lauralee came up from behind him and butted him in the back with her throbbing, aching head.

Clint scrambled to his feet. He looked desperately through the trees and saw that he had lost sight of Soft Wind, then looked quickly at Lauralee as she tried to run past him.

"You ain't goin' nowhere," Clint said, grabbing her by the arms, backing her up toward the bed. "You're mine. All mine." He laughed throatily. "I bet that Injun is goin' wild about now, wonderin' where you are, and who with. He won't find me. My cabin is well hid. No one knows about it except for me and Soft Wind . . . and . . ."

He looked over his shoulder, having almost forgotten about Brian Brave Walker.

But when Lauralee kicked at him with her moccasined feet, he knew that he had enough on his hands here in the cabin. Let Soft Wind go. He'd be glad to be rid of her. And she knew enough not to tattle on him. He had warned her often enough about never telling anyone about how he treated her and the kid.

"Seems not only my kid, but now my wife, has run out on me," Clint said, laughing boisterously. "Well, I was glad to be rid of Brian Brave Walker. I'm just as glad that my squaw is gone." He leaned into Lauralee's face. "Since you were so willin' to be Dancin' Cloud's squaw, surely you won't mind bein' *mine*."

Lauralee's head was spinning. Not so much from pain, but from discovering that this man was Brian Brave Walker's father!

Now she understood all too well why Brian hated and mistrusted white people so much. Surely he had been terribly mistreated by his father who was a white man!

She wished that her mouth wasn't gagged. She had so much that she wanted to say to Clint McCloud!

Instead, she closed her eyes and prayed that Dancing Cloud would find this cabin and rescue her from this vile man. As she lay there she could not help but relive over and over again the rape and the murder of her mother all those years ago. She could hardly bear to think that she might follow in her mother's footsteps and be victimized by the very . . . same . . . man. He surely would not want her to live to point an accusing finger at him.

Sobbing and frightened, Soft Wind ran blindly through the forest. She looked continuously over her shoulder, fearful of the moment that her husband would catch up with her. He would kill her. She knew that he would kill her. Had he not told her often enough that he would if she left him?

Even when he had left her for weeks and months at a time she had been too afraid to leave. She had known that he would search until every stone in the forest was upturned to find her.

"My people!" she sobbed, gazing up at the smoky haze that circled the mountain. "So near, yet so far. I must not go to them. I will bring danger to their very doorsteps!"

She stumbled over the roots of a tree that grew gnarled across the ground, then regained her balance and ran onward. "Brian Brave Walker!" she cried. "My son! My son! Where are you, my son? My baby. Where did my husband take our baby?"

She ran up a steep path. When she heard the sound of horse's hooves behind her, she made a sharp turn and ran at breakneck speed through the trees.

Then her breath was stolen away and she screamed as she came to the brink of a cliff that plunged into a chasm cut by an ancient stream. She tried to stop, to steady herself, but toppled over and found herself hurtling through space.

She grunted with pain as she fell hard against the rocks below, her head making a cracking sound as it fell back against a boulder.

The black void of unconsciousness followed.

Dancing Cloud drew a tight rein and listened. His eyes narrowed. He had just heard the bloodcurdling scream of a woman.

"Lauralee?" he whispered, his blood turning cold at the thought of what may have happened to her.

He wheeled his white stallion around and edged his horse through the denseness of the forest and followed the route of the scream. He stopped again when he saw a cliff a short distance away.

Securing his horse's reins beneath a rock, he ran to the ledge and looked downward. He was too high up to tell who lay on the rocks far below him.

Breathless, his pulse racing, he began making his way down the side of the cliff. . . .

29

While we live, in love let us so persevere,
That when we live no more, we may live ever.
                                    —ANNE BRADSTREET

Finally at the bottom of the cliff Dancing Cloud ran to
the woman and knelt beside her. Now knowing for certain that this woman was not Lauralee, he breathed in
a heavy, quavering breath of air. Her skin was copper
and through the threads of red blood running through
her hair he could see that it was coal black.

With trembling hands he smoothed her hair back
from her face just as her eyelashes fluttered slightly
open.

"Clint ... and ... woman," Soft Wind said raspily.
She looked wildly up at Dancing Cloud and lifted a
shaky, weak hand, pointing in the direction of her
cabin. "Cabin. Go. Help woman."

Dancing Cloud's eyebrows raised. This woman
knew a man named Clint? Could it be Clint McCloud?

And she had spoken of a woman.

Was that woman Lauralee?

He turned his eyes where she was still pointing, then
looked down at her again.

"You said the name Clint," he said guardedly. "Is his
last name McCloud?"

She slowly nodded, then slipped back into unconsciousness.

"Clint McCloud," he ground out between gritted teeth. "*He* is here. He abducted Lauralee!"

He was torn with what to do. This woman was in no shape to be put on his horse and carried as he searched for the cabin where he might find Lauralee.

Yet he feared leaving her there, unprotected.

His mind was scrambled.

He wanted to do what was right for this woman.

Yet Lauralee's life lay in the balance if he waited much longer!

Lifting Soft Wind into his arms he found a narrow path that led up the side of the cliff that he hadn't known was there when he had come to her rescue. He held her close and climbed the steep path.

When he reached the top of the butte, he knew that he had no choice but to leave the woman and come back for her later. Hopefully he would have Lauralee with him. A travois could be made and the woman would be transported to his village. There she would be among people of her own skin coloring. She would be cared for.

Hopefully she would survive.

He gently laid Soft Wind beneath a tree, then went to his horse and took the blanket from his saddle. He spread this on the ground on a soft bed of leaves, then placed Soft Wind there and turned the corners of the blankets up over her.

Knowing that she had arrived there by foot meant that she had surely not traveled that far. He would go by foot in search of the cabin. His arrival would be less noticed that way. He would surprise Clint McCloud. He would rescue Lauralee.

Wonder of how Clint McCloud could be there, so close to Dancing Cloud's mountain, and why this woman had apparently been with him, filled Dancing Cloud's thoughts as he grabbed his rifle.

He glanced at the woman once again, worried about her welfare.

But knowing that Lauralee's own welfare was in

question, he ran through the tangled vines and thick
brush, his eyes constantly searching for signs of a
cabin.

Clint shoved Lauralee onto his bed and straddled
her. He smiled smugly down at her as he untied her
wrists, his wicked eyes telling her everything that she
needed to know about what he had planned for her
next.

She had to get away.

She could not allow herself to die the same hideous
death as her mother!

She had too much to live for now.

Her Cherokee chief.

Oh, what a life they could have together.

And Brian Brave Walker.

She wanted to mother him into loving her!

"I can't get over how much you look like a woman
I came across during the war," Clint said, jerking the
rope away from her wrists. He held her down by the
force of his body as he continued straddling her. "I
raped more than one Rebel woman. But there was this
one woman in particular I will never forget."

He grabbed Lauralee by her hair, causing her to
wince. "The hair was the color of yours. Her eyes were
the same," he snarled. He jerked her face close to his,
so close she could feel the heat of his foul breath.

He released his hold on her hair and traced her facial
contours with a finger. "And by damn," he said huskily. "She looked just like you in the face."

Breathing hard, waiting for the right moment to
make her move, and seeing him as quite foolish for releasing her bonds, Lauralee glared up at him. She tried
not to hear him paint the same description of her
mother in the same breath that he had spoken of raping
her. Her anger was fueled enough already to kill him.
If he didn't stop his bragging she knew that she could
not stop at just killing him. She would humiliate him
first in the worst way a man could be humiliated.

If . . . only . . . she got the chance.

If only she could grab his pistol and disarm him.

She knew where she would like to shoot him, right where his thoughts seemed always centered, as well as his ego!

For her mother, for all of those other women he had raped and murdered, for herself and the life she had been forced to lead because of him, she would make him pay.

And for his son, Brian Brave Walker, whose life had probably been filled with abuse and pain, she would make him pay.

Even for this Indian woman who had surely been forced to be his love slave, Lauralee would take care of this man and make sure he never fulfilled his lusts with another woman's body.

Once his body was mutilated worse than having been maimed in the leg, he could lust, but would never again be able to act upon those loathsome feelings.

Clint jerked his shirt open, causing buttons to pop off. His eyes narrowed into Lauralee's. "See these scars on my chest?" he said between clenched teeth. "This woman, the one you resemble, gave them to me. She was a hellcat, that one." He laughed boisterously. "These scars? I wear them proudly. They are a reminder of my victories in the South. And I ain't speakin' about the sort gained by shootin' off firearms. My favored victories were those I found while with the beautiful southern ladies."

Not able to take any more of his bragging, and seeing that he was somewhat off guard as he glanced down long enough to admire the long, lean scratches that ran like paths through his thick, dark, and kinky chest hairs, Lauralee reached for his face and went for his eyes with her sharp fingernails.

Before he could stop her she had drawn blood around his eyes.

Grabbing for his face, he let out a loud cry of pain.

Seizing the opportunity, Lauralee gave him a shove, causing him to lose his balance.

She then raised a knee and planted it squarely in his groin.

This sent him from the bed yowling and clutching himself.

Lauralee rolled from the bed. Her eyes were on a holstered pistol that hung from a peg on the wall.

Her heart pounding so much that she felt as though her body was one large throbbing, she made a lunge for the pistol.

Just as she had it in her hand she screamed with pain when Clint grabbed her by the hair again and gave it a hard yank. The pain was so severe it felt as if her entire scalp had been pulled from her head.

He dragged her to the floor.

He released her hair and placed a foot on her stomach as he bent over to reach for his pistol.

"Ain't you a hellcat?" He chuckled. "Just like that lady I was tellin' you about."

In Lauralee's mind's eye she recalled her mother fighting off the Yankee, only to be knocked to the floor over and over again.

Lauralee had been too afraid to move as she had gazed at the man's holstered pistol. She had wanted to run from beneath the staircase to the man and grab the pistol. But her father had always taught her the dangers of firearms. He had told her never to touch his pistol. He had warned her that curious children accidentally shot themselves every day.

He had put the fear of God in her about firearms; so much that she had not been able to take the man's firearm away from him when she had the opportunity while . . . he . . . was raping her mother.

The guilt tore at her heart even now for having not saved her mother. She remembered closing her eyes and saying the prayer that she had said with her mother every night before she went to sleep. . . .

"Now I lay me down to sleep, I pray the Lord my

soul to keep, if I should die before I wake, I pray the Lord my soul to take."

She had said that prayer over and over again until suddenly it was quiet in her house.

From her hiding place beneath the staircase she had peeked out and found the man gone and her mother lying lifelessly still, her clothes torn, her arms and legs spread out strangely, her eyes staring, forever staring.

These thoughts crashing through her mind, like wildfires raging through prairie grass, gave Lauralee the courage and strength to knock Clint away from her.

When he fell, she grabbed his pistol, then scrambled to her feet.

Breathing hard, huffing and puffing, she stood over him.

"Now do you want to tell me again about raping my mother?" Lauralee said venomously, not even recognizing her own voice. With her free hand she wove her fingers through her hair. "See this hair? My mother's hair was the same color." She glared at him, her eyes narrowing. "See my eyes? My father's eyes were the same color as mine. But so were my *mother's*."

She waved the pistol toward him. "See those scars you are so proud of on your chest?" she cried. "My mother's fingernails inflicted those wounds. I look at them proudly. At least she was able to inflict some measure of pain on you before you . . . before you . . ."

She stopped. There were more urgent things on her mind besides reliving that dreadful day over and over again. She steadied her pistol with her other hand, keeping a steady aim on Clint.

"Get undressed," she flatly ordered.

"What?"

"You heard me," Lauralee said, her voice breaking. "Get undressed. I have something to do to repay you for what you did to my mother and countless other women and people of your past."

"What are you going to do?" Clint whined, slipping his shirt off. "Please don't hurt me."

"Listen to you beg," Lauralee said, laughing. "Did those women beg? Did you enjoy hearing them beg as I am enjoying hearing you plead with me?"

Clint cowered beneath the threat of the gun, and the sound of her voice, so cold, so ruthless.

Lauralee cocked the pistol. "Damn you, Yankee," she hissed. "Get undressed. I'm not going to shoot you dead. I only intend to make it impossible for you ever to rape women again."

"You don't plan to shoot my . . ." Clint stammered, paling.

"Exactly," Lauralee said, a slow, smug smile lifting her lips. "My father taught me long ago not to touch firearms and I never disobeyed my father." Her eyes glimmered into Clint's. "But I'm a big girl now. I need no one telling me what or what not to do. I have my own mind. I have my own need . . . for *revenge*."

"Lord," Clint gasped, his breeches dropping to his ankles.

Lauralee's gaze moved slowly over him, disgusted at the sight of him. When her eyes reached that part of him that she planned to remove with a bullet, maybe *two*, she found his hairy hands covering his manhood.

"If I have to, I'll shoot right through your hands to get to that disgusting part of your anatomy that you've misused all of your ugly life," Lauralee said, shrugging nonchalantly.

The sound of rushing feet approaching the cabin outside, took Lauralee off guard. Instinctively, she looked over her shoulder.

That gave Clint enough time to jump her, his wooden leg dragging clumsily behind him as he grabbed Lauralee by a wrist.

When she dropped the gun, it went off.

Lauralee wrenched her wrist free and turned to Clint. Her eyes widened as he sank to his knees, blood seeping through his fingers as he clutched at his chest.

"You . . . damn . . . bitch," Clint managed to say in a sour whisper. "You . . . damn . . . *Rebel*."

Lauralee jumped back as Clint's body spasmed, then fell forward.

Her pulse racing, her eyes wide, Lauralee stared down at the Yankee. His body was still. She was almost certain that he wasn't breathing.

She inched back from him, afraid to feel for a pulse in his throat. If he was still clinging to life, he could grab her wrist. He might even reach for the pistol. It lay only a few inches from one of his hands.

Lauralee turned quickly around when she heard someone enter the cabin behind her. When she found Dancing Cloud there, her feelings rushed out in a torrent of tears.

Sobbing, she ran to him and flung herself into his arms.

Dancing Cloud held her tightly, his eyes locked on Clint McCloud. Totally nude and lying in a pool of blood, the man was slumped over, his knees drawn beneath him.

"Dancing Cloud, is he dead?" Lauralee asked, clinging tightly to him, her cheek pressed hard against the soft fabric of his buckskin shirt. "I dropped the pistol. It went off. Is he dead? Truly dead?"

Dancing Cloud leaned a bit sideways, enabling him to see Clint's eyes. "His eyes are locked in a death stare," he said thickly. "*Ii*, yes, I would say that he is dead."

Lauralee crept from his arms. She moved behind him and leaned out only enough to see Clint. "Please make sure for me," she murmured. "I've got to know that we have nothing else to fear from that man."

She shivered and clasped and unclasped her hands nervously as Dancing Cloud went to Clint and kicked him over onto his back. She bit her lower lip nervously as Dancing Cloud stooped down onto his haunches and placed his fingertips to Clint's neck.

"There is no pulse," he said, turning to give Lauralee a reassured stare. "We are finally rid of this vermin. The growth of the cancer stops here, today."

He went to Lauralee, gave her a comforting hug,
then stepped away from her and held her at arm's
length. "Your nursing skills are needed," he said
thickly.

"What do you mean?" Lauralee said, seeing the concern in his eyes. "Who needs me? Where is this person?"

Dancing Cloud explained about having found the
Indian woman at the foot of the cliff. He explained that
she had helped him find the cabin.

Lauralee paled. "Oh, no," she cried. "That must be
Brian Brave Walker's mother. Where is she? I must go
to her."

"Brian Brave Walker?" Dancing Cloud said, arching
an eyebrow.

"Clint McCloud was his father, the Indian woman
was Clint's wife, Brian's *mother*," Lauralee blurted out,
seeing the disbelief in Dancing Cloud's eyes.

"He . . . ?" Dancing Cloud said, numb from the
knowing.

"Yes, he," Lauralee said, taking his hand. "Now let's
go to Brian Brave Walker's mother. I shall do what I
can for her while you also work your magic with your
herbal medications."

Hand in hand, they left the cabin and the man who
had been like a dark thundercloud over both their lives
for too many years to count.

30

A mind at peace,
A heart whose love is innocent.

—LORD BYRON

The sound of a steady beat from a drum filled the evening air just outside Dancing Cloud's cabin. Low chants rose and fell in rhythm with the drumbeats.

Several days had passed and Lauralee had hardly left Soft Wind's bedside after Dancing Cloud had brought her to the bed on the loft. Lauralee had bathed her fevered brow and force-fed her broth when she barely awakened.

But no matter what Lauralee did, nor no matter how dedicated she was to her patient, she had seen Soft Wind slowly slipping away. The head wound had been too severe to heal. There were other broken bones, and one of her lungs had collapsed. The end seemed inevitable. It would come soon. Very soon.

Lauralee realized today that Soft Wind lay closer to death than ever before. She could tell by the strange sort of rattling sounds emerging from deeply within her one lung.

And it had been a full day and night now since Soft Wind had been able to take any nourishment.

Brian Brave Walker edged in next to Lauralee and gazed down with tear-filled eyes at his mother. He fell to his knees beside the bed and clutched her thin, frail hand in his.

"Mama, please don't leave me," he cried. "Papa is dead now. You can live a life of peace. You are among your own people, Mama. Can't you hear their chants? Everyone wants you to live."

A knot forming in her throat, her heart going out to this small child, Lauralee tried to take Brian Brave Walker's hand to draw him into her embrace.

She jumped with a start and gasped when he turned and gave her a look that made her want to shrink away to nothingness. The hate in his eyes was so intense, it seemed to burn into Lauralee's very soul!

"Leave me alone with my mama," Brian Brave Walker said, his voice low and even and emotionless. "She will hear me if I talk long enough today. I know it."

"Brian Brave Walker, darling, your mother can't hear anyone now," Lauralee said, knowing that he must be prepared for what would soon transpire.

Yet Lauralee also knew that Brian Brave Walker must not be denied these last moments with his mother.

"But stay and talk to her as long as you wish," she quickly interjected. "I will leave you alone with her. You shan't be disturbed."

Lauralee pushed herself up from the chair, and when she placed her feet on the floor and she felt suddenly dizzy, she realized just that quickly how worn out and weary she was. She had not slept all that much. When she had, she and Dancing Cloud had laid on a pallet of furs before the fireplace, taking what little comfort they could in the lonely midnight hours by holding each other while they slept.

Lauralee sighed and walked toward the ladder that led from the loft. She wiped her eyes with the back of her hands. She wove her fingers through her tangled hair. She looked down at her drooping, wrinkled cotton dress.

While caring for Soft Wind so feverishly, she had neglected herself. In the end she had hoped that it would be worth it. She had hoped that she could help Soft Wind pull through this crisis.

Yet all along Lauralee had known the severity of Soft Wind's wounds and had truly never thought that she would live.

Turning to back herself down the steep, narrow ladder, she gave Brian Brave Walker and Soft Wind one last, lingering look.

Then feeling empty and useless, she went on down the ladder.

She was glad to find Dancing Cloud sitting in the plush overstuffed chair beside the fire. As never before, she needed his arms around her now. She had not been able to win Brian Brave Walker's friendship, much less his love.

Did he see his father when he looked at her?

She wondered now if he could ever see her in any other light.

The damn Yankee had harmed the child in so many ways without even having to touch him physically. It had all been inside the child's head.

That was not the sort of illness that Lauralee knew anything about. She had just learned how to treat physical wounds. Not those inflicted on one's soul by a mad, twisted father!

Lauralee moved listlessly over to the chair, then sank down and rested her head on Dancing Cloud's knee. She became warmed through and through when he began lovingly stroking her hair.

"There is nothing more than I can do for Soft Wind," she said, blinking tears from her eyes. She stared into the fire. "When she dies, Brian Brave Walker is going to blame me."

Dancing Cloud bent low and placed his hands at Lauralee's waist and drew her up to her knees, then lifted her onto his lap. "My *o-ge-ye*," he said, cuddling her close. "No one could have put such heart in caring for someone as you cared for Soft Wind. I have stood back and observed Brian Brave Walker watching your gentleness toward his mother. Deep down inside himself he knows that you have gone way beyond what most would do for someone who is ill."

"When your Shaman came and spoke over Soft Wind, Brian Brave Walker thanked him," Lauralee said, her voice breaking. "Darling, he has not given me the courtesy of one thank you, even though I have spent countless hours at his mother's bedside. I haven't done this for his mother to receive thanks. But I deserve some sort of courtesy, don't you think? I truly don't believe he understands my feelings, nor *me*. He may hate me forever only because my skin is the same color as his father's."

"At present he cannot see past his fear of losing his mother, nor beyond his grief and despair," Dancing Cloud said, brushing a soft kiss across Lauralee's lips. "Give him time, my *o-ge-ye*. He *will* move into your arms for comfort."

An involuntary shiver swam across Lauralee's flesh. "She *is* going to die," she murmured. "Before the night is over, she will be dead. The poor child. He will feel that he has lost everything in the world when he loses his mother." She swallowed hard. "I know. I experienced it, myself."

"It is different for Brian Brave Walker," Dancing Cloud said. "He has someone who wishes to take him in as 'family.' He will never be an orphan."

Lauralee gazed up at the loft. Candlelight wavered from a candle beside the bed, the soft light spreading. "Soft Wind was conscious enough, enough times, to tell me that she was originally from this village," she said, shuddering when she caught the sound of Soft Wind's death rattles as they became more pronounced. From her experience with seeing patients die, Lauralee knew that Soft Wind had hardly any time left at all.

"I questioned around," Dancing Cloud said, releasing Lauralee as she eased from his lap and sat down on a chair beside him. "None of her relatives survived the massacre brought onto my people by Clint McCloud and his Yankees. She escaped. She was found by some Confederate soldiers. She was too much in shock to make any sense when they questioned her. She was placed with other children who had been misplaced during the war and taken to an orphanage in Kentucky."

"Had I been found by the same men as she, Soft Wind and I could have been raised in the same orphanage," Lauralee said sullenly. "She perhaps thought that she was one of the lucky ones when Clint McCloud found her there and took her away, to be his wife."

"Damn the railroads that were built through Cherokee country," Dancing Cloud said, his teeth clenched. "If not for the railroads, Clint McCloud would never had cause to come to the land he had devastated when he was a Union officer. As it was, he traveled with the railroads, a railroad man even before the war broke out."

"He had some nerve marrying a Cherokee after having massacred so many during the war," Lauralee said, her voice filled with venom.

"I am sure Soft Wind was beautiful and entrancing before she married Clint McCloud. He was taken by her innocent loveliness. He was blinded too much by her sheer beauty to even think about her being Indian," Dancing Cloud said, glancing up at the loft.

"Until Brian Brave Walker was born," Lauralee hissed. "Then he realized just what it meant to marry someone with a different skin coloring. His wife bore him a son who he could never love because his skin was copper instead of white."

"I don't believe it was the color so much as Brian Brave Walker's physical attributes," Dancing Cloud mumbled. "Surely if the man had any guilt whatsoever about the havoc he wreaked during the war against the children of our village, seeing Brian Brave Walker could be the same as looking at those children his horse ran down, or his bullets pierced."

Lauralee looked quickly at Dancing Cloud. "Darling, you have spoken so often of your people as full-blooded Cherokee, and your pride of that," she said, her voice guarded. "Have you ever stopped to think about the children *we* might have? They would not be full-bloods. How would you feel about having a son with white skin, instead of copper?"

Dancing Cloud gave her a sudden, stunned look, as if someone had splashed cold water onto his face. Like a thunderbolt inside his mind the remembrance of that day in the spirit world with his father came to him, and what his father had said to him about children. He had forgotten the warning, until now.

He stared at Lauralee a moment longer, then rose quickly from the chair and went and stood at the open door. He clasped his hand so tightly to the door, his knuckles were rendered white.

He thought back to that day with his father in the spirit world. James Talking Bear had reminded him that this woman to whom he had given his heart was white. If she had children born of their union, the child could be white.

Never before had mixed bloods lived among his Wolf Clan of Cherokee. Never before had any of their braves married a white woman.

This was the first for his people.

Only briefly after Dancing Cloud had discovered that he loved Lauralee had he stopped to consider the consequences of marrying her. And all through these weeks of other more pressing issues he had forgot to worry about the skin color of a child born of his and Lauralee's love.

Lauralee came to him and took his hand. "Dancing Cloud, what is it?" she murmured. "Tell me what's wrong. You're frightening me."

"I want children," he said, turning slow eyes to her. "But white-skinned?"

She went cold inside. Fear grabbed at her heart. What if he changed his mind about marrying her? What if he sent her away?

Again he turned his eyes from her and peered out the door, at the throng of people who were kneeling around a large outdoor fire not that far from his cabin. They were now quiet, in a soft communion with the Great Spirit. It was as though even they knew that Soft Wind was taking her last breaths.

Dancing Cloud felt suddenly guilty for thinking of what color children he and his woman might bring into the world, when one of his very own people would soon enter the spirit path of the hereafter.

"Darling Cherokee," Lauralee murmured. "I know you too well to allow what you have said worry me any further. You know, as well as I, that the color of *our* children will not matter. Even if it means that we will bring the first mixed-blood into your people's lives, it will be a child who is loved . . . who is revered, because it will be the child born of an intense love, the first child of your people's *chief*."

She sighed heavily. "I still am not your wife," she said, feeling selfish to even think about that at this time.

"Soon," Dancing Cloud said. He took her hands and drew her around to face him. "Soft Wind is dying. When our mourning for her is behind us, we will speak words of togetherness. We will have brought Brian Brave Walker into our circle of life. We will then look toward a future of our very own children, be they white, or copper-skinned."

"Oh, darling, I knew that you would never allow such a thing as skin coloring or bloodlines stand between our happiness," Lauralee said, easing into his arms. "And I promise you, Dancing Cloud, that we will have many beautiful children."

"There is something more I wish to do," Dancing Cloud said, gazing down at her.

"Yes? What is it?" Lauralee asked, searching his eyes.

"I have recently learned about an orphanage that lies

only a half day's ride from the base of my mountain,"
he said hoarsely.

"Yes, I believe I know the orphanage. It was a topic
of conversation many times among those of us who
were in the orphanage in Saint Louis. It was built only
a few years ago. The orphanage where I was raised donated a good sum of money to get this newest one established. I remember talking among the girls at our
orphanage about whether or not those at the new one
fared better than we did at ours."

"There may be small children there from Cherokee
villages where there is much starvation among their
people because of white people's interference in their
lives. White people who stole their land and their live-
stock," he said thickly. "Let us go there soon. Perhaps
we might find a child or two to bring back with us to
be Brian Brave Walker's brother or sister?"

Lauralee stared up at him, stunned by his suggestion.
She was torn with how she should feel. If he brought
more orphaned children to his house to father, would
this give him an excuse to ask her not to bear children
of their own whose skin might not match his?

"Do you mind, my *o-ge-ye*, if we go soon and see if
there are Cherokee children who need family and loving?" he said, his voice filled with an anxious hope.
"While you have sat at Soft Wind's bedside those long
hours I have thought of what a sad life she had. Like
you, she witnessed the death of her mother. Not only
her mother. Her whole family. She was wrenched from
her home and placed in an orphanage. Then she lived
a hellish life with Clint McCloud."

He stopped and nervously cleared his throat. "While
you saw to Soft Wind's needs these past days I have
thought hard and long about other Cherokee children
whose destiny is colored by sadness because they are
in orphanages. An orphanage must be the loneliest of
places. But of course you know that it *is*."

Feeling selfish and guilty for having thought that
Dancing Cloud had motives other than what he said, to

bring more children into their home, Lauralee leaned
into his embrace. He had not *just* thought up taking in
more orphans after thinking about bringing a mixed-
blood child into this world that was born of his and
Lauralee's love. He had been thinking about the orphaned Cherokee children for days!

"My sweet, gentle Cherokee," she said, tears streaming from her eyes. "Your heart is so big. Your heart is
so good. Yes, my beloved, I will go with you to the orphanage. I will take within my arms as many children
that will fill them."

She clung to him. "If you wish, we can even delay
our wedding day awhile longer so that we can go and
get the children," she murmured.

"I knew that you would say that," Dancing Cloud
said. "I only wish that I had known about Soft Wind,
where *she* had been taken as a child. She would have
been spared that dreadful life with Clint McCloud."

Lauralee turned and gazed up at the loft, then turned
to Dancing Cloud again. "One thing wonderful came
from that marriage," she said, her voice breaking.

"Brian Brave Walker," Dancing Cloud said thickly.

Lauralee nodded.

A sudden cry of despair wrenched Dancing Cloud
and Lauralee apart. They ran toward the ladder that led
to the loft, Brian Brave Walker's hysteria squeezing
their insides.

When they reached the loft, Brian Brave Walker was
bent over his mother, desperately hugging her.

"You can't be dead!" he cried. "*Tla-no,* no! You
can't leave me! Without you I have nothing! You have
been my world. I'm sorry I ran away from home.
Please forgive me and come back to me now. I will
never leave you again!"

Lauralee felt frozen to the floor. Trembling, she
placed her hands to her throat. She watched Dancing
Cloud go to Brian Brave Walker and clasp his hands to
the small brave's shoulders. With a slight yank he

managed to wrench Brian Brave Walker's grip from his mother.

"Come now, son," Dancing Cloud said, his voice gentle, but filled with command. "It is time to allow your mother's spirit to begin its journey on the path to the hereafter. We must help her spirit along by singing songs and praying. Cry, my son. Cry it all out. Then we will go among our people. You will be taught the true ways of mourning that your people, the Cherokee, practice."

Remembering why his mother had named him "brave," Brian Brave Walker willed himself to stop crying. He left his mother's bed, his chin held high, his shoulders squared.

"Show me how it is done," he said, looking up at Dancing Cloud with his trusting dark eyes. "Show me everything Cherokee. I wish now to be your son. My mother would want it that way."

Lauralee moved slowly toward Brian Brave Walker. "Child, I also want to help you adjust," she murmured.

She jumped with alarm and almost fell backward down the ladder when Brian Brave Walker glared up at her, his eyes and pursed lips revealing how he still hated and mistrusted her.

Dancing Cloud was as stunned as Lauralee by the intensity in which Brian displayed his hate for Lauralee. It was hard for Dancing Cloud to accept, or overlook. He wanted to shake the child and scold him for treating Lauralee in such a callous way.

But he knew that this trust and loving had to be learned, not forced on him.

Lauralee stepped slowly around Dancing Cloud and Brian Brave Walker. "Take him downstairs and I shall see to Soft Wind," she said, her voice breaking. "I shan't be long."

"No! No! Leave her be!" Brian Brave Walker screamed, trying to jerk himself free from Dancing Cloud's tight clasp so that he could go to his mother again. "It's your fault that she's dead! Why did you not do more for her? You were supposed to heal her! Instead, you killed her!"

Lauralee grew dizzy beneath such a horrendous tongue-lashing and accusations. She grabbed for her head, her heart racing so fast that she felt it might leap from her throat.

"Brian Brave Walker, you . . ." Dancing Cloud began, but Lauralee interrupted him.

"Leave him be," she said, stepping past them, toward the ladder. "I shall go and inform those who will prepare Soft Wind's body for burial that she has left us."

Dancing Cloud's eyes were soft with love for her as he nodded and watched her go down the ladder.

Then he knelt down on his haunches and turned Brian Brave Walker to face him. "You are filled with much hate," he said, his voice firm, yet gentle. "Do you realize the strength of such hate and what it can do to a *a-s-ga-ya,* man?"

"A . . . man . . . ?" Brian Brave Walker said, his eyes widening. "You are talking to me as though I am a man?"

"Do you feel deeply within your heart that you deserve to be called a man who would one day be a great Cherokee warrior?" Dancing Cloud asked softly.

"*Ii,* I wish to one day be a Cherokee warrior," Brian Brave Walker said anxiously. He wiped his eyes dry with the backs of his hands. "I wish to be called a *man.*"

"Can you say that moments ago when you were shouting at Lauralee and saying unkind words to her that you were being a child, or a man?" Dancing Cloud said. "Did saying such things make you feel big, or little?"

Brian Brave Walker sighed heavily. He shuffled his feet nervously. "I do not want to hate," he said, glancing over at his mother who lay peacefully and as lovely as he could ever remember. "Mother would not want me to hate. She never even instructed me to hate my father. She said that hate is like a sore that spreads and spreads."

He looked into Dancing Cloud's eyes once again. "I want no sores within my body, especially my heart," he said innocently.

"Then you must place your hate for Lauralee behind you, my son, for it is very misplaced as it is," Dancing Cloud said thickly.

Brian Brave Walker hung his head for a moment, then he moved slow eyes up at Dancing Cloud. "But I *do* hate her so much," he said, his voice breaking.

"And why do you think that you do?"

"I do not think. I *know*."

"Search your heart, Brian Brave Walker. Search long and hard. Do not tell me now what you find. I will wait for you to tell me later."

Brian Brave Walker nodded. He went to his mother's bedside and gave her a lingering stare, then turned and took Dancing Cloud's hand and looked trustingly up at him. "Please teach me about the spirit world and how my mother will get there," he said softly.

"Come," Dancing Cloud said, walking toward the ladder.

Brian Brave Walker followed Dancing Cloud down the ladder.

"Dancing Cloud?" Brian Brave Walker asked softly.

"Yes, my son?"

"Can you also teach me how not to hate Lauralee?" Brian Brave Walker asked, placing his feet on the floor and gazing up at Dancing Cloud. "Because of you I do wish to know how to like her."

Lauralee had just entered the cabin with two women and had heard Brian Brave Walker. Her lips quavered as Dancing Cloud turned and gave her a soft, reassuring smile.

Brian Brave Walker clung to Dancing Cloud's hand, his eyes wary as he looked over at Lauralee.

He turned again to Dancing Cloud. He tugged on his arm so that Dancing Cloud would lean down close to hear what he had to say. "She is almost as beautiful as my mother, is she not?" he whispered.

"Yes, I would say so," Dancing Cloud whispered back.

"It should not be all that hard to like her, should it?" Brian Brave Walker whispered again, giving Lauralee a quick glance over his shoulder.

Dancing Cloud chuckled.

Lauralee sighed with relief, for Brian Brave Walker's whisper had not been as much of a whisper as he would have liked.

She had heard all that had mattered!

For now, that was enough.

31

What's the earth with all its art,
verse, music, worth compared with
love, found, gained and kept.

—ROBERT BROWNING

Soft Wind had been buried. The journey to and from
the orphanage was behind Lauralee and Dancing
Cloud. When they had arrived there, Lauralee had been
thrust back in time as she had walked the corridors.
While looking into the rooms, seeing the children, it
had been reminiscent of times not that far past. She
could see it in the children's eyes as they gazed back at
her that they envied her and wished to be taken away
to a different world where they would find a true home
filled with love.

There had been no way they could have known that
she had been one of those children at another time, in
another orphanage, with her own dreams, with her own
envies.

She only wished that she could have embraced them
all and brought them back to the village with her, to offer them the sort of life that she had found among
Dancing Cloud's people.

All of the Cherokee children had been taken from
the orphanage and were even now with various families in this village.

Lauralee and Dancing Cloud had taken one child to
raise as their own. She gazed down at the tiny bundle
that she held in her arms. Her eyes sparkled with tears

as she unfolded the blanket and looked at the tiny copper face that was framed already by straight, black hair.

"We found her on our doorstep only recently," the superintendent in charge of the orphanage had told Lauralee and Dancing Cloud. "There was no note. Only the child lying wrapped in a blanket in a wicker basket. If she is taken now by a family, she will never know that her mother chose to give her away."

Lauralee and Dancing Cloud's thoughts had been of one mind and heart. At that very moment their arms had collided as they had both reached for the infant.

That was then.

This was now.

"Our very own daughter, Dancing Cloud," Lauralee said, smiling over at him as he held Brian Brave Walker on his lap before the fire in their fireplace. "Isn't she a small miracle? Isn't she beautiful?"

"She belongs in your arms as though you were the one who gave her life," Dancing Cloud said, lifting Brian Brave Walker to the floor. He placed a gentle hand on the young brave's shoulder. "Go. Go and see the child. You will grow up as brother and sister."

Brian Brave Walker shied away from the suggestion. Instead, he went and stood behind the chair so that he could not see the child.

"Brian Brave Walker, please come and become acquainted with Hope," Lauralee said, puzzled over why he was acting this way. Nothing about his reaction to the child was normal. He even refused to look at the baby, much less touch her. "Brian Brave Walker, Hope is so sweet. So precious."

"No," Brian Brave Walker said, refusing to come from behind the chair, his attitude seeming to be steeped in a deep sadness. "I do not want to see the *u-s-di-ga*, baby. I wish not to *hold* or *touch* any baby."

Lauralee rose from the chair. She slowly rocked the baby back and forth in her arms. "I must take her to the loft and put her in her cradle," she murmured. "But before long she will be crying to be fed. Brian Brave Walker, will you go with me to prepare her milk and warm the bottle for her feeding?"

"No, I will stay in my bed while you take care of her," Brian Brave Walker said, running now and throwing himself down on his bed. "Just leave me be. I wish never to call that baby my sister."

Dancing Cloud's eyebrows arched. He rose from the chair and turned and gazed questionly at Brian Brave Walker. He did not think that the child was jealous. There seemed to be more to his behavior than what jealousy would cause.

Dancing Cloud could only conclude from that, that Brian Brave Walker's behavior stemmed from something else in his past, but he could not fathom what it might be.

As Lauralee waited for Dancing Cloud at the foot of the ladder, he went to Brian Brave Walker and moved to his knees beside his bed.

"My son, we will talk about this tomorrow," Dancing Cloud said, removing Brian Brave Walker's moccasins and placing them on the floor beside the bed. He shoved the child's fringed shirt over his head, then scooted his breeches down and covered him with a blanket.

Dancing Cloud smoothed the palm of his hand over Brian Brave Walker's brow. "Find solace in sleep, my son," he said thickly. "Soon all of the battle scars from your past life will heal. Then you will accept things of your new life with much ease. Even *sisters*."

Brian Brave Walker gazed up at Dancing Cloud with defiance, then he sobbed and lunged into his arms. He held onto Dancing Cloud as if his life depended on it. "I love you," he sobbed. "You are more father to me already than my true father ever was. Thank you, Dancing Cloud. Oh, thank you. But do not make me look to that baby as my sister."

Dancing Cloud held the young brave close to his heart, his hand caressing his tiny back. "If you wish, call me Father," he said softly. "I already proudly call you my son. And I would never force anything on you. Not even a sister."

"Thank you, Father," Brian Brave Walker said, looking past Dancing Cloud's shoulder at Lauralee. His feelings for her were softening as each day passed, yet he still could not let her know that he was ready to be friends, even perhaps more than that.

The word "mother" came to him at times when he envisioned himself in her arms.

Then his true mother's face would flash before him, but his feelings for her were still too intense, too real, to replace her with another woman.

"Good night, Brian Brave Walker," Lauralee said, smiling at him. "Sleep tight. Tomorrow is going to be a wonderful day, darling. Dancing Cloud and I are going to be married."

Brian Brave Walker smiled weakly at her, then eased from Dancing Cloud's arms and snuggled beneath his blankets.

Dancing Cloud rose from him and went to Lauralee. He started to take her by an elbow, to help her onto the ladder, then was taken aback when he saw a sudden grimace on her face.

"What is it?" he said, taking the child from her arms. "You are in pain. Where? Tell me where you hurt."

Lauralee inhaled a quavering breath. Afraid of what she had felt, she placed a hand to her abdomen. Tonight she had wanted to be able to tell Dancing Cloud that she thought she might be with child. She had missed her last monthly flow.

And, ah, what a perfect time to tell him that they would have another child, one born of their love. When they had already been blessed by two children, being able to tell him that they would soon have one of their very own would have been wonderful.

Now, as the pain passed on through her abdomen, leaving only some small, vague cramping, she had to believe that she was going to have her monthly flow after all.

"What *is* it?" Dancing Cloud persisted as Lauralee silently pondered over what had caused the pains.

"I'm not sure," she said, smiling awkwardly up at him.

The pain had stopped.

The cramping was gone.

Surely what she had experienced had been caused by the excitement of the day, of bringing home a daughter, and seeing the other children being taken into homes where they would find the love they had never known before.

Now feeling totally all right again, Lauralee flipped her hair over her shoulders and walked over to Brian Brave Walker's bed. "I'm fine," she told Dancing Cloud over her shoulder. "Go on up to the loft with Hope. I have something else to do before coming to bed, myself."

Dancing Cloud gazed at her for a moment longer.

He then held Hope in the crook of his left arm while pulling himself up the ladder with his right hand.

Lauralee knelt on her knees beside Brian Brave Walker's bed. When she reached a hand to his brow and he flinched, she drew her hand slowly away.

She gazed into his large, dark eyes. "I do love you, Brian Brave Walker," she murmured. "And because I do, I wish to teach you a bedtime prayer that my mother taught me so many years ago."

"Is a prayer like a story?" Brian asked, leaning up on an elbow.

"Something like that," Lauralee said, laughing softly.

"I like stories," Brian Brave Walker said, scooting closer to Lauralee. "My mother told me stories at bedtime . . . stories of her people, who are also *mine*. Will you be telling me a prayer of your people?"

"I will be teaching you a prayer that belongs to all people, whether their skin is white, copper, red or black," Lauralee said, smoothing the blanket up to his chin as he stretched out on his back.

The prayer had brought back memories of that day, when she had recited it over and over to help get her through the horrible ordeal of her mother's rape. Now, however, Lauralee felt that maybe something as innocent as this prayer might bring her and Brian Brave Walker closer.

As she began saying the prayer, she watched his expression softening. "Now I lay me down to sleep, I pray the Lord my soul to keep . . ." she began, smiling to herself when his eyes drifted closed. "If I should die before I wake, I pray the lord my soul to take."

She placed a gentle hand on his brow, which he now allowed because he was asleep, then lightly kissed his lips. "Sleep well, my son," she whispered. "Have sweet dreams of angels."

As she rose from the bed she grabbed at her abdomen and gasped when pains shot through it, so severe, she became dizzy.

Then the ugly, pressing down cramping began in earnest. Soon it fully emcompassed her abdomen. She teetered as she gazed up at the loft. She tried to cry out Dancing Cloud's name.

But her voice came out as no louder than a harsh whisper, the intense pain having robbed her of her ability to talk normally.

Slowly, perspiration rolling from her brow, Lauralee inched her way to the ladder. She panted and sucked in a wild breath of air as she locked her hands on the sides of the ladder.

Gazing upward, wishing that Dancing Cloud would decide to look down to see if she was coming, she began slowly climbing the ladder. She pulled herself up one rung after another. She closed her eyes and panted hard, trying to bear the pain, a pain that was now an intense pressure, as though everything within her might fall out of her at any moment.

This isn't any ordinary menstrual period, she thought desperately to herself.

"Lord, surely I am miscarrying," she whispered. Despair filled her at the thought of losing hers and Dancing Cloud's child before having even told him that she thought she might be pregnant.

When she finally reached the top of the ladder, Lauralee could just barely see beyond the small, dimly lit space. Then she realized why Dancing Cloud had not been aware of her efforts to climb the ladder, nor had he heard any of her muffled pleas for help. He was totally engrossed in the child. The baby was on the bed beside him, her blanket thrown aside, her fists and arms kicking as Dancing Cloud talked and played with her.

When Dancing Cloud sensed Lauralee's presence, he turned to her. "She is awake but I do not believe she is hungry yet," he said.

His words drifted off and he lunged from the bed when he saw the fear in Lauralee's eyes, the sweat pouring from her brow as she tried to climb the rest of the way into the loft.

"*O-ge-ye!*" Dancing Cloud cried, rushing from the bed. He bent low over Lauralee and placed gentle hands to her waist and helped her on up the ladder. "What is happening? You look as though you are in such pain. Why, my *o-ge-ye*? What is the matter?"

Tears pooled in Lauralee's eyes as she stretched out on the floor of the loft on her back. She groaned as the pain worsened. She turned to her side and hugged her knees to her chest. The bearing down pain was so bad she felt she might truly faint at any moment.

Grabbing Dancing Cloud's arm, she looked wildly up at him. "Warm some water over the fire," she managed to breathe out between pains. "Bring me many towels. Many will be needed to soak up the blood."

Dancing Cloud paled. His shoulders swayed from dismay. "Blood?" he said throatily. "What blood?"

Lauralee placed a hand to his cheek. "My darling

Cherokee chief," she managed in a drawn-out whisper. "I believe I am going to miscarry our first child. No . . . no . . . monthly flow has ever caused me such pain. It has to be more. I have seen it before. Miscarriages. This is the way a woman's body reacts before aborting a child."

Dancing Cloud wanted nothing more than to gather Lauralee into his arms and wipe away her pain and the knowledge that what she suspected was more than likely true. She was wise in ways of medicine and health. Their child. A child he had not even yet known about. It was going to be taken from them.

Lauralee moaned and grabbed at her stomach again. Dancing Cloud rushed down the steps. He placed a kettle of water over the flames of the fireplace. He grabbed an armload of towels from a shelf and placed them at the foot of the ladder.

Then he went to his store of herbal medicines. He mixed up a concoction of meadow rue roots and wild alum in water, which was used for hemorrhaging.

He carried these things to the loft. He gasped when he saw the pool of blood in which Lauralee was now lying. He panicked when he saw that she had lost consciousness.

He gazed up at Hope where she lay on the bed. He went to her, gathered her gently into his arms, and placed her safely in her cradle.

He then lifted Lauralee onto the bed.

The next moments seemed to flow by without thought as Dancing Cloud did what he could to save Lauralee's life. He forced the medicinal herbal mixture through her lips and down her throat.

Alone, he continued to care for her, cleaning her up, placing towels between her legs to soak up the blood.

And after several crucial moments of thinking blood flow would never stop, the towels that he brought out from between her legs were finally free of blood.

He stared down at Lauralee, his heart skipping a beat

over how pale she was. He was not sure now if she would survive.

Covering her with a warm blanket, he knelt down beside her and began a soft chant.

His eyes never left the stillness of her face.

32

For love is heaven,
and heaven is love.

—SIR WALTER SCOTT

Lauralee was aware of someone singing as she slowly emerged from her deep sleep. The voice. It came from afar, as if from a distant land.

Dancing Cloud.

It was Dancing Cloud's voice

Where was he? She wished to reach out and touch him, to tell him that she was going to be all right.

The child, she despaired to herself. Their beloved child they both would never hold or love. It had been taken from her.

She refused to open her eyes. She did not want to face reality just yet. She just wanted to listen to the song, to the voice singing it. She wanted to draw it around her like a protective cloak and never let it go.

Dancing Cloud. Oh, how I love you, Dancing Cloud, she thought lethargically. Do you still love me? Although childless now, do you still love me?

She hugged herself with her arms and turned on her side, the song reaching her, touching her, calming her. . . .

"Listen! On high you dwell, On high you dwell—you dwell, you dwell," Dancing Cloud sang as he sat on a cliff that overlooked his village. "Forever you dwell, you *anida-we,* forever you dwell, forever you dwell. Bring us relief. Bring my woman relief. *Hay!*"

He gazed down at his cabin. His eyes never left it as he continued to sing. "Listen! In the pines you dwell, In the pines you dwell—you dwell, you dwell. Forever you dwell, you *anida-we,* forever you dwell. Make my woman well. *Hay!*"

"Listen," he continued. "O now you have drawn near to hearken, O little whirlwind, *O-ada-wehi,* in the leafy shelter of the lower mountain, there you repose. You have come to sweep the great intruder, my woman's pain, into the great swamp on the upland. You have laid down your paths toward the great swamp. You shall scatter my woman's pain as in play so that it shall utterly disappear. All is done. *Yu!*"

The sun was a vast splash of orange along the horizon as evening grew in lengthy shadows along the land. Dancing Cloud pushed himself up from the rocky precipice.

"Hear my prayers, *Wah-kon-tah,* Great Spirit," Dancing Cloud said, walking dispiritedly down the angled path that led from the cliff. "My child has been taken. Do not also take my wife."

A soft hand on Lauralee's arm drew her eyes open. The hand. It was warm. It was comforting. But . . . it was so small, so much smaller than Dancing Cloud's powerful hands.

Turning over, Lauralee found herself gazing up into Brian Brave Walker's troubled, dark eyes. The candlelight from a fluttering candle on the table beside her bed revealed not only *tears* in Brian Brave Walker's eyes, but also a deep look of concern.

"You are finally awake," the young brave said, his voice filled with a sudden relief. "You have been asleep for way too long." He hung his head for a moment, then looked slowly up at Lauralee again. "You slept soundly like my mother. Then she died."

He eased onto the edge of the bed and placed his

tiny arms around Lauralee's neck. "Do not die," he sobbed. "I need you to be my mother. I am sorry for having hurt you with my words and actions. I now know that my life would be empty without you. I no longer care if your skin is white like my true father's. The difference is in the heart. Yours is pure. His was black and evil."

Touched to the very core of herself over Brian Brave Walker's declaration of love for her, Lauralee's eyes filled with tears. This made it easier for her to brush aside her sadness over having lost one child, for she had just gained another!

"Don't cry, Brian Brave Walker," she said, stroking his coarse, midnight-dark hair. "I understand why you felt the way you did. Shhh. Please don't cry. Everything is going to be all right."

"No, it is not," Brian said, slipping out of her arms. He gazed sadly down at her. "The baby you carried inside your body. It is dead. I feel to blame. I treated you so badly. Your hurt feelings made the baby come from inside you, did it not?"

"Heaven's *no*," Lauralee said, gasping softly. She placed her hand gently on his cheek. "Dear, I'm not sure why the child was taken from me. All that I know for certain is that it was God's choice."

"Your God was mean to you," Brian Brave Walker said, wiping his eyes dry with the backs of his hands.

Then he smiled at Lauralee. "But you still have two children," he proudly announced. "Myself and Hope."

He glanced over his shoulder at the cradle, where Hope slept.

Then he looked guardedly at Lauralee. He had yet to hold the baby. He had most certainly refused to look at her face. To do so would hurt him too much. He had not long ago been forced to say farewell to his own baby sister.

The worst of Brian's feelings and fears and the fruit of many of his nightmares was that his evil father may have taken his sister out into the forest and left her for the wild animals to feed on.

He did know for certain that his sister had been taken from his mother. His father had stated that he would do this. By having said that, it had even at that moment been the same as done. His father's hate for both Brian Brave Walker and his baby sister had been that deep.

"I shall get Hope and bring her to you," Brian Brave Walker said, knowing that doing what he had so adamantly refused to do before might be enough to prove to Lauralee the depths of his feelings.

"You will bring Hope to me?" Lauralee asked, her eyes wide. She had yet to see Brian Brave Walker even get near the child, much less take it from its cradle. That meant so much to Lauralee. So very much.

She wiped tears from her eyes when he anxiously nodded.

"Then, yes, I do wish to hold her," she murmured. She moaned from pain as she tried to get more comfortable on the bed, so that it would be easier to hold the child.

Brian Brave Walker crept over to the cradle. His little heart throbbed with a deep longing for his sister when he gazed down at the sleeping child. She was wrapped snugly in a blanket, a loose corner drawn down partially over her face so that he could not actually see her face.

He turned his eyes to Lauralee. "Susan Sweet Bird has gone to her dwelling to prepare corn bread dumplings and bean bread for our supper," he said, purposely delaying picking up the child. "Father . . . Dancing Cloud? He has gone to sing to the heavens."

He paused and listened.

"He sings no more," he murmured. "Perhaps he will come now and discover that you have awakened."

"I heard him singing even when I was still partially asleep," Lauralee said, the remembrance making her feel warm and wonderful inside, and very, very

wanted. "My Cherokee warrior is gifted in many ways.
I am sure I will discover many more of his hidden tal-
ents after we become man and wife."

"The wedding will be soon now," Brian Brave
Walker said matter-of-factly. "Father told me that as
soon as you are well, we will have us a wedding and
a large celebration. I will even dance with other young
braves. Will that not be a grand time for us all,
Mother?"

Lauralee sucked in a wild breath of wonder when he
addressed her as "Mother" as easily as it had been for
the words to slip across his lips.

And Father?

He definitely looked to Dancing Cloud as his father.

Yes, now they were a true family.

And so they should be.

They had all gone through hell and back to have
such, to *become,* a family.

His arms trembling, Brain Brave Walker bent over
the cradle and slipped them beneath the child. In his
mind's eye he recalled the first time his mother had allowed him to pick up his small sister. He had grown
accustomed to the feel, had even rocked her in his
mother's rocker. He had so enjoyed having a sister.

"Sweet baby," he whispered as he so very carefully
lifted Hope from the cradle. "I will not drop you."

Lauralee scarcely breathed as she watched Brian
Brave Walker. This might be the first time for him to
have ever held a child.

But as he received Hope within the crook of his arm
and carried her toward Lauralee, Lauralee's eyebrows
raised. Brian Brave Walker seemed practiced at han-
dling babies.

She wondered how, and *when*?

There had been no children at his house. And if he
was so practiced at carrying a child, why had he acted
as though he despised even the thought of getting near
Hope until now?

"Here she is," Brian Brave Walker said, slipping the

child from his arms, into Lauralee's. "Does holding her take some of your sadness away?"

Lauralee's insides melted at the feel of the baby in her arms. Although a part of her mourned the loss of her true child, this baby that was also hers, would help erase the pain that her empty womb caused her within her heart.

"Yes, holding Hope helps to take my sadness away," Lauralee said. She smiled up at Brian Brave Walker. "Let's see if she is still asleep, or if taking her from her cradle has awakened her. If she is awake, she is a good girl, isn't she, Brian Brave Walker? She isn't crying."

Brian Brave Walker fought the emotions that were building within him ... emotions that were raw and bruised from having recently lost his baby sister. His little heart throbbed at the thought of looking at the face of this baby. Seeing such sweetness could cause the lonesome ache to begin all over again that he had felt for endless days after having said his last goodbye to his sister. He had been haunted by where his father would take his sister, whether or not she was even alive today.

But to please Lauralee he must make this one more sacrifice. He would take a quick peek, then make up an excuse to go downstairs away from the baby while Lauralee held and fussed over her. He could say that he was going to prepare the baby's milk for feeding.

Yes, that is what he would do. That excuse would be perfect and more understood by Lauralee.

Lauralee's fingers went to the corner of the blanket that lay loosely over Hope's face. She slowly eased the blanket aside, sighing and loving the child all over again when she saw the tiny copper face with the tiny nose, lips, and the darkest of eyes as the child gazed back at her.

Brian Brave Walker stared disbelievingly down at the baby. His knees went so weak they almost buckled beneath him when he recognized the child. "My ...

sister. . ." he gasped, taking a shaky step away from the bed.

"Yes, your sister." Lauralee sighed, thinking how grand it was that Brian Brave Walker had even gone this far today, in that he had not only accepted Lauralee and Dancing Cloud as his parents. He had also accepted the child as his *sister*.

"Brian Brave Walker, I'm so glad that you . . ." she said, but when she looked up at him and saw the utter dismay in his eyes, and saw how he seemed in such a state of shock, her smile and her words faded.

She reached a hand out for him. "Brian Brave Walker, darling, what *is* it?" she asked, her voice drawn. "Does seeing Hope bring back some sort of terrible memories? And if so, why did you call her your sister?"

Brain Brave Walker continued staring at the baby. "My sister," he said again. "My little sister."

"Brian Brave Walker, if calling her your sister causes you such pain, wait awhile longer. Wait until later," Lauralee encouraged. "No one is forcing you to call her your sister."

Brian Brave Walker shifted his eyes. He gazed into Lauralee's as a smile fluttered onto his lips. "This is my *true* sister," he said, now on his knees, taking a closer look at Hope. His hands rolled the blanket fully away from her and he touched her tiny fingers, her tiny toes, her soft face.

"*U-lv-no-di,* Wilnota. It is my sister Wilnota," he said, his eyes dancing happily. "My father did not kill her after all. Instead he took her to the orphanage!"

Lauralee's head was spinning. "This is your true sister?" she asked, her voice filled with wonder. "Actually your true sister? And what is this about your father? Clint had threatened to kill Hope?"

"Yes, it is Wilnota," Brian Brave Walker said, picking up the child. Holding her close, he began rocking her in his arms and explained everything to Lauralee. About his father having said that he was going to take the child away; about Brian Brave Walker having run away before he witnessed such a sight as his father wrenching his baby sister from the arms of her mother; why Brian Brave Walker had not wanted to talk about his sister—because it pained him too much to even be reminded of her.

"If Mother could have only known that my sister did not die," he said, his voice breaking. "If Mother could have only known that my sister is going to be raised by those who will treat her special ... who will treat her as their very own."

In awe, Lauralee watched Brian Brave Walker cuddle the child. "Your sister? And her true name is Wilnota?" she murmured. "The good Lord must have led us to that orphanage. Or else how could this miracle have happened?"

Dancing Cloud came up the ladder and pulled himself into the loft. He stood back, his mouth agape at what he saw. Not only was Lauralee on the speedy road of recovery and not burdened with sadness over losing their child, but Brian Brave Walker's attitude had also made a complete turnaround about Hope, and most surely Lauralee. The mood in this small room was that of sweetness and delight.

"Miracles?" he said, having heard Lauralee say something about a miracle. He went and knelt beside the bed and took one of Lauralee's hands. "Just look at you." He turned and gazed at Brian Brave Walker and Hope over his shoulder, then looked down at Lauralee again. "Today seems *filled* with miracles."

He swept Lauralee into his arms and held her close. "Thank you for coming back to me, my *o-ge-ye*," he said thickly.

Lauralee clung to him. "Wait until you hear what Brian Brave Walker has to tell you," she murmured, smiling over her shoulder at the sight of the boy still rocking Hope back and forth in his arms, now singing to her.

"Oh?" Dancing Cloud said, easing from Lauralee's

arms. He turned and watched Brian Brave Walker with the child.

Lauralee then told Dancing Cloud everything that Brian Brave Walker had told her.

"And so our baby's true name is Wilnota," Dancing Cloud said, rising to his feet. "Shall we, ourselves, call our small daughter Wilnota?"

Lauralee nodded.

Dancing Cloud rose to his feet. He placed an arm around Brian Brave Walker's waist and led him to the bed, encouraging him to sit down beside Lauralee.

Brian Brave Walker gave the baby back to Lauralee, then in one wide sweep Dancing Cloud had his arms around his family.

He closed his eyes and whispered, "O, Great Whirlwind, you listened well today, and ... you ... gave...."

33

And so, all the night's tide,
I lie down by the side of my darling—
   my darling—
My life and my bride.

—EDGAR ALLAN POE

Several weeks had passed and Lauralee had regained her full strength. The day prior to today's wedding activities she had been required to perform one of the Cherokee's most frequent medicinal-religious ceremonies in connection with a prayer for long life. She and the Shaman had fasted the previous day and then she had bathed in a running stream, or "going to water," so called by the Cherokee.

While she had been in the stream, dipping herself completely under the water seven times as was required, the Shaman had gone through his ritual on the banks of the stream, drawing omens from the motion of colorful beads that he held between his thumb and forefinger.

She had been told that this was deemed the most suitable season of the year for the ceremony. It was late autumn, when the leaves that covered the surface of the stream supposedly imparted their medicinal virtues of the water.

And now the time had finally arrived, the day that Lauralee had been dreaming of ever since she had realized just how much she loved this wonderful Cherokee chief.

Several candles made of fragranced beeswax lighting the cabin, Lauralee stood patiently still as Susan Sweet Bird prepared her for the wedding. Although Susan Sweet Bird's eyes could not see, her fingers were her eyes. She worked diligently, feeling out how she was making Lauralee beautiful for her special day.

Lauralee was dressed ceremonially in a knee-length skirt woven from feathers, edged at the bottom with down plucked from the breast of a white swan.

Her hair was plaited in a wreath that was turned up and fastened on the crown, with a silver broach forming a wreathed topknot.

Her lips were red from the juice of the bloodroot, her cheeks just faintly colored from the juice of the same plant.

Tiny woodland autumn flowers of various brilliant colors had been tied together, making a bracelet for both of her arms, and a necklace around her neck.

Lauralee turned her eyes to the open door. Her heart pounded wildly as she listened to those who were already loud with merriment outside. The drums and rattles were beating out their rhythm as feet thumped soundly on the stamped-down earth before the Wolf Clan Town House.

The holy house had been readied for the ceremony and the ensuing celebration, the tantalizing aroma of food being cooked in the village.

Her thoughts were drawn back to the task at hand when Susan Sweet Bird said something that made her happiness waver somewhat. She stiffened as she listened.

"To safeguard the virility of our Wolf Clan of Cherokee, a member of our clan never mates with a member of his clan," Susan Sweet Bird said, her excitement having caused her to rattle on. "Instead, a mate is chosen from the Deer, Bird, Twister, Blue, Red or Wild Potato Clans."

Lauralee relaxed again. She did not belong to any of the Clans that Susan Sweet Bird mentioned. Nor any *others*. But that had never mattered to Dancing Cloud. She was his choice regardless of her color.

Susan Sweet Bird once again ran her fingers over Lauralee, studying every nuance of how she had made her beautiful.

She checked to see that every lock of her hair was in place.

She checked to see that all of the feathers of her dress lay flat and beautiful against the curves of Lauralee's body.

Susan Sweet Bird's hands trembled as they moved softly over Lauralee's face. "My fingers tell me that you are beautiful," she murmured. "Are you ready now to step out and allow my people to see how wisely their chief chose his woman? Shall we walk now together to the Wolf Clan Town House?"

Lauralee nodded nervously, her eyes wide. It thrilled, yet frightened her somewhat, to know that the marriage ceremony would take place close to the sacred fire inside the Town House. She knew the meaning of that fire to the Cherokee, *and* she hadn't yet seen it herself, much less been married in its presence.

Susan Sweet Bird placed an ear of corn in Lauralee's hand, the wedding gift that Lauralee would give to Dancing Cloud as she accepted the one that he would give her.

"You have Dancing Cloud's gift, you are beautiful, so let us go now so that my people will not have to wait any longer," Susan Sweet Bird said, her voice filled with warmth and excitement.

Lauralee swallowed hard. She held the corn against her bosom and walked outside with Susan Sweet Bird. Her gaze went past the throng of people, to the cabin where Wilnoty would stay until after the celebration was over. Lauralee already missed her, her arms aching even now to hold her.

Wilnoty. Yes, she thought to herself, it was best that the child's name had been changed back to her former name. For Soft Wind's sake this had been agreed upon between Dancing Cloud and Lauralee. When Wilnoty had lived a full life, then joined her true mother in the hereafter, the mother must know her child by her name. Calling the child anything else would have been like placing one's back to the remembrances of Soft Wind.

Lauralee's gaze searched out Brian Brave Walker who stood with a gathering of young braves his same age. Tears stung the corners of her eyes to see how he so belonged. His smile was genuine as he gazed back at her. He was a child who had finally found his way in life, a place where he could fulfill his destiny.

Then she gazed at the Wolf Clan Town House. Dancing Cloud was already there, waiting for her arrival. Her cheeks grew hot with an anxious blush as she walked with Susan Sweet Bird toward it.

The people were quiet now. They parted and made space for Susan Sweet Bird and Lauralee to walk. Lauralee could feel their eyes on her and knew they were thinking about this white woman who would soon be as one with them. She felt a genuine friendliness reaching out between herself and Dancing Cloud's people. She had been accepted. She felt as though she belonged.

Out of the corner of her eyes Lauralee saw Brian Brave Walker and his friends move closer to her. She could feel the sea of their proud faces tilted up to her like flowers to the sun.

Lauralee was bubbling over with joy from having finally reached this day. Now her life would finally come together.

One thing, however, would be missing from hers and Dancing Cloud's joined futures. Their very own children born of their union. The miscarriage had been way too devastating ever to believe that she could get pregnant again.

She never allowed herself to dwell on this for long, for she would think herself cheated of the blessings that a child of her very own could bring into hers and Dancing Cloud's life.

While she had been tormentedly alone in the orphanage, she had looked forward to having children of her own. She had vowed that she would give to them what she had so cruelly been denied as a child.

Her eyes wavered even now at the thought of not being able to give birth to a child, yet she just as quickly remembered the two children that she *had* been blessed with. She loved them no less than had they been formed inside her womb and nourished by her very own body. They were the world to her.

Whenever the thought of who their true father was came to Lauralee with dread, she just as quickly brushed the thought away.

Clint McCloud had been no more a father to them than had he not fathered them at all.

Lauralee regretted having not had the chance to have known their mother better. There had to be much good in that woman to have brought Brian Brave Walker up with such a caring and loving nature. His mother had truly been both mother and father to the child.

Lauralee walked up the incline that led to the Wolf Clan Town House. She sucked in a wild breath of excitement as she went inside.

Susan Sweet Bird parted from her and took her place among the others who were seated on "sophas," or seats. Those who had seated themselves before the greatest throng of people entered, were the clansmen, elders who were spokesmen for Dancing Cloud's Wolf Clan of Cherokee.

Lauralee's gaze met Dancing Cloud's as she walked slowly toward him. He sat at the right side of the sacred fire that was kindled atop a cone-shaped mound of earth in the center of the Wolf Clan Town House.

Lauralee smiled at Dancing Cloud, her gaze then slowly sweeping over how he was dressed. Her heart skipped a beat at his grandness. His attire was the ceremonial dress for a chief, a gold-dyed buckskin shirt and leggings with a matching feather headdress. He sat on a platform that was covered with beautiful pelts, autumn flowers sprinkled along the base of the platform.

His eyes were filled with warmth and pride. His back was straight, his arms folded across his majestic chest.

As Lauralee stepped up next to Dancing Cloud, she could hear the shuffling of feet behind her and knew that the Wolf Clan Town House was quickly filling with his people.

Out of the corner of her eye she caught the sight of the musicians as they gathered opposite the fire from Dancing Cloud's platform. The musical instruments consisted of a wooden water drum, a cane flute, and several long-handled gourd rattles.

She looked beyond. People were settling down in a wide circle on blankets, leaving room for dancers who would soon perform.

Lauralee had been told that the wedding ceremony would be simple. There would be an exchange of gifts, in lieu of vows, which would last only a matter of minutes. She clasped her hand gently to the ear of corn that she was going to give to Dancing Cloud.

As he stepped from the platform and stood before her, Lauralee saw the ham of venison that he was going to give to her.

Susan Sweet Bird had explained to Lauralee earlier that the groom's gift of venison symbolized his intention to keep his household supplied with game from the hunt.

The bride's ear of corn signified her willingness to be a good Cherokee housewife.

They smiled into each other's eyes as they exchanged their gifts.

Brian Brave Walker came and took the ear of corn away.

A young and beautiful Cherokee maiden came and took the gift of venison.

Both of these gifts were then taken outside and placed with the food that was being prepared beside the large communal fire, where many pots simmered over the flames.

Lauralee felt giddy with happiness as Dancing Cloud took her hands and gazed down at her with his midnight-dark eyes. She felt the intense hush behind her as the people awaited the exchange of vows between their chief and this white woman who they had finally accepted into their hearts.

Lauralee had proven time and again that she was a woman worthy of walking among them as though one with them. She had relentlessly cared for Soft Wind day and night, trying to save one of their very own women. She had taken into her heart and life two Cherokee children, to raise as her own.

Today she would bond with their chief, forever—totally, heart and soul, as if she were born Cherokee, herself.

And the people were glad. Each and every one had given Lauralee and Dancing Cloud their blessings.

Dancing Cloud drew Lauralee close. He held her hands and gazed down at her as he began to sing.

She melted inside, touched deeply by his song as she listened intently to the words.

"*Ku!* Listen! You great earth woman," Dancing Cloud sang. "No one when with you is ever lonely. You are most beautiful. *Ha!* The clan to which I belong is the one alone allotted for you. Woman, with me no one is ever lonely. Put your soul into the very center of my soul, woman, never to turn away. Your soul has come into the center of my soul, woman, never to go away. *Sge!*"

Tears pooled in Lauralee's eyes. She whispered a soft thank you up at Dancing Cloud.

Then, knowing that what she had planned to say could never compare to that which had just been said to her, she hesitated.

She also briefly thought about whether or not this ceremony made her truly married in the eyes of *her* God. When she had worried about this to Dancing Cloud and had said that she wished to at least have a Bible to cling to during her exchange of vows with

Dancing Cloud, he had said that the white man's Bible seemed to be a good book, but strange that the white people were not better after having it so long.

She had said no more to him about the Bible, or her concerns over not having a preacher present.

It was enough that she was marrying Dancing Cloud, no matter in which way the ceremony would be performed. She felt at peace with herself; God had indeed reached down from the heavens and touched her very soul with his blessings.

Dancing Cloud's fingers lightly squeezed hers, bringing Lauralee's thoughts back to the present. She did not sing. She just spoke gently and lovingly as she said her piece, glad that what she said pleased Dancing Cloud.

"My sweet Cherokee," she murmured. "I give to you today my love, my devotion, my very soul. I will never turn away from you. My heart is yours. My every thought and desire is yours. Oh, my sweet Cherokee, I give my all to you. Our love will be like the stars, undying and forever. I come to you today with my gift of corn as a promise to you that I will be as you want me to be, not only for you, my beloved, but also for our darling children. Take me, my sweet Cherokee, mold me as you wish me to be, for I wish to please you, forevermore."

Her words warmed Dancing Cloud's insides. "You please me as you are," he said thickly. "My woman, my wife."

Realizing that those exchanged words had made them man and wife, Lauralee drifted into his arms. He placed a finger to her chin and tilted her lips to his. Before his people he claimed Lauralee with a tender kiss.

They responded with loud chanting and songs, the drum and rattles now beating out a rhythm that brought dancers to their feet, the flute eerie and magical in its sound.

Dancing Cloud took Lauralee's hand and swung her around to the platform. He made sure that she was comfortable on the plush pelts, then sat down beside her. He reached for her hand and held it on his lap as dancers began to perform, while people clapped, chanted, and sang in time with the beat of the musical instruments.

Some of the women dancers were dressed in robes of chaste white deerskin, ornamented with beads. They wore bracelets and a profusion of gay ribbons, while others wore short skirts and jackets.

The male dancers wore brief breech clouts, their bare chests and arms painted and ornamented with silver bracelets, gorgets, and wampum. They wore high-waving plumes on their heads, and tortoise shell leg rattles.

Facing Dancing Cloud and Lauralee and the musicians, the women stood hand in hand in a semicircle before the sacred fire. They began moving slowly round and round in time with the music, the men joining them.

The dance proceeded beautifully and mystically while Lauralee watched, entranced by the grandeur of it all.

After closely studying the dancers for a while, Lauralee felt some unseen force drawing her to her feet. The dancers stepped aside and made room for her when she began dancing, the rhythm of her footsteps seeming to be a separate song over the drumbeat. She sometimes felt as though one foot was suspended, gliding back and forth, the other pulsing up and down, alternating, a most subtle syncopation.

Dancing Cloud's heart raced as he watched his woman, the exquisite grace in every movement of her lithe, slender body, of the look of wild abandon on her angelic face. He watched the rise and fall of her breasts as they pressed against the inside of her feather dress. He watched her tapered ankles.

His gaze followed her superb arm gestures, her right hand upraised majestically, then swooping down like a rush of rain, and then pulling up again, like growing corn.

Male dancers who wore buffalo head masks soon joined Lauralee. Dancing Cloud rose to his feet, his spine stiff as he watched as the male dancers diagonaled away from his wife, circled back, their horned-headed masks leaning close to her, following her smooth, dreamy movements.

Dancing Cloud entered the circle of dancers. The masked dancers fell back into the crowd. Everyone was quiet, the instruments mute as their chief picked his wife up into his arms and carried her away.

Lauralee clung around Dancing Cloud's neck as he took her from the Wolf Clan Town House, past the fires where the wondrous aromas of cornmeal dumplings, hominy, beans, and chestnut bread were being kept warm by the hot coals, and into Dancing Cloud's cabin, which by marriage, was now also Lauralee's.

Dancing Cloud kicked the door closed with a heel and did not take the time to carry his bride up the ladder to their loft bedroom. He set her down before the fireplace on a thick pallet of furs.

In a frenzy, their fingers trembling, they undressed each other.

Dancing Cloud released Lauralee's hair from the tight bun so that it tumbled free across her shoulders, a few fronds falling over her breasts.

Bending to a knee before Lauralee, Dancing Cloud gazed up at her, his eyes smoke-black with passion. He smoothed the hair from her breasts and cupped them within the palms of his hands.

Lauralee sighed, the sudden onslaught of pleasure spreading a delicious warmth through her body. As he kissed her hard and long, she closed her eyes as ecstasy swam through her in wild, warm currents.

She melted into his hands as he slid them down to her waist and lowered her onto the warm pelts before the fire. He leaned over her and made love to her as if it were their first time together.

She ran her fingers over the expanse of his copper, sleekly muscled back, then reached for his finely chiseled face and feathered her fingers across his lips.

She giggled and felt currents of rapture swim through her when he sucked one of her fingers between his lips, his tongue wrapping it inside his mouth.

"It has been so long, my *o-ge-ye*," Dancing Cloud said huskily, his body momentarily pausing in its movements. "It has been hard waiting for your body to heal."

He gazed at her small, ivory-pale breasts, then down at the cloud of shadow between her legs, and up again where her ribs were brushed with the softness of the fire's glow.

Lauralee tremored beneath the scrutiny of his eyes, seemingly being touched by them, as if they were hands, themselves, stroking her.

"Do I look well enough now for lovemaking?" she murmured. She ran her fingers through his thick, black hair. "It is so wonderful, my darling, to feel your body next to mine."

"You look and feel well enough for this that we are now sharing," Dancing Cloud said, leaning a soft kiss to her brow.

And then his mouth covered her lips. His body moved rhythmically against hers again, his kiss deepening, almost frenzied.

"My wife," Dancing Cloud whispered as his lips now rested against the long, delicate column of her throat. He kept his steady pace within her, his arms now holding her imprisoned in his embrace.

"My husband," Lauralee whispered, the drugged passion making her blood quicken. She laced her arms around his neck and whispered against his cheek. Her voice quivered emotionally in her excitement. "Oh, how I adore calling you my husband."

Dancing Cloud's mouth brushed Lauralee's cheeks and ears and lightly kissed her eyelids. His fingers reached up and entwined them in her hair as he brought her mouth to his again. His mouth forced her lips open as his mouth grew more and more passionate. Desire shot through him, acutely aware that the urgency was building inside him. His head began to reel.

He held her close as her body answered the call of his. She swayed and rocked with him into paradise.

Soon Dancing Cloud rolled away from her and lay on his side facing her. He reached for her and drew her next to him, sculpting himself to her moist body.

"And so it begins, ah, it truly begins," he said, smoothing some locks of her hair from her eyes. "Our future and that of our children."

He paused and kissed her softly. "The damn Civil War was good for something, after all," he said. "Though under tragic circumstances, it brought us together."

"I am so very thankful that you were my father's best friend," Lauralee said, cuddling close. "If not, we would have never met. Ah, the trust that man had in you. I am certain that he is smiling from the heavens even now, Dancing Cloud, to see just *how* devotedly you looked after me since his death. How more devoted than to take me as your wife?"

"And the children," Dancing Cloud said, leaning away from her, to gaze into the fire. "Our destinies also included the children that we now call ours."

"*Ii,* yes, that is true," Lauralee murmured. She cast her eyes downward and placed a hand on her flat tummy. "There could have been another child. It just wasn't meant to be."

She cast him a half glance. "My darling, can you truly accept that you will never have a true son, one who carries your blood through his veins?"

"I have a son," Dancing Cloud said, turning to give her a soft smile. "As I see it, as I feel it, Brian Brave Walker is my son in every sense of the word. He will be raised in my image. And, yes, that is enough. I would never risk losing you just to gain a child."

Lauralee drifted into his arms. She lay her cheek

against his chest. She loved the smooth texture of his skin, and the swish-swishing sound of his heartbeat. "You are more than wonderful," she murmured. "I am so blessed to have you."

He lifted her chin with a finger. His mouth covered hers with a gentle sweetness that made her insides melt. Trembling, she wrapped her arms about his neck and returned the kiss.

Lauralee came alive again with his touch, with his kiss, with his passion, each caress, each kiss, promising more, assuring fulfillment.

Tremors cascaded down her back as he made love to her again, gently, tenderly, warmly, wonderfully.

Afterward he sang to her as he held her close before the fire. She gazed up at him, her eyes, heart and soul filled with him as she listened. . . .

"Oh, I am thinking, oh, I am thinking I have found my love," Dancing Cloud sang softly. "Oh, I think it is so . . ."

And then he kissed her, the whole universe seemingly spinning.

34

The heavens reward thee manifold, I pray
—ANNE BRADSTREET

Ten years later.

Black smoke belched into the sky from the train's engine as Lauralee sat beside a window in one of the passenger cars. She gazed wistfully at the countryside as the train rumbled along its tracks through the never-ending flat land of Illinois.

Autumn had arrived with its magical, vivid colors. In this brief fleeting moment at sunset, when the orange sky became a canvas for the autumn trees, Lauralee was rendered breathless as she peered at them through the window. Along the horizon were a scattering of trees, their leaves resembling a patchwork quilt from this distance, the colors of red, purple, bronze, and yellow intermingling.

From her experience of having traveled through Illinois on horse and buggy, she knew that high in those trees there were secret hollows, where bushy-tailed squirrels made their residence. Toasty warm in their thick, gray coats, the squirrels busied themselves putting together their private store of acorns and hickory nuts. Woodpeckers would also he nestled in their own secret places, as also would owls.

Illinois was a beautiful place, and Lauralee had enjoyed discovering more about the state while traveling in the comforts of a train instead of how she had arrived there the first time, in her horse and buggy.

And not only was she not arriving by horse and buggy, other things about her arrival had changed. Her Uncle Abner would not be there to greet her with his open, muscled arms.

She stifled a sob behind her gloved hand. Uncle Abner had died recently and was already buried.

Guilt spread through her, paining her heart, over having not made time to visit her aunt and uncle enough times through the years.

And she would never forget how wonderful their surprise visit at the Cherokee village had been. Dancing Cloud had known of their visit prior to their arrival but had not told Lauralee.

She inhaled a quavering breath. Nervously, she placed her hands on the brim of her hat, slightly repositioning it on her head where her hair was circled into a tight bun beneath it.

"My *o-ge-ye,* I can tell that you are fighting your emotions," Dancing Cloud said, reaching over to take a hand. He affectionately squeezed it. "Remember that although your Uncle Abner has crossed over to the other world, he is here with you even now, in spirit. Allow that to give you comfort."

Lauralee turned to Dancing Cloud. "It's so difficult," she murmured. "And how I hate to see the grave. It will be hard to accept that he is in the ground, in a . . ."

She placed her free hand to her mouth and turned her eyes away from Dancing Cloud again. "I just find death hard to accept," she said, her voice drawn. "I doubt that it shall ever be any other way for me."

A soft hand on her face made Lauralee force a smile. She gazed at her ten-year-old daughter as Wilnoty came and knelt before Lauralee. Wilnoty was the picture image of her mother, so beautiful and petite.

"Do not be sad, Mother," Wilnoty said softly. "It makes *me* sad."

"I know, I know," Lauralee said, leaning a kiss to

her daughter's brow. "And we don't want you to have a sad face when we arrive at Mattoon's Union Depot. Your Aunt Nancy will be there with her carriage, waiting for us. We must smile for our Aunt Nancy. I am certain she has seen enough sadness these past weeks to last her a lifetime. To lose one's husband must be a devastating, horrible thing."

"I wish Brian Brave Walker were here to share the excitement of the train ride, and of seeing Aunt Nancy once again," Wilnoty said as she settled back on the seat opposite her mother and father.

Demurely, she clasped her hands together on her lap, the ruffles of her petticoats spreading out beneath the fully gathered skirt of her gingham dress. She wore a bonnet that tied beneath her chin with a yellow satin bow that matched the color of her dress.

"But I understand why my brother stayed behind," she said, lifting her chin proudly. "He is assuming the role of chief in the absence of Father."

She smiled, her dark eyes dancing. "Is he not a smart, handsome brother?" she asked, gazing from her mother to her father. "Will not Brian Brave Walker one day make a *true*, great leader of our people?"

"He has listened well to the teachings of his father," Dancing Cloud said, stretching a long, lean leg out before him, revealing new, shiny boots, and dark, snug breeches.

Lauralee gazed over at him, pride swelling within her heart as once again she realized how noble and magnificent a man he was. And he was always so generous. Whenever he would return from the trading post, he would always bring her a surprise.

One of his finest surprises was a sewing machine. She loved to sew on the newfangled contraption, and not only did she make Dancing Cloud and Brian Brave Walker's breeches and shirts, she made herself and her daughter lovely dresses and petticoats.

Dancing Cloud had even built a new, larger cabin for his family and had cut windows out of the logs for

Lauralee, to give her more true light for which to sew her creations. She had even sold several dresses and suits to the trading post, having begun to make quite a profit now from her sewing skills.

Today she wore a blue silk dress that was full and flowing from her tiny waist. The silk fabric had been one of Dancing Cloud's gifts to her that had came directly from China during one of Dancing Cloud's transactions with his abundant crop of ginseng.

Lauralee's thoughts were catapulted back to the present when the city of Mattoon came into view as houses began to multiply along the sides of the tracks. She watched from the window, her mind drifting back to the past and to the events that had taken place after she and Dancing Cloud had arrived there those ten long years ago.

She smiled to herself when she thought of helping Dancing Cloud escape from the jail, and of coming face to face with Paul Brown during the escape. From the kindness of Paul's heart he had allowed them to escape.

Paul was married now to Jana. Jana with the long and flowing brilliant red hair and turquoise eyes. She wondered if they had been blessed with children?

The melancholia that always swept through her heart at the thought of not being able to give birth, herself, came to her at the thought of Paul and his wife possibly having children.

Never wanting to labor long over anything that reminded her of her womb being barren, she thrust those thoughts aside.

Leaning closer to the window, her eyes widened as she spotted the Union Depot a short distance away. Her gaze swept over the large depot, the trains' smokestacks having blackened the building as they steamed through town. Not only did the building house the train depot, but also the Essex House Hotel.

The trains always stopped at the Essex House, to

feed their passengers since the trains did not offer a dining-car service.

The train shuddered to a stop as it came directly in front of the depot. Lauralee felt the excitement building to see her Aunt Nancy, while still deeply inside her lay the grieving she felt for her uncle.

But she loved her aunt dearly. Who could not get excited over seeing her once again?

And it was almost like going home every time she came to Mattoon. Her aunt had become her mother in all ways that mattered.

"We're here," Wilnoty said, her eyes brimming with excitement. "I love coming to Mattoon. I so enjoy the people on the streets and the big buildings. It is nothing like living in the mountains."

Dancing Cloud frowned at his daughter. He did not like to see her taking to this environment as she so obviously did. He never wanted her to choose this way of life over that which his people offered. The white community had too many ways that corrupted their people. He never wanted his daughter tempted with that which corrupted!

"We will stay only long enough for you to extend your condolences to your aunt, and then we must return to our people," Dancing Cloud said, his eyes intent on Lauralee.

Lauralee understood. She had heard the same envy in their daughter's voice that Dancing Cloud had obviously heard. She, too, did not want her daughter to get caught up in this world that could in one breath falsely welcome her, and in the other condemn her for the color of her skin.

"Yes, I see that as best, and I am sure that my aunt will not expect more from us than that," Lauralee said, clutching her purse as others began filing from the train.

She looked from the window again and her heart frolicked in her chest when she not only saw Aunt Nancy standing outside the train, but also Paul Brown and his lovely wife, standing with Nancy.

Lauralee's eyes shifted. Standing beside Jana was a child. It had to be their son. He was the exact replica of his father. The blond hair. The blue eyes. The long, straight nose. And squared shoulders.

Yes, the young man was already handsome. He was perhaps now five years of age. It had been six years now since Lauralee had visited Mattoon.

Dancing Cloud moved from the seat and took a travel bag down from overhead, then reached a hand to his daughter and led her out into the aisle.

Lauralee smiled up at Dancing Cloud as he then offered her his hand.

She left the seat, moved down the aisle, then stepped quickly down the narrow steps.

Hearing her name being spoken, Lauralee turned and found her Aunt Nancy running toward her, Paul and his family following at a brisk clip.

She ran to her aunt and hugged her tightly.

"Aunt Nancy," she murmured, nurtured by the warmth of her aunt's fleshy arms, yet feeling the absence of her uncle so heavily within her heart. "Oh, Aunt Nancy, I'm so sorry about Uncle Abner. So very, very sorry. And I wish that we could have gotten here sooner, to be here to comfort you during the funeral."

"There, there, child," Nancy murmured, stroking Lauralee's back. "It's all right. I'm learning to accept my loss. Abner wouldn't want me grieving forever over his death. I'm comforted in my loneliest hours with remembrances of what we shared those many years we were married."

"I wish to place flowers on his grave," Lauralee said, as she eased from her aunt's arms. "Perhaps you can tell me where I might purchase a lovely bouquet?"

"Abner would be happier with flowers from our own garden," Nancy said, patting Lauralee on the arm.

Then Nancy knelt down and gathered Wilnoty into her arms. "My, my, but you have grown," she murmured. "You were just a tiny thing the last time I saw you. Now you are such a lady."

Then she moved from Wilnoty and hugged Dancing Cloud. "Thank you for bringing my precious Lauralee to me," she said, tears swelling in her eyes. "You have made her such a fine husband."

"I wish we could have been here for you sooner," Dancing Cloud said, brushing a tear from Nancy's eyes as she stepped away from him. He gazed at her at length, seeing how she had so aged since he had last seen her. Her hair was gray and her eyes were sunken.

"But where is Brian Brave Walker?" Nancy asked, looking past Dancing Cloud, as though expecting to see Brian come from the train at any moment.

"He is practicing being chief in my absence," Dancing Cloud explained.

Nancy nodded. "I see," she murmured. "Oh, but I do wish I could have seen him, too."

When Paul reached Lauralee, she was swept into his powerful arms. "It's good to see you again, Paul," she murmured, then slipped away from him, having felt a sort of desperation in the way he had held onto her.

As she gazed into his eyes she became somewhat uneasy. She knew now without a doubt that he still cared for her. Even with the gorgeous woman at his side who seemed to adore him, he could not hide the fact that he still cared for Lauralee.

"And thank you, Jana," Lauralee blurted, reaching a handshake toward her. "Thank you for thinking enough of my aunt to accompany her to the train station."

"It has been my pleasure to look after your aunt's needs," Jana said, gently shaking Lauralee's hand. "She has been a comfort, also, to Paul. First his mother passed away from a lung ailment. Then his father passed away a short while ago. He had a heart attack."

"Oh, I am so sorry," Lauralee said, turning back to Paul as she slipped her hand from Jana's. "I didn't know."

"It's been hard," Paul said, nervously shuffling his

feet. And to change the subject, he reached a hand to his son's shoulder and scooted him over to stand before him. "We have another Noah in the family. Meet our son Noah."

Lauralee bent over and placed a hand to Noah's cheek. "Hello," she murmured. "I'm so glad to make your acquaintance."

"As I am yours," Noah said politely as he smiled at Lauralee. He looked over Lauralee's shoulder at Wilnoty. His eyes locked with hers for a moment, then he went to Dancing Cloud and offered him his hand. "It's a great pleasure meeting *you,* sir."

"It is *my* pleasure to make the acquaintance of such a fine young man," Dancing Cloud said, thinking it refreshing to find the young man so polite, so earnest in his offer of friendship.

Lauralee watched young Noah's eyes. They always shifted back to Wilnoty. Her insides tightened when she saw the sudden interest both children had in each other. Her only consolation was that her daughter was way older than Noah. Nothing could ever transpire between them except friendship.

Wilnoty stepped forward. "Noah, my name is Wilnoty," she said, taking his hand. They ran off together toward the carriage that waited at the curb.

"Seems they have made a fast friendship," Nancy said, smiling. She slipped an arm through Lauralee's. "Shall we now go to my house? We shall pick flowers for Abner's grave, then we shall pay him a visit before it gets totally dark."

Paul and his family said their goodbyes and left in their horse and buggy.

Because she wanted to sit beside one of the windows, Lauralee was the last to board Nancy's carriage. Nancy had given the driver instructions to travel slowly down Broadway Avenue, giving Lauralee and her family time to enjoy this grand street and its changes.

Lauralee gazed from the window as the carriage left

the curb. Just as it began to make a left onto Broadway, she gazed out the window at Brian's Place Saloon at the very end of Broadway. It had grown in size. It now had two stories. And with its fresh coat of paint it had such a look of respectability.

When the carriage swung onto Broadway Avenue, with other horse-drawn vehicles and men on horseback, Lauralee once again enjoyed riding along the street that was the center of Mattoon's commercial and society activities.

She settled back against the seat and admired the majestic brick buildings and the displays in the plate-glass windows of the shops on the lower floors. She marveled at the various hats with their decorations of plumes and artificial flowers. She gasped at the display of the frilly dresses and underthings in other windows.

Now past those tempting, somewhat daring displays, she gazed over at the Byers Hotel. Remembering having been there to try and find Clint McCloud, she shivered.

She looked quickly elsewhere, at the Dole Opera House, the first real theater and largest building in the town. She had heard that many famous actors appeared on the stage of this opera house.

They rode on through town, past Gibbs's Livery Stable, more general stores and saloons, and The Pennsylvania House, a three-story building that had been brought in piece by piece on a railroad car.

And then the business district was left behind and the carriage passed lovely homes on each side of the street where trees towered over them like large, opened umbrellas.

The colors of the maple and oak trees were magnificent, a blending of crimson reds and yellows. Birches lent their yellow colors to the backdrop of the city. Flowers of all various colors and designs bloomed in flower boxes and along the borders of the yards.

Lauralee gazed from the window when the Peterson House came into view. A deep sadness engulfed her at

the remembrances of why she was there, and who she
would never see again in his upstairs study inside the
stately house.

Her Uncle Abner.

Somberly she watched the horse and carriage approach the circular driveway in front of the house.
When it stopped, the driver opened the door on the
side of the carriage on which Lauralee sat.

She crept from the carriage, feeling timid in her de-
meanor, her eyes wavering as they swept to the second
story of the house where the curtains and blinds were
drawn at the windows of Abner's study.

Lauralee walked slowly toward the house as everyone else left the carriage. Dancing Cloud came to her
left side while Nancy went to her right, Wilnoty skipping on ahead of them.

"I've decided not to live in this house any longer,
Lauralee," Nancy said, stopping to gaze wistfully at
her home. "Without Abner, it is so vastly empty at
night, and so quiet."

"You will leave this wonderful house?" Lauralee
gasped. "But it is so lovely."

"It is so *quiet*," Nancy stressed as she turned and
placed a hand on Lauralee's arm. "It is best that I live
elsewhere. I have already purchased a house in
Charleston. I have kin and friends there for which to
fill my empty hours."

Nancy paused and cleared her throat, then said,
"And by making my residence in Charleston, I will be
close to Abner. You see, he was buried there, in the
Mound Cemetery."

Lauralee swallowed hard, then again stared up at the
two-storied Italianate home, memories of her scarce
times there rushing through her mind. After today she
would never enter the house again. It would belong to
someone else.

"But, my dear, do not fret over my moving from this
beloved house," Nancy quickly interjected, drawing
Lauralee's eyes quickly back to her. "It *and* twenty-

two acres of land around this house have been given to the city of Mattoon to be used as a public park. It was my husband's dream that this land one day be a park. He bequeathed it to the city in his will. I have seen that his dream will come true."

"Such a marvelous thing to do for the city," Lauralee said softly. "The name of the park. Will it be named after Uncle Abner?"

"Yes, it will carry *both* our names," Nancy said, flicking tears from her eyes with a gloved hand. "It will be called Peterson Park. It should serve the people of Mattoon well from generation to generation."

Lauralee walked to the back of the house and gazed across the vastness of the land. Towering trees were everywhere, as well as a vast carpet of grass. She went to the huge flower garden and fell to her knees and began to gather a bouquet of snapdragons that she would place on her uncle's grave.

When a hand touched her shoulder, she turned smiling eyes up at Dancing Cloud. "I feel him here even now, Dancing Cloud," she murmured. "I feel my uncle in the gentle breeze and in the soft whispering sound of the wind through the trees."

Dancing Cloud smiled and nodded to her, seeing that she finally understood about the spirit path and how no one ever truly left you once they entered that other world where there were no sorrows, no prejudices, no hatred.

Once her flowers were gathered, they boarded the carriage once again. As they rode toward Charleston, to go to the Mound Cemetery, Lauralee no longer feared going to her uncle's grave. She did not feel that she had truly lost him after all.

Yes, he was there with her even now, the power of his smile reaching down from the heavens.

35

Thou art my own, my darling, and my wife.
—ARTHUR JOSEPH MUNBY

Several months later.

All was perfectly content in quietness as Dancing Cloud and Lauralee rode a one-horse sleigh in the moonlight. They were buried deep under a buffalo robe blanket. Bells rang and jangled as the runners of the sleigh hissed upon the crisp, new-fallen snow.

Lauralee snuggled against Dancing Cloud as he tended the reins. Nothing was better than a winter blanket and her man to share it with. There was nothing more comforting against the cold. It was as if the great buffalo were still alive, sharing its great, ungainly body heat.

"I've never been happier," she said, slipping a gloved hand through the crook of Dancing Cloud's arm, clinging to him. "And look how lovely everything is? It is as though we are traveling through a vast wonderland."

The bare branches overhead silently spoke of a new year. The tall, stately trees, veterans of so many winters, had quietly bent under restless winds and heavy ice. Hidden beneath the crusty earth were wiry roots of spring.

Bulbs beneath a thick blanket of brown leaves covered by the snow were patiently waiting to burst forth in the spring with their lovely flowers.

When the earth was still and bare, the somber gray-brown bark of a hickory tree trunk could be quite magical and breathtaking.

"It is beautiful now, but as you know, come spring and our people return to planting their crops, some will curse the thawing ground," Dancing Cloud said, flicking his horse's reins.

"Yes, I have learned that with each frost and thaw the earth heaves up a new crop of stones that must be cleared before the spring plowing can begin," she said, proud of all of the knowledge that she had absorbed since she had made her home in these Great Smoky Mountains.

Dancing Cloud smiled at her. "'Picking rocks', it is called," he chuckled.

He then looked around at the serenity of the day. "Winter is a favorite time of mine," he said, nodding. "It is a time to gather thought."

More snow fell. Lauralee felt the magic, the stillness, and excitement, when the winter turned its world into a blank white sheet upon which one's imagination could range free.

"Let's make love out here in the snow," she blurted, hearing the creak of the snow-laden branches.

Dancing Cloud gazed ahead and caught sight of an antlered buck and his doe. They turned their quick eyes to the horse and sleigh, then away they suddenly went, tails up, with long leaps over the snow, lovely and slow.

"I am happy in the company of our forest friends," he said.

He turned his dark eyes to Lauralee. Her skin was as pale as the snow, all blushed with the evening's quiet pinks. "You would like for your husband to warm your body beneath the buffalo blankets?" he asked, his eyes dancing into hers.

Snuggled and hooded in a coat of rabbit's fur, Lauralee nodded anxiously, her pulse racing. "Please, my darling, I need you," she murmured. "But not for warming my body. I want you, for wanting's sake, alone."

Dancing Cloud drew a tight rein beneath a snow-laden maple tree. He dropped the reins to the floor of the sleigh, then took the buffalo blanket and drew it entirely over himself and Lauralee as she stretched out on the sleigh on another thick layer of blankets.

Dancing Cloud and Lauralee laughed as they shook off clothes that impeded their lovemaking. When they were ready, Dancing Cloud ran his hands up and down the satiny flesh of Lauralee's thigh, her skin warm, smooth, and inviting.

Lauralee seemed to be in a state of suspended animation as they began making love. While the wind moaned and whistled around the sleigh, the air beneath the buffalo blanket was charged with heat and excitement.

Dancing Cloud's mouth covered Lauralee's with a heated kiss. She moaned with passion against his lips. She lifted her hips and rocked with him, his arms holding tight.

As he moved with her, their bodies joined as one. Lauralee abandoned herself to the torrent of feelings that swam through her. She nestled close to him, her breathing quickening as she already felt the pleasure mounting and spreading.

Dancing Cloud's kiss became more demanding. Lauralee trembled with a quickening rapture, the curl of heat tightening inside him.

As Dancing Cloud's passion rose, he felt himself being drawn into the feeling of a vast, spreading fire.

And then the explosion rocked his whole being as he came to that moment of wild abandon, when nothing but giving and taking total pleasure was the ultimate goal. He clung to Lauralee. He moaned against the long, sweet column of her throat.

Lauralee tossed her head back and forth, the intensity of the pleasure filling her, spilling over, spreading, her gasps long, soft whimpers into the still snow-filled air on the mountain path.

Their bodies then subsided exhaustedly into each other's. The sharp cry of a blue jay jerked them out of their reverie. Lauralee giggled. Dancing Cloud laughed.

"Did I warm you enough, my *o-ge-ye?*" he teased.

"More than a dozen fires in a fireplace." Lauralee laughed.

The horse whinnied. The bluejay cried again. The wind howled more feverishly outside the covering of the buffalo blanket.

"I guess it's time to return to the real world." Lauralee sighed. They quickly dressed. "I believe Brian Brave Walker has plans tonight. He said something about using our horse and sleigh, to take a friend from the neighboring village for a ride."

"She is a woman friend?" Dancing Cloud asked, pausing to frown at her.

"Yes, a woman friend," Lauralee said softly.

"He is too young to think so seriously about women," Dancing Cloud grumbled.

"Darling, life is too short to measure one's love by age," Lauralee said, gently touching his cheek. "If he's in love, let it be."

"Just like I should allow our daughter to continue corresponding with that Brown boy from Mattoon?" Dancing Cloud said, sarcasm thick in his voice.

"I've told you time and again that nothing but a sincere friendship can ever come of that relationship," Lauralee softly argued. "Remember how much older Wilnoty is than Noah."

Before they threw aside the buffalo blanket and returned to their seat, Lauralee framed her husband's face between her hands. "Darling, let our children enjoy their young lives," she murmured. "*I* had no life, till you. I was robbed of so many sweet moments that most young people share. Please relax with our children. Please?"

Dancing Cloud drew her suddenly into his arms and held her close. "I want what is best, always, for our children," he said, then tilted her lips to his. "And your words about what is best for our children are wise. I find that I am a selfish father sometimes."

"You are a wonderful father *and* husband," Lauralee quickly corrected. "Ah, but how I would love another kiss, my darling."

He chuckled, then gave her a kiss that made her head spin, the shared bliss always there between them, gently sweet and wonderful.

Dear Reader:

I hope that you have enjoyed reading *Wild Abandon*. My next Topaz book will be *Wild Bliss,* about the Chippewa Indians. This book promises much adventure and true, undying romance. *Wild Bliss* will be available in the spring of 1995.

June 1995 marks the date of the second annual Cassie Edwards International Festival. If you wish to know more about the festival, my fan club, or would like to have a copy of my latest newsletter, please send inquiries and a legal-sized, self-addressed stamped envelope to:

Cassie Edwards
R#3 Box 60
Mattoon, Il. 61938

HAPPY READING:

Cassie Edwards

ANNOUNCING THE
TOPAZ FREQUENT
READERS CLUB
COMMEMORATING TOPAZ'S
1 YEAR ANNIVERSARY!

THE MORE YOU BUY, THE MORE YOU GET

Redeem coupons found here and in the back of all new Topaz titles for FREE Topaz gifts:

Send in:

 2 coupons for a free TOPAZ novel (choose from the list below);

☐ THE KISSING BANDIT, Margaret Brownley
☐ BY LOVE UNVEILED, Deborah Martin
☐ TOUCH THE DAWN, Chelley Kitzmiller
☐ WILD EMBRACE, Cassie Edwards

 4 coupons for an "I Love the Topaz Man" on-board sign

 6 coupons for a TOPAZ compact mirror

 8 coupons for a Topaz Man T-shirt

Just fill out this certificate and send with original sales receipts to:

TOPAZ FREQUENT READERS CLUB-1ST ANNIVERSARY
Penguin USA • Mass Market Promotion; Dept. H.U.G.
375 Hudson St., NY, NY 10014

Name_____

Address_____

City_____State_____Zip_____
Offer expires 5/31/1995

This certificate must accompany your request. No duplicates accepted. Void where prohibited, taxed or restricted. Allow 4-6 weeks for receipt of merchandise. Offer good only in U.S., its territories, and Canada.